DECEIVED

Stella Barcelona

To Mom and Dad, Thank you, with all of my heart, for creating a daydreamer and teaching her to appreciate, at a very young age, the life-enhancing value of reading.

To Bob, Thank you for...everything, especially for your unwavering understanding of my need to write, for encouraging me every step of the way, and for regularly taking me to beaches with crystal-clear blue water so that I can replenish my soul.

Prologue

Wednesday, June 29
New Orleans, Louisiana

Young mothers don't deserve to die as collateral damage for the misdeeds of others. He shook off the random thought, blaming it on his fatigue and the mind-game that it played. He couldn't afford to dwell on the tragic circumstances of what he was about to do. Lisa Smithfield, a graduate student who happened to be the single mother of a two-month old baby, was a gateway to freedom, which would come through the emotional destruction of others and also result in financial gain for him. By the fourth day of July, the lives of four women would end. Lisa Smithfield was first. Then he'd move on to the next three, the ones who really mattered. No one who needed to die bore responsibility for that necessity. They were simply the best pawns he had to play.

The 2800 block of Melody, a narrow, one-way street with potholes, had broken lights and sagging power lines. A few blocks away, the manicured grounds and stately buildings of Tulane University gave way to mansions. In the opposite direction, equally close, were slums. On Melody, abandoned homes sat amidst wood-frame doubles and cottages, where lights shone from within. Despite the dumpiness, a beautiful essence from sweet-olive trees infused the night's moist air.

No humans were in sight.

Brilliant lightning etched the dark sky into a sizzling and ever-changing canvas, signaling a thunderstorm's approach. Surveillance had indicated that Lisa worked on campus on weeknights in the student-faculty office. She left the office at ten, and she normally ran a few minutes late. He waited for her behind a hedge. Soft-soled shoes padded on the sidewalk. She walked past him without noticing he was there. The small bit of baby weight that remained on Lisa made the blue-eyed student even prettier. She juggled her backpack while searching her purse for keys, oblivious even as he walked towards her.

He gripped her ponytail with a gloved hand and wound it tight around his wrist. Before her sharp intake of breath could become a scream, he placed his pistol flush against her temple and braced for recoil. The silencer muted the noise. Particles of flesh, blood, and bone flew back, away from him. She fell against her car, then slid to the grass between the street and the sidewalk. He picked up her keys, then took her purse and her book bag. Lightning flashed as he drove away in his car. Two seconds later, thunder broke.

A few blocks away, he pulled over to check her book bag, where he found her laptop. Its data was part of his prize. Within minutes he was at Lisa's tiny rental. As he let himself in with her key, the sky opened with dense sheets of rain. He shut her door then locked it and leaned against it, savoring his post-kill, pulsing energy. Most, if not all, of her belongings were in moving boxes. He took a mental snapshot of each room. Once Lisa's body was found, the police would look to her home for clues. He had to make sure that he left no sign that he'd been there. Her murder needed to look like an armed robbery that went bad. While he wanted certain others to wonder about Lisa's murder, he didn't need the cops to think it was anything but random.

He opened and resealed boxes, taking research material. Under her mattress, he found the smoking gun, the document that proved that Lisa's theory was correct. He stood still, holding the letter to his chest, shutting his eyes while relief and anticipation churned through him.

Time passed. He lost track of how many minutes.

Move. Get out of here. Now.

This deep inner voice was his failsafe compass. It moved him forward. He stuffed her research into his duffel, then reorganized the rooms.

He left, getting back in his car and heading to Central City. Calliope Street, which bordered high-rise projects, was suitably quiet and disreputable. Rain fell so fast and hard that not even dogs were out. Narrow rivers of water swirled along both sides of the street, heading to drains that were clogged with old newspapers and beer cans. He pulled over, but couldn't toss her stuff out of the window because the water in the street and gutter would carry it away, and the cops needed to find it here. He opened his car door, stood, took a few steps onto higher ground, and dumped Lisa's purse on the sidewalk, along with the book bag, which he had robbed of all but meaningless papers. He drove to his boathouse, parked in the garage, put a new license plate on the car, dismantled his firearm, then got into his boat. Under the shelter of the boathouse, he waited out the worst of the rain. Guided by moonlight, he enjoyed the trip, with only the whirr of the boat's engines for company. Along the way, he dropped the weapon's pieces into the dark, murky water. A weight that he tied to the old license plate made it sink. As the plate disappeared underwater, an idea formed. One of his next three victims would sink, drowning, beneath murky water. More weights, he thought, adding that item to his ever-growing kill list. At the camp, he cooked eggs, bacon, and toasted fat slabs of bread. He made a phone call. "Got it."

"Lisa?"

"As planned."

"Dear God."

"He has nothing to do with this. Two million, from you, now. I'll deliver my demand in the morning. Twenty-five million."

There was a long pause. "These men are not that desperate. George Bartholomew will never agree to that figure."

He thought of his next three targets, particularly the one who George Bartholomew would care about the most. He smiled. "We'll see."

Chapter One

Upon seeing his home, Taylor Bartholomew received her first clue that her expectations of Brandon Morrissey were off. At eleven a.m. she approached the address that she'd been given by New Orleans Police Officer Joe Thompson and his partner Tony Abadie, the homicide detectives who were working the prior night's murder of Lisa Smithfield. The address was in a tree-filled neighborhood of spacious homes and meticulous gardens, a few hundred yards outside of Orleans Parish. Taylor double-checked the number that she had scribbled, glanced again at the residence that bore the address, and parked on the street, behind Joe's unmarked white sedan.

Morrissey was a lawyer. He defended high-profile criminal defendants and represented plaintiffs in class action, personal injury cases. He used television commercials to feed his firm's personal injury practice. Every night, in the middle of the local news, he sponsored "The Morrissey Minute," in which he reduced complex legal problems to understandable terms, then asked the public to hire his firm. Taylor shuddered at the thought of his commercials. The very nature of a plaintiff's personal injury lawyer was antithetical to Taylor's old-line, well-bred world. Morrissey's manner of practicing law had led her to expect crass and tacky, yet his modern-styled residence blended green-gray flagstone, creamy stucco, and etched glass windows into a subtly elegant and tasteful home. The house was centered on a corner lot with sprawling oaks, camellias, azaleas, and clusters of white caladiums.

Taylor checked her reflection, wiped away a faint smudge of mascara, ran her fingers through her long hair, and applied a fresh swipe of coral-colored lipstick. Once out of the car, she smoothed the knee-length skirt of her butter-yellow linen suit, checked to make sure that the kick-pleats were folded, buttoned the sleek bolero jacket, and reached for her purse and matching portfolio. If she had known that she'd end up at a murder interrogation, she might have chosen a suit in a more conservative color, and maybe she wouldn't have worn nude patent peep-toe shoes with six-inch heels. She shrugged. At least the style of the suit was conservative. She breathed deeply, pushed her shoulders back, went to the front door, glanced at the security camera that was poised above it, and rang the bell.

From inside the house, there was a baby's cry. The sound was jarring, loud, and unhappy. The door opened and the star of the Morrissey Minute barely glanced at her as he tried to console a baby who was nestled in the crook of his arm. The baby wore nothing but a diaper. Bare feet, balled-up hands, and fat legs were exposed. He had a plump belly with a tiny bellybutton and a face that was red from crying. The unhappy infant presented a human package that seemed improbably tiny next to Morrissey.

Tiny, but loud.

"Thank God you're here," Brandon said. "I can't calm him. I changed him. He ate." Light green eyes glanced into hers for a second, then returned to the baby. "Here. Let's trade." At first, she had no idea what he meant, but it became obvious fast. With his free hand, he reached for her purse and portfolio and took them from her, then leaned forward with the arm that held the wailing baby, so that the baby and his arm almost touched her chest. Surprise at the quick exchange momentarily robbed Taylor of the ability to react.

"Take him," he said. "You've got to be better at this than me."

Her arms closed around the wriggling baby, whose miserable state became more important than introducing herself. The baby weighed ten, maybe twelve pounds. He had fat cheeks, full lips, and a full fringe of eyelashes that would have made a supermodel envious. His face was flushed, and tears flowed from his unfocused, gray-blue eyes. She held him against her shoulder as she turned her face to his ear.

"Aw, you're going to be fine. You're okay, sweet little thing. All good," she said, inhaling the sweet scent of baby lotion. She pressed her palm against his tiny back, attempting to soothe his warm, bare skin. Taylor wasn't a mother, but she had volunteered throughout high school in church nurseries. She drew upon that experience, and after a couple of seconds where the only thing she did was hold him tightly and whisper to him, his cries became less desperate. Her hair had fallen over the baby, and when she tried to push it back with a head shake, she discovered that he had grabbed a clump. She let him hold onto it.

Taylor continued whispering to the baby as she followed Brandon into a living room with flagstone floors, cream-colored walls, high ceilings, crown molding, and soft light. Modern furniture alongside antiques provided an eclectic feel, but the large room was too sparse to seem finished. No pillows were out of place on the creamy linen couch. There were no photographs or other personal touches. The room overlooked a pool and gardens. She could see silver reflection orbs of a tall garden sculpture moving in a slow, graceful dance that reflected the pool's glistening water, and lush green gardens, under a bright blue summer sky.

Either the Morrissey family consisted of neat freaks, Taylor thought, or they had other issues. There was no hint that an infant lived there, but for the moment, the baby didn't seem to mind. He was quiet, his head was turned to hers, and his eyelids were getting heavy.

She looked at Brandon, who was looking at the baby, and she whispered, "Success."

"Amazing," he said, studying her hold on the baby, how the baby's chest hit right above her chest, and how his fist was entwined in her hair. When Brandon glanced at her, his green eyes captured her attention. Serious, tired undertones flooded his eyes, as his gaze travelled over her suit, the rings on her fingers, and his eyes fell to her high heels. "The set-up for him is in the kitchen and the casual living room that's next to it, for now," he said. "The nanny service said it would be at least two hours before someone could get here, but they'd try to be faster. I appreciate that you got here so quickly."

Forget that his home far exceeded her expectations. The man was nothing like what she'd expected. She met his gaze, where there was none of the cocky bravado that he showed on his commercials. Instead, he looked like a man who had more than a healthy dose of frustration and fatigue. In person, Brandon seemed nothing like the slick, uber-confident man who appeared on television in crisp white shirts, subtle silk ties, and expensive business suits. Faded jeans and an untucked, close-fitting t-shirt revealed a lean, yet muscular, body. He was as sturdy and rugged as his home was neat. He was tall, with broad shoulders and a narrow waist, and looked younger and slimmer than he did on television. A large, multi-colored fleur-de-lis art-like tattoo covered the part of his right bicep that was visible beneath his short sleeve. The tattoo was bordered in black, or something lighter, maybe midnight blue, while the inside resembled an intricate, stained-glass mosaic. The colors shimmered, as though layered with gold dust.

Keeping her voice just above a whisper, she shook her head and said, "I'm not with the nanny service."

"If you're not with the nanny service, who are you?"

"Taylor Bartholomew," she said, keeping her tone soft as she kept a firm hold on the baby. "I'm an assistant district attorney, and I'm here for your interrogation. The police are already here, right?"

He frowned. He still held her purse and portfolio. "I'll take him. Sorry." He reached towards the baby, gently pried her hair from his grasp, and took him from her with one strong arm. "I made an assumption that I shouldn't have."

He returned her purse and her portfolio to her and, even before the feeling of the baby's weight and warmth faded from her arms, the baby started crying.

She studied his one-armed hold on the infant. "Use both arms," she said, realizing that he had no clue what to do with the child, and she wondered why. "Security is what it's all about. Think swaddling."

He glanced at her. "What?"

"Wrapped for comfort. Place him against your shoulder with a hand on his back. Hold him tightly. He really needs a blanket. Clothes, at least."

The baby's cries began to fade as he made adjustments with his arms. The front door burst open, and a thirty-something-year-old woman charged into the house, wearing loose-fitting black pants and a button-down white shirt. Her long, dark hair was pulled into a ponytail. She entered the foyer, then halted. Her eyes widened as she focused her attention on the baby, then Brandon, then the baby. Brandon crossed through the living room, towards her. He kissed the woman on the cheek while he patted the baby on the back. From the infant, there was a faint whimper, almost a sigh, then silence. "Kate, meet Michael. My son," he paused, "your nephew. And this is..." his eyes fell on Taylor, then he was silent.

"Taylor Bartholomew," she said, realizing that he hadn't listened when she first said her name, and that even now he wasn't focused on her, or her name, or really anything about her. He was focused on the baby, and holding his breath and hoping like hell the baby was going to be quiet.

Kate nodded to Taylor. "I'm Kate Morrissey. Brandon's sister."

"This is my son, Michael." Brandon said the words slowly, as though they were new. He whispered, "Shush," in the baby's ears, and looked again at his sister, whose eyes had welled with tears. Taylor was intruding on a personal moment, but she couldn't stop staring at Brandon, Kate, and Michael. Kate's hands were shaking. Brandon shifted the baby off of his shoulder, giving both Taylor and Kate a view of fat cheeks, a tiny turned-up nose, and eyes that were almost closed, as he shifted the baby into Kate's arms.

"Hold him against your shoulder. Talk to him." He turned his attention to the baby and said, "This is your Aunt. Kate. Aunt Kate's got you." He stroked his son's cheek as he said to Kate, "We have plenty to talk about, but later. Thanks for coming. I need to be in this meeting. The nanny service is sending someone. It wasn't a problem for you to get off of work, was it?"

Kate shook her head. "Oh, my gosh. He's so tiny."

"For now, this is between us." Brandon and his sister shared a long, silent glance.

"Mom doesn't know?"

"Not yet."

Worry lines appeared on Kate's brow. "Have you heard anything about Victor?"

"No," Brandon frowned, "I haven't heard anything yet, but Sebastian's company is checking on his whereabouts. They'll find him."

"Mom's frantic. I talked to her earlier today," Kate said. "He's never not called her on her birthday, and now it's been a month."

"Let's talk about it later," Brandon said. "For now I really need your help with Michael, because I can't put off this meeting any longer." With a glance that encompassed Taylor and Kate, but mostly Kate, Brandon said, "Michael has finished the last of the final bottle that Lisa had fixed, which gives me about three hours to figure out what brand of formula he's on. I changed him a few minutes ago. Esme was off today," he explained, referring to his housekeeper, "but she's coming in this afternoon. She'll run to the store, once we figure out what we need. When this interview's over, I'll see if I can get a better handle on things from Lisa's house."

Kate and Michael disappeared down a hallway. *Lisa*, Taylor thought. *Lisa*'s house. Taylor knew from information that Joe had given her that Lisa Smithfield, the murdered Tulane graduate student, had been a new mother. She had only known that Brandon was a person of interest, but there had been no explanation regarding why. Now she understood that Brandon was the father of Lisa's child, a fact that no one had told her. While understanding dawned, Brandon stared at her, arms folded, full lips drawn together. Dark lashes made his light eyes inviting, but his razor-sharp gaze was a caution sign. He had high cheekbones, hollow cheeks, and enough stubble on his square jaw to reveal that the lawyer who was always sleek and well-groomed in his television commercials hadn't shaved that morning. A thin white line formed a three-inch scar that traveled along his right cheekbone. His hair looked as if nothing but his fingers had been used to comb it. A small bit of gray that shot through the temple-region of his black, wavy hair could have given him a distinguished look. Instead, the gray, coupled with the hard expression in his eyes, gave him a tough edge.

There were reasons why their social circles didn't overlap, why Taylor had never met Brandon in person. Yet for one reason in particular, she knew of his family, and he, no doubt, knew of hers. His grandfather had been in business with

Taylor's grandfather at one time, and had been convicted of attempting to sell military secrets to the Nazis. Besides his unfortunate family history, Brandon had chosen a path that would have him shunned by people in her circles. Brandon's commercials had frequently aired as Taylor sat by the sickbed of her mother, Rebecca Marlowe Bartholomew, Bitsy for short. Each time the lawyer with the rock-star good looks reduced legal concepts to a sound bite, Bitsy would shudder and say, *"Those people are not our type. We are kings and queens of Mardi Gras. The Morrisseys, well, they'd be lucky to get a good viewing spot on the street."* Her father, George Bartholomew, was not as concerned about social graces, or the lack thereof. George hated plaintiff's lawyers in general, considering them to be parasitic bottom-dwellers that fed off the hard work of legitimate businessmen. Two years earlier, in the last month of her mother's life, in the long evenings when Taylor and her father had kept vigil over Bitsy's sickbed, George would say, during the Morrissey Minute, *"The arrogance. How dare he purport to teach the public about the law? That bloodline should have been eradicated when his grandfather was convicted."*

Taylor handed Brandon her business card. He glanced at it, gestured in the direction she should head, then walked with her. "Bartholomew. Any relation to the B in HBW Shipbuilding Enterprises?"

"Yes," she said.

He reached a closed door. He studied her for a second before opening it. "Really? An assistant D.A.?"

People had a hard time reconciling the Bartholomew name with the government-service job. She didn't bother explaining. On this last Thursday of June, before the upcoming Fourth of July holiday on Monday, most of the assistants, along with the D.A., were attending a bar association convention in Florida. The Deputy Chief was scrambling for bodies and had passed by Taylor's office with the options of misdemeanor court, a guilty plea hearing, or making sure a subject and his defense lawyer stayed in check in a homicide interview. Taylor had chosen the interview and left before someone with more seniority could steal the assignment. Hands down, it was the most interesting of the options, even before she realized that Morrissey was the subject of the interview, arrived in his gorgeous house, figured out that he had fathered a child with the murder victim, and way before he had placed the baby in her arms and gazed at her with eyes that were the color of pure, expensive jade. Now, the quick assignment had become downright fascinating.

"Yes," she said, "an assistant district attorney."

"Why?"

People couldn't get past the fact that she could be described as a debutante, an heiress, former Queen of Carnival, and an assistant D.A. Most, though, didn't so blatantly ask why. She folded her arms and met his stare. "I'm here for your interview, Mr. Morrissey. Not mine."

His serious gaze softened. Without the full weight of untold worries in his face, his eyes became riveting and his lush lips worth more than a passing glance. Yet he didn't smile. "Good for you," he said. "Not so great for me."

He opened the door for her, revealing a large, lived-in, legal war room. Two conference tables could seat fourteen people. Four computer monitors filled work stations along one wall. Laptops were on one of the conference tables. Large-screen televisions were mounted on one wall. Audiovisual equipment was encased on sleek shelves. Against another of the walls there was a jury booth, with seating for twelve. The mock-trial courtroom also had a judge's bench and a podium. Joe and Tony, the homicide detectives, were seated at one conference table. She recognized Brandon's lawyer, Randall Whiteman, seated with them. All three men were on their phones, and it took a minute or so for them to end their conversations. The detectives nodded hello to Taylor, while Randall crossed the room to introduce himself.

Brandon focused on Joe. "You said you had a few questions. That's it. So why is the D.A.'s office here?"

Joe answered, "We do things differently than when you were on the force."

"That's nice, considering my last day on the force was more than fifteen years ago. Glad to see there's been some evolution. Still," Brandon said, "why? You're not seriously thinking that I had anything to do with Lisa's murder, are you?"

"The new policy is that when an interviewee in a murder

investigation has a lawyer present, the D.A.'s office sends a lawyer. You have Randall, so the D.A. sent Taylor, who will ask whatever questions she sees fit and make sure the new protocols are followed."

Brandon made no move to sit. He remained standing, next to Taylor, arms folded. "Randall's here because he's my friend."

When she heard the tension in his voice, warning bells flashed. Part of her job there was to make things go smoothly, and his tone indicated that her task could prove tricky. Taylor glanced at Randall. He wore a conservative, navy-blue business suit. She knew from her work that he was no stranger to criminal law courtrooms. He might be Brandon's friend, but he was also one of the best criminal defense lawyers in the city and, at least for now, his quiet, calm demeanor indicated he was willing to let his client have free rein.

"If Randall were only a friend, he wouldn't be allowed in the interview," Joe said, "and you know it. You made it perfectly clear that you wouldn't answer questions without Randall present."

"I talked to you last night," Brandon said, "before Randall arrived."

"And now we need an official statement," Joe said.

Brandon glared at Joe, Tony, and Taylor. "You've all lost it if you're seriously thinking of me as a suspect."

"Mr. Morrissey," Taylor said, drawing green-eyed ire, "insults aren't going to move this process forward."

"I told Joe everything that I knew last night," Brandon said. "This is insane."

"We need an official statement," Taylor shrugged as she stated the obvious, "and we have to record the interview."

Joe flipped on a recorder as he set it on the table and said, "We won't start until you sit."

Brandon's face flushed red. He didn't sit. He stared at the recorder, then at Joe, then his gaze fell on Taylor. He gave her a long hard glance, then he turned his attention back to Joe. The silent stare that Brandon and Joe shared had a current of mutual respect, but also wariness. "You're kidding. A recorder?"

To corral Brandon she decided to threaten the one thing

that she guessed was priceless to the unshaven father, who had overnight become an infant's sole parent. Time.

"We can do this downtown, Mr. Morrissey," Taylor said. "The detectives agreed to conduct this interrogation in your home as a courtesy, but we can go downtown and reconvene at the station." Her comment won her a hard glare and a clenched jaw. She squared her shoulders, lifted her chin, and said, "You decide. Here, now, and relatively quickly, or downtown, and," she paused, as she watched a pulse throb at his temple, "not so fast."

***

Well, damn.

Taylor had him, and he'd been easy to get. He had worked for years on controlling his temper, and just like that, he had regressed. Brandon gathered control as he drew a deep breath and studied her. He was used to smart, pretty lawyers. Taylor, though, was off-the-charts gorgeous, and, as he studied her, he bet that her good looks didn't always work in her favor. Golden strands streaked through thick, honey-colored hair that fell midway down her back. Her subtle, tasteful tan complemented the warm tones in her almond-shaped, brownish-green eyes. Her ultra-feminine suit showed off her curvy figure, but she also looked professional. Natural sultriness was toned down by good taste, time, money, and effort, which made her even more alluring. She was a stunning beauty and, for the life of him, he couldn't figure out why a Bartholomew would be an assistant D.A. His eyes fell on the card that she had handed him. Taylor Marlowe Bartholomew. He digested all three of her names. What the hell? His gaze bounced back to her. She wasn't only a Bartholomew. Her other two names were family names. Filthy-rich, upper-crust family names.

She raised a perfectly arched eyebrow. "Well? Here, or at the station?"

He sat at the conference table, across from Joe, with the recorder between them. "Here."

Focus on their questions, he told himself, as he'd told countless clients in similar situations. So many other thoughts, though, sizzled through his brain. Murder. Fatherhood. Lisa, a perfectly nice woman. Murdered. Damn. Parenthood. *Single* parenthood. Damn it. *Sole* parenthood. Murder, and the police were interrogating him.

Joe, gray-haired, barrel-chested, and olive-complected, was frowning. Brandon had prior experience with Joe, and, if he had to put money on it, he'd have bet that Joe wasn't happy to be there. Joe's partner, Tony, sat on Joe's right. Unlike Joe, Brandon didn't have experience with Tony, a younger man with dark hair and dark eyes. His glance fell again on Taylor, who sat next to Joe. *Damn.* She was a distraction. Joe gave introductory comments for the benefit of the recorder, then asked, "Tell us for the record why you arrived at Lisa's home last night at one forty-five in the morning."

"I received a call around midnight from a girlfriend of Lisa's who was babysitting. She said that Lisa hadn't returned from work to pick up Michael. Lisa never ran late. She was concerned. Lisa doesn't have family. She didn't know who else to call."

Taylor said, "Tell us about your relationship with Lisa."

Brandon hesitated. He didn't want his relationship, or lack of a relationship, with Lisa becoming public record.

She arched an eyebrow. "Well?"

"Look," Brandon said, "the reality is that some thug wanted Lisa's purse and killed her for it. The city might have a new D.A., a new police chief, and new procedures, but what you're doing with me, here, tells me that the city has the same damn ineffectiveness." He glared at Joe. "Go do your job, find the thug, and put him away before he kills someone else."

"Don't criticize," Joe said. "Not that long ago, when you needed good police work you came to the NOPD."

"And the NOPD almost cost me my life," Brandon said. "All you guys had to do was confirm what I knew and make an arrest, but the NOPD didn't do the job. You left me to do the dirty work."

"Don't forget that you were in it up to your ass," Joe said. "You're not a stranger to violence, Brandon, and if you hadn't come to the NOPD back then, there's a strong chance that you'd be doing prison time right now." He paused. "If you'd like, we can make that violent incident part of the record in this investigation."

Randall interrupted. "Ask your questions, detective. Stay away from irrelevant history."

"No," Joe said, his face flushed. "We'll do this at the station."

As Joe stood, Brandon's anger ebbed. The simple fact was that given Brandon's history, Joe wouldn't be doing his job if he didn't talk to Brandon. Plus, as Taylor had figured out, today's reality was that he didn't have time to cool his heels at the police station. Brandon ran his fingers through his hair, took a deep breath, and said, in as apologetic tone as he could muster, "Wait. Please. Sit down."

Some of the red left Joe's cheeks and neck. He gave Brandon a hard stare, then plopped into the chair with a sigh.

In a calm voice, Taylor asked, "Did you know Lisa well?"

"No."

"When did you first meet her?"

"About eleven months ago," Brandon said. "Our son is two months old. Lisa and I slept together the night that we met, and," he paused as Taylor frowned. She tried to conceal her disapproval with an impassive expression, but not before Brandon guessed that one-night stands were beneath her well-bred upbringing. "I didn't talk to her again until two weeks ago, when I learned about Michael. It was a one-night thing. I'm not proud of this. It's not the way I ever anticipated becoming a father."

The room was quiet as Taylor's eyes held his with a serious look that made him feel cheap, which was exactly how he had acted with Lisa. Joe's cell phone rang, shattering the silence. He turned off the recorder, answered his phone, stood, and gestured to Tony to step out of the room with him. Taking advantage of the break, Randall stood, stretched, then turned his attention to his phone.

Taylor. Marlowe. Bartholomew.

Any New Orleanian knew that Taylor was oil, Marlowe was shipping, and Bartholomew was shipbuilding. The businesses of Taylor and Marlowe had been sold in the early eighties at prices that had put the families on the Forbes lists. As a Bartholomew, she was also heir to her father's position in the shipbuilding company, the same company that had been the downfall of Brandon's grandfather, and, by association, the entire Morrissey family. To Brandon's knowledge, Taylor wasn't simply an heir to George Bartholomew and the Bartholomew fortune. She was George Bartholomew's only heir.

Now, luminous hazel eyes held his in a steady gaze that reminded him of the distance between his world and hers. He was the grandson of a convicted traitor. The son of an alcoholic, who had never amounted to much and who had taken the coward's way out of life. With each word that Brandon articulated, the distance between their worlds would grow greater, and, as he returned Taylor's stare, he realized that her beauty was no competition for her sobering, unsmiling eyes. The focused attention that she gave him was unsettling, and the last twelve hours had been disturbing enough. Joe's reentry into the room gave Brandon a needed break from her.

Joe switched the recorder back on. He heard Joe whisper to Taylor, "I'll take over. We've got to hurry and get out of here." To Brandon, Joe asked, "Where did you first meet Lisa?"

"At my office. She came with questions." Brandon paused, then decided that he'd said enough.

"How the heck does a trip to an office for legal advice become a one-night stand?" Joe asked.

Randall said, "Detective, we don't need judgmental attitude coloring your questions."

Joe glanced at Randall with more than a little disgust. "Answer the question, Brandon."

As Brandon replayed Joe's poorly-worded question in his mind, he glanced at Taylor. Joe's question assumed that Lisa had approached him for legal advice, while Brandon hadn't meant to give Joe that impression. Taylor was staring at Brandon, one eyebrow arched, with a slight frown, as though she knew that Joe's assumption needed confirmation. Damn it. He had to stop looking at her. She was a distraction.

Brandon focused on Joe's dark-eyed, weary gaze. Joe wasn't asking him whether Lisa had sought legal advice. Joe was assuming that Lisa had been to his office for legal advice, then asking how Lisa's visit to his office had become a one-night stand. Brandon felt more comfortable focusing on the how and why of the one-night stand than on the real purpose behind Lisa's original visit to his office. "I couldn't help her," he said. "She was disappointed. I took her out on one of my boats for a cruise. One thing led to another." Brandon watched Taylor lean towards Joe. Before she could make her point, Joe continued, "So after your boating trip, which became a one-night stand, you had no contact with Lisa until two weeks ago?"

"That's correct. She tried to call me a couple of times, but I didn't take her calls."

"Why not?"

Brandon drew a deep breath. There was no way to sugarcoat the reality of it. "I was busy, and I wasn't interested."

Joe continued, "Why did you decide to talk to her two weeks ago?"

"The message she left was, 'I had your baby,'" he said, again glancing at Taylor. She was frowning. "That got my attention. I confirmed what she was telling me, and in the last ten days or so, I've seen her several times."

"How many times?"

"Six," Brandon paused. "Maybe eight."

"Did you resume your relationship?"

"There was no relationship." Brandon felt like punching Joe's obtuseness out of him. "Not at first and not in the last two weeks. Never."

"Why did you see her so frequently in the last two weeks?"

"I was trying to get things settled."

"What do you mean by that?"

"Proper care for the child."

"Money?" Joe asked.

"Of course, money," Brandon said. "He's my child, Joe. She was a student. She had no money."

"Were you angry?"

Brandon felt some of the color leave his face as he realized how bad it looked. "Yes. With myself. With Lisa? Hell no. He's my *child*, Joe. Hell. This is a nightmare. I had no idea that she was pregnant. I used precautions, damn it. I didn't believe it at first, but DNA's confirmed it. As soon as I knew about him, I knew that I had to take care of him, and because she is — was — his mother, I needed to take care of her as well. Lisa was living in a dumpy little rental. I had to persuade her to take my money and move. She had no family. She needed help. Money, and more. Sitters. Good, reliable help. A support system."

Joe asked, "So it was a nightmare to you?"

Brandon winced at Joe's use of his own word, then shrugged. "I've been through nightmares before, Joe. You know about them. This was one that I could handle. Without killing anyone."

Joe placed his elbows on the table and leaned toward Brandon. "Were you and Lisa fighting over visitation rights?"

Brandon shook his head. "She was in favor of joint custody. At least for now, I had full access. We weren't fighting over anything. I was doing whatever I could do to help her."

"This was going to cost you a lot of money."

"I have it," Brandon shrugged.

"Where were you last night," Joe asked, "when you got the call from the babysitter?"

"Sleeping on my boat. It was docked on the wall in Madisonville, on the Tchefuncte River. Yesterday was my birthday. I left Orleans Marina at three, and about an hour and a half later, I arrived in Madisonville. I had friends over to the boat for cocktails. We went to dinner, and returned to the boat around nine."

"You were alone after nine?"

"No. I had a date," he said. "She was with me when I left New Orleans, through dinner, and she returned to the boat after dinner. She was with me when I got the call, and she rode across the lake with me. In a taxi. I dropped her at the marina where I picked up my car and she picked up hers. Then I headed Uptown, to the university, then to Lisa's house, to see if I could find her. That's when I ran into you. Lisa was supposed to pick up the baby at ten-fifteen or so and she was hours overdue by that point."

"You said that you had visits with Lisa. Were you in her house?" Joe asked.

Brandon stared at Joe. In the early morning hours he had pulled up to Lisa's house at the same time as Joe, and Joe wouldn't let Brandon in. Brandon guessed the police had found prints, and they wanted to know whether Brandon's were a match. "Yes. Most recently Tuesday night, two nights ago. I watched Michael at her house while Lisa worked. I interviewed a few ladies from a nanny service. I didn't realize until this morning how lucky I was that he slept the whole time." He glanced at Taylor, whose expression softened at his slight joke. "I interviewed a few ladies from a nanny service."

Tony reentered the room. He whispered to Joe. To Brandon, Joe said, "I'll need names and contact information for everyone who can verify your whereabouts yesterday. Also anyone who might be able to verify that in the last two weeks you were helping Lisa. The ladies you interviewed for the nanny position. Did you hire one?"

"Yes. Actually, there's two sisters. They were going to tag team for a couple of months. They were supposed to start Monday, but now I need them sooner." He glanced at Taylor. "They were both unavailable today, so the nanny service is sending someone else.

Joe paused, and Tony asked, "You have handguns?"

"Two Glocks and a Hammerli." Good, Brandon thought. The cops could have the damn guns. His weapons didn't kill Lisa, and the sooner the cops figured that out, the better.

"Are they registered?" Joe asked.

"Of course."

"We'll need them."

"Two are here. You can have them now. The other's on the boat. Pete St. Paul, one of my investigators, can bring the one from the boat downtown."

Joe stopped the recorder. Brandon went to his bedroom and retrieved one of his Glocks and the Hammerli. He returned to the study and handed the weapons, in their carrying cases, to Tony, who bagged each of them, then turned his attention back to Brandon. Joe turned on the recorder and identified the weapons for the record.

"I need to take care of some things at Lisa's house,"

Brandon said. "Now."

"You won't get into Lisa's house until late tonight, or tomorrow," Joe said, glancing at his watch, "at the earliest."

"What's the rush?" Tony asked.

Tension built in Brandon's shoulders and snaked up his neck. He stood, rubbed his neck, and drew a deep breath. Hold it together, he told himself. Stay calm. "I can't wait that long. I need supplies for Michael."

Joe said, "There's a drugstore down the street."

"No shit, Joe, but I don't know what to buy. I don't know what formula he takes. Lisa made the bottles from packaged powder, and that's at her house. Michael finished the last bottle that she prepared about an hour ago. I can't change his diet. His stomach will give him fits. Plus, Lisa had mentioned that he was taking medicine for a cough." He looked at the cops, who didn't seem to give a damn, and Taylor, who looked like she didn't have a problem in her life except choosing which thousand-dollar designer suit to wear. He hated to ask them for help, but this wasn't for him. "He's coughing, and there wasn't any medicine in the bag that she packed for him. I don't know his pediatrician's name. I was in the process of figuring all of this out, before last night, but I certainly wasn't expecting that overnight I'd become his sole parent."

Joe made closing comments, then turned off the recorder. "Crime lab techs are done there, but I haven't gotten the official word that the scene's released. Tony and I have to go to the Ninth Ward. Now. We have new leads on last week's triple murder, and that could take the rest of the day. I can't let you go there alone. Not until the scene's released."

"There's got to be somebody," Brandon said, "who can go now."

"I could call a uniform," Tony said, "but that could also take hours, and the reality is that we need to have someone connected with the case as an escort. I'm sorry, Brandon. You'll have to wait."

"I can't," he said, but he realized that he'd have to.

"I have a short meeting at one, but I can be there in an hour and a half," Taylor said. "I'll go with Brandon."

"*Aw hell,*" he muttered to himself, as his help came from an unlikely source.

Joe and Tony shared a glance. Joe shrugged and nodded to Taylor. He pulled her to the side, and after a short conversation, Joe handed Taylor the key to Lisa's place, which he had taken from Brandon the night before. Joe and Tony left, along with Randall.

With no others in the room, Brandon became aware of her poise and her quiet, formal manner. "Thank you," he said. "I couldn't wait."

"You're welcome," she said. "I'll meet you there. But before I leave, Mr. Morrissey, I need the list of people who can verify your alibi."

Brandon made the list and handed it to Taylor. He gestured for her to step ahead and walked her to the front door. Before he shut the door, he watched her walk away. Her high-heeled stride showed off long legs, tapering, curvy calves, and with each step, her form-fitting skirt cupped the cheeks of her high, full butt. He'd come off of twelve colossally tragic hours, but he couldn't stop looking. *Hell.* The pale yellow, slim-fitting skirt begged for an eye glide, and her high heels were more stripper-like than lawyer-like. Not noticing her long, perfect legs would be something to worry about, so he forgave himself. He shut the front door before she turned to get in her car, before she saw him watching.

To the side of the kitchen, in the area that doubled as a casual dining and sitting area, Kate was sitting in Brandon's favorite barrel chair, feet up on an ottoman, with Michael in her arms. Michael was snoozing against her chest, with a fat fist held against a pink cheek. When Brandon bent to listen, Michael's breath sounded less raspy than it had earlier. *He could handle this,* he told himself. Single fatherhood, sole parenthood, wasn't something he had anticipated. It was one hell of a speed bump, he acknowledged, but not a problem.

Kate gave him a worried glance, with eyes that matched the color of his. "Are you all right?"

"All good."

She gave him an uncertain smile. "Convincing yourself?"

Brandon nodded. "Yeah."

Chapter Two

George Bartholomew had only allocated twenty minutes of time for his daughter. That was fine with Taylor, because she didn't need much time to tell her father that she was going against his wishes. Her plan was to walk in, tell him what needed to be told, then leave. Such conversations with her father rarely had produced success on Taylor's part, and the faster she handled this, the better off she'd be.

The district attorney, Paul Connor, a family friend, had been Taylor's criminal law teacher. He'd taken office the month before Taylor graduated from law school. Once in office, he had fired half of his legal staff, attorneys who were loyal to his political opposition. Connor had been desperate for lawyers, and Taylor had used his desperation as a bargaining tool with her father. After heated argument over the issue, George had given Taylor one year to get her need for public service out of her system. One year, then Taylor, his only child, was to take her place as heir-in-waiting to his position on the Board of Directors of Hutchenson, Bartholomew, and Westerfeld Shipbuilding Enterprises. The shipbuilding company had been founded by his father and was one of the country's largest builders of cargo ships, military vessels, and oil industry service boats. Given the energy that he had poured into the argument, Taylor had realized then that no matter how great Taylor's accomplishments were in the world outside of HBW, George would see her achievements as a waste of time.

The year for which Taylor had fought so hard would be over in one day. Connor had offered her a permanent position in the division that handled felonies and violent crimes. She was going to accept the offer, but she needed to tell her father of her decision first. She wasn't seeking permission, she reminded herself, as she entered her father's office. She was only there to tell her father of the offer and that she planned to accept it.

George was on the phone. He was standing for the call, glancing out of the floor-to-ceiling windows at the views of the city skyline, the Mississippi River, and the HBW shipyard, that were visible from his corner office. He turned to the doorway when she entered, nodded, then, as she drew a deep breath and tried not to be nervous, he continued his telephone conversation. George had a full head of gray hair that was clipped short. He wore navy-blue linen slacks, a crisp pink dress shirt with French cuffs, and a silk tie with pink and blue stripes. His tailor-made clothes accented his tall stature, which Taylor had inherited. She had also inherited his high cheekbones and the almond-shape of his eyes, but her olive coloring and hazel eyes came from her mother.

Traditional taste permeated the space, with hardwood floors, oriental rugs, and heavy furniture. Oil paintings of boats and ships, all built by HBW, adorned the walls that weren't windows. Taylor found the atmosphere oppressive, even with two walls of floor to ceiling windows. She knew better than to sit. George rarely sat, and she didn't want him towering over her for this conversation.

He ended the phone call. Her father's skin was ivory, which made the brown-black hue of his eyes seem even darker, and with a humorless glance from him, her resolve started to slip.

"I'll make this short," he said as he walked away from the window and towards her.

"I requested the meeting," she said, feeling control slip.

"Earlier this week," he continued, as though she hadn't spoken, "Connor let me know that he would be making you an offer for a permanent position. He said that you're one of the most talented lawyers he's ever seen. You'd be a great asset to the office."

She hadn't anticipated that the District Attorney was going to talk to her father. Breathe, she told herself. Breathe. She should have known that her father was going to keep tabs on her. It was consistent with his style.

"The attorneys there love working with you," George continued, "the staff adores you, and Connor informed me that your persona coupled with your legal skills means that juries will do anything you request. I, of course, know how great you are. You have so many natural gifts."

Only her father could make all of those compliments seem like a prelude to an insult. Taylor knew her father well, braced herself, and said, "I've decided to accept the position."

His cheeks became flushed. A pulse started to beat at his temple. The pulse signified irritation, the default emotion that George displayed whenever he and Taylor discussed serious matters. "That's not possible. When you started there, we agreed," he said, his words in a monotone, with emphasis on *we* and *agreed*. "You would only be there for a year. Your year ends tomorrow, and your position here starts with Saturday's board meeting. We agreed that when your year was over, you'd take your place as general counsel, overseeing litigation and transactional matters, most of which are currently farmed out to law firms. The general counsel position is one that I created for you, at your insistence, and it is waiting on you."

"I'm not sure how much of an agreement we had," she said. "As I recall, you told me what I would do." Her worst professional fear was that she'd become a glorified personal assistant to her strong-willed, energetic father, who showed no signs of slowing down, even at seventy-three. He was a micro-manager who didn't delegate important decisions.

George paused, softened his expression, walked closer so that he was only an arm's length from her, and said, "Let me give you some context."

As her father adopted a calm, reasonable tone, Taylor's eyes smarted with tears. She wasn't going to win. She knew it, he knew it, and painful misery simmered deep within her. She bit the inside of her lower lip and found the strength to squelch the crying instinct. Ignoring her self-doubt, she stood straighter, and folded her arms.

"I've been working on obtaining navy contracts for submarines. The congressional committee that is in charge is talking ten submarines. I'm convincing the committee members that twenty would be more cost effective. They're revising the requests for proposals. The negotiations are delicate. The contracts mean hundreds of millions of dollars of revenue for HBW. We need these contracts. If you had been paying attention to business over the last few years," he paused, "I wouldn't have to explain to you how dire economic realities have been or how important these contracts are to our future."

"Dire? Please don't overstate the circumstances to manipulate me."

He frowned. "You decide whether dire is an overstatement. The simple fact is that if we don't get these contracts, by December we'll be out of production in two of our yards. We'll have to reduce the permanent work force by at least five hundred positions. Doesn't that sound dire to you?"

Taylor drew a deep breath, pushing past breath-stealing anxiety. "There's no other option?"

He shook his head. "No. Our failure to obtain the contracts will hurt HBW, it will hurt employees, and it will hurt the economy here. I'm pressing these points now with the decision makers. I need your help," he looked deep into her eyes, "and you need to be a part of this company to provide meaningful help."

The tight, anxious feeling in her throat built as the door to her dream of being an assistant district attorney started to close. "I didn't know that so much was at stake."

"Only because you haven't been here," George said. "Many of the decision makers for the submarine contracts will be in town for the museum opening on the Fourth of July and the events that are a prelude to it. I cannot afford for you to be a distraction right now. All those attributes that Connor spotted are needed here at HBW, and they're needed now, this weekend and over the next several months, while we negotiate these contracts. This company is my legacy and your future. HBW is at a critical juncture. I'm sorry, Taylor."

George wasn't sorry, though, and Taylor knew it. Her father had what he wanted. Control.

"You no longer have the luxury of chasing a dream that is ultimately only a detour," he said. "You belong here. Sooner rather than later."

She squared her shoulders, glanced deep into his eyes, and nodded. "I understand." She drew a deep breath as she almost choked on the words, "I'll let him know that I won't be accepting the position."

As she turned and walked towards the door, his words

followed her. "You don't have to look as though you've been sentenced to prison," he said. "Most young lawyers would be thrilled to step into the position of being general counsel for a Fortune 500 company."

She stopped walking, glanced at him, and nodded. George had gotten what he wanted from her, like he always did. It was time for her to leave, before she attempted to explain that the reason she didn't want the job was because it had nothing to do with merit. She'd been handed the position because she was his daughter, and, as long as her father was alive, the position would be meaningless.

***

Brandon parked behind Taylor's white Mercedes convertible, in front of a narrow, wood-framed shotgun double, half of which had been Lisa and Michael's home. He and Taylor stepped out of their cars at the same time and walked towards Lisa's house, where bright yellow crime scene tape marked an X in her doorway. A bike was near the front door of the other half, which was open. Before Brandon and Taylor made it up the steps that led to the porch, Lisa's neighbor stepped out, swinging a book bag onto his back. Taylor and Brandon introduced themselves. Taylor added, "I'm an assistant D.A."

"Hey. I'm Kevin." Worried blue eyes bounced from Brandon, to Taylor. Thick brown curls fell over his forehead. "The crime lab cops said that they don't think the murderer came here. You know any differently?"

"We can't talk about a pending investigation," Taylor answered, as Brandon asked, "Were you here last night?'

Taylor shot Brandon an arched-eyebrow glance. Brandon shrugged, focusing his attention on Kevin, who answered, "I left around nine-thirty last night and didn't get back until ten this morning."

"Did you sense anything unusual?" Brandon asked.

"No. Nothing."

Brandon pulled his wallet out of his back pocket, slipped out a card, and said, "If you can think of anything."

As Brandon held out his hand with the card, Taylor reached forward and snatched it before Kevin could take it. "If you think of anything, call the police, or call the D.A.'s office," Taylor said to Kevin. "Mr. Morrissey here is with neither office. He's simply a friend of the victim."

Kevin shrugged. "Sure. No problem." He unlocked his bike, carried it off the porch, and peddled down the street.

Taylor held Brandon's card between her thumb and index finger, raised it in the air, and blocked the entrance to Lisa's side of the house. "What was that?"

Brandon shrugged. "That's my business card, and I only asked him a couple of questions."

"Why?"

Brandon stared at her, wondering if she was serious. "Well, the questions were obvious. Kevin was there, and someone has to ask Lisa's neighbor questions. Based on what I knew about the overworked state of the NOPD's investigative force, I'd put money on the bet that Joe and Tony haven't interviewed him. They were here in the middle of the night, and Kevin didn't return until the morning. They haven't had time to return here, and now they're working on another case. So why not ask him a few questions?"

Sparks fired from her eyes. "If being a lawyer doesn't give you the knowledge to know that what you did was police work, then you should have picked that up when you were a police officer." She folded her arms and said, "It's called interfering with a police investigation. Don't you understand what I'm talking about?"

Well, damn it. She was gorgeous and poised and, he thought, more than a little indignant about her beliefs. He asked, "Police work?"

"Yes."

"As an assistant D.A. you have somewhat of an insider's view of the NOPD. Tell me, Taylor Marlowe Bartholomew, in your honest opinion, what kind of police work is getting done, or is likely to get done anytime in the near future regarding Lisa's murder?" As he waited for her answer, he decided that her wide eyes were more green than brown, and, although her body language suggested composure, the angry sparks that fired from her eyes indicated that she was ticked. "What's wrong? Don't want to admit that the over-worked, turmoil-driven office of the NOPD is not doing a damn thing on Lisa's murder right now?" He shrugged. "I don't blame you. It's a hard reality to face. Hell, Taylor. I asked the kid some questions because I'm curious. Aren't you? Why the hell not ask Lisa's neighbor a couple of questions?"

Her cheeks developed a light flush. She gave a slight shake of her head. "Because you gave him the impression that you're a cop, when, in reality, you're a suspect."

"I'm not a suspect and," he drew a deep breath, "my card, which he didn't get a chance to look at because you snatched it, states exactly who I am. How long have you been an assistant D.A. anyway?"

"One year," she said. "Why?"

"That explains it. You're inexperienced."

"What has my experience got to do with whether you're a suspect?"

"It explains why you're not getting the fact that Joe cleared me."

She shook her head. "Now that's a leap. Who said that?"

"Look," he paused, studying her eyes, which burned with anger, "it was a royal pain to deal with, but Joe did it in the best way possible, which was on the record. The most important thing is I have no motive. Besides that, he'll shortly have all of my weapons, which did not kill her. Also, the lab techs probably found my fingerprints in this house, but I admitted being here before last night. Best of all, I have an alibi, which can be easily verified, and my actions over the past two weeks, which Joe can also verify, indicate that I was making every effort to help Lisa. Not hurt her. My guess is, though, that Joe won't even take the time to verify my actions over the past two weeks or my alibi, because he believes me, and he has too much other work to do. Agree?"

She frowned. "I'm not agreeing, so don't gloat."

"I'm not. I'm simply stating facts that we both know are true." He paused. "Look. I don't want to argue with you. I really appreciate that you're helping me by being my escort here, when you're certainly not obligated to do so." He undid one half of the taped X that blocked the doorway. "You have the key, so, if you don't mind, please open the door so that we can do this and then each get on with our day."

She pulled the key out of her purse. Before she could use it, he said, "Wait. Give it to me. Doorknob's dirty." She handed him the key. He unlocked the door. Black fingerprint dust smudged his hands as he opened it. He glanced at Taylor's suit as he held the door open and slipped the dirty key into the pocket of his jeans. "Be careful," he said, "I expect there's more of this inside. It won't go well with your suit."

The crime lab techs hadn't wrecked the place, which made him wonder just how much work had been done there. The house looked much the same as it had on Tuesday night, with neat stacks of boxes and packing supplies. Brandon stepped around the boxes and went to the kitchen, where he found a list of emergency numbers for Michael taped inside a cabinet door. Lisa had shown it to him on Tuesday. The pediatrician's name was on the list. He peeled the list from the cabinet door, folded it, then placed it in his wallet. Next, he opened the kitchen cabinets, and found the name of the formula. He photographed the unopened canister with his phone, then sent it in a text to Kate and Esme.

Brandon turned towards the room that doubled as Michael's bedroom and the study. He paused at the threshold. For a second, a grief mixed with anger threatened to choke him. Damn. Lisa deserved better than this.

So did his son.

He cleared his throat, "I'll return for Michael's things later, when Joe gives me the green light, but for now, I want to get a few things that will make him feel like his mother is with him."

They had been standing shoulder-to-shoulder in the doorway. He turned to her and almost did a double-take. Brandon could think of any number of reasons why he didn't like Taylor. Status-conscious women who armored themselves with designer clothes usually weren't to his liking. Plus, the frown of disgust that had marred her perfect features when she learned of his one-night stand with Lisa and his ignorance of Lisa's pregnancy was etched in his memory. Now, though, her eyes had welled with tears and she was letting a couple of them fall, without caring that her mascara was running.

"God," she said, "this is hard. Maybe you could take something that she used to hold him when she was putting him to sleep. The texture and smell might comfort him."

Well, she was prissy, but she was human. Brandon stepped to the rocker, where there was a soft mint-green blanket. He went to the baby bed and pulled a creamy-white, cottony-soft stuffed bear from the corner. "Do you mind if I take these two things with me?"

She reached for the items, studied them, and squeezed them in her hands. "No problem."

"Thank you." Brandon turned and brushed too close to a stack of boxes. The top three fell off the stack. The boxes were sealed, they were labeled research, and they made hollow sounds when they fell. He lifted one. It was too light to be full of research. He lifted the next box and the next, placing them as they'd been stacked. Both boxes felt lighter than they'd been on Tuesday night, when he had stacked the boxes so that Lisa had space in the small room.

Taylor glanced at him. "Is something wrong?"

"These boxes seem lighter than they were the other night. I'd like to look in them," he said, "but I'd bet that you wouldn't go for that."

"You're supposed to be getting the pediatrician's name, a list of medications, and the brand of formula. That's it, until the scene is cleared."

If it weren't for Taylor's efforts, he wouldn't be there now, so he wasn't going to argue with her. Brandon walked past her, out of the room, and out the front door.

After he locked it, she held her hand out. "The key, Mr. Morrissey."

She was pretty, Brandon thought, but a righteous pain in the ass. "Call Joe. He'll tell you I can keep the key."

"Joe said he'd call me when the apartment is released, and I haven't gotten a call. I'm not disturbing him while he's interviewing witnesses."

Brandon willed himself to not be angry. She was only doing her job. He wiped the dirty key on his jeans, then handed it to her. "Thank you for your time."

"You're welcome," she said, then drew in a deep breath. "Mr. Morrissey, I was wondering-"

"Brandon. Lose the last name thing."

"It's not personal. I'm being professional."

"You're making me feel old."

She gave him an easy smile. "Well, you said in the interview that you had a birthday yesterday. Which one was it?"

"Forty."

"That makes you thirteen years older than me."

"Great," he muttered, staring at her. She was too damn young to look so sophisticated.

"Anyway," she paused. "When Joe questioned you, he assumed that Lisa went to your office for legal advice. Did she?"

"Are you interrogating me?"

"No," she paused. "I'm just trying to clarify something. You skirted around Joe's assumption in your answer."

Well, hell.

Taylor wasn't only gorgeous, she was astute and unafraid to follow a trail of curiosity. She was also out of line for continuing a police interrogation, when his lawyer wan't present. "I'm not here to answer questions. You had your chance in the interview to get clarification. It was a rookie mistake, not interrupting Joe, if you felt that I hadn't answered appropriately."

Irritation flashed across her face. He didn't wait to hear what she had to say. He stepped off the porch and into his car. Taylor was nobody's fool, he thought, and she was correct. He *had* skirted around Joe's assumption. The simple fact was that the real reason why Lisa had originally appeared at his office needlessly complicated things. He drove home, trying to focus on the myriad of things he had to do for Michael, but he couldn't help being bothered that Taylor was still wondering why Lisa had gone to his office, because if she figured out the truth, it would look like he was hiding something. He wasn't. He just didn't feel like talking about it. *What if* thoughts invaded his mind, and he couldn't push them out. What if Lisa's murder was related to the reason she had contacted him in the first place?

Once his mind went down that path, he couldn't stop thinking about it. Lisa hadn't come to him for legal advice. She was working on her dissertation and wanted to ask Brandon questions that were related to her research. Eleven months earlier, Lisa was asking questions that he hadn't heard since his childhood, the same questions that had tormented Marcus Morrissey, Brandon's father. The questions were about facts that had destroyed the life of Benjamin Morrissey, Brandon's grandfather and Marcus's father. The topic had been a systemic part of Brandon's young life. His mother would not allow conversation about it after a fire stole his childhood home, and after Marcus's suicide, which stole what remained of Brandon's innocence. Tuesday night, one night before her murder, Lisa had told Brandon she'd made progress. He had again shut down her comments. He wasn't interested in the conspiracy theory that had stolen his father's sanity. Now though, Brandon wondered, what if Lisa's research had revealed that Marcus was correct, that an injustice had been committed when his grandfather had been convicted? Who, after all of these years, would care, and would anyone care so much that they'd kill her?

***

On Thursday morning he disguised his appearance with eye contacts, touristy clothes, bad hair, and a cap. He journeyed back to the city, merged in with the ten a.m. walking tour of the Garden District, and slipped the demand letter into the mailbox of George Bartholomew's mansion. His demand was plain and simple:

I have an original of the Hutchenson Letter of DECEMBER 1979. I will go public with the letter if you do not deposit, by wire transfer, 25 million U.S. dollars in the Bank of Switzerland, Antigua, account BSTBBSITW 101108072809 before 12:01 a.m. on July 4th.

Afterwards, at The Chocolate Croissant, on Magazine Street, he stopped for a good cappuccino with thick, creamy froth and an almond croissant, that was crumbly, buttery, and sweet. The local newspaper had an article about Lisa's murder. There were no leads and, so far, no witnesses. The police were pleading with the public to come forward with information.

He flipped to the society section. Taylor Bartholomew, pictured with Andi Hutchenson at a party for the opera guild, was in the largest photograph in the paper's society section. He scanned the other photographs, but did not see a picture of Collette Westerfeld, the other filly in his trifecta. As usual, although Andi was pretty, his eyes were drawn to Taylor. Her hair was down in the picture, falling past her shoulders in gentle waves. The full attention that she had given the photographer revealed confidence. Her almond-shaped eyes had a knowing look. Her cocktail dress exposed a hint of cleavage, a small waist, and the graceful curve of her slender neck.

So perfect.

Her special, sultry beauty aroused him, which few women now did. Yet, he despised her for having the name, the wealth, the prestige, and the confidence that came with being untouchable by the mortal world, where people worried about mundane things like having to pay a mortgage.

Taylor's elevated stature had come simply by breathing her first breath of air when she was still sticky from birth. He detested her for it. He was going to destroy George Bartholomew by killing his only child. He was going to kill Taylor, whether or not George Bartholomew complied with his extortion demand. His apocalypse plan was in motion. There was no turning back. Before Taylor, though, there was Collette. Then Andi. One plum from each of the three HBW families would die. He started to fold the paper, but paused when an article about the upcoming party caught his eye.

Gala Honoring Local Families Will Precede July 4th Opening of New Wing at the National World War II Museum

On Sunday evening, the third of July, a black-tie gala will honor Andrew Hutchenson I, George Bartholomew Sr., and Charles Westerfeld, the founders of HBW Shipbuilding Enterprises. Thanks to the current HBW families, the new wing of the National World War II museum, the Infamy Wing, will soon be a reality, and will more than double the size of the original museum. In addition to expanding the museum's historic collections, the new wing will feature the HBW Pavilion, which will house a three-hundred seat movie theater and a restaurant. The HBW families made the financial contributions in honor of their forefathers, who designed the Hutchenson Landing Craft, the unique boat that enabled the United States to develop a winning strategy for World War II. Coveted invitations for the gala, on ecru paper with engraved, royal blue lettering, and red lined envelopes, have been hand-delivered to select locals. In addition, public officials, military men, and veterans from around the country will be attending. Other attendees will include World War II historians and celebrities who are students of history. A patron reception is being held at the Bartholomew mansion on Saturday, July 2nd. The Infamy Wing will be open to the public on Sunday, July 4th.

How fucking pretentious, he thought. The myth of HBW Shipbuilding Enterprises was built upon lies. He held the cards that could expose the lies, but the final play would be dictated by George Bartholomew Jr., Andrew Hutchenson II, and Claude Westerfeld, the three current members of the HBW board. The men who so proudly bore the names of their ancestors. He believed that those three men would comply with his extortion demand. They would pay him so that there was no tarnish on the HBW legend, so that the legend remained for future generations. Once he had their money, and destroyed them by killing their loved ones, he would simply walk away. He would disappear. He would never have to work again.

He would rest.

Finally.

Chapter Three

Upon returning to her office, Taylor shut her office door and drew a deep, calming breath. At least the District Attorney was out of town. It would be easier to remain composed in a phone call than in person. She called Connor, thanked him for the offer of a permanent position, but informed him that she had to decline. Framed diplomas were easy to remove from the walls. Desk accessories fit into two packing boxes. A crystal set that included a paperweight, letter opener, vase, and clock, given to her as graduation gifts by Andi and Collette, went into one box after Taylor wrapped each piece in paper.

Don't think, she told herself. *Get through today. Don't think about what you're leaving, or where you're going.*

She typed a short memo regarding her observations of the Morrissey interview, the trip to Smithfield's house, and ended with Brandon's list of alibi contacts that he had provided after the interview. She proofread the document, but instead of seeing words, she saw high cheekbones, jade green eyes, and Brandon's attempt at appearing nonchalant when answering Joe's questions about his initial contact with Lisa.

Joe's questions had hinted at past problems with law enforcement, while Brandon's responses had indicated a lack of faith in the NOPD. After a few computer searches, she found news articles that explained both Joe's questions and Brandon's responses. Two years earlier, news accounts stated that Brandon had killed, in self-defense, an intruder who had entered his Old Metairie home on Northline Street. The residents of the quiet, secluded neighborhood were panic-stricken at the violence. A few days before the incident, the NOPD had issued an arrest warrant for the man who died, due to his alleged involvement in a murder-for-hire scheme. He had eluded capture. No charges were filed against Brandon.

A current-day news search revealed the latest media

account of Smithfield's murder. Taylor's eyes were drawn to Lisa's photograph. Earlier in the day, when Taylor had first received the assignment, she had only managed to find Lisa's driver's license photo. The media had printed a larger photograph that looked more current. Lisa had sleek, dark-brown hair, blue eyes, and a fresh smile. She'd been pretty, in a natural, studious way. She'd been twenty-six. One year younger than Taylor. Tears welled in Taylor's eyes as she remembered Michael's cries. Now she understood that he was missing his mother, that he'd never know his mother's love.

God. How awful.

If only she could work in the D.A.'s office longer. Maybe she could somehow make a difference in the avalanche of violent crime that had seized the city that she loved. Connor was instituting reforms in the way the D.A.'s office conducted prosecutions. She wanted to be there to help his policies succeed. More convictions would lead to fewer crimes. Eventually there'd be fewer victims like Lisa, young, pretty mothers whose children needed them. If only she had more time.

She didn't. Her father had made that perfectly clear.

Taylor shook the thought away, swiping the tears from her eyes as she did so. HBW duty called, starting Saturday, at the July board meeting. She had to do what she had to do and she couldn't feel sorry for herself, not with Lisa's photograph staring at her from the computer. She reminded herself that she was fortunate, but still, she was restless. She picked up the memo she had drafted, stared at Brandon's alibi list, then glanced at Lisa's photograph. She read the article. Lisa was working on her doctorate degree in history and concentrating her studies on World War II era spies. Tulane students from the history department were preparing a memorial service for her.

Her heart skipped. *History. World War II. Spies.* Of all things.

Brandon and Taylor shared a piece of long-ago history, involving World War II, and involving spies, or one spy in particular. If that was the reason that Lisa went to Brandon, it could mean something. Maybe Brandon didn't like when people asked him about his grandfather. *But would he kill someone who did so?*

Taylor made a phone call to Lloyd Landrum, long-time family friend and history professor at Tulane University. Lloyd would be able to tell her the specifics of Lisa's research, but he didn't answer his office phone. At the beep, she said, "Lloyd. It's Taylor. I have a couple of questions regarding the murdered Tulane student, Lisa Smithfield. Please return my call."

She dialed Joe's cell number. When it went straight to voice mail, she tried Tony's cell. He didn't answer. At a minimum, someone should verify the alibi information, and Joe and Tony were too busy to do it anytime soon. The D.A.'s office had a pool of investigators that helped to fill gaps in police work, so that holes in police investigations didn't become acquittals. Taylor didn't have authority to assign the matter to an investigator, even if she could find one in the office. She figured she could do it. There couldn't be any harm in a few questions. Right?

Brandon had said that he had docked his boat and had dinner on the north shore of Lake Pontchartrain, in Madisonville. She took the box of crystal items, nestled it into the trunk of her car, then headed to the North Shore. Along the way, Taylor called Anna and Laura Maloney, the nannies whose names Brandon had provided. They confirmed that Brandon had interviewed them on Tuesday evening at Lisa's house, he had hired them, and that they'd be reporting for duty at Brandon's house the following day. Brandon had said that he had dinner at Fernando's, a restaurant on the Tchefuncte River. When she arrived there, the young hostess indicated that Brandon and five others had dined there the night before.

"It was Mr. Morrissey's birthday," she said. "He doesn't seem like he's forty. I mean, gosh, that seems old. I'd have guessed early thirties. He's nice," she said. "He comes here often. We all like him." She gestured towards the plate glass windows, and pointed down the river. "That's his boat. The Frayed Knot."

Taylor followed the hostess's gesture to one of several boats that were docked along the river's edge. She told the hostess goodbye and walked along the river to the motor yacht that bore the name Frayed Knot. A fit and tanned man sat at a table on the aft-deck, working on a laptop. He wore khaki shorts, a white polo shirt, and had short, dark hair. He eyed Taylor as she approached. A black lab bounded off the boat and rubbed moist fur against her skirt.

"Jett. Come." The dog did two bouncing laps around Taylor, another rub against Taylor's skirt, then jumped back on the boat. "I'm sorry," he said. "We're trying to train her, but she's young. Did she get you dirty?"

"It's fine." Taylor glanced down at her skirt, swiped at an enormous smudge, then shrugged. "She's a beauty."

"Jett or the boat?"

"Both," Taylor introduced herself and handed him her card. "Is this Brandon Morrissey's boat?"

"Yes. And his puppy." He glanced at her card. "I'm Pete St. Paul. Brandon told me that someone might be calling."

She asked, "What did Brandon tell you to say?"

"He didn't tell me what to say." He met her eyes with a solid glance, and a shrug. "But I guess he expected that I'd tell the truth."

She thought of the way Brandon's intense green eyes studied her as he listened to her. "Of course." She paused. "What kind of work do you do for Brandon?"

"I'm an investigator for the Morrissey Firm, boat sitter, dog sitter, captain, first mate, mechanic. Whatever Brandon needs."

Pete looked to be in his mid-twenties. Despite his easy manner and natural smile, his dark brown eyes had deep undercurrents that suggested a troubled past and a strong will. It was the same kind of serious look that Brandon had. The look made Taylor think that the "whatever" part of Pete's job description was the most important part. Taylor remembered that Brandon had said Pete would be bringing a pistol from the boat to downtown. "Did you bring the pistol to the police?"

"I'm heading there in a few minutes."

"When did the boat arrive here?"

"Yesterday around five."

"Did Brandon drive the boat himself, or were you the captain?"

"Brandon drove. I came over this morning to work on it and so Jett could have some exercise. I'll take the boat back to the city in the morning."

Pete's time line and facts matched Brandon's. She should stop, but she had one more question. "Do you have any idea why Lisa Smithfield originally went to see Brandon?"

"No. I sure don't."

"That's all the questions that I have. Thank you," she said.

"I'll tell Brandon that you came by."

Brandon's alibi had checked out, but there was still one missing piece. Brandon's date had been Sandra Gaines. Taylor placed Sandra's mid-city address into her GPS system, then crossed the lake. She was there by six-forty-five. No one answered Taylor's knock. As she stepped off the porch, a lone female jogger approached. She was tall and lean, with auburn hair in a ponytail.

"Sandra Gaines?"

Sandra nodded. "That's me."

Taylor introduced herself and handed Sandra her card.

"Brandon told me someone might have questions. I'm happy to talk, but I need water." Sandra pulled a key out of a waist pack and unlocked her front door. Taylor followed Sandra into a room that doubled as a kitchen and a dining room, where papers were strewn across the table. A laptop was open and on. Sandra reached into the fridge and pulled out a bottle of water. She offered one to Taylor.

"No, thank you," Taylor said.

Sandra opened the bottle, drank several large swallows, then her light brown eyes fell on Taylor. "Ask away."

"You were with Brandon yesterday?"

"Yes."

"From when to when?"

"About three in the afternoon to one in the morning."

"Are you and Brandon good friends?"

Sandra shrugged. "I met him a couple of years ago. He was opposing counsel on my first big case with the firm. I was second chair. He kicked our asses. We didn't go out until after and we've gone out a bit since then. He's honest and straightforward. He fights hard. He's got this simple, direct style that plays well in front of a jury. He's amazing, actually. A forceful advocate. He has killer instincts when ferreting out cases and questioning witnesses."

All good to know, Taylor thought, but Sandra hadn't answered her question. "How close are the two of you?"

Sandra was quiet for a second. "Not very." She drank what was remaining in her water bottle, then walked across the kitchen to throw it away. "Brandon doesn't get close." She paused. "His wife died in a bad accident five years ago. The trucker was hyped-up on amphetamines. She was six months pregnant. She and the baby both died, but it wasn't an instant death for his wife. She lasted a few days. I've never heard him talk about his wife, the baby, or the accident. Not once. Ever." She held Taylor's gaze. "I tried to get him to talk about it, thinking that's what a friend would do." She shrugged. "Now I respect his privacy and don't pry. I know about it because I know some of the lawyers who worked on the defense side. The tragic facts led to a huge judgment, which Brandon put into a foundation that provides educational grants for underprivileged children."

Sandra shuddered. "I didn't know him before the accident, but I don't think he's ever gotten over it. So are we intimate? Yes. Close?" She shook her head. "No. Brandon stays remote." Sandra continued, "Would I lie for him?" She leveled her gaze on Taylor. "No. So, Brandon and I crossed the lake, we had drinks, went to dinner, and we weren't apart for more than fifteen minutes. When we weren't with friends, we were alone together. You know."

Taylor felt a blush on her cheeks, yet Sandra seemed non-plussed. Brandon's alibi was established. She should stop asking questions and move on, but she thought back to Joe's questions that hinted that Brandon had a violent past, and Brandon's ability to kill an intruder. "Do you think Brandon has a temper?"

Sandra glanced at Taylor and shrugged. "Don't we all?"

"I mean more than most."

Sandra shot Taylor an annoyed look. "That guy that Brandon killed was a beast who went after Brandon to kill him. Brandon isn't a victim, but he's a nice guy, Taylor. He wasn't involved in any way with last night's murder."

Taylor thanked Sandra and left. As she drove away, she glanced at her watch. It was ten after seven. Thanks to the smudges left on her skirt by Jett, she had to change before attending the Blues and Bar-B-Que dinner that was being hosted by the Society for the Prevention of Cruelty to Animals. Taylor, along with her friends, Andi Hutchenson and Collette Westerfeld, were on the fundraising board for the SPCA.

She crossed town, pulled into the garage of her Garden District home, and went straight to her second-floor bedroom. She shut the door. Within minutes, there was a soft knock. Taylor braced herself. The person on the other side didn't wait for permission to enter. Bitsy had hired Carolyn Sweeny as a live-in nanny when Taylor was five, and Carolyn and Taylor had been together ever since. As Taylor grew, Carolyn's duties evolved from being a child's nanny to a professional woman's personal assistant. Taylor paid enough that Carolyn could afford her own home, and she could afford to live well. Carolyn chose to live with Taylor, and she was more than welcome. More than a paid employee, Carolyn was her friend. She'd been the mother that Taylor's own mother wasn't capable of being, the one person who had always given Taylor unconditional love, who listened to her, who was always there.

Taylor had shut the door to her bedroom because Carolyn was one person from whom she couldn't hide her emotions, and her disappointment over the end-result of the meeting with her father was still too raw. Carolyn's blue eyes gave Taylor a quick once over, then her brow furrowed with her frown. "You were going to call me. I'm guessing the meeting didn't go well?"

Taylor shook her head.

"Oh, Taylor," Carolyn said. "How bad was it?"

"Actually, he was nice, for him," Taylor said. "But you're looking at the next General Counsel of HBW. Starting Saturday."

Carolyn was silent for a second as she absorbed Taylor's news. "I'm sorry. How are you doing?"

"I'm fine," Taylor said.

Carolyn shook her head. "You don't need to pretend with me."

"I was foolish," Taylor said. "I should've known this would be the result. When have I ever had a backbone with my father?" Carolyn didn't need to respond, because they both knew that the answer to that question was never. "The good news is that I don't have time to feel sorry for myself. I was supposed to be at this event twenty minutes ago."

Taylor changed into black linen palazzo pants, a matching halter top with fat straps, and high-heeled, strappy sandals. Taylor's phone rang. When she answered it, Andi didn't waste time. "I can't believe that you're not here."

"I'll be there in twenty."

"That long? This is painfully boring," Andi said, "and it is really hot out here."

Andi, who loved the kind of partying that happened in dance clubs and bars, hated organized fundraisers and only attended when Taylor insisted. "I had to change," Taylor paused. "Is Collette there?"

"Yes, she's trying, but she's having a rough time." Collette's mother, Alicia Westerfeld, the daughter of HBW co-founder Charles Westerfeld, had never married and had adopted three children. Alicia and her oldest son, Charles Westerfeld II, had died in a plane crash two months earlier, leaving Claude, who was thirty, and Collette, who was twenty-three, as the only remaining direct descendants of Charles Westerfeld. Alicia, while a tough-as-nails director of HBW, had put together a close-knit, happy family. Collette and Claude were struggling with the loss of their mother and brother.

"Well," Taylor said, "at least she's out. I'll be there as soon as I can."

"Wait. How did it go with your father?"

"Don't ask."

"Ouch. I feel terrible for you."

"No sympathy. I don't want it," Taylor said. "Let me go. I need to get there, right?"

Taylor broke the connection, then studied her backside in the three-way, full length mirror. "Do I look fat?"

Carolyn said, "Don't be ridiculous."

"Too much cleavage?"

"You're not a nun." Carolyn squinted her eyes as she studied Taylor. "Put your shoulders back."

Taylor did, then Carolyn nodded. "You look fabulous. Only the expression in your eyes shows how terrible this day really was."

Taylor sat at her vanity, grabbed a tube of eye liner, and said, "I'll try to fix that."

Carolyn chuckled. "I don't think eyeliner is a cure-all for disappointment. Have you eaten?"

Taylor shook her head. "No time."

"I'll have something in the fridge for you for when you get back."

"Thanks," she said, "but go light."

As Taylor paddle-brushed her hair and smoothed it into a black rhinestone ponytail holder, Carolyn gave her a run-down of housekeeping details, pending meetings, and personal appointments. Taylor listened as she moved the contents of her day purse into an evening clutch. She switched out her pearls for diamonds. Taylor applied coral lipstick, a shiny gloss, and made sure the key to Lisa's house made it to her evening bag, in case Joe needed it. Taylor kissed Carolyn's cheek when she was finished. "Good bye, and thank you."

She pulled alongside Lafayette Square at eight-fifteen and into the event's valet parking area. Her phone rang, with an unknown number.

"Yes, Taylor," the caller didn't introduce himself, but there was no need. Brandon's deep voice was distinctive, it conveyed a punch of sarcasm, and she had spent part of the day listening to it. She had given her card with her cell and office numbers to two of Brandon's friends, and she guessed they had called him to report on their conversations with her. "I have a temper. A bad one. In the past, I had difficulty controlling it. It hasn't given me problems recently. Since you asked Sandra that question, I figured I should answer it myself."

"I was simply verifying your alibi."

"My temper has nothing to do with my alibi," he said, "and neither does the reason behind Lisa's original visit to my office, which you felt the need to ask Pete about. So, tell me. Did you get all the information that you need?"

"Well, I did verify your alibi," she said.

"That's not what I asked. Is your curiosity abated?"

"No," she said. "I still want an answer to the question that I asked you earlier. Why did Lisa originally go to see you?"

"You should leave police work to the police."

"That's what I told you earlier today. If I recall correctly, you asked, what's the harm. So what's the harm?"

"Damn," he said. She detected more than a little frustration in his tone as he asked, "You could keep going all night, couldn't you, with question, after question, after question."

"Absolutely."

"Can you meet me at Lisa's house at ten this evening?"

"Why?"

"So that I can answer your question."

Her heart did a stutter beat. "Really?"

"No," he said. "Joe called a few minutes ago, gave me free access, and you have the key. I don't feel like climbing through a window or breaking in, and I'd like to get in there tonight."

"Do you expect me to take your word for this?"

"Joe said he'd call you. For the moment, though, he's busy on another case, which shouldn't come as a surprise. There's always another case."

"If Joe calls me," she said, "I'll be there."

As Taylor walked towards the party, Andi and Collette were walking towards the valet stand. Andi, a tall, thin brunette, with dark green eyes, had an easy smile. Collette, a shorter red head, with large blue eyes and a few freckles on her nose, looked more serious. "Sorry that I'm late," Taylor said. "Time got away from me."

"We've been here since seven," Andi said. "We've traipsed through tree roots in high heels for long enough."

"Where are you going now?"

"My house," Collette said.

Andi added, "We're going to drink wine, order a pay-per-view comedy, and get pizza. Stop by when you're done here, if you'd like."

Andi stared intently at Taylor, conveying a silent message of worry about Collette. Taylor glanced into Collette's blue eyes. "Are you all right?"

"I'm fine. Really. Please don't look at me like you're trying to gauge my depression level," she smiled. "Come to my house when you're done here. Andi told me about your day. I'm sorry, Taylor. I know how badly you were hoping to stay in the D.A.'s office. You need a drink and a pizza binge more than we do. We're ordering extra pepperoni."

Taylor groaned. "I can't eat carbs until Monday and especially not pizza. My dresses for Saturday and Sunday are form-fitting nightmares."

"Then we'll only allow you to eat Greek yogurt," Collette said. "Please come by."

"I'll call first if I can, but it will be late." She gave both of her friends a kiss on the cheek. "Love you guys."

As they left, Taylor scanned the crowd and walked to where it was most dense. She was starving, but eating wasn't an option. As her mother would have said, Taylor was there for more important things than being photographed with food in her mouth. Marlowe money provided significant grants to this nonprofit, and Taylor was the only Marlowe who was present. Taylor's attendance was a nod to the importance of the organization.

"Hello, beautiful," Claude Westerfeld's voice came from behind her. The newest member of the HBW Board was blue-eyed and blonde-haired. He looked younger than his years, and his summer tan suggested an athletic life. Long hours on tennis courts had given him natural, athletic grace. In the last few months, with the sudden deaths of Alicia and Charles, Claude had turned to alcohol to ease the pain. Now, he had a tight grip on a glass that held a double-shot of undiluted, golden-amber liquor. His eyes were blood-shot. The Times-Picayune photographer walked by, spotted the two of them, and waited for a nod. Taylor obliged. She stood straight, squared her shoulders, and smiled for the camera. When the photographer moved on, Claude took a deep swallow of whiskey.

"Hey," she said, her voice low. "You're hitting it a little hard for a Thursday, don't you think?"

"Thursday's the new F-Friday, haven't you heard? Besides, Friday's going to be a dud because of the board meeting on Saturday," he winced. His smile was replaced with a marked frown. "Call your father now. Tell him no. You know, it isn't too late."

"What do you mean?"

"Tell him you're not going to join the family business. Don't attend Saturday's board meeting."

Taylor said, "I wasn't aware of how bad the economic realities are. He made me aware. I'm going to be HBW General Counsel because that's what I want to do."

"And if you say that enough," Claude said, "maybe one day you'll believe it?"

She couldn't fool her friend and she wasn't fooling herself. She drew a deep breath, but it was hard to push past the tightness in her throat.

"You'll see," Claude said. "When your father dumps the full HBW weight on those gorgeous shoulders of yours," he said, "you'll see."

"Now isn't the place or time," she said, "for you to be saying this."

"Why? Afraid someone might overhear the newest member of the HBW Board express disillusionment? Forgive me, Taylor. I've had cocktails and dinner with your father, Lloyd, and Andrew. I'm all done with pretension for one night." Claude looked over her shoulder. The expression on his face brightened. "There is a God. My dates have finally arrived." Her gaze followed his to a cluster of three young women who wore beat-the-heat sundresses, revealing yards of limbs and skin.

Taylor's phone dinged with a text. She pulled it out of her purse and read a text from Joe. *"Brandon's correct. He has access. Will call in a few minutes."* Claude's dates drew closer, but she didn't focus on them. Joe's text had made her think about Lisa, who should be roaming around a fundraiser in a sundress. She glanced at Claude, and her heartbeat raced. If

Lisa had been questioning Brandon about the history behind his grandfather's treason case, Lisa may have also talked to current members of the HBW board. "Did you hear about that Tulane student who was murdered?"

Claude's eyes slid back to her. "Yes. Terrible, huh?'

"Did you ever meet her?"

He shot her a surprised glance. "Why are you asking about her?"

Before she could answer, the trio of party girls arrived and clustered around him. Claude introduced them to her, then grazed Taylor's left cheek with his lips. "I'll talk to you tomorrow. For now, things are looking up. See you later."

They left her in the thick of the party, alone. She felt eyes on her, but when she glanced at the crowd, no one in particular was looking at her. Attending a fundraiser by herself was nothing new, and being an object of curiosity in a social setting also was not unusual. After all, it seemed that everyone that Taylor met in New Orleans knew of her. Tonight, though, as she worked the fundraiser crowd, she couldn't shake off the feeling that she was being studied from afar. She looked to see whether someone was staring, but no one seemed to be hyper-vigilant. Because she was there to be seen, she made several slow circles through the crowd. Along the way, she shook hands and exchanged pleasantries. She left the party at 9:30 p.m., intentionally giving herself extra time before her meeting with Brandon. Rather than head straight to Lisa's house, Taylor drove to the 2800 block of Melody Street, where Lisa's life had ended.

Pavement on Melody Street was broken and the narrow street was cramped with cars. Taylor found the closest parking spot, which was on the far side of the block from the wood-frame house that bore the address of 2813. Pink paint was peeling. Tall weeds had overtaken the yard. There was no light in the windows. The front door gaped open. Some houses on the street looked the same, but others were better maintained. It was the type of neighborhood where she shouldn't be alone at night, and she hesitated before stepping out of her car. She thought about driving away without getting out, but her memory of the feeling of Lisa's tiny baby, resting on her shoulder, kept Taylor there.

Her phone rang, startling her. "Sorry it's taken me all day to get back to you. Brandon's correct," Joe said, with the call automatically defaulting to her car's audio system. "He has access to the Smithfield home, but you don't have to meet him there. I'll do it."

"It isn't a problem. I'm on my way," she said. "Is there anything new?"

"Let's see. Fingerprints there belonged to Lisa and Brandon. There were hairs. Lab reports on that won't be in until tomorrow. They're likely hers, though. If the murderer went there, he didn't leave signs of his presence. I'm thinking that the perp more likely was someone who frequented the Melody Street neighborhood and happened to see her." Joe paused. "Brandon told me you checked his alibi. I'm not one to kill initiative, but you didn't need to do that."

"Tomorrow's my last day. My legal work is finished," she said, "so I had time. I knew that you and Tony didn't. None of the D.A. investigators were around. I'll put my notes in the file and send you an e-mail in the morning."

"I wish that you'd stay. The D.A.'s office needs lawyers who care," Joe said.

"I would if I could," she said, sighing with a sharp pang of disappointment, then shaking it off. She clicked the call to hand-held and stepped out of her car, phone in one hand, keys in the other. "Did you find anything at the scene?"

"No. Last night's storm was a deluge. When we got to her, she was soaking. The water didn't even leave her blood behind."

Night had reduced the day's heat to just below miserable. Taylor was careful not to let her heels catch on the ridges and cracks in the uneven sidewalk. Only one streetlight worked on the block, and it was a few houses away. Joe wouldn't be happy if he knew where she was, so she didn't tell him. The yard of 2813 was bordered with sweet olive trees. The normally pleasant fragrance was cloying in the humid air. As she stood there, inhaling the night's perfume, a tear fell for Lisa, then another. Taylor knew from the police report that the impact had thrown Lisa against her car. Now, another car was parked in its place. Lisa had fallen on the narrow swatch of grass between the sidewalk and the street. There were no indications of the prior night's violence. Nothing marked where Lisa had died.

Joe continued, "The perp either picked up the shell, or rainwater carried it away. We have the bullet, though. It went through her skull and lodged in her car. Ballistics aren't back. Her car doesn't look like he touched it. We talked to a few residents last night. No one saw or heard anything. I'll go back to the neighborhood tomorrow, if I have time between meetings."

Taylor shook her head, pushing past her sadness and keeping her voice from wavering. "Did Brandon seem evasive to you?'

"Brandon didn't do this, Taylor." Joe was silent, then said, "Lisa was in the wrong place at the wrong time, and that happens way too often in this damn city. There's a strong chance that we'll never get near the perp, unless someone talks. The problem is that no one talks to us, and we don't have time to make people talk. Tomorrow I'll be in federally-mandated reform meetings most of the day."

Joe's words painted a horrible truth that Taylor had heard before. The NOPD was under federal scrutiny for ongoing civil rights violations. Department morale was low. Violent crime had multiplied exponentially, and the conviction rate was at an all-time low. Connor's reforms were in place, but had not helped the conviction rate, as the cases that were filed in Connor's regime were just starting in the judicial process.

Joe said, "I'm exhausted. I'm going home and having a cold beer. I'll catch up with you tomorrow. Thank you for meeting Brandon."

As they broke the phone connection, a black four-door sedan appeared on the cross street, thirty yards or so away. Taylor didn't move. The car slowed, as though it was going to turn onto Melody. It looked like there was only one person, the driver, in the car. It was too dark for her to make out features, but the driver's size suggested that he was a broad-shouldered man. His skin was white. From the position of his shoulders, he gave the impression that he was tall.

The sleek car began its turn and its headlights illuminated where Taylor stood. It stopped and stayed in one spot while the beams from its headlights bounced off of her, blinding her. While Taylor stood in bright light, the driver was in shadows. The skin on the back of her neck crawled. He could be looking at where Lisa had been killed. Worse, he could be looking at her. Taylor wore black, but her outfit revealed shoulders and bare arms, plenty of skin to reflect light. As her heart pounded, she repressed the urge to hide in the shadows.

Chapter Four

He was lost, Taylor told herself. It was easy to get lost in the uptown area, with its maze of one-way streets. He wasn't looking at the crime scene, she told herself. He wasn't looking at her. It was her imagination that had her heart racing, that had her certain that she was his focus. He wasn't interested in her.

The driver flashed the bright lights, refuting her denial.

Taylor dismissed the flash. She glanced around the neighborhood, looking for some signal of comfort. There was no one outside, no one in a car, no one looking out of a window. The neighborhood suddenly seemed more abandoned than lived in, the houses more dilapidated than cared for.

The second flash of high beams sent chills up her spine.

Run.

Taylor knew that she needed to get out of there, but she couldn't move. She was rooted to the sidewalk, an arm's length from where Lisa had been killed. She squinted into the glare. The engine of the car were barely a hum, no louder to her than her own fast breaths, drawing in fragrant air that became sickly sweet, perfumed by the overabundance of sweet olive trees.

The third time the driver flashed the lights, he left the brights on, shining on her. Iced blood pulsed through her veins as she lifted a hand to shield her eyes.

Run.

Dear God, she couldn't move.

He inched the car closer to her. His forward motion propelled her to move. She turned and ran as fast as her high heels would allow. At her car, she pressed the unlock button on her key, slipped into the seat, and started the car, before realizing that he was gone. Still, she didn't breathe easier until she was several blocks away and even then, her hands shook with certainty that she had just encountered Lisa's murderer.

He had returned to the scene.

Taylor pulled onto Lisa's street a few minutes later. She had clutched the steering wheel so hard her fingertips were numb. She breathed easier, and her shaking slowed, until she spotted, across the street from Lisa's house, a sleek, four-door, black sedan, with the headlights on. It looked like the car from Melody Street. She grabbed her cell phone. As she passed alongside the car, her hand was poised to call 9-1-1. On Lisa's street, the streetlights worked, and there was enough light for her to see into the black sedan. She could make out the features of the driver enough to know that he was Brandon. He glanced at her as she drove past, nodding as he spoke on the phone.

Adrenaline turned her fear to nerve-crackling fury as she realized that Brandon had been the driver who had frightened her to death. How dare he stalk her at the murder scene and scare the living bejeezus out of her. Taylor parked in the nearest space, slammed her car door shut, and charged towards Brandon's car.

***

The lovely, lovely Taylor. She was the one and only thing, other than business, that George Bartholomew, the most powerful member of the HBW Board, cared about. He wanted to destroy George, and Taylor was how he was going to do it. Between Collette, Andi, and Taylor, his favorite was Taylor. She was that gorgeous. Tonight he was following her, watching her from afar while she was at the fundraiser, planning how he was going to use her.

Taylor shone, even in the midst of hundreds of beautiful people. Mingling in a social setting appeared easy for her, yet even as she greeted others she seemed remote. When Claude and the young ladies left, he watched Taylor collect her breath under the oak trees of Lafayette Square. Her vulnerability struck him. He sensed that she was not only alone, but that she was lonely. The thought made him smile. He had followed her to Melody Street and watched her. She was talking on a cell phone, not paying attention to anything more than her next few steps.

Stupid. Stupid. Stupid.

When she stood where he had killed Lisa, he couldn't resist flashing his bright lights on her.

Hello, precious. I'm here. Watching.

Wide-eyed fear had crossed her face. It was his best moment of the day. He drove away when she ran like a scared, high-heeled jack rabbit. He circled the block, then followed her. When she parked across the street from Lisa's house, he hung back, a block away. Taylor charged out of her car and, in short, purpose-driven strides, she walked towards a dark sedan. Not many things surprised him. He was used to changing circumstances. He could adapt. When Brandon Morrissey stepped out of the four-door Mercedes and approached Taylor, his heart skipped a beat.

What the fucking hell?

He left. He'd love to stay and watch the two of them together, but he did not have that luxury. Collette's hours were numbered. He had to create the perfect ending to her tragically-short life.

***

Brandon stepped out of his car as Taylor charged at him. "Are you ok?"

"You jerk."

"Excuse me?" He stopped his forward motion.

"You heard me," she said, closing the distance between them. He thought that she was going to push him back, forcibly, with her hands, but instead she folded her arms against her waist. "Jerk." None of her poise that had been evident earlier in the day was there as she drew a deep, steadying breath, then another. Her face was flushed. Her shoulders shook. "You scared the hell out of me."

"Whoa. What is it that you think that I did?"

"You know. A couple of minutes ago. On Melody Street."

"Melody Street?" There could only be one reason why she was there, but he needed confirmation before he believed it. "You went to where Lisa was killed? Alone? This late?"

"Yes."

"Are you nuts?"

"You were there. You blinded me with your headlights." She held up three fingers. "Three times."

"Like hell I did."

"Don't deny it. I saw you." She hesitated. "Well, I saw your car."

"Taylor, I wasn't there." Her glare softened, then her eyes widened. Her flushed cheeks became pale. When she started to look more scared than angry, he said, "Tell me what happened."

Her sentences became shorter as her explanation progressed, and her poise returned as her words became matter-of-fact. He glanced around the neighborhood as she told the story, but he didn't see a car that was similar to what she described, except his. When she was through, she did a two-second bite on her lower lip, then shrugged off her uncertainty. Finally, she leveled calm eyes on his. "I didn't see the license plate, but it looked like your car. I know a newer model Mercedes when I see one. It was either a Mercedes, or a look alike."

"That narrows it."

"Don't be sarcastic," she said.

"There's plenty of cars that look like this on the road," he paused. "Did you see the driver?"

She shook her head. "It was too dark, then the glare almost blinded me. I had the impression that the driver was a male. He wasn't small. He had broad shoulders. Like you. He was white. Or maybe a light-skinned black man." She paused. "I thought nothing of it, until he flashed his brights at me, as though he was telling me that he was watching me."

"I didn't do that. Didn't, and wouldn't. I'd lower my window and ask you what the hell you were doing there, but I wouldn't do that."

She drew a deep breath. "Now it seems silly that I got so scared. After all, if he had wanted to hurt me, he could have. There was no one around. Good God, have you been there? That street is awful. Brandon," she said, her eyes holding his, "Joe said, wrong place, wrong time. He might be right."

His blood started a slow simmer. *Wrong place, wrong*

time. He'd heard the phrase often when he was a cop. Hell, he'd probably used the self-defeating phrase himself. If the NOPD was already being so dismissive, they'd never find Lisa's murderer.

She continued, "It's a run-down, dark, deserted neighborhood. Not anywhere a female should be walking, alone, at night."

"Yet you were," he said, focusing on the problem at hand and not the attitude of the NOPD, which he could do nothing about. "Lisa had to get to work, and she had to park her car. The campus is crowded, and that was the nearest spot she could find. I was trying to get her to park in a pay garage, but she said that her contract wouldn't start until July. She had no choice. You, on the other hand, didn't have to be there." He admired the tenacious, curious streak that had Taylor going to a murder scene, at night, alone, yet he was angry that she was so damn reckless. "You're driving a convertible Mercedes, for God's sake. If your diamond rings don't get a thug's attention, your ponytail shows off the rocks on your ears. NFL players would be jealous of those stones. You look like an easy grab for a big pay-out. Lisa was killed in that neighborhood, if the cops are right, because she might have had a few dollars in her cheap purse and a laptop in her bookbag. Compared to Lisa, you're the jackpot, and you go to the same spot, alone, not twenty-four hours later?"

Luminous eyes stared into his. Her cheeks were flushed. He should shut up, but he couldn't. "Hell. You got spooked by a Mercedes, for God's sake. What the hell do you think happens in those kinds of neighborhoods?"

"What happened was odd. I reacted," she said, arms folded, "and I don't deserve ridicule. I wanted to see where Lisa was killed."

"Why?"

She bit her lower lip. "I can't stop thinking about her," she said. Then her vulnerability disappeared as she squared her shoulders and almond-shaped, green-brown eyes held his gaze. "And if I want to keep looking into the circumstances of her death, I will."

"Well," he said, "while you were busy checking my alibi, I

made a few calls of my own. Your last day in the D.A.'s office is tomorrow. You're going to be working with your father, doing God-knows-what HBW executives do. You're the president of the Taylor Foundation and the Marlowe Foundation. You're gliding into the cushioned life for which you were born." She flinched, then her face flushed with pink. "Why the hell do you even care about Lisa's murder?"

Taylor narrowed her eyes. "My feelings aren't dictated by my job or my social standing. I want to make a difference."

"Great. A clueless do-gooder, throwing out lines from a beauty pageant segment on goals and aspirations."

She gasped. She opened her mouth, but then clamped it shut. When Brandon saw her eyes well with tears, he felt like a heel. Then he remembered who he was talking to and shook the feeling away.

If life was a beauty pageant, she was Miss Universe, and she didn't need him to coddle her. The rest of the world did that. He did, however, soften his tone. Slightly. "Look, it's noble of you to want to make a difference. I appreciate the fact that you're bothered by this. More people in the city should be." He hesitated, then decided that there was only one way to say what was really bugging the hell out of him, and he shouldn't have taken a round-about, insulting way to do it. He just couldn't figure Taylor out. "You don't know what the hell you're doing. Bullets won't go around you, Taylor. Bullets won't give a damn about your social standing. Acting as an amateur sleuth will get you killed." Brandon glanced at his watch, which read ten twenty.

Damn. He was going to be late. He didn't have time to worry about Taylor, or be annoyed by her, or even to think about her. "Would you please give me the key?"

She opened her clutch and handed it to him. He turned to get back into his car. He opened the driver's door and slid into the seat. Taylor hovered in the space of his open car door. "Aren't you going in?"

"I only had a few minutes, which I spent arguing with you. I'll return when I'm done with my appointment."

"What kind of appointment does someone have at this time of night?" He shot her a narrow-eyed look that he hoped conveyed his irritation with her questions. "Well?"

Damn it. He tried to pull his door shut, but she was blocking it. "Please move."

"*United States v. Morrissey.* Your grandfather's treason case. That's why Lisa went to see you. Correct?"

Brandon kept his mouth shut as he gazed at the woman whose stature had climbed with her question. He wondered whether Taylor had made a lucky guess, or whether she really knew. He kept all expression off his face. He was under no obligation to answer her, but damn it, if she kept her nose to the ground along this path, it wouldn't be long before she found her answer. She arched an eyebrow. "I have a call into a family friend. Professor Lloyd Landrum. He's with the history department at Tulane University."

Brandon frowned. "I know of him."

"Lloyd oversees graduate students. It's only a matter of time before I know exactly what Lisa was researching."

Son of a bitch. Taylor had one-upped him. Now, it looked like he was hiding something, and he didn't want anyone to think that. Damn it. He tried for a delay tactic, instead of answering her question. "Please move. I'm late."

She didn't budge. Her eyes shone. High cheekbones reflected street light. The dewy gloss on her full lips was distracting. Her halter-top bared long, lean arms, strong, yet graceful shoulders, about two inches of tight cleavage, and a tapering waistline. She must have looked like an apparition in the Melody Street neighborhood. He shouldn't do what he was about to do, yet she wasn't moving. He drew a deep breath and told himself no.

No. Aw. Hell.

He blamed his weakness on her damn cleavage. He couldn't resist. If Taylor was so hell-bent on doing investigative work, he wanted her to know what she was getting into. "Get in the car."

"Why?"

"My appointment is about Lisa. If you want to come, get in. Or step away and let me leave. Your choice." As he turned the key in the ignition, Taylor walked around the front of the car, then slid into the passenger seat. In seconds the car's interior filled with the fragrance of gardenia, vanilla, and spice. It was a lush, languid scent, as heady for Brandon as a long sip of dark amber rum. It made him want to find the places on her body where she had rubbed the perfume.

"Son of a bitch," he muttered, as the scent provoked mental snapshots of what she might look like underneath that halter top. Blood flowed to places in his body where it had no business going.

"What's wrong?"

He drew a deep breath, blocking the images that flashed through his mind. "We're late."

They rode in silence for a few minutes, until he pulled onto the interstate. "Where are we going?"

"The East. Off of Downs Road. Black-Eyed Jack's. A video-poker joint that features topless dancers and easy heroin scores. You know the place?"

He took his eyes off the road long enough to catch an arched eyebrow and a frown. "Of course not."

"Oh, I forgot. You're a woman with family names that are so important that no one bothered to give you an ordinary first name, like Cathy or Katie or Bridget. Strip clubs are way beneath your stature."

"Are you always rude, or are you intimidated by debutantes and carnival royalty?"

Brandon chuckled. "Neither. I'm teasing," but he wasn't telling the whole truth. Women like Taylor reminded him that he wasn't born into polite society and, no matter how hard he worked or how much money he donated to good causes, he'd never be welcome there. "Look. You should stay in the realm of luxury you were born into. Your type might play-act as ballsy assistant district attorneys, but you really would never dream of hitting the real neighborhoods of New Orleans, where the vast majority of its people live."

"So this is a lesson for me?" She spat out the words. He thought about denying the truth, then decided to evade her question by ignoring it. She muttered, "Patronizing jerk." Louder, she said, "How did you ever make anything of yourself with that Goliath-sized chip on your shoulder?"

Yet another good question from Taylor. "It isn't a chip. It's a deep, shattered canyon. Usually, it fuels my ambition. Evidently, with you, it makes me want to show how skewed your perception of reality is."

"I don't need lessons from anyone as arrogant as you. You don't know me. You've only made assumptions," she said, "and your assumptions are way off base."

"Well, that may be true, but I'd bet that you'll never understand what it's like to be born ten insurmountable steps below polite society, but . . ." he shut up. He sure as hell didn't need to explain the source of his attitude to her.

Not now. Not ever.

So he had a lot of incentive to do better than his grandfather, a notorious convicted felon and his father, a delusional, suicidal alcoholic. So it gave him more than a little attitude when he was around society queens like Taylor. He was never going to be so old that he forgot where he came from, which didn't amount to anything positive. Big fucking deal.

"But? But what?"

Damn it, damn it, damn it. Deep-seated curiosity was imbedded in her nature and on-target questions bubbled out of her as naturally as water from a well. *Damn it.*

"Well?"

Brandon rubbed the left side of his neck, trying to ease the feeling that a wrestler had a stranglehold on him. "But nothing." He drove in silence until he approached the exit.

"So why are we going to a strip club?"

"My friend Marvin knows everything about what happens on the streets. Later, he's going to where Lisa was killed to put out feelers. He'll talk to people who would never talk to the cops, or me for that matter. Right now he's at Black-Eyed Jack's." Brandon's cell phone rang. He answered it without putting the call on the audio system.

"Yo, Brandon. Marvin. Where the fuck are you?"

The phone gave a stutter signal, indicating that another call was going straight to voice mail. "Just a few minutes away."

"I'm leaving the bar. Headed home, but I won't be there long. Go there."

As Marvin broke the connection, Brandon fought the 'oh-shit' feeling that formed in his belly. Taking Taylor to Black-Eyed Jack's, a nasty and seedy, but public, establishment, was one thing. Taking her to Marvin's home was another thing entirely. He braked at a red-light. He could return uptown, drop Taylor at her car, then backtrack to Marvin, but it would be at least a half hour round trip. Once Marvin disappeared from his home, finding him wouldn't be easy.

Hell. He'd finish what he started. He reached into his glove box, pulled out a money pouch, settled it into his lap, opened it, then started counting cash as he drove. "Here," he said, handing Taylor a stack of hundreds. "There are envelopes in the glove compartment. Double count for me, if you don't mind, make sure there's twenty here, and put this in an envelope."

He stopped at a red light, counted out another two thousand dollars, and watched her glance into the pouch. "How much cash is in there?"

"Fifteen thousand."

"Why do you carry so much?"

He handed her the other stack of two thousand dollars before answering.

"In another envelope?" she asked.

He nodded. "Do you know anything about plaintiff's work?"

"In theory, but I can't seem to get past the tacky television commercials."

Brandon slid the money pouch into the bottom of the glove compartment. Four thousand would be enough for Marvin for tonight. "So you think my commercials are tacky?"

She arched an eyebrow. "Oh, come on. This can't be the first time you've heard that your commercials are cheesy."

He glared at her, but he really felt like laughing. She certainly called it like she saw it. "Tacky and cheesy? I should kick your well-dressed ass out of my car." He nodded in the direction of a mini-skirted, tube-topped hooker on the near street corner. "Maybe you'd like to hang out with her."

"You would not leave me here." She turned her head slightly to the side, looking for confirmation. She was right, but instead of nodding, he scowled. "Actually," she offered, "your commercials aren't terrible. The legal tidbits are accurate, and you've tamed some of that used-car salesman persona you used to have."

Her tone wasn't exactly convincing as she extended the verbal olive branch, but he took it anyway. "I have toned the commercials down," he shrugged, "and I really don't care what you think of them. You're not my target market."

"What is your target market?'

He drew a deep breath, then thought, well, hell. She asked. His commercials weren't geared towards his criminal clients. Those people seemed to find him, no matter what he did. They were geared towards his personal injury clients. "My market is that person who is suffering because of someone else's carelessness, negligence, or greed. The person who wouldn't otherwise get a lawyer and sue the son of a bitch who broke his life. That good client might be one in a hundred. Or one in five hundred." He shrugged. "I love to find that person and make the bad guy pay. You've never done without. I've never done without. Some of my clients have, though. Money doesn't fix everything, but it helps. When the really down-on-their-luck ones come to me, I front them money until the bad guys pay. That's where the cash comes in. Not everyone has checking accounts and credit cards." He paused. "Investigators like Pete handle the dirty work, but I like to do some of it. If I stay close to the harsh reality, it helps when I need to persuade a jury."

For once she was silent. He counted to ten, wondering how long she could last. Eleven. Twelve. Thirteen. Fourteen.

"Then you understand," she said, "the feeling of wanting to make a difference, to make things right."

Well, she'd gotten his point, and now he understood hers. Damn. She was good. He glanced at her. Her gaze was unwavering and serious as she said, "I don't know how to make a difference."

He had to concentrate on his driving, because he could just keep looking at her, wondering what she was thinking. Staring at Taylor, though, wasn't going to get them to Marvin's house.

"I'll give the vote of confidence, Taylor, that you'll figure it out."

"Thank you," she said, and for once, she didn't ask a question.

Brandon checked his cell phone. Damn. The call that had signaled when he was on the phone with Marvin had been from Sebastian Connelly, his best friend and one of the founding owners of Black Raven Private Security Contractors. The company's title suggested limits on Black Raven's activities that didn't really exist. In addition to providing security, the company had an elite intelligence division. Brandon had gone through Ragno, the head of Black Raven's intelligence division, for information on Victor's whereabouts. Although he'd told Ragno not to bother Sebastian with his query, Sebastian's call made him wonder if she'd kept it to herself.

In polite conversation, and with Rose, his mother, and Kate, Brandon would have said that his brother Victor worked with an international security agency. In reality, Victor was a mercenary who worked for anyone who could afford his price, doing whatever they needed him to do. He was a brilliant hired gun with no morals. According to Sebastian and Ragno, Victor didn't simply protect people. He killed their enemies. Black Raven knew this sort of information, because people like Victor often targeted Black Raven's clients. Victor and Brandon didn't talk frequently, if at all, but Victor managed to stay in contact with Kate and Rose. His failure to call Rose on her birthday, one month earlier, had worried Kate, because on Victor's last few visits, both women thought he had seemed sick.

Sebastian's voice message to Brandon was simple. "Hey. I talked to Ragno. I'll try you later. Don't bother calling me."

The cryptic message was typical of Sebastian when he was on a job. Brandon passed Black-Eyed Jack's and stopped at the next traffic light. Taylor shot him a questioning glance. He explained, "Marvin left the bar. His house is about a mile away. If you don't mind, put your rings and earrings in the glove compartment with the cash."

She at least had the good sense to give him a worried glance. "Seriously?"

"If your purse will fit, put it in there, as well," Brandon said. "I trust Marvin, but I have no idea who, or what, might be at his house."

Chapter Five

Brandon slowed as he approached Marvin's dead-end street. The one-story red brick ranch house was in decent shape, but aside from weed-filled grass, there was no landscaping. Two cars were in the driveway, one a Cadillac, another a Land Rover. Brandon recognized them as belonging to Marvin. A shiny red truck was parked in the front yard. Brandon thought it belonged to Marvin's son, but he wasn't sure. A large plate-glass window was front and center. A split in the draperies revealed a television's flashing light. Brandon grabbed the two envelopes that Taylor had stuffed with twenties. He shoved them into his rear pocket. He pulled a Glock that he had borrowed from Pete from under his seat, along with his holster, which he snapped onto his belt.

Taylor gasped. "I thought that you gave your weapons to Joe."

He grabbed a legal-sized envelope that he had wedged between his seat and the center console when Taylor had gotten into the car. "I did. This one's from Pete. Joe didn't tell me I couldn't get another weapon, did he? I'll come around to get you," Brandon said, "and stay close."

Brandon stepped out of the car, then met Taylor on the passenger side. A wide-chested Rottweiler ran from the corner of the house to them. The dog slowed within a few feet of them, then continued walking in their direction. The animal was Boy, Marvin's pet. Boy gave a low, fang-bared growl. Taylor pressed close against Brandon, half behind his back and half smashed against his right arm, with fingernails cutting through his shirt into his forearm.

"Hey, Boy," Brandon said, bending to let the dog smell his hand.

Boy snorted, licked Brandon's fingers, then turned his

muzzle to Taylor's leg, against which he gave a loud, mucous-accented sniff. Boy stepped aside as a young man stepped from behind the home. Brandon nodded at Corey, Marvin's twenty-year-old son, who held a black automatic pistol. "Dad's inside."

Marvin was in the front room, watching the Animal Planet channel, with an Uzi resting on the couch next to him and a laptop computer resting on his legs. He rose when they entered, putting aside the computer, but lifting the Uzi with him. Taylor was so close to Brandon he felt her body heat and smelled her perfume. Girl, another Rottweiler mixed with something else, was nursing a litter of puppies in a nest of blankets in the corner of the room. Girl lifted her head and glanced at them, then set it down again when she sensed no threat. Marvin was a solid block of a man, tall, with bulky arms, long black hair that was yanked into a ponytail, and dark, close-set eyes. After his gaze fell on Taylor, his glance returned to Brandon.

Brandon introduced Taylor, who managed to put a few inches between herself and Brandon. She extended her hand to Marvin, who shifted the Uzi from his right to his left hand and shook hers.

To Brandon, Marvin said, "Is this your idea of a date?"

"Not a good one, and not because of the location." Brandon glanced at Taylor. She was wide-eyed, but otherwise expressionless, a cardboard cutout of the woman who had charged at his car earlier in the evening, bursting with anger and adrenaline, or the woman who couldn't stop pressing his buttons with her questions. She was too far removed from her comfort level to even give Brandon an annoyed look for his glib comment. It was time to do their business, then leave. Brandon handed Marvin the legal-sized envelope. "Inside are photographs of Lisa."

Marvin nodded. "I made calls. None of my soldiers did it. Still no leads?"

"No. Police are thinking crime of opportunity. Lone woman on a dark street. Two known crack-houses within three blocks. A suspected meth lab within a half mile."

As Brandon relayed the information that he'd been given from a source on the NOPD drug squad, he heard Taylor draw a deep breath. He watched the last color leave her face. Brandon guessed that Joe hadn't bothered to tell Taylor about the meth lab and the crack houses.

Brandon asked, "Second guessing your field trip to Melody Street?"

She bit her lower lip and looked away.

Brandon took that as a yes.

"So the cops think some druggie or thug grabbed her purse. If that's it," Marvin smiled, revealing gold caps on his top front teeth, "I should be able to find out who. My people don't pop women for a few bucks. The better gangs don't. Others," Marvin shrugged. His eyes fell on Taylor. "They'd kill only cause they could. Some for a purse, some for a notch, or maybe because they want the cops in a neighborhood where a competitor has a lab. There's a war now over prime turf on the river side of Claiborne and your friend might have been caught between the bullets."

"Don't help me if it causes trouble for you," Brandon said.

Marvin rolled his eyes. "There's already trouble. Those inner city fuck-ups have no respect for nothing. I'm happy to look into this. It'll stir shit up. I'm sending Maria and Anna Maria away to the beach. Don't want them here, at home." He put the Uzi on the couch, opened the envelope, looked at a photograph of Lisa, then shook his head. "It's a damn shame." Dark eyes met Brandon's gaze. "If there's really no talk," Marvin said, "that's odd. Everybody talks here. Not to any cops, but to each other. If there's no talk, well, that would be interesting, wouldn't it?"

"Absolutely." Brandon handed Marvin the two white envelopes. "There's two thousand in each. One envelope is for you, for tonight. The other is for you to spread around. Make it clear that there's a reward for solid information. Not bullshit. Something that leads to the trigger man."

Marvin nodded, as Boy barked in the front yard. He put the envelopes down, picked up his Uzi, and was still a minute. Brandon held his breath, listening as the barking stopped. Marvin's cell phone rang. He answered it, then laughed. He ended the call. "Fucking cat," he explained, as Marvin's wife, Maria, and their young daughter, Anna Maria, entered the living room. They were olive-complected, with long dark hair and dark eyes. Maria rolled a black suitcase, while Anna Maria, a miniature, five-year-old replica of her mother, rolled a small pink suitcase. Brandon had met them before. He told them hello, and introduced Taylor. Anna Maria had a long ponytail, with a big pink satin bow with chartreuse polka dots. She wore pink pajamas, with bright green trim.

Anna Maria glanced at Brandon and Taylor, then scooted to her father, who bent and lifted her with his free arm. *Aww hell,* Brandon thought, as he got an eye full of the beautiful child in Marvin's arm and the Uzi that Marvin held in his other hand. This wouldn't sit well with Taylor. Anna Maria pressed her face into her father's chest, then turned back to gaze at Taylor, to whom Anna Maria whispered, "You're pretty."

"Thank you," Taylor said. She was pale. Brandon could see that her hands were shaking, yet she managed to focus on Anna Maria and give the child a smile. "So are you. I bet that you're a smart little girl, too."

The little girl beamed. "Anna Maria Paquin is my name. I can spell, too. P-a-q-u-i-n."

"That's very, very good," Taylor said.

"I can spell dog too. D-o-g."

"That's great."

Anna Maria rested her head on her father's chest, while her gaze stayed on Taylor. Brandon stared at the young girl, the big man, the pink satin bow, and the Uzi that seemed like it was as much a part of Marvin as his hand.

Damn it.

He glanced at Taylor. She had kept her voice steady when she spoke, but she was so pale that she looked like a wax mannequin of herself. She glanced at Brandon. Her hazel-green eyes were wide, her expression was blank. She lifted a shaking hand to smooth her already-perfect hair. Jesus. He had to get her out of there.

"Anna Maria," Maria said, "kiss your daddy." The girl obliged. "We gotta go."

Maria kissed her husband on the cheek, then took her daughter's hand as Marvin stooped and steadied Anna Maria on the ground. The child broke free from her mother's grasp and ran to Girl and her puppies.

Brandon said, "We're going."

Marvin nodded. "Wait." He pulled his phone out of his pocket, made a call, and asked, "Clear?" He broke the connection and nodded to Brandon. "You're good. I'll be in touch in the morning, or sooner," he said to Brandon, "let you know what I figure out." Marvin walked out with them, with Maria and Anna Maria at his side.

Brandon guided Taylor by the elbow to the passenger side of the car, then opened the door. She sat without a word. He hesitated, waiting for a question, like *what the hell were you thinking, taking me to a place like that?* If not that, he expected a retort, a sharp, sarcastic comment like *Gee, thanks, Brandon, for that lesson. I really needed that.*

Taylor stayed silent, though, and glanced at him with pained eyes as he shut her door. He walked around to the driver's side. Once again, in the confined space, he became aware of the lush scent of her expensive perfume. It wasn't overpowering, and that was the problem. He wished that he didn't like it, but it was delicious, a subtle siren song that vaporized her into his thoughts. He started the car and lowered his window for outside air. He didn't want to be distracted. He drove away from Marvin's, past Black-Eyed Jack's, and stopped at a red light. Her gaze was fixed on a distant point. Her jaw was set, but he detected a slight tremble in her lower lip, and her shoulders shook. She lifted a hand to her eye and ran her index finger along the corner, blotting away a tear.

Aw hell. It was the second time that evening that he had reduced Taylor to tears, and, although he hadn't cared much about it the first time, now he felt like a heel. Hell, the sight of Anna Maria and the Uzi had made even him queasy.

"I'm not stupid," she whispered. "I know that this is a high crime city. I also know that I lead a privileged, pampered life." She pulled her purse out of the glove box, fished out a folded, monogrammed handkerchief, and dabbed at her eyes. "My foundation work keeps me aware. I don't delegate everything. I study the grant requests. I analyze the needs. I visit the sites. I go to public schools and community centers. I wanted to be an assistant district attorney so that I could make a difference. It's my dream job and yet tomorrow is my last day. I haven't made a difference. When I see a sight like that I realize that I'll never really make a difference. I don't know how."

As she wiped the tears from her eyes, Brandon considered the possibility that Taylor might be nothing like what he expected her to be. The thought was disturbing, because so far that evening he had ridiculed her for going to Melody Street and patronized her by trying to teach her a lesson. He had acted upon assumptions involving her names and her wealth, and he wasn't usually so judgmental. In his business, he couldn't afford to be, because assumptions distorted cold, hard facts, the kind that either won or lost cases. His uneasiness prompted him to say something nice. "I'm sure that you do a lot more good than you're giving yourself credit for."

Taylor gave him a half smile. She straightened her shoulders. She sniffed softly, wiped at the corners of her eyes, then unfolded the handkerchief and gave a delicate press between the tip of her nose and her upper lip. She had either been trained regarding the ladylike way to cry in public, or she was born with knowledge of how to look pretty while crying. Either way, it worked, as her eyes found his. "I don't often come face to face with that kind of reality."

"I'm sorry," Brandon said as he tore his eyes from hers and focused on the road. "I shouldn't have taken you there."

***

Brandon had accused her of being naive and silly, and crying only proved him correct. Taylor willed herself to stop, and somehow, the tears did. "Once I realized what kind of man you were dealing with," she said, "once I saw that watchdog and that young man, a boy, really, with the gun, I braced myself for violence. Or even to see a drug addict, on some kind of trip." She drew a deep breath. "I could have handled that kind of thing, but not that beautiful little girl. He was holding an assault rifle while he held her. That little girl shouldn't be exposed to that."

"Marvin's not usually on edge like that, and Anna Maria isn't normally around when he is." He gave her a sideways glance, a serious one, and a slight head shake. "I wanted to keep you from hurting yourself with your investigative efforts and thought the seedy scene at the bar would do that. I shouldn't have taken you there. I'm sorry, and I really mean it."

She decided to take advantage of his remorse by pressing the question that had been bothering her ever since Joe's interview. "Lisa didn't originally go to you for legal advice, did she?"

He gave her a serious glance, one that was even more penetrating than the non-smiling, analytical gaze that seemed to be his default expression. "No." He parked in front of Lisa's house as Taylor digested the fact that her hunch had been correct. He continued, "She did not. How did you know?"

"Joe's question assumed that she went to you for legal advice," Taylor said, "and you hesitated when you answered."

"I did not."

"Yes. You did," she said. "And something in your eyes made me wonder. She was a post-graduate history student, she's studying spies of World War II, and the rest is a guess, given your family history. You can either confirm that she was looking at your grandfather's treason case now, or not. I'll know exactly the subject of her research, when Professor Landrum returns my call in the morning. Once I know, Joe will know, and if we have to go the long way around to figure this out, well," she shrugged, "that's going to make you look like you were hiding something. I don't think that's a position you want to be in, is it?"

He frowned. "Your questions can really wear a person out."

She shrugged. "But I'm correct. Right?"

"On all fronts. I wasn't hiding anything, though. I was answering Joe's question, as he asked it," Brandon said, "and I'll call Joe now and tell him, so no one really thinks that I was trying to conceal anything."

"He was going home when I talked to him earlier."

Brandon shrugged. "I have his duty number. He'll get the message in the morning, if he isn't sleeping with his cell by his bed." Brandon pressed a few buttons on the display on his car's dash, directing the phone to dial the fourth most recent number. The car's speakers relayed the rings, then Joe's voice directed the caller to leave a message. "Joe. It's Brandon. Nothing urgent. Only an update. I put some feelers out on the streets, as I said I would. I also thought you might want to know about Lisa's research project, because Taylor is asking me about it. It involves my family history, and also Taylor Bartholomew's family history."

Taylor hadn't thought about it that way, but Brandon was right. If Lisa was looking into the Morrissey treason case, she was also looking into the history of HBW Shipbuilding Enterprises. Anything involving HBW history involved Bartholomew family history.

Brandon continued with his message to Joe, "That's why Lisa came to see me in the first place. She didn't come for legal advice. She was researching spies of World War II, and, in particular, my grandfather's treason case. Call me when you get this message. Or call Taylor. She thought that you might be interested in this." He broke the connection. "Satisfied?"

"Yes," she said, "You really wanted Joe to hear that from you rather than me, right?"

He nodded. "After Joe interviewed me, I couldn't seem to stop thinking what-the-hell-if. What if her murder could have been related to her research? It's a long shot, but given my family history, I can't get it out of my mind. So, I sure as hell didn't want Joe to think I was hiding something, as you insinuated. I might not worry much about the NOPD, but I also do not play games with homicide detectives."

With the touch of one button he made another phone call. "Hello, Esme. Is Michael sleeping?"

"Soundly. He finished a bottle a half hour ago and now he's out. I think that gives us another two and a half or three hours."

"Call me if you need me."

Brandon pulled the key out of the ignition, and reached into the backseat for his laptop case. "Look. I really feel bad about what happened at Marvin's house."

"Don't," she said, taking in the serious set of his jaw and the apologetic look in his eyes. "I can handle it."

He gave her a glance that said that he wasn't so sure, then said, "If you're still interested in Lisa's research, come into the house with me."

"You must really feel bad to be this nice."

He shook his head. "I do feel bad, but that isn't why I'm inviting you in. I want to show you how easy it would have been for Joe to figure out what Lisa was researching, if Joe had been interested."

"Ah," she said, "so you're still trying to teach me a lesson."

He shrugged, but didn't deny it. Taylor was curious, so she followed Brandon into Lisa's house, which looked as it had in the afternoon. As Brandon went to the study and flipped on the lights, Taylor typed a text for Carolyn. *"Hey. I'm running late. All good."* She hesitated. *"Be home in a couple of hours."* She thought she'd be home in an hour, but it was best to overestimate. She didn't want Carolyn to worry. Her next text was for Andi. It was late, but Andi and Collette would be up, watching movies. *"Are you guys all right?"* What Taylor really meant was, is Collette ok, and Taylor knew that Andi would know what she meant.

Andi's reply was instant. *"All good here, but I might spend the night."*

Spending the night meant that Andi was worried. Taylor replied, *"Let me know if you guys need anything."*

"I can handle this," Andi answered. *"We can talk in the morning. Get some sleep before your last day of work, and the first day of the rest of your life. You'll be the best general counsel ever. :)"*

Her good friend was trying to make her feel better about her current funk at switching careers. Taylor wanted to hug her. *"Love u."*

Taylor dropped her phone in her purse. Brandon was standing over a stack of boxes. "Joe and Tony could have done this. In a minute." He pulled something out of his pocket, then pressed a button that revealed a shiny six-inch blade.

"Do you always carry that knife?"

He glanced at her. "Almost always." He used the blade to open boxes that were labeled research. After looking in the boxes for a minute, he said, "Well, it would have been hard for them to piece it together from what's in these boxes."

At the small couch, he sat and reached for the ottoman. He lifted the top portion of it, which was hinged. "I saw this the other night when I was babysitting." He pulled out a binder and slipped a jump drive from a plastic pouch. "There's more binders in the ottoman, with more jump drives."

Brandon pulled his laptop out of the case, and slipped in a jump drive. Taylor sat next to Brandon as he opened the files. She asked, "You read her work?"

"I didn't read it, but I did see it. I moved the ottoman with my feet, the weight of it was odd, and I opened it when I realized the top was hinged. I thought it was a clever hiding space and that it would be a good thing to have on a boat, where storage is always a challenge. Here," Brandon said, "this folder was labeled background." He positioned the screen so that they both could read Lisa's text.

> *The names of the four men - - Andrew Hutchenson I, Benjamin Morrissey, George Bartholomew Sr., and Charles Westerfeld - - who designed and built the Hutchenson Landing Craft are legendary. The Hutchenson, Bartholomew, and Westerfeld families remain prominent in New Orleans's elite social circles.*

Seeing the Bartholomew name in print wasn't unusual for Taylor. The Bartholomew family, and HBW Shipbuilding Enterprises, were woven into New Orleans history and were current day newsmakers. The story of HBW and the Morrissey treason case had been told before. Seeing it in black and white, in Lisa's apartment, made her wonder why Lisa had focused on it and whether she could have shed new light on facts that had been aired again and again.

As Brandon and Taylor shared the small couch and the laptop, his leg pressed against hers and his arm touched her bare skin. He had shaved his face since she'd been at his house. Loose, thick waves of dark hair were neatly combed. Black pants and a pure white, long-sleeve, button-down shirt perfectly draped over his long-limbed, lean, and muscular body. His skin was smooth and clear and his cheeks had natural color, as though he spent time outdoors. He emitted warmth and his scent, well, it was fresh and light, and she paused. She inhaled, focusing. Despite his tough-guy masculinity, he smelled like a baby.

She started laughing.

Jade green eyes studied her. "What's funny?"

"You smell like baby powder."

With the first real smile that Taylor saw from Brandon, the weight of untold problems fell from his eyes. He chuckled, then shrugged. "I've gotten more on me today than on Michael."

He was gorgeous when he smiled. He had straight, white teeth, full lips, and the smile didn't end there. His eyes lightened, and his smile brought a few crinkles to the corners of his eyes. It was simply a smile, she reminded herself, but as he held her gaze for a few extra seconds, and looked into her eyes, she couldn't stop looking at him. It was only a smile, but the lightness of it stood in sharp contrast to his hard-edged masculinity. He didn't conform to the norms of the men with whom she typically associated, and his individualistic attitude, coupled with his rough good looks, was intriguing. Sweet-scented baby powder had no business falling on this man, whose eyes revealed a serious soul. As she drew a few breaths laced with the out-of-context scent, she became aware of how close they were sitting, and how his sharp focus on her eyes made her feel as though he saw straight through her pretensions. As though he could tell that her pretty clothes, her careful make-up, and the polished image that she projected were her way of shielding her ultra-vulnerable self from the world. Suddenly, the lack of distance between them was too intimate. It was wrong, on many levels, especially there, where both Lisa's presence and her tragic end were palpable. Taylor shifted to the right, placing a few inches between them, as he shifted to the left.

"I didn't mean to crowd you," Brandon said, as his smile faded. He gestured to his laptop. "Lisa was focusing on home-grown spies of World War II. In particular, the Hutchenson Landing Craft, how it changed the war, and how the craft that won the war for the Allies almost landed in Hitler's hands, thanks, as most people say, to my grandfather."

"And that's what Lisa went to see you about?"

Brandon nodded. "A year ago, when she came to see me, she was beginning her research. I didn't want to talk about it," his eyes flickered with intensity, "but I met with her because I wanted to make sure that she didn't go to anyone else in my family."

Taylor thought about letting it go. She couldn't, though.

She followed her natural inclination to ask, "Why?"

He was silent, then let out a long breath. "My father was obsessed with his belief that his father was falsely convicted. He was unable to cope when real adversity hit. Now, my mother is sixty-nine years old. She's still sharp, but I didn't want her to be bothered with this. I wanted to spare Kate from dealing with it and," he drew a deep breath, "my brother, Victor," he paused, "doesn't live here and is generally unavailable. So I headed Lisa off at the pass by meeting with her."

A pulse throbbed at his temple, revealing an emotional toll that wasn't detectable through the flat tone of his voice. Taylor felt a twinge of nervousness. It wasn't polite to ask such personal questions. Yet she was fascinated, because she'd never thought about her luck at being born a Bartholomew, on the good side of history, and the bad luck of being born a Morrissey, with a notorious war criminal for a grandfather.

Brandon turned his attention to Lisa's text. Taylor followed his gaze.

World War II would ultimately require the cancellation of Mardi Gras for two years. However, in New Orleans, in 1937, during carnival season, despite current world events being grim, Mardi Gras revelers filled the French Quarter and spilled into the surrounding streets. It was the Monday before Mardi Gras when Andrew Hutchenson returned to HBW&M Shipyard's main office on the bank of the Mississippi River, where Canal Street met the river. He brought with him a design for a boat that the Japanese were using. He believed it could be adapted to carry modern tanks and land on beaches. For three years, the partners of HBW&M worked on designing the boat that would ultimately be known as the Hutchenson Landing Craft. Morrissey alone was convicted of attempting to sell the design to the Nazis. My research looks into whether Morrissey was framed.

Taylor glanced at Brandon. "Whether your grandfather was framed? Now that's a novel idea."

"Seriously?"

"I've never heard anyone suggest that your grandfather was framed."

He shook his head. "Maybe that idea isn't trumpeted in your circles, but you wouldn't think it was so original if you had grown up with Marcus Morrissey as your father."

There was something about him, something that made the history of HBW and the Hutchenson Landing Craft, even the preposterous idea that Morrissey was framed, downright fascinating. She glanced at her watch, where the hands had drifted past midnight. Seven a.m., when she needed to awaken for her last day of work, was going to come fast, but something about Brandon made her not mind that it was late. She hadn't eaten dinner, but also wasn't the least bit worried about food. His patronizing, teach-her-a-lesson motivation that had caused him to take her to Marvin's house was now only a distant memory. Maybe it was his rough good looks, the body warmth that he emitted, and his intense stare with those light eyes, but as he focused on the computer screen, she couldn't deny that she was attracted to him, and that realization made her uncomfortable. He wasn't the type of guy to whom she should be attracted. She forced herself to read Lisa's words.

> *Hutchenson, Bartholomew, and Westerfeld held engineering degrees and were from old New Orleans families. Bartholomew and Hutchenson had wealth, but the depression had drained their family fortunes. Westerfeld did not have the family wealth that Hutchenson and Bartholomew had, but his family had strong political ties. In the late 1930s and 40s, Westerfeld's father was a senior member of the Senate and a close friend of President Roosevelt. In contrast to the other principals of HBW&M, Benjamin Morrissey had no formal schooling and no family wealth. He was from Galliano, a small town in South Louisiana and had experience designing and building a wide range of boats. The role each man took in the design, production, and contract procurement of the landing craft, that is ultimately credited with winning the war, varies depending upon the source of the information.*

Taylor read the last sentence again, then glanced at Brandon. "What is your version of the facts?"

"I only know what my father used to say, as he rambled on and on. It can be reduced to a few facts. Benjamin designed the landing craft's innovations, the other men gave him none of the credit, and Benjamin was falsely accused of being a traitor." He shrugged. "I told Lisa what my father used to say." Both pulled away from their locked gaze and turned back to the screen.

> *The official version in the National World War II Museum credits Hutchenson as the design leader. Hutchenson and Bartholomew had the capital to produce the test hulls; Westerfeld had the government connections to secure the contracts. Morrissey was also involved. In fact, in 1935, when the company was formed, it was called HBW&M. Morrissey was a self-taught boat building genius with an aptitude for designing boats that fulfilled various functions. He was given a share in the company to keep other contractors from stealing him away. The M was dropped after Morrissey was convicted.*

"If your grandfather's ownership interest hadn't been taken away, there would still be a Morrissey on the board." She thought about Brandon's tattooed bicep that she had viewed earlier in the day and contrasted that with the country club, conservative look that the three existing members of the board shared. "That would certainly make it a more interesting board."

He chuckled. "We'll never know, will we?"

Her eyes followed Brandon's, back to Lisa's words.

> *In the official version, none of the ingenuous innovations, such as the ramp in the bow that enabled men to walk out of the boat, rather than climb out, are credited to Morrissey. The design drawings that have been made public in the National World War II museum are signed by Hutchenson, and Morrissey receives no credit for the design. If Morrissey did not participate in the design, how is it that he knew enough to sell the design to the Nazis?*

"My father had Benjamin's drawings," Brandon said. "Benjamin designed the boat, according to those drawings. Not Hutchenson." He shot a questioning glance at Taylor. "Does the corporation have the original documents?"

"I don't know," she answered. "I've never looked for the original design drawings, but there's a private library at corporate headquarters, and my father has an extensive collection of historic documents at his home. The documents could be in either place."

If Morrissey had let Hitler's spies know in 1940 that the United States had plans to build more than 20,000 of the Hutchenson Landing Craft, the strategy of our enemy would have been different. The World War II Museum has excerpts of memoirs of Phillip Rorsch, one of the lead U.S. Government agents whose undercover work led to Morrissey's arrest. Did Rorsch testify at trial? Is there a more complete collection of his notes? Did he publish memoirs?

They had reached the last of the text on the jump drive. Taylor looked at Brandon. "How far did Lisa get with her conclusions?"

"I don't know. Remember, I talked to her briefly about this when we first met, then didn't talk to her at all until two weeks ago, and then we only talked about Michael. I'm pretty sure, though, that her pregnancy derailed her efforts. She sat out last spring, but she hoped to have her dissertation complete this November. She was due for a preliminary presentation sometime this summer."

"This subject matter has been reviewed, time and time again," Taylor said. "Where was she going with it?"

"It sounds as though she was making a case that Benjamin wasn't the person who tried to sell the design."

"If your grandfather didn't do it, then who did?" As soon as Taylor asked the question, she realized the most likely answer. If Morrissey didn't do it, the obvious answer was one of the other three original founders of HBW did it, or maybe all of them.

***

At one in the morning, when the lights in Collette's bedroom went out, and Andi's car remained parked in the driveway, he gave up on waiting for Andi to leave Collette's house. His plan was Collette first, then Andi. He hadn't come up with a plan to kill them together and, for the moment, he was too tired to be flexible. He wanted to go to Lisa's house, anyway, and make certain that last night he had uncovered all of the research that would help him destroy HBW.

Brandon's car was in front of the house. Taylor's white convertible was there as well. Lights were on. He parked on the street behind Lisa's house, and walked through the neighboring yards. Lisa's house was so close to her neighbor's house that the width of the path between them could not have been to code. He'd been in tighter spots, though. Staying still and silent was a skill that he'd had since childhood. He stood at an angle. He allowed himself only short glimpses. It wasn't the first time that he had watched Taylor through a window.

It was, however, the first time that he had watched her with Brandon. Their backs were to him. He watched Brandon reach into the ottoman. His pulse quickened. He hadn't realized that Lisa had used the furniture as storage. Fuck. He almost panicked, worried that there could be a duplicate of the Hutchenson letter in the ottoman. He didn't know what Brandon would do with the letter if he had it, but he damn sure would bet it wasn't going to be something that he'd like. The letter could not become public before the HBW Board paid him. It was only worth twenty-five million dollars if they believed they could keep it quiet. Son of a fucking bitch. As Taylor and Brandon read, they were interested, but, judging from their reactions, the material didn't seem earth-shattering. He breathed easier. Brandon would have visibly reacted to the Hutchenson letter.

He had expected challenges. Every project had obstacles, but he hadn't expected that Taylor and Brandon would join forces. Whoa. Whoa. Do not jump to conclusions, he told himself. Taylor and Brandon were on opposite sides of history. Their interests were diametrically opposed. They couldn't join forces. He quieted his instincts and forced himself to think.

Think. Think rationally.

He turned back to the window and watched.

Chapter Six

"If your grandfather didn't do it, then who did?"

Brandon wondered if she was serious. He answered her question anyway. "The most likely suspects are Hutchenson, Bartholomew, or Westerfeld. Maybe all three conspired against my grandfather, the least sophisticated of the four."

"Why would they sell secrets to the Nazis?"

"Money," he said. "Why else? Unless they were Nazi sympathizers, but I doubt that. Even my father didn't suggest that."

"But they were getting money from the United States government," she said. "They didn't need to get it from the Nazis."

"You're right," he said, "but my father's theory, which he told me again, and again, and again, was that the United States hesitated on the contracts. Hutchenson, Bartholomew, and Westerfeld had high lifestyles. When they first would have come up with the idea to sell it to the enemy, the landing craft wasn't the great military secret that it ultimately became. They had spent a lot of money and effort on research and development, and for a while it looked like no one was going to order their product. Economic times were tough. Then, when the government placed the orders, it was a really bad idea to be selling the idea to the Nazis. So whoever had initiated the contact, they, or he, blamed it on my grandfather. They used my grandfather's mind to design the perfect boat, and his skills to work out the kinks, then they accused him of treason."

"I'm not buying it. Not one bit. Your grandfather was tried by a jury. He was convicted."

"Juries are fallible. Sometimes they get it wrong. That's why we have appeals courts." Brandon said, wondering whether Taylor had yet, in her short legal career, witnessed a case where a jury got it wrong. "When the world wants to punish bad guys," he shrugged, "it is easy to find a man guilty. Think of today's current concerns about terrorism. Our jury system has safeguards. Hell, even the international tribunals have safeguards, but one of the reasons that they're so damn scary from the viewpoint of a defendant is the finality of their decision."

He was referring to the tribunals where countries joined forces to try criminals whose crimes threatened world-wide security. As a recent law school graduate, he knew that Taylor was aware of the tribunals. He had twice represented defendants in tribunal cases. They'd been the most difficult cases of his life.

"In 1944, when my grandfather was tried, the world was at war. People were scared, and that includes the people on the jury," Brandon shrugged, "hell, even the judge. They're people. People make mistakes. The jury in my grandfather's case may have gotten it wrong. In his appeals, the judges may have gotten it wrong."

"That's a theory. Your father's theory. Maybe it was Lisa's theory," Taylor said. "But we'll never know, really, unless we manage to piece together her research, and," she lifted her hand and gestured to the room, "even then, this is all hypothetical, unless Lisa uncovered cold hard evidence."

Brandon put his laptop to the side, lifted the stack of material that had been in the ottoman, and found three more jump drives. He downloaded each onto his laptop, then scanned the contents.

"Let me see," Taylor said, attempting to turn the screen so that she could see it.

Brandon held the computer firm, studying her, wondering if she had heard enough to make her worry that maybe, just maybe, there was legitimate doubt regarding his grandfather's conviction. "Don't trust me?"

Taylor shrugged, but her hands remained on his laptop. "If you're going to insinuate that my grandfather could have been involved in treason, I need to be aware of what Lisa uncovered."

"I'm not hiding it," he said, and turned the laptop to Taylor. "We're on the same side when it comes to finding Lisa's murderer. Right?"

She arched an eyebrow and shook her head. "How can this possibly be related to her murder?"

"I don't know, just like I don't know whether Marvin's efforts will uncover anything, but I don't want to rule it out. So," he said, "getting back to my question. If Lisa's research is related to her murder, are you and I on the same page?"

"Meaning?"

"Expose the truth at all costs."

She hesitated for a second too long. He had no real reason to think that she'd be as interested in the results of Lisa's research as he was. After all, her family was on the hero's side of history. "I've got to do this, Taylor, for my son. I've got to make sure the murderer is caught. History, and what Lisa was researching, is collateral to the end goal, but I've got to consider everything. I'm not sure whether you care as much as I do about finding her murderer," he said, "and I'd understand if you didn't. It's late. This isn't your worry."

She drew a deep breath, held his gaze, and squared her shoulders. "You brought me in here because you felt bad about what happened at Marvin's house. Please don't shut me out now, right when it's really getting interesting. To answer your question, if the historical truth differs from what is regarded as historical fact, and if the truth is related to her murder," Taylor held his gaze, "of course it should be exposed."

Well, he thought, maybe she'd been straight-to-the-gut sincere, earlier, when she'd thrown out her line about wanting to make the world a better place. He had ridiculed her comment as a sound-bite from a beauty pageant. As he studied her, he decided to test her. "The truth should be exposed, even if the truth is related to our history and it exposes your grandfather's involvement in treason?"

Taylor shook her head. "Exposing my grandfather as such is not likely, and you know it."

"But even if?"

"Your A doesn't lead to B," she said. "You're not being logical."

"A, if Lisa's research revealed that your grandfather,

George Bartholomew, Sr., was the person who committed treason, or one of the other founders of HBW, then he or they covered it up by blaming my grandfather," as Brandon said the words, he was met with a stoic and beautiful wall of skepticism, yet he continued, "and our current-day murderer killed Lisa because he didn't want that secret exposed, then B, finding our current day murderer could expose the original traitor, who could be your grandfather. How is that not logical?" He drew a deep breath, hating that he had said those words aloud, because he suddenly sounded like his father.

Taylor frowned. "There are too many unknowns in what you're saying. Besides, if Lisa had proof of your grandfather's innocence, wouldn't she have told you?"

"No. I made it clear to her that I didn't want to talk about anything having to do with my grandfather's treason case."

He gave her the laptop. "It's been over seventy years since my grandfather was convicted in 1944. I don't believe that anyone will ever prove that my grandfather was falsely convicted. Lisa could have made a case of plausible doubt, but I don't think she would have changed the history books. I do think, however, that if someone killed Lisa based upon what she knew," he paused, "and that's a really big if, then I need to figure out what she knew. Joe and Tony won't figure this out. It's too speculative. They don't have time, especially when Lisa's murder could have been exactly what they suspect — a random act of violence. They'll impound all of her work, and it will sit in some office, and weeks and months will go by. If there's anything there and we leave it up to them, we'll never know."

Taylor didn't argue. He watched her attention turn to the laptop. After a minute, she said, "There's only a small bit of material on each of the drives, and most of it seems to be class notes."

Brandon stood. He walked into the room that doubled as the baby's room and study, where earlier in the day he had knocked over the stack of boxes that had seemed lighter than he remembered. He turned in the tight space between the crib and the changing table. Each box was sealed, as the boxes had been on Tuesday evening, and each box was labeled research. On Tuesday, he remembered that the boxes were heavy, as though packed full. Tonight, he lifted each box and carried them to the living room. They were lighter than he remembered, but then again, Lisa had been home on Wednesday. Maybe she had reorganized the material.

He sliced through the tape with his knife. The first box that he opened contained binders that were labeled research, but there was no material in them. Lisa had been a student, with a baby, on a tight budget, and she was supremely organized. The fact that she had packed empty binders in a moving box seemed odd. The next two boxes were mostly empty, containing only a few notebooks and loose papers. Taylor placed his laptop on the couch, stood, and said, "The first jump drive that you had contained information on her World War II project. The other drives have unrelated information."

"There should be more here than what I'm finding," Brandon said. "I'm not even finding hard copies of documents, references, or notes."

"Maybe she stored everything on her laptop," she said. "People don't hit the print button as much as they used to. I took entire law school classes without one piece of paper to show for them."

He thought about his days in law school, more than fifteen years earlier, with each class producing thick binders of lecture notes. "You're making me feel old."

"Paper addiction is inconvenient," she shrugged, "and ink is expensive."

He nodded. "Those law school classes with no paper notes. How much back-up did you have?"

"Lots," she said. "Jump drives that were transportable and external drives that I left at home."

"Then that's what we should be finding." Brandon opened desk drawers, while she moved around the room. He had left his knife open on a box. She lifted it to cut through tape on other boxes. "Be careful, it's sharp."

"You're not kidding," she said, as the blade easily sliced through tape and cardboard. She opened boxes and sifted through the contents. "There's no back-up here," she said, "but I found a few onesies that you might want to take home."

"Excuse me?"

She held up a tiny piece of pale yellow fabric. "Don't you know what this is?"

"Clothes. Sure." But he didn't know. Good God. Her show and tell reminded him that he had a baby to care for. A child to raise.

"Are you okay?"

He shook off the in-too-deep feeling that had been clawing at him ever since he had realized that Lisa was gone. *All good*, he reminded himself. He could handle this. "Yes."

She opened another box. "More clothes for Michael. Wait." Taylor reached deep into the box. "I feel hard plastic, like an external hard drive." She pulled out a box of baby wipes and frowned. "Nothing."

"She was organized. I don't think she'd have put a hard drive in things for the baby."

"Unless she was trying to hide it."

He nodded. "Good point."

Brandon's cell rang. He recognized Sebastian's phone number. "If you're calling this late," Brandon said, "it can't be good. Are you at home?"

Sebastian had been working in Europe for two months. Brandon didn't know details of Sebastian's most recent job, but an international tribunal had recently announced a decision in a terrorism case, and Brandon guessed that Sebastian's job was related to the case. The tribunals were secret while in session, but given the high profile subject matter of the trials, security was of paramount importance, and Black Raven was often hired to provide security.

"Yes. I just returned to Denver," Sebastian said, "Sorry I missed your birthday dinner."

"Make it up to me next time you see me."

"Look, I talked to Ragno, and I've made some inquiries of my own in the last few days, based on what she uncovered. I thought that you'd want to know as soon as I knew."

"Bad news?" It had to be bad news, because otherwise Ragno would be providing the information. Instead, his best friend was calling with it. Brandon walked out of the study and over to the couch, where he sat and mentally braced himself.

"Analysts are still looking at financial data," Sebastian said, "but indications are that Victor is dead."

Brandon let out a long breath. He leaned back, rested his head on the back of the couch, shut his eyes, and asked, "When?"

"My intel tells me six weeks ago. A couple of weeks before you asked Ragno to find him."

"What happened?"

"He worked for Ali bin Laden, part of Osama's surviving family, in Pakistan. Ali's complex was bombed. Your brother, Ali, and others died in the explosions. The place, and the people in it, were incinerated. An Egyptian group claimed credit. Ali's list of enemies includes some of the more notorious al Qaeda splinter groups. It's a quagmire, one not easily unravelled."

Brandon provided legal advice to Sebastian on Black Raven's contracts and knew the intricacies of Sebastian's business. His friend's current reality was worlds removed from the days when they had worked together on the New Orleans police force.

Sebastian continued, "I think the financial data will confirm that Victor is dead, but Ragno is only now getting started with those searches."

"So why are you sure that he's dead?"

"I've hired two people who previously worked with Intrepid, the firm that Victor worked for before he left and went to work for Ali bin Laden," Sebastian said, "Your brother left Intrepid and started working for Ali about a year ago. These two guys were shadowing Victor at the time of the explosion."

"Why?"

"Once he left Intrepid, some of Victor's targets for Ali were people he'd once been paid by Intrepid to protect. Victor had killed one too many of Intrepid's clients, and Intrepid had a bounty on him. The two men who I hired were at one time shadowing Victor to kill him for Intrepid. That's the ugly reality of this business. These guys are good. They're sure he's dead, and so far, Black Raven's data searches confirm that he's dead, but we've only got preliminary results at this point." Sebastian was silent for a second. "You okay?"

Brandon hesitated, but only for a second. "Yeah. Victor and I didn't have a relationship. It's been years since I spoke to him. This is going to hurt my mom and Kate, though, and I hate to do that. They had no idea what an amoral son a bitch he was."

He caught a glimpse of Taylor in the other room, then she disappeared in the direction of more boxes. He thought about telling Sebastian of everything happening in his life right now — Lisa's death and his new status as a parent. He'd been friends with Sebastian since first grade. They'd been on the police force together and had gone to law school together. Sebastian had been his best man at his wedding and his best friend when, five years earlier, Brandon's life became a living hell.

Sebastian had been working and out of contact when Brandon learned about Michael. Brandon could have gotten word to Sebastian about the life-changing event of having a child through Ragno, but Brandon hadn't wanted to bother Sebastian until he got a grip on things. He decided against telling him on the phone. Letting Sebastian know about Michael would be the stuff of a longer conversation, face-to-face, maybe with good rum. It would be one that had to take place soon, so that Uncle Sebastian could enjoy babyhood.

"Hey," Brandon said, "You should come for a visit this weekend."

Sebastian said, "Not a bad idea. I'm dying for some good food and I'd like to see what your sorry ass looks like at forty."

"Don't get cocky. You'll be there soon."

"Are you sure you're okay? He was your brother, Brandon. It's got to be weird, at least."

Brandon drew a deep breath, then let it out. "I'm fine. You knew him. Except for mom and Kate, and their feelings for him, the world's a better place without him." Brandon broke the connection. He watched Taylor reappear in the doorway of a study, then lean against it as she leafed through a notebook. He asked, "Find anything interesting?"

When Taylor looked up, something behind him and over his shoulder caught her eye. All color left her face. He leapt to his feet, as she said, "Someone. Someone's there."

Brandon turned and looked in the direction Taylor was facing. Beyond the glass pane there was darkness, yet he didn't doubt that she saw something. He lunged across the room, grabbed his knife, then ran out of the house. He jumped off the porch and into the narrow lane that the window faced.

No one was there.

The backyard wasn't fenced. If someone had been there, they could have disappeared in any direction. A car started on the street behind Lisa's house, but by the time he ran there, it was gone. He backtracked to the empty front yard, where the street was dead still. He returned to the lane between the two houses. Beneath the window, lush grass revealed slight indentations that could have been his own footprints. He thought about doing a run around the block, but when he stood, Taylor was at his side. He didn't want to leave her alone. He shut the switchblade, but gripped it in his hand instead of pocketing it.

"Did you see anyone?" she asked.

"No. If someone was here, he moved fast."

"I saw only a flash. Someone ducked and turned when I looked up."

"You didn't see his face?"

"No," she shook her head. "I only saw part of his forehead, hair, and shoulders."

"Describe what you can."

"Maybe white, or a light-skinned black man. His hair was black," she said, "but maybe," she bit her lower lip. "Maybe it was a cap."

Brandon eyed the window. He could see into the raised house without an assist, but he was six four. There were no signs that the person had used a prop. "He was probably about your height," she said. "I think I saw his face as he turned. His chin hit at the sill." She lifted her hand to her forehead and rubbed her temple. Her hand shook. He reached for her shoulder and gave her a reassuring squeeze. "I'm really, really certain that I saw someone." She shivered. "He was watching us."

She stepped closer, as though seeking comfort. He

pocketed his knife, then wrapped his arms around her. She stepped into his hug. *Hell.* Want simmered through him.

Want? This wasn't a want. Want was something that happened when he encountered the usual females with whom he surrounded himself, women who treated sex as casual fun. This thing that made his nerves sizzle wasn't merely want. There was nothing awkward about the way their bodies fit together. She wore high heels, but he was still a good five inches taller. Her face fit in the space between his shoulder and his head. Full breasts hit him where his ribs started tapering. He lifted her thick ponytail and bent his head to where her hair met the delicate, soft skin of her neck. Behind her ear, and down, he found where she had applied her perfume. He inhaled the heady scent of gardenia, and once again became an instant addict. Damn. If he died with that scent wafting around him, with her lush body pressed against his, he'd die happy.

He opened his lips and touched the spot with his tongue, tasting her and that heavenly scent. *Wrong. This was wrong.* Taylor wasn't his type. High expectations oozed from her pores. There was nothing casual about her, from the flawless streaks in her hair to the tips of her shiny toenails. She'd been handed a perfect world at birth, and he'd bet that she wasn't used to compromise. When a woman was with him, she better be ready to settle for less. His capability for intimate relationships and enduring love died five years earlier, when he had buried Amy. In the first few years after she died, he'd been too hell-bent on destroying himself to be interested in women. In the last couple of years, he enjoyed women who were amenable to a no-strings-attached way to have fun, and, from the frown on her face when he had told of the one-night stand with Lisa, he knew that Taylor would never be the sort of woman who had learned to expect zero in terms of feelings from a man. There were plenty of those women, women who were happy to have a good time and casual sex and go about their life without expecting much of anything from him. Those women came in all shapes, sizes, and ages, and once he was able to start looking for them, he didn't have a problem finding them.

Brandon started to ease out of the bad-idea hug, but before he released her and moved far enough away so that he wasn't drowning in her scent, she lifted her arms over his shoulders

and turned so that her face was only inches from his. *Damn it.*
He hugged her tighter, pressing more of her soft flesh into him.
She raised her face a bit more, holding his gaze while offering
lush lips. He touched his lips to her forehead, cheek, then her
lips. They were full, soft, and dewy with sweet moisture.
Brandon ran his tongue along the gentle curve of her full lower
lip, then he slipped inside her mouth, where she met him with a
silk-like touch of her own.

More.

He wanted more. *More* tastes, more touches with his lips,
his tongue, and any other part of his body that he could rub
against her. *More. Damn it. More.*

She moaned. It was softer than a kitten's purr, yet it
screamed *wake-the-hell-up*. He eased away from the kiss,
pulled his arms away from her, stepped back, and tried to
squelch the need for her that had seized his body. They stood,
frozen, staring into each other's eyes.

She found composure before he did, with a half-smile, a
deep breath, and squared shoulders. "Well," she said, with a
shrug, as though mentally wiping away whatever had
happened. "That's one way of forgetting about being scared."

"Then mission accomplished," he said, glad he could sound
normal, like his body wasn't screaming for her.

"This has been the oddest of nights, wouldn't you say?"

"Yeah. Damn odd." But there was nothing odd about his
body's reaction to hers. There was nothing to be done about his
desire, though, because now that sanity had returned, he wasn't
going anywhere near her anytime soon. She might taste like
nectar of angels, but for him, she was about as good as arsenic.
"Let's go inside and lock up."

They walked through the alley and into Lisa's house. Taylor
crossed the living room and picked up the notebook that she
had dropped on the floor. "Is your mother named Rose
Morrissey?"

"Why?"

"She lives in Folsom, Louisiana?" Taylor held up the
notebook.

"Aw hell," he said, knowing where Taylor was going.

"Lisa spoke to her."

Brandon's world, for the billionth time in the past twenty-four hours, tilted. He sat on the couch. Taylor sat next to him. He made sure that he didn't touch her, because space was a good thing for a man with a hard-on and no hope for release.

"At least once, maybe twice. This notebook is sort of a calendar, sort of a to-do list. Anyway, it looks like ten months ago Lisa visited Rose Morrissey, in Folsom, and three months ago, she met with someone named Rose on Magazine Street."

"Ten months ago was after I talked to Lisa, after I asked Lisa not to contact my mother."

She lifted a perfectly-arched brow. "And it was also when you weren't returning Lisa's phone calls, right?"

Son of a bitch.

He hadn't returned Lisa's calls, so Lisa did exactly what he didn't want her to do, which was go to Rose with her questions. "My mother didn't mention that she met with Lisa."

"Would she?"

He thought about it. "No, and I wouldn't typically mention anything about this to my mother. My mother hated what my father's theories did to him, and she didn't talk about it with us. She didn't want it to warp our existence. It was bad enough that HBW was everywhere. One of your shipyards was even down the street from where we lived. My father's theories about HBW were a cloud over our daily existence," he paused, "and my mother hated it. We only stayed in the area because we never had the money to leave. My mother wouldn't have twice revisited the subject with Lisa."

Taylor handed him the notebook. The entries were there, as she said. Ten months earlier Lisa had scribbled an entry with Rose's address in Folsom and a time. The entry of three months earlier said, "Rose. Ten o'clock. PJ's. Magazine Street."

"Once I can understand, because my mother is gracious. Twice? No." He shook his head as he studied the entries and persuaded himself that he was correct. "The second entry for Rose doesn't say Rose Morrissey. My mother didn't meet with Lisa twice." The notebook didn't provide details regarding whether any information had been gathered from Rose

Morrissey, three months ago or from Rose, seven months before that. Brandon thumbed through a few pages, then glanced at Taylor. "Lisa also talked to your father. Two months ago. Three weeks ago. There's also a scribbled entry that says Rorsch and document, but there's not enough here to know what she was talking about." He paused. "The jump drive text that we looked at earlier indicated that she was wondering if Rorsch had documents."

"Maybe she found them." She chewed on her bottom lip for a second, then glanced into his eyes. "If Rorsch testified at your grandfather's trial, do you think he could still be alive?"

"My grandfather's trial was in 1944. Rorsch could be alive is if he was really young then. Even so, he'd be well into his nineties." He turned more pages. "Over the last year there are entries here for meetings with Alicia Westerfeld. Claude Westerfeld. A Mr. Hutchenson."

"The current Mr. Hutchenson is actually the second," Taylor said. "Like my father, he's the son of the Hutchenson who was the original founder. All of the original HBW Board members are deceased."

"Well, it looks like she talked to someone from each of the HBW families."

"I saw that," Taylor said. "She also had recent appointments with Lloyd Landrum, which is something that I expected earlier today when I learned of the subject of her graduate work. He's an expert in that area and on the faculty at Tulane. I've placed a call to him to ask what he discussed with her. He hasn't returned my call. I could also make inquiries with the people in the HBW families whom she talked to. You and I certainly won't be able to figure out how far she had gotten by looking through these boxes."

He glanced around the apartment. "Maybe she made a preliminary report to the school."

"I'll ask Lloyd."

As he glanced at her, a distant caution bell clanged in his mind. "I wasn't intending to encourage you to become an investigator."

She shrugged. "We're talking about my father and men I've known all of my life. Why wouldn't I ask them a couple of questions?"

"I can't imagine that your father had much time for her."

Her expression turned serious. She narrowed her eyes a bit, enough to tell him that his words had hit a sensitive spot. "Do you know my father?"

"No," Brandon said, "but I've sued HBW quite a few times. I've tried to take your father's deposition for legitimate reasons. He resists. He sends corporate henchmen and tough lawyers who play dirty. I assume they're following his orders."

She held his gaze. "My father's tough with everyone, including me. Especially me."

He shrugged. "I don't take it personally."

"I do." She gave him the slightest half-smile, the kind of expression one gave when attempting to make light of a really, really painful subject. She looked away, stood, and paced a few steps away from the couch. "My father may not be happy when I ask him about this." She turned back to him. Small worry lines appeared between her brows.

Hell, if he hadn't realized it before, he knew now. *Stay the hell away from her.* Taylor had father issues, George Bartholomew was widely regarded as a prick of epic proportions, and he didn't need that kind of drama.

She continued, "The other men, though, they'll humor me. Besides, I know that you're going to talk to your mother about this."

He nodded. Damn right he was. Taylor's coral lipstick had long since faded. A bit of eye make-up had smudged below her left eye. Her tight ponytail had become loose, and wisps of hair had slipped through the black-rhinestone holder. She looked so freaking kissable that he almost groaned. Instead, he asked, "Tired?"

"Yes. Exhausted. Suddenly."

Without glancing at his watch, he wouldn't have known that it was well past midnight. He wasn't tired. A few hours a night usually got him through the day, and even when sleep didn't come at all, he could make do without it for several nights in a row. His ability to work through the night had served him well in his legal practice, but his restless energy hadn't been his friend during turbulent times of his life. Taylor, though, looked like she needed the serious kind of refueling that only came with several sound hours of sleep.

She glanced at the window and shuddered. "There really was someone out there."

"I believe you."

"Before that happened," she said, "the phone call. Was it bad news?"

"My brother, Victor, died."

She drew a deep breath. "I'm so sorry."

"We weren't close, Taylor. As a matter of fact..." he searched for the right words, then abandoned his attempt to describe his relationship with Victor. "The worst part, for me, is I have to tell my mother and my sister." She studied him, and, for once, she was silent. Smart woman, he thought, because she sensed that questions on this subject wouldn't provide answers. "This will all be here tomorrow," he said, glancing around the room.

"Here," she said, pointing to two boxes that she had pulled to the side. "You might want to take these. They're baby clothes, wrapped in tissue. They're folded so neatly." Her voice broke, and he watched her try to compose herself. "The items are precious." She swiped a tear away with the tip of her index finger. When she glanced at him, he saw heartbreak in her eyes. He could see in that one glance that she understood how awful Lisa's death was for her son. She might have all the composure of a beauty queen, but her eyes revealed her real emotions. "Would you let me do something for Lisa?"

She looked so vulnerable at that moment that he'd have agreed to anything. "Of course."

"Let me help you decorate the nursery."

Nursery? *Fuck.* He hadn't even picked out a room for Michael, and God knew that he had enough spare rooms. The space between his shoulder blades and his neck tightened. *This wasn't how he should have become a father.* Life had thrown him yet another curve ball that he didn't quite know how to hit.

Taylor continued, "My decorators are good, and Sarah, the female part of the team, has three children. She can assess what

Lisa had already acquired and know what you need from there. I can probably persuade them to start this weekend, and they're fast." He felt so damned inept that he didn't know how to respond. Taylor, misunderstanding his silence, blushed. "I've overstepped, haven't I? Never mind."

"No, no. I hadn't even thought about this. I'd love your help. Thank you for offering. I accept." He looked at the boxes that she had pointed out. "I'll get all the baby stuff delivered to my house tomorrow. Your decorators can work from there. Let's lock up and go."

He opened the door, did a quick visual surveillance of the street, then walked Taylor to her car. "I'll follow you home."

"That isn't necessary. I drive straight into a secure garage and the alarm is set."

He shrugged. "Humor me. You've been rattled tonight, for good reason, and part of it is my fault. Let me watch you drive into your garage. Call me on my cell when you're in and your alarm is armed."

"Well, thank you." She gave him a teasing smile, but her tone was one of appreciation.

Damn. With those almond-shaped eyes, high cheekbones, and lush lips — forget that killer body — she was irresistible.

Hell.

Irresistible? *No.* It had been a long turmoil-driven day. His brain was playing tricks on him, because the one and only woman in his life who had been irresistible had been Amy.

He shrugged off the thought. He turned away from Taylor, followed her in his car, but didn't wait for her to get home and call him. Instead he dialed her cell once they entered the Garden District, as they neared the huge, Greek revival monster of a home that locals called the Bartholomew mansion. When she answered, he said, "Please tell me that you don't live in the mansion with your father."

She laughed and did not slow her car at her father's three-story home, which dominated the block. The mansion had elegant curves at each corner, spacious balconies, and galleries. Meticulous gardens surrounded the home and a tall, heavy, wrought iron fence separated the lawns from the sidewalk. "I have gained at least enough independence that I do not live there," she said. "Go two blocks up, take a right, then go three more blocks and take a left. Cross Prytania, then I'm on the first corner."

"Wow," he said. "Four whole blocks away from dad. That's pretty far for a girl with three last names and no first name of her own."

"I am all three of my names, Brandon, and they're sufficient for me." As she spoke, it occurred to him that the Southernness had been schooled out of her voice. She articulated each word with crisp precision. Yet schooling hadn't stripped away the natural sultriness that came with her low pitch, slightly throaty tones, and breathy catch when she started her sentences.

Damn it.

There was that throb again, as his body reacted to her voice, and she continued, "And my house is five blocks away from my father's home, not four."

The Bartholomew mansion was on Saint Charles Avenue, a brightly-lit main street with four lanes of traffic and a center neutral ground through which streetcars travelled. Taylor's home was on a lesser-travelled, narrow street that didn't seem to have enough lights. An oak-tree canopy blocked light from the nighttime sky. In the darkness, he saw the outline of a symmetrical, two-story house sprawled across a large yard that, for the most part, lacked a fence. Gas lanterns on the porch revealed white masonry, light-colored shutters, and lacy, wrought iron balconies. Fluted Corinthian columns soared from the base to the second floor ceiling of the balcony. The lines were clean, feminine, and elegant. Leaded-glass front doors sparkled from an interior light. "You live in that big thing by yourself?"

"With Carolyn," she said. "My friend, personal assistant, housekeeper, surrogate mother, you name it. It was built in the 1890's. I inherited it a few years ago. It's huge, I know, but it was my grandfather's house. I couldn't let it go." She hesitated, then said, "And I know that it's ridiculously opulent and light years away from where we were earlier tonight, in Marvin's house, where little girls get hugs from a father who is holding an assault weapon."

The sadness in her voice made his gut twist. "I'm sorry for taking you there. Again."

"Thank you for that, but I'm not angry." He rounded the corner as she did. She waved at him before she drove into a side garage. "And thank you for following me."

"Let me know when you rearm the alarm," he said. The house looked anything but secure. It wasn't a sprawling monstrosity like her father's house, but it was still large. There were too many floor-to-ceiling windows, too many French doors, too many shadows in the yard.

"I'm almost in the house. There. I'm in." Brandon heard three persistent beeps through the phone. "Well," she said, "there's a bit of dysfunction with the alarm. What can I say? The system's new. Okay." She drew a deep breath, then he heard a piercing electronic wail. "Great. Now I've set the darn thing off."

"Need help?"

"No, but thank you." She spoke to someone and he assumed that it was Carolyn, the housekeeper she had mentioned. "Okay. I've put the password in, and," she paused. He heard a short beep. "Now the numbers. It's rearmed. Finally. Sorry about that. Carolyn is here, we're fine, and it was just a glitch."

"Check the zones."

She gave a low, throaty chuckle. "If you think I know how to do that, you are far overestimating my capabilities. I'll call the alarm company tomorrow, but, for now, it is on. I humored you," she said, "now will you humor me by listening to some unsolicited advice?"

"Do I have a choice?"

"No. Look. I don't know how you can think straight. First Lisa, now your brother." Brandon listened to Taylor, but he wasn't focusing on either Lisa or his brother. Taylor's landscaper had done a good job of back-lighting the oak trees that sprawled across the yard, but there wasn't enough light for safety. Hell. Sitting there, Brandon could map out a shadowed-path through the yard to a side gallery where he had a choice of brainless entries, either through French doors or floor-to-ceiling windows. Sebastian had told Brandon that Black Raven agents could work through most home security systems in under ten minutes. Better systems could be cracked as well, but they took more time. No matter how good the system, one of Black Raven's agents only needed a few minutes, and they could rig the system for their future silent ingress and egress. After that conversation, Brandon had Black Raven agents design the system that he used in his home and his boats, and they did semi-annual maintenance checks. "Go home," she continued. "Go to where Michael is sleeping, kiss his cheeks," she said, "and try not to think about anything else but him. Watch him breathe. *Watch him.*"

"How is it that someone who is only twenty-seven is so wise?"

She laughed. "I was an only child, with parents who were very, very social. Most evenings were spent with adults when I was growing up, at dinner parties. I was taught to be a good conversationalist. Which means that I know how to ask questions-"

"Yes," he chuckled, "you certainly do."

"-and listen to the answers," she said. "As a child, I enjoyed the company of adults, and," she hesitated, "maybe some of their wisdom took. I like the patina that comes with age."

Good to know, he thought, because he'd become hard again by listening to her voice. Maybe their age difference wouldn't be a big deal to her. If only he could convince her that casual sex was a good thing. He shook off that thought, though, because the vulnerability of her house was still bugging him. "Do me a favor. Open a window on the first floor. Any window. Don't disarm your alarm system. See what happens."

"Really?"

"Really." He heard her heels clicking on the floor, then he saw her in one of the side windows.

She reached up, unlocked it, then lifted it. Brandon let out a breath of relief when he heard the alarm.

"It's working," she waved at him, then disappeared from the window. "And now I've rearmed it. I'll get the alarm company in here tomorrow."

Chapter Seven

At home, Brandon found Esme pacing in the casual sitting area that joined the kitchen, with Jett at her heels and Michael in her arms.

"He woke up about a half hour ago. I fed him and changed him," she shifted the baby into Brandon's arms, "and now he's falling asleep again. Jett won't leave his side."

Michael stirred when Brandon touched his lips to the baby's cheeks. Blue-green eyes opened for a second and focused on him. *Good God.* He lost his breath as he held his son's gaze. Michael's eyes shut again. Brandon held his baby against his chest, and told himself that he'd become the father that this child needed. Somehow. He'd figure it out, minute by minute, just as he'd gotten through the last five years. He drew a deep breath. "Esme, I've got it from here. Get some rest. The nanny arrives at seven. I'll be good until then."

Esme disappeared in the direction of the guest apartment, which was above the garage. She didn't normally stay at Brandon's house, but with Michael's sudden arrival, she had told him she'd stay overnight for the next week, or longer, if needed. Brandon lay Michael on his back in the pack-n-play that Kate had purchased on Thursday. Jett settled on a nearby rug. Brandon sat in a leather barrel chair next to the pack-n-play and put his feet up on an ottoman.

In the dim lamp light, he watched Michael's chest rise and fall with the gentle breaths of an easy sleep. After a few minutes, Brandon felt himself drifting. Relieved, he shut his eyes. His thoughts wandered to Lisa, whose research echoed the long-silent sentiments of his own father.

His son's mother.

Murdered.

One day Michael would ask Brandon about her. He had no

idea what he'd say. He only hoped that he'd be able to tell Michael that his mother's murderer had been caught.

His thoughts shifted to Victor. His eyes opened. The world was a better place without his brother in it, but he didn't expect Kate and his mother to feel that way, because Victor had been careful to conceal his true self from them. He had to break the news about Victor to them. Sooner was better than later, before the burden of carrying the information became heavy. He drifted ever closer to sleep. Thoughts that Brandon didn't allow while awake came as he drifted.

Victor had been a sneaky, cruel, and smart child. Brandon had learned at an early age, when Victor was thirteen, and Brandon was six, that Victor was more than mean. Bad, bad things happened in River's Bend, a rural area that was twenty minutes outside of New Orleans that wasn't yet starting to see gentrification. Neighborhood dogs were maimed and left to die. Cats, on occasion, would hang from trees. To Brandon's knowledge, no one suspected Victor. No one except Brandon, who followed Victor at night through the quiet streets of wide, empty lots, sleepy, half-developed cul de sacs, wooded fields, and slow bayous that outlined the area that the developers called Woodmere. At least he tried to follow his brother. Victor was quiet, fast, and elusive.

Brandon's dreams led to the fire that destroyed their family home. It had occurred when Brandon was seven and Victor was fourteen. Time had not diminished Brandon's memories of the fire's heat or the stink of smoke. Kate had been two, sick and staying in the room with their mom and dad. Catherine, his older sister, had been ten and her room had been the closest to the fire source, a hot water heater. She died of smoke inhalation. Brandon awoke with a start, his mind racing to reality. He'd lost them all. Catherine was dead. Amy and their unborn child were dead. And now, Lisa was dead. Murdered. But this time, with death, there was also life. Their baby was sound asleep, and he was in charge of the impossibly small life.

He stood, stretched, then paced. Sleep was, as usual, bad for him. Tonight, being awake was worse. He stopped at the refrigerator, found chicken salad that Esme had fixed, and spooned some into a plate. As he leaned against the kitchen counter and ate it, his thoughts wandered to Taylor. Twice tonight someone had frightened her, or she had momentarily been victimized by her imagination, sparked by the harsh reality of Lisa's murder.

That hug. That kiss. Taylor's body, pressed against his.

Brandon went upstairs, took a quick shower, then returned to the living area that adjoined the kitchen, where he sat in a barrel chair, put his feet on an ottoman, and focused on the rhythmic movement of Michael's impossibly small chest. Up. Down. Up. A little higher up. A pause. Then down. Up. Down. Brandon's eyes became heavy.

Taylor.

His last waking thought was of Taylor, wondering how she'd known that on this night, the vision of Michael's soft inhale and exhale would be his ticket to peaceful sleep.

***

Joe called Taylor at 8:30 a.m. as she was pulling into the D.A.'s office parking lot. "We've got a lead in the Smithfield case. I need you to grab an assistant from juvie, get them to pull a file on a Marquis Rochard, and get here, fast. Rochard's mom brought him to the station about an hour ago, saying he has information regarding Lisa's murder. Rochard wants outstanding warrants against him dropped in exchange for the information. I can't do anything without the D.A. being involved."

"Marquis Rochard," Taylor repeated. "Got it. I'll be there in a few minutes." She parked in the ten-minute zone, went to the hallway where the five assistants who handled juvenile cases had offices, and stopped at the office of Colleen Dunbar, the senior juvenile assistant. Colleen had salt and pepper hair, large brown eyes, and she wore a conservative business suit. "The police have a juvenile who wants to get rid of warrants in exchange for information in a murder case. Who should I talk to?"

Colleen grimaced. "Me." She listened while Taylor gave her background, then said, "I heard you decided not to stay."

Taylor nodded.

"We'll miss you."

"Thank you," Taylor said, warmed by the nice words from

the normally-serious assistant. "The Deputy Chief will be appointing someone else for the murder case, probably by the day's end, but for now, I'm the contact."

Colleen put down her coffee mug. She pecked at the keyboard, then paused. "Well, Rochard's not an angel," she said. "He had three shopliftings before age fifteen. Then a burglary of a dwelling, a car theft, and a year in detention. He's been out only three months, and he's already scored a couple of pickpocketing incidents in the French Quarter. He's wanted for another burglary. He's screwed if these cases get prosecuted." Colleen clicked more keys on her keyboard. "At least he doesn't have weapons or drug charges. The D.A. might let me deal for murder-related information. I'll call while we're on the way."

Taylor drove to the police station. Colleen, in the passenger seat, called the Deputy Chief. By the time they arrived at the station, Joe was in the interrogation room with Tony, the witness, and his mother. Joe and Tony stepped out of the room to talk to Taylor and Colleen. Colleen received a phone call, listened, then told Joe, "We'll agree not to prosecute on his outstanding warrants, but only if he provides information that leads to an indictment. Want me to go in with you?"

Joe shook his head. "His mother's refused legal counsel for now. We'll get started without you. He's more likely to talk without you in the room. If they request a lawyer, I'll want you to step in."

Taylor and Colleen stood in the observation room, watching through a one-way window and listening through speakers. Marquis's skin was dark black. Short dreadlocks stood at odd angles from his scalp. He chewed on his lower lip and stared at the wall. Carettta Rochard, in a neon blue, skin tight halter and tight jeans, had her arms folded over her large midriff. When Joe and Tony reentered the room, she said, "Y'all tell me my boy's charges are dropped or we be leaving. Now."

"Don't threaten us, Caretta," Joe said. "If he has information regarding a murder..."

"He do."

"Then legally, we'll hold him until he gives it to us," Joe said. "Now, we are grateful that you're here. In exchange for your voluntary appearance, the D.A. will drop the outstanding charges against Marquis, but only if he provides information that leads to an indictment."

"It will," Caretta frowned, "if you do your job."

Joe nodded. "If Marquis lies to us, if he sends us on a wild-goose chase because he's making stuff up, we'll charge him with providing false information to law enforcement."

Caretta said, "We understand that."

Joe's attention focused on Marquis. "Do you?"

The boy mumbled.

"Look me in the eye," Joe said, "and say yes or no."

"Yes," Marquis said, "I understand."

"Then tell me what you know."

"I saw Tilly Rochelle last night at midnight. He claimed the kill."

"He did what?" Joe asked.

Marquis rolled his eyes. "He said that he shot her through the head. The Tulane student."

Joe paused.

From their place behind the glass, Colleen asked Taylor, "Was she shot in the head?"

Taylor nodded, her heart racing.

"Was that made public?"

"Not anywhere that I know of."

"Why would Tilly tell you that?" Joe asked.

"Because he's a stupid motherfucker," Marquis said.

Caretta gave Marquis an open-palmed whack on the top of his head. "You say what you told me, without the cursing, or you are not living in my home no more."

Marquis looked at Joe, pursed his lips together, then shook his head. "Me and Tilly used to be friends, until he stuck me with one of his burglaries, and that's why I'm here. He's bragging about killing that Tulane student like he brags about everything. He thinks the murder's his way into the Gravier Street Kings. Stupid ass doesn't even know how to get into the Kings."

Colleen glanced at Taylor. "Have you been around long enough to know the Rochelle name?"

Taylor nodded. "It sounds familiar."

"The Rochelles breed violent miscreants. We probably have had twenty cases in the last five years involving Rochelles. I know Tilly without even looking him up. Tilly is eighteen." Colleen gestured to the window. "Tilly makes Marquis look like an honor student." As Joe wrapped up the interview, Colleen stood. "Well, back to the office." Taylor glanced at Colleen, who was heading towards the door of the surveillance room.

Taylor stood, but reluctantly. "Do you think Marquis is telling the truth?"

"I have no idea," Colleen said, "he could be fingering Tilly for any number of reasons. Tilly is certainly capable of murder. He's been on the fringe of several," she shrugged. "But figuring it out is Joe and Tony's job. I have a hearing at one this afternoon. I've got to prepare."

After Colleen and Taylor parted ways at the D.A.'s office, Taylor went to her office and pulled up Tilly Rochelle's files. She wasn't interested in his crimes. She wanted a picture. In the fourth file that she opened, she found it. It was from a year earlier. He was a small and wiry man-child. His skin was ebony and his hair was short, in a tight, black afro. A physical description put him at five nine. Taylor exhaled, releasing pent-up anxiety. Tilly Rochelle was not the person who'd been staring into Lisa's house. His face wouldn't have reached the window. She placed a call to Joe and left a message for him to call her. She needed to tell him that she thought she saw someone last night who wasn't Tilly Rochelle, but that required explaining about her trip to the murder scene, the car, and what had happened at Lisa's house.

A few attorneys stopped by her office. News had travelled fast regarding her decision to leave the office and, it seemed, that was all anyone could talk about with her. A couple of her closer friends asked her to go to lunch, but she declined, saying that she had a prior engagement. The secretary who she shared with some of the other assistants came into her office. "Your files are now reassigned. I have the list of who gets what. Are there any documents on your private drive that need to be e-filed?"

Taylor shook her head. "I don't believe so, but I'll double check after lunch. Who is going to have the Lisa Smithfield file?"

"That one's going to the Deputy Chief for now."

Taylor called him and updated him on the morning's events. Then, because Taylor had told others that she had a lunch engagement, she felt the need to act as though she did. She left the building and started walking, without a firm plan as to where she was headed. Her phone rang as she was slipping on sunglasses. It was Lloyd.

"Hello, dear. I am sorry that I didn't return your call yesterday. Time got away from me with last minute details for the museum's new exhibits and the gala." Lloyd, at seventy-five, did everything fast, including speaking. He was athletic and energetic and had a tireless zest for life that defied his age. "I can't believe that the gala is two days away, and the opening is in three days. It is all going to be simply fabulous."

He was semi-retired from the university, but he still worked with graduate students. He also kept busy as a consultant for the World War II Museum, and she knew he was writing a book on President Reagan. Taylor turned in the direction of the museum and started walking. "Are you at the museum now?"

"Actually, I'm leaving there," he said, "but I have a few minutes to talk now, if you'd like."

"Well, yesterday, I was calling to ask you about the Tulane student who was murdered the other night. I thought you might know her." Today, she thought, as Marquis Rochard was fingering Tilly Rochelle, questions regarding Lisa's research were not so important to the question of who murdered Lisa. There was silence. "Lloyd?"

"Yes. I'm here. What a tragedy. Lisa Smithfield. Such a beautiful, smart young woman."

"She was researching spy scenarios in the World War II era, in particular the Morrissey treason case."

"I'm aware of that." He was silent for a few seconds. "If you don't mind me asking, why are you interested in Lisa's research?"

The heat was stifling. Taylor started to think that her midday walk wasn't such a great idea. "Well, you know I'm wrapping up my work at the D.A.'s office, right?"

"Yes."

"I covered a police interview yesterday for her case. Her research led her to the current-day Morrissey family," she paused, "and she had contact with Brandon Morrissey, which led the police to ask him questions."

"Now that is interesting. Is Morrissey a suspect?"

Taylor thought back to Joe's statement to her last night. *Brandon didn't do this, Taylor.* The lack of evidence supported Joe's assessment, and, after being with Brandon yesterday evening, her intuition also told her that Brandon had no part in the murder. "No. He's not a suspect. I was wondering, though, if her research could have been a factor in her death."

Taylor stopped at a red pedestrian light. Lloyd asked, "Is that an angle that the police are pursuing?"

"I can't speak for the police. I also no longer speak for the D.A.'s office. I'm just wondering. Lisa met with you, didn't she?"

"Of course. As recently as a couple of weeks ago. I *am* an expert in the area. Some would say *the* expert in the area."

"Well, did her research reveal anything new?"

Taylor received the green light, and walked across Poydras Street. "No," Lloyd said. "Based upon the questions that she asked me, I don't think that Lisa was anywhere close to breaking new ground."

"Is there another professor in the history department I should speak with regarding the status of her research?"

"No one would be able to give you a better idea than me. She was really in the preliminary phase. She wasn't scheduled to make a report until the fall. When we last spoke, it was only in general terms. As a matter of fact, I was encouraging Lisa to focus on other areas of interest."

Taylor stopped walking. "Really? Why?"

He chuckled. "Well, she wasn't covering new territory. I wrote it all before, Taylor. The facts about Morrissey's treasonous activities are exactly as I wrote them, which is how the jury found them. Lisa was not going to uncover anything new. No matter how hard she tried. Now," he paused, giving Taylor a moment to dwell on how pompous he sounded. "I have arrived at my destination. I don't think that you should be troubling yourself with thoughts of murder. The police really need to get a handle on the crime in this city, and that's the hard reality of it." He paused. "On a lighter note, your father and I talked this morning, and you are slated to address the audience at Sunday night's gala. Nothing too serious. Only a few casual remarks on behalf of the HBW families, from," he paused, "the prettiest member." Taylor flinched. Her father and his friends would never, ever stop patronizing her. No matter what she accomplished. Lloyd continued, "It will be an easy delivery. I'll help you with the remarks, if you'd like. I don't know if your father mentioned it to you?"

She shut her eyes in exasperation. Her father had left a message for her while she was at the police station, but she hadn't returned his call. "No. He didn't."

"I'll help you with a draft, so that we can tie in your remarks with the subject matter of the new wing." Of course he'd help her, she thought. God forbid they'd trust her to get even a light-toned speech correct. "Why don't we sit down tomorrow morning, after you're through with the board meeting?"

She managed a curt, somewhat polite, "Sure." Her phone rang before she dropped it back into her purse. Brandon's voice was smooth and deep. "Good morning, Taylor."

"It's afternoon," she corrected him before she could conceal her irritation, then said, "Sorry. Didn't mean to snap."

"No worries," he said. "I talked to Marvin. I'm leaving a status conference in civil court, which puts me about a block from your office. Are you there?"

"No," she said, "I'm on Magazine, six blocks from the World War II museum."

"Want company?"

***

Brandon's car glided to a halt at the nearest crosswalk. Taylor slipped into the passenger seat and eyed Brandon's crisp white dress shirt, navy-blue pants, and red silk tie. His dark hair was neatly combed in a nod to the professional decorum of court. He was on the phone, talking to an associate about a discovery plan. As the air conditioner blew chilled air in her direction, she caught the subtle aroma of earthy cologne, without a hint of baby powder. She savored the scent, as the car's audio system picked up the associate's matter-of-fact questions. Brandon held up one finger. "Sorry," he mouthed, "one minute more."

He answered the associate's questions and asked a few of his own. Something in the way he held his lips, as he thought through the questions, prompted memories of their late night kiss. With the touch of his lips, her entire body had sizzled. She'd fallen asleep thinking about the kiss and had awakened wanting another one. Her reaction confirmed her belief that she had to *just do it*.

When she was seventeen years old and had promised herself that she'd be a virgin until marriage, she hadn't thought through how long it might take her to find someone to marry. She certainly hadn't anticipated how it would feel to be twenty-seven years old with no marriage prospects in sight. As she, Andi, and Collette had figured out, now that she was out of law school, and had time on her hands, Taylor's virginity was officially messing with her head. She needed to be done with it before she could have a normal life, one where she didn't hope that every man was the right one. Andi had advised her to find a hot guy, have sex, and move on.

Just do it and move on.

Brandon could be a *just-do-it-and-move-on* candidate for her, because, from yesterday's interrogation, Taylor knew that he treated sex as a casual pastime. From talking to Sandra Gaines, she knew he didn't do relationships. There was no danger of her confusing the having-sex part with something more serious, because, even if she wanted something serious, Brandon wasn't a candidate for a relationship. Her father would have a fit if she ever dated Brandon. His words as the Morrissey Minute aired one evening were unforgettable. *That bloodline should have been eradicated when his grandfather was convicted.*

If last night's kiss was any indication, Brandon knew what

to do if she wanted to *just do it*. He broke the phone connection as her stomach twisted with the possibilities. She fastened her seat belt and tried hard to stop thinking about sex. His eyes lost some of their deep-from-within seriousness as he glanced at her ivory linen skirt, matching short-sleeved, bolero jacket, and high-heeled sandals. He did a visual trace of the lines of her jacket, which showed a small amount of collar-bone and a pearl choker. When his gaze rested on her hair, which she had styled in a French twist, Taylor lifted a hand to press stray hairs into place.

"Don't bother. It's perfect," he paused, then looked again at her eyes. "Take off your sunglasses."

"Why?"

"I can't see your eyes," he said, "so I can't tell what you're thinking. Your body language doesn't reveal it. Your eyes do."

She shook her head without touching her sunglasses. "A woman's got to have some mystery."

He gave her that face-transforming smile, the one that she'd caught a glimpse of the night before, the smile that took her breath away. With a lightning-fast movement he reached, pulled off her sunglasses, folded them, and handed them to her. "You have plenty enough."

She laughed as she slipped the sunglasses into their case. "What Brandon Morrissey wants, he gets?"

His smile disappeared. Something close to weariness flashed through his eyes. "Not all the time."

She held his gaze, remembered Sandra's comments about the accident that had claimed his wife's life, and realized that she had said something that was stupidly glib. He might not talk about the loss, and she guessed that he worked hard to conceal his feelings about it, but at this moment his pain was palpable. If it wasn't his wife's death that caused the pain, she knew that Lisa's death was weighing on him, as well as his brother's death. "Sorry. I know the answer to that is no."

The rawness left his eyes. He re-armored himself with a serious gaze, then broke eye contact as he pulled his car on to the street. "Where are you headed?"

"The World War II Museum."

He glanced at her. "Really?"

"I was trying to avoid last-day lunches with coworkers. I figured that I'd go see what Lisa saw when she was there. Anyway, after the phone call that I had with Lloyd, I'm not hungry." She told him what Lloyd had said, then added, "He was dismissive of Lisa's efforts. I'm used to my father and his friends patronizing me. I thought, though, that as a professor, Lloyd would have treated a graduate student with a little more respect and not like a pompous old man who had written all that needed to be written on the subject."

"If Lisa had uncovered something new," Brandon said, "it would mean that the esteemed professor missed something all those years ago when he wrote the book on the years leading up to World War II. Wouldn't it?"

Taylor hadn't thought of that, but Brandon was right. "Yes, it would."

"And given his close relationship with your family," Brandon said, "you did say that he is a close family friend, right?"

"Yes."

"Lloyd would not only have professional embarrassment; he'd lose credibility, and my gut tells me that he should lose a little. To come clean, I'm biased. I have a seven-year-old's memories of his name, a general dislike of Lloyd Landrum, based on my father's rants."

"Well, Lloyd basically told me not to worry my pretty little head on such serious subjects as murder."

He glanced at her and frowned. "Please tell me that you're kidding."

"Well, he didn't use those words, but he told me not to worry in the same breath that he asked me to be eye-candy with a mouth at Sunday's gala to celebrate the opening of the new wing of the museum. I'm giving a speech. Not a serious one, God forbid. A nice one. I'm tagged for it not because I'm articulate, or smart. I'm doing it because," Taylor drew a deep breath, trying to keep her frustration in check, "as Lloyd says, I'm the prettiest member of the family. I aced law school. My father wanted me to be a business major and get my MBA, though, so anything I did in law school was a waste in his eyes.

Does anyone even care that I worked night and day to be number one? Number one out of one hundred and thirty-five very bright people."

Brandon stopped at a traffic light and gave her his full attention. She should stop her rant, she knew, but Brandon was giving her a sympathetic ear, and it felt good to unload.

"I'm not giving the speech because I'm more than capable of addressing this crowd of important people. I'm giving the speech because," she said, "according to Lloyd, I'm pretty, and I'm sure my father thinks the exact same thing. Lloyd said that he'll help me with my remarks. Evidently, I'm not smart enough to compose the words myself."

The light turned green, and he directed his attention to driving. "Don't be bothered by the fact that people are patronizing you. Part of it is the image that you project."

"What is that supposed to mean?"

He shrugged. "You don't look brilliant. You're too damn gorgeous and too put together, in a stylish way. You look like you care more about the latest fashion than anything serious."

A slow simmer of anger burned a flush into her cheeks. The truth underlying his words made the day from hell worse. When he stopped at another traffic light, he glanced at her.

"Don't get mad. Use it to your advantage. Look so good that you dazzle them, then kick them in the balls when they're not looking. I don't know how many juries you've been before, but I'd bet money that your track record is going to be a winning one. Men won't focus on anything in the courtroom but you, which is a nightmare for opposing counsel. As long as you keep that rich girl prissiness in check..."

"Gee," she interrupted, "thanks a bunch."

"Hey. I'm only being honest. But, once they look into your eyes," he said, pausing as he held her gaze, then slowing his words, "even women jurors will love you. They'll want to wear what you're wearing, or fix their hair like yours. It's close," he narrowed his eyes, studying her, "but I don't think they'll be jealous, because when you do speak, you do it with such conviction, it even makes me pause. Your eyes are so real. They're a compelling reflection of all of your thoughts. You'd persuade them all, women and men, to do whatever you wanted them to do. I'd hire you for my firm in a flat second," he gave her a smile, "but I don't think you'll be applying for a job."

"Wow," she said, momentarily at a loss as to how to respond to his honest assessment. "Thank you. I guess."

"So why do you want to avoid last day lunches with co-workers?"

"I think others believe I'm leaving to start a dream life, but I know I'm actually leaving my dream life. Given how down I am about leaving," she paused, "the thought of polite, lunchtime chatter makes me ill. I'm not close enough with any of them to tell them the reality of how I feel about leaving this job. It's hard to explain without sounding pathetic."

"You wrapped it up in a few sentences to me," he said, his eyes on the road as he maneuvered his car through lunch-time foot traffic and a construction zone. "Succinctly, without sounding pathetic."

"There's something about you that makes me capable of saying exactly what's on my mind," she paused. It was because he was nice. Really, really nice. "And I'm sorry. I really shouldn't blab. I don't usually, you know."

"You'll figure it all out."

With the disappointment of leaving the district attorney's office so fresh, she wasn't sure. "I hope so."

The stark, khaki-green exterior of the museum came into view, reminding her of Lisa's research. Taylor asked, "Have you spoken with Joe this morning?"

"Briefly, to tell him what Marvin has uncovered. Since I dragged you to Marvin's house last night, I thought I'd keep you in the loop, if you're interested." He glanced at her. She nodded. "Evidently, according to Marvin, some bad-ass named Tilly Rochelle went around town last night bragging about killing Lisa as his entry into a gang called the Gravier Street Kings. Marvin also told me that one of the kids that Tilly bragged to is at the station, trying to help himself. You may already know that."

Taylor nodded as Brandon pulled into the parking lot. Marvin really was good. So far, he had picked up on everything the police had learned.

"Also," Brandon continued, "Marvin called to tell me that someone found Lisa's backpack and purse in Central City, yesterday, on Calliope Street, not five blocks from Tilly's last known address."

"That's news to me," Taylor said, "Does Joe know that?"

"If he doesn't know it yet," Brandon said as he parked the car, "according to Marvin, he will shortly."

"So if Tilly killed her as a gang-initiation rite, it makes the theorizing that we did last night about Lisa's research somehow playing a part in the murder seem far-fetched, doesn't it?"

He shrugged. "I'm not sure I'm ready to forget about the theory, because I'm not sure it's as simple as a gang thing. The Gravier Street Kings don't require murder as an entry fee. The Kings are a pretty sophisticated bunch and, from what I've learned from Marvin, Tilly is well-known on the streets as a stupid punk from a long line of dumb criminals. The Kings wouldn't let Tilly anywhere near them, but Tilly might not know that and want a kill to impress them. According to Marvin, Tilly is claiming on the streets that Lisa was shot in the head," Brandon paused, "and as far as I know, that fact hasn't been released to the public. So Joe and Tony have to take this news about Tilly seriously, because Tilly knows a critical fact that hasn't been released to the public."

"Well, it is logical for the police to focus on Tilly," Taylor said. "How would Tilly know that she was shot in the head, if he wasn't involved?"

"Small-town mentality runs rampant even in the big city. Hell. I know that Lisa was shot in the head, and I didn't learn it from Joe or Tony. I know it because Marvin talked to the right people. Tilly may know it because people who work in the coroner's office have talked. Or," he shrugged, "Lisa was there for a while before her murder was called in. Tilly or one of his punk friends could have seen her before the police received the call, and, as far as I know, the police still don't know who made that call." Brandon paused. "The kicker is that if Joe and Tony focus on Tilly, they won't be focused on Lisa's research."

"I looked up Tilly Rochelle's picture," Taylor said, "he's not the person who flashed his lights on Melody Street while I was there. Tilly also isn't the person who was looking in the window at Lisa's house."

He gave her a kind but doubtful glance. "Last night you couldn't describe either man to me."

"I know," she said, "but as first impressions go, I'd say no. Tilly is small, almost scrawny, and he's dark black. The person on Melody Street and at Lisa's house was either a light-skinned black man or a white man, and he wasn't small." She shrugged. "I'm not sure what that means, but after I saw the photograph of Tilly, I placed a call to Joe. I figured I better tell him what happened and my observations regarding Tilly."

Brandon asked, "Is there any reason why anyone would be following you right now?" She shook her head. "Did you get the alarm company to your house?"

"They're coming at three. Carolyn will meet them."

The stark lines of the museum beckoned them. Taylor stepped out of the car, as Brandon did. The complex had sprawling buildings that covered two city blocks. Three of the buildings were open to the public and had been, in various phases, since 2000. The fourth and largest building would be open on July 4th. Taylor gestured with her chin in the direction of the original building, as her phone buzzed with a text message. She pulled her phone out of her purse.

Andi wrote, *"I have a date this evening. Can you do something with Colette?"*

Taylor responded, *"Sure."*

"Good. C. promised she'd go for a walk today. She was down last nite, but better this a.m. Even said she might try to stop taking so many meds."

"Great news. Really."

Collette was on antidepressants and, after Alicia's death, she had a habit of mixing them with anti-anxiety medicine and sleeping pills. Taylor and Andi had grown concerned to the point of being alarmed.

Taylor sent a quick text to Collette, *"Hey. Want to do something tonight?"*

She held onto the phone as she and Brandon walked towards the main entrance. Collette did not reply. Taylor dropped the phone in her purse. She made a mental note to call Collette after she left the museum.

Chapter Eight

Brandon had been to the museum before, but not for history's sake. The museum and especially the Paul Taylor Atrium, named after Taylor's maternal grandfather, was a popular venue for large fundraisers. The atrium was the official entryway and led to the museum's other exhibits. Glass ceilings were three stories high. World War II era fighting planes hung from steel supports. Military craft were parked on the floor. A red, white, and blue banner announced the July 4th opening of the new Infamy Wing. The only names of benefactors that warranted placement on the banner were Hutchenson, Bartholomew, and Westerfeld. The HBW names were also carved in a marble wall that displayed the museum's original founders.

When he could, Brandon avoided the museum, the same as he avoided anything that related to his family's history. His presence had been required there at a handful of large political fundraisers over the last few years. He usually walked in late, found the people he needed to see, said what was necessary, then left.

Now, the atrium wasn't nearly as crowded as it was for fundraisers. His stomach knotted as Taylor walked through the atrium and straight to a Hutchenson Landing Craft, which was part of the museum's permanent display. The boat's functional simplicity seemed archaic when compared to modern military transportation devices and high-tech weapons, yet there was genius in the simplicity. The stark atrium paid proper homage to the large vessel, isolating it from other displays.

Minimalist signboards explained the features that made the boat unique. The khaki-green, flat-bottom craft had a ramp in the bow, which was open in the display model. The ramp enabled troops to disembark, combat ready, and enabled jeeps to drive into and out of the boat.

"When I was young," Brandon said, "my father built a tabletop model of the boat and explained to Victor and me how my grandfather had designed the ramp. It seems like a simple concept now, but at the time, it was revolutionary. According to my father, my grandfather came up with the idea to put a ramp in the bow and to make the ramp extend across the beam of the boat. The width of the ramp was important, because it meant that there wasn't a bottleneck of troops."

Taylor's attention was focused on him. She had a slight frown. "I've never had the impression that your grandfather designed anything on the boat. As these displays explain, it was named the Hutchenson Landing Craft because Hutchenson was the primary designer."

Brandon shook his head. "My grandfather didn't have money to invest or connections with people in charge of military contracting. Why else do you think they made him a partner?"

"I don't know, but the exhibits here don't support your father's theory."

Brandon hadn't expected the museum's exhibits to make long-forgotten memories return, but they did. "My father had original design drawings. I can still see them in my mind. He'd unroll them on the kitchen table, and go through each line, each idea, each concept, explaining how his father was a maritime genius, despite the lack of a formal education. He even had the original stamp that my grandfather used to mark his drawings."

The museum's signboard that explained the landing craft's features told of how Hutchenson, Bartholomew, and Westerfeld built the prototype for the boat, with Hutchenson being the primary designer.

"Thank God the museum wasn't built in my father's lifetime. The absence of my grandfather's name would have killed him." He returned his attention to the signboard, which explained that the landing craft that had enabled the United States to secure a victory on the Normandy beaches was a hybrid of a Louisiana swamp boat and a combat boat that was used by the Japanese. Below the description, President Eisenhower was quoted as saying that the Hutchenson Landing Craft had enabled the Allies to change the course of the war.

The next signboard explained that when it was developed, the boat had been a tough sell to the United States armed forces, and the men of HBW faced financial pressure. Hutchenson, the original founder of HBW and an engineer with boat-building expertise, was nearly bankrupt from the depression. Bartholomew had family money and an engineering degree. Westerfeld, also an engineer, had contacts in the Government and political savvy. Westerfeld persuaded his Government contacts to attend a secret beach trial on Lake Pontchartrain around the same time that Hitler succeeded in seizing major European ports. After a 1940 trial showed that the landing craft could enable an army to land on a beach and therefore make ports irrelevant to an Allied landing, the Marines placed an order for 20,000 units. Bartholomew was credited with developing plans for assembly-line, mass production, while Hutchenson was credited with the major engineering innovations that were incorporated into the boat.

One small signboard near the rear of the display explained that somewhere between the perfection of the design and the beginning of its production for the military, one of HBW's workers and a partner in the early days of the business, Benjamin Morrissey, had contacted the Nazis. Brandon's heart pounded as he read the short account of his grandfather's criminal offense.

Only words on a board, he told himself. *Only words.*

The board said that before Morrissey managed to give the Nazis the design plans and tell them that there were 20,000 boats on order, he was arrested. Benjamin Morrissey was charged with attempting to sell military secrets to a known enemy. A jury had convicted him of the crime in 1944. Morrissey died in prison. The company that was once named HBW&M became the modern day HBW Shipbuilding Enterprises.

Son of a bitch. One day he'd have to explain this bullshit to Michael. His gut twisted as he stepped away from the exhibit. He sure as hell hoped that he did a better job than his own father had.

"Tough to read?" Taylor placed a hand on his arm, a soft gesture of compassion as he absorbed the reality of the hard facts that pre-dated his existence.

"Not easy to see in black and white," he said, "but I have my mother to thank for the fact that those words, and my grandfather's misdeeds, didn't wreck my life like they wrecked my father's."

"How is she doing, with the news of your brother?"

Taylor's soft tone, the quiet pause in her words, combined with her expressive eyes, conveyed genuine concern. "I haven't told her. I'm going to visit her after my hearing," he shrugged, "Kate will go with me. I'm taking Michael. You know, bad news with good." He glanced around the atrium. "Lisa's notes indicated that part of Rorsch's memoirs were here," he said, referring to the U.S. Government agent who, according to Lisa's notes, had been instrumental in his grandfather's arrest. "And I don't see design drawings of the landing craft."

"There's more upstairs," she arched an eyebrow, "where I'm guessing you've never been."

He looked into her eyes. "Not once."

Taylor led the way, stepping through a troop of cub scouts, then into a time-lined exhibit room. Brandon stopped at a spy exhibit, remembering that Lisa's notes had a cryptic notation that included Rorsch, documents, and Dallas. Brandon found Rorsch's name amidst timelines and graphic depictions of people who had been caught by government agents in treasonous activities. The exhibit indicated Rorsch oversaw the investigation that had resulted in his grandfather's arrest and conviction. A few pages of handwritten notes were displayed, one describing that South Louisiana, with the port of New Orleans, was a hotbed of spy activity, and another describing a meeting that took place in 1940, in the restroom of Antoine's Restaurant. According to Rorsch, he worked undercover as a Nazi sympathizer when Benjamin Morrissey had attempted to sell to Rorsch the design drawings for the Hutchenson Landing Craft.

"Lisa was looking for a complete copy of Rorsch's memoirs, right?" Taylor asked.

Brandon nodded. "And now Pete is tracking that down, along with trial transcripts and other open-ended questions from Lisa's notes."

They entered another room, where display cases housed

architectural drawings of the landing craft. His heart pounded as he paused at each one. "My father had these drawings."

The first drawing depicted the landing craft with the ramp sealed shut. Along the left margin, his grandfather had marked neat, hand-written measurements for every conceivable angle of the boat. He could hear his father's voice.

Look Victor. Look Brandon. In this drawing, the landing craft is an ordinary boat. But your grandfather's numbers, here, tell of the possibilities.

The second drawing had two renderings. In the first, the ramp was one-third of the way open. In the second, a side view, the ramp was half open and the boat was approaching a beach.

You see, the Allies had lost control of the ports. To have any hope of beating Hitler, they needed to land troops, weapons, and vehicles on the beaches. Your grandfather's boat could land on a beach, bow first, the ramp would open, and troops could walk off.

The third and final drawing had been the best, the one that always held Brandon's attention the longest. It was a frontal view with the ramp wide open, and it showed men in full uniform stepping off with weapons ready for combat. Centered in the bow, a jeep was driving onto the beach.

Your grandfather understood the mechanics, the weights, the measures. The boats never failed, Brandon. Remember that, Victor. Your grandfather's boats delivered the men who made World War II turn in our favor. Don't you ever forget that.

Brandon retraced his steps, stopping at each drawing. With each short step, his heart pounded harder. "My father showed these drawings to us. Night after night. He didn't teach us the alphabet, or how to throw a baseball. He didn't help us with our homework. He showed us these drawings," he paused. Other museum patrons stared at him. He stood closer to Taylor and dropped his voice, "And the original drawings that he had were signed by his father." Brandon pointed to the signature at the bottom of the maps. "Not Hutchenson, as these are signed. Benjamin Morrissey signed each drawing, and his name isn't on any of these."

Taylor shook her head. "Maybe each engineer prepared

their own drawings."

Her eyes were leveled on him, her arms were loose at her sides, and she was as composed as he'd ever seen her. It would take way more than his childhood memories to make her doubt the story that the museum told. Still, what she was saying didn't make sense to him. "They would have had duplicates, but not multiple, competing versions. That's not how engineers work."

"Maybe your grandfather's plans weren't used, or maybe they all played a part in the design."

"And maybe my father got it wrong?"

"Maybe," Taylor's voice dropped to a low whisper, "until now, I didn't think that you believed your father."

Her words hit deep and brought to the surface complex feelings from his childhood when he was faced with a parent whose mental thought processes were less than healthy. "I don't know that I ever disbelieved him. I do know that his obsession scared me. As for now," Brandon paused. He breathed in deep, then exhaled. His pulse slowed, thank God. He lost the feeling of being a vulnerable kid and he was able to focus on the reason why he was roaming through the World War II museum with Taylor. His son's mother. Lisa. Her research. Her questions. "I'm not sure whether I believe his theory. Until now, I can't say that I cared one way or another. But now, Lisa was asking the same questions, and I'd like to know if she found answers."

"Lisa's notes indicated that she was looking for the original drawings." He paused, staring at the uniform, black ink on the drawings. He'd have sworn that his grandfather's drawings were in blue ink. The paper in the museum wasn't aged. "These documents look like copies to me." He glanced at the explanatory signboards, retracing his steps to the room's initial display regarding the Hutchenson Landing Craft. Taylor followed him. "The archives of HBW Enterprises are credited with providing documentation regarding the landing craft. Last night you mentioned that the corporate office has documents and your father has a private library. These copies are probably from documents that are in one of those places. I'd like to see the originals."

Taylor folded her arms and turned to him. "You're insinuating that the museum is selectively displaying historical artifacts. Are you suggesting that someone from the World War II museum, or HBW, or possibly my own father, removed your grandfather's name?"

"Yes," Brandon said, "That's exactly what I'm suggesting."

Her back was straight, her shoulders were squared, and her eyes were narrowed. "That's offensive."

He shrugged. "Sorry. I know what I saw. I know what my father's documents indicated, and he had originals."

"Where are your father's documents now?"

"Our home burned in a fire when I was seven. The documents were destroyed."

"You said that your father died when you were seven."

"He did," Brandon said. "It was one hell of a bad year."

Greenish-brown eyes held his gaze, imparting sympathy. "I'm sorry about that."

"It was a long, long time ago. I'm past it."

He guessed that his callousness was contagious, because her eyes hardened as she studied him. "You can't use your memory from when you were seven years old to accuse people of forgery."

It sounded implausible, he knew, but he remembered staring at his grandfather's rough signature. Night. After night. After night. "I think that I can."

She shook her head. "I'm not buying it."

"We need to find the original documents from which these exhibits were copied, if they still exist. You have access. I don't. Will you either include me in the search," he paused, "or tell me what you find?" He hesitated, then thought through what he had learned about Taylor. Despite his preconceived ideas of her, she was a compassionate, caring person who wanted to make the world a better place. His gut told him that she wouldn't lie to him, no matter what she discovered. Yet she was a Bartholomew, which meant that she had a stake in the outcome, so he added, "Honestly tell me."

Taylor drew a deep breath, as his phone vibrated with a call. "I would never be anything but honest," she said. "How dare you suggest otherwise?"

He removed the phone from his pocket as Taylor turned and headed to the stairs. He told Pete to hold for a second, then caught up to Taylor. "Look-"

"Take your call," she said, walking down the stairs and to the exit. "We're done here."

"I'll give you a ride."

She shook her head. "I'd prefer to walk."

"Hey," he said, as they stepped outside, "I didn't mean to imply that you'd lie."

She didn't look at him. "But you did."

"I'm sorry. I didn't intend to insult you. It's too hot to walk ten blocks, and I'm going to court, which is next to your office." He paused. "Besides, Pete's been looking into some things that were mentioned in Lisa's notes, and you might be interested in what he's found. That's what this call is about."

"Fine," she said, "Then take your phone call and give me a ride."

Once they were in the car, the audio system picked up the call. "Pete, find anything?"

"Rorsch's daughter, Madeline Rorsch, has all of her father's documents, which include transcripts of your grandfather's trial. By the way, going through federal court cold storage would take weeks. If you want to look at the transcripts, Madeline is the way to go. So, Madeline was upset when I told her that Lisa was murdered. Lisa had made a couple of trips there, once in the beginning of the year, then three weeks ago, for a day."

"Where is Madeline?" Brandon asked.

"Outside of Dallas." Brandon and Taylor shared a glance. "Near the airport that you usually fly into."

"Something had to be important for Lisa to spend money that she didn't have and take the time to go all the way to Dallas," Brandon said. Taylor nodded, indicating that she was thinking the same thing. "Especially considering that she had a five-week old baby at home."

"Madeline wouldn't tell me why Lisa went there, and she was reluctant to open her father's collection to you," Pete said.

"I convinced her by pressing the issue that you were not only a friend of Lisa's, but you were Benjamin Morrissey's grandson. She said to tell you she'd expect you to arrive tomorrow or Sunday. The documents are part of her father's collection of war memorabilia, which is kept under lock and key in a secure storage facility. She will not allow copies. I arranged for you to have the jet tomorrow. The pilots are booked and the flight plan, which might be adjusted slightly, calls for you to leave at 11:30," Pete said, "then return here by 4:30."

Brandon thought through his schedule for Saturday. "I was going to work with Steve and Noel on trial prep. Can you see whether they could be free on Sunday?"

"I'm already rearranging that. Steve would prefer to do it tonight. Are you open for a late night session?"

"Plan it at my house at ten-thirty. I was going to use that time to work on an oral argument that I'm giving next week, but I can wait. Mitch is coming by at ten to talk through discovery strategy on another case," Brandon said, referring to one of his more senior associates. "And he might need your help with that."

"I'll pull it all together." Pete said. "Oh. One more thing. I looked for an obituary on Rorsch. I wasn't able to find one. I asked Madeline whether he was alive. She said yes. When I asked whether I could talk to him, she said no. Not under any circumstances." Brandon detected silverware sliding on a plate, as Pete finished talking.

"Are you eating?"

"Yeah. I stopped by your house to check on the little guy." Pete paused, and Brandon imagined him standing in the kitchen, as he usually did, with a plateful of food.

"How is Michael?"

"Awesome. I gave him a bottle, he fell asleep in my arms," Pete said, "and now he's sleeping. Esme insisted that I eat. Lasagna. It rocks. She made two pans, so we can eat it tonight as well. Getting back to Lisa's research, I checked the Secretary of State's historical records. Benjamin Morrissey was a principal in the company, as Lisa's notes indicated, and I've confirmed that he forfeited his share in the company upon his conviction. Do you realize how wealthy you'd be today, if he hadn't been convicted?"

Brandon glanced at Taylor, who arched an eyebrow back at him, and frowned. "I have an idea."

"You know, if you could prove that your grandfather was wrongfully convicted," Pete said, "you may have a claim against HBW for wrongful termination of his ownership interest. Or would that be prescribed?"

Brandon lucked out with a parking spot that was between the courthouse and Taylor's office. Taylor said, "This is downright fascinating."

"Brandon?" Pete asked.

Brandon chuckled. "I forgot to mention that Taylor Bartholomew is with me and you're on speaker. Emphasis on Bartholomew. As in HBW. You two met yesterday evening in her capacity as an assistant district attorney. Today she's leaving that job. Tomorrow, she'll be working for HBW."

"Um, when you have my call on speaker, don't you know that you're supposed to tell me when someone else is in the car with you?"

Brandon laughed.

"Hello, Taylor," Pete said. "I hope that I didn't offend you."

"No offense taken," Taylor answered Pete, but her gaze was on Brandon. Her eyes were serious, but she had a slight, amused smile "As general counsel for HBW, it's important for me to stay informed of potential adversaries."

"Whether I could, or would, ever claim an interest in the company is, like Taylor said, fascinating. But that isn't what this is about. We want to know what Lisa knew," Brandon said, his words as much for Taylor as for Pete, "and whether it was worth killing her."

"So you're not buying the idea that Tilly Rochelle did it?" Pete asked.

"No," Brandon said, "Not yet."

"I don't blame you. The Kings claim that they have nothing to do with Tilly Rochelle, who, by the way, is gone. Even his mom claims that she doesn't know where he is. Says she hasn't seen him in months."

"I'm getting ready to walk into court. Call Marvin. Tell him I'll pay him to find Tilly and deliver him to the NOPD so that Joe doesn't waste too much time looking for him."

As he broke the connection with Pete, Brandon checked his watch. He had five minutes. Taylor said, "Nice to know you might be gunning for an ownership interest in my company."

He laughed. "I'm not at all."

"If that changes," she said, "give me fair warning."

"You won't need a warning. I'll make damn sure that you know."

"You plan work sessions that begin at ten-thirty at night?"

He shrugged. "I'm an insomniac with a bad habit of multitasking during the day. The other lawyers in my firm know they'll have my full attention at night."

"I'd like to look at Rorsch's documents myself. Is there room for one more on your jet?"

"Not mine. I lease it on an as-needed basis, mostly for the firm. And yes, there's room for one more. You're welcome to go to Dallas with me," he paused, "as long as you let me know what those original design drawings tell you."

"Deal," she said, "and I was always going to do that."

"I know," he said. "Hard feelings?"

She shook her head. "No. Just be careful with that lack of trusting thing."

"Will do." Brandon and Taylor stepped out of the car and into the breath-stealing heat of the first of July. They said goodbye, then turned to walk in opposite directions, until her voice halted his forward movement. "I forgot to tell you about tonight."

Brandon turned back to her, then froze. A car was pulling away, not twenty yards from where she stood. The car caught his attention, because it was a black, four-door Mercedes, the type of car that Taylor had described the night before. The side windows were tinted. He couldn't see the driver's features. As though the driver saw that Brandon was looking, the car accelerated, cutting across three lanes of traffic before Brandon could see the license number. Other drivers protested the maneuver with blaring horns.

Taylor turned to the commotion. "What was that?"

"Nothing," he said, shaking it off before alarming Taylor. There had to be hundreds of cars like that in downtown New Orleans, even though tinted windows were illegal. He made a mental note to talk to Joe about it though. His observations, coupled with Taylor's observations from the night before, could mean something in the scheme of the investigation. "You were saying?"

"I'll be at your house at 6:30 this evening. With my decorators. They're on board to decorate the nursery." Taylor gave him a soft smile. "Remember, last night, you said that I could."

"I remember," he said, even though Taylor's offer had slipped his mind. "That's great."

"You don't need to be there. Arrange for me to get in and let me know which room is Michael's. I'd welcome your input, though," she paused, "any theme you'd like, and, of course, an amount you'd like to spend."

"Of course," Brandon answered. He had to get into court, but he lingered as he watched her walk away. Her skirt hit a few inches above her knee, giving him a view of plenty of long, lean calf. She was sleek and elegant, and even in the godawful heat, she made the parking lot seem like a runway. He turned from her, but he didn't try to deny that he was attracted to her. His gut said no though, because she was a Bartholomew and would one day lead the company that had destroyed his grandfather and, by proxy, his father. Her name, and what it stood for, should give him enough of a reason to stay away, and the problems didn't end with her name. For all of her put-on airs of sophistication, she seemed naive, as though she hadn't been in the real world long enough to develop a shield.

He was broken, with sharp, jagged edges. One way or another, he'd hurt her. He was better than he'd been in a long time, but he sure as hell wasn't whole. He entered the courtroom as the judge took the podium. As he waited for his case to be called, he told himself that he'd stay away. No more long looks. No more thinking about last night's kiss and how his body had responded.

No more.

***

Collette Westerfeld stepped out of her home, which bordered Audubon Park. She locked the door, then wandered to the park's jogging path, toying with ear buds and her phone as she walked. She wore athletic shorts, tennis shoes, and a thin exercise tank top. Her red hair was in a ponytail. She didn't see him, even though he didn't bother hiding. While many twenty-seven year olds had work to keep them occupied at two on a Friday afternoon, jobs were for lesser, poorer mortals. Collette was a Westerfeld, and that meant that she didn't have to work.

He had already been in the Mediterranean-style home long enough to know that this would be an easy kill. Collette was grieving for her mother and brother with the aid of doctor-prescribed antidepressants and anytime-she-wanted-it alcohol. Those two drugs were in addition to her normal rich-girl-fixes of anti-anxiety medication and sleeping pills. Since she possessed the ingredients for a lethal mixture, all he had to do was persuade her to take the shit. Persuasion had never been a problem for him. He went into the kitchen and put odorless gamma hydroxybutyrate into a glass of water.

He liked to use the full name of the date-rape drug, always amused when the people who supplied it said, huh? Stupid fucks. GHB, dummy. Huh? *Date-rape shit. Oh, they'd say,* that's easy to get.

He dissolved some of her anti-anxiety pills into the liquid. Her refrigerator was stocked with bottles of drinking water, one of which was separate from the others and was only three quarters full.

Could it be that simple?

If she reached for that bottle of water first, he wouldn't need to work hard at persuading her to take the rest of the stuff that would kill her. If she didn't reach for that bottle first, he'd be there to make sure that she drank it anyway. He shrugged.

What the fuck? Why do hard when one could do easy?

He emptied the bottle that she had already started, filled it with some liquid persuasion, then waited for her return.

Chapter Nine

Rose was on a porch swing waiting for Brandon and Kate as they pulled into her driveway. She walked towards the car. Two young labs, Jett's litter mates, ran circles around her. Rose was tall and lean and, at sixty-nine, she still had more black in her hair than gray. She had a stoic calmness about her that disappeared when she took in the fact that Kate was sitting in the backseat with Michael. "Brandon? Kate? What's going on here?"

As Brandon got the baby out of the car seat, he said, "This is Michael, mom. He's my son."

"Good Lord." She was still. "Seriously?"

He nodded. She took Michael out of Brandon's arms. "Well, I was wondering why an impromptu visit on a Friday afternoon was warranted." Puzzled eyes, a color that matched Brandon's own, held his gaze, "but I never would have guessed this." They walked into the house. Rose sat at the kitchen table, holding Michael, smiling as he gazed into her eyes. "He is the most beautiful baby I've ever seen." She redirected her attention to Brandon and Kate. Her smile disappeared. "Brandon, you're scaring me with that godawful look of seriousness in your eyes," she glanced at her daughter, "and Kate, you look about as somber as I've ever seen you. If the looks from the two of you are any indication of what's coming, this conversation is going to be harsh. For five minutes, please let me drink in this gorgeous infant."

Brandon handed Rose a bottle then, when he saw that Michael was taking it, he sat next to his mother. Kate sat at the table with them. As he let Rose have her time, he focused on Michael's steady progress through the formula. When Michael had taken most of the bottle, and seem uninterested in the rest, Rose lifted him onto her shoulder and patted his back. Her gaze rested on Brandon. "Tell me why you look so miserable."

His mother appreciated directness, so that's what he gave her. "His mother and I didn't have a relationship. Her pregnancy was an accident. I didn't know about him until a little over two weeks ago. His mother's name was Lisa Smithfield." Rose drew in a deep breath, which he took as a a signal that she recognized the name. He hesitated. He knew that she didn't pay attention to the news, and he bet that she didn't know what happened. "She was murdered a couple of days ago."

Her face became pale. "Oh good God."

"You met her, didn't you?"

She nodded. "Last summer. She came here, doing research. She mentioned that she went to you, but that you couldn't, or wouldn't, help her."

Michael started whimpering. Kate reached for him. Brandon watched the baby settle into Kate's arms, become quiet, and start to work again on the bottle. "What did you and Lisa talk about?"

"I told her that I wouldn't talk about anything having to do with Benjamin Morrissey," she paused, "or what your father believed. She came here anyway. She was such a nice young lady. She seemed smart. Oh Brandon," Rose shook her head, "this is terrible."

"I know," he said. "Terrible doesn't begin to describe it. I have to ask whether you talked to her about dad's theories. Did you?"

Rose stood and walked to the refrigerator.

"Mom?"

"No," she said. "Nothing good ever came of that. Are you two hungry?"

Brandon shook his head, not surprised by his mother's total avoidance of the subject. Kate said, "No."

He thought about Lisa's notes, which indicated a meeting with Rose in New Orleans three months earlier. "Did you see Lisa again, more recently?"

Rose pulled a pitcher of tea out of the refrigerator. "No."

"Did dad ever have dealings with Lloyd Landrum? He's a

professor of history at Tulane.”

"I know," Rose said, placing ice in three glasses. "He's an authority on the Allied invasion of Normandy. A book that he wrote on the subject came out around the time of your father's death." A memory sizzled through Brandon's mind of his mother, up late, crying as she looked at a thick book. He remembered the incident, not because of the book, but because of his mother's tears. With his father gone, Rose had been his rock. Her tears had disturbed him. Later, when she'd gone to bed, he found the book. He'd fallen asleep looking at the pictures of the landing craft that, according to his father, his grandfather had built. When he awakened, the book was gone. He never saw it in their home again.

"Did dad meet with him?"

"Your father met with anyone who would listen to him."

He decided to ask a more specific question. "Mom. Do you know whether he met with Landrum?"

Rose handed them glasses of iced tea. She sat back down at the table. "Can we please not talk about your father?"

Michael finished the bottle. "He hasn't burped, but," Kate wrinkled her nose and handed the baby to Brandon, "this diaper has dad's name written on it."

Brandon set up a spot on the floor and changed Michael. As he did, Rose asked, "Do the police know who murdered Lisa?"

"They have a suspect," Brandon said. He stood and burped Michael before handing him to Rose, who took him with a soft, uncertain smile. He drank the minty, sugar-sweetened tea, poured more for himself, and hesitated before asking Rose another question, one that she wouldn't like. "Mom, all of dad's documents were destroyed in the fire. Right?"

Her smile disappeared as he mentioned the fire. She looked in Brandon's eyes. "The fire destroyed everything. Please, Brandon. Enough. I do not want to revisit the past." Michael cooed and stole her attention. With her gaze on Michael, she asked, "Where are Lisa's parents?"

"They died in an automobile accident a few years ago. She was an only child, and as far as I've been able to tell, she didn't have close relatives."

"So much tragedy," she whispered, then visibly shook off her sadness. "And now this beautiful infant. I could hold him forever. If there's anything you need or want from me, let me know." She asked about Brandon's child care arrangements, whether he needed help with Michael, how much Michael was eating, and whether he was sleeping through the night. He answered as best he could, listened to her advice when she offered it, and wondered how and when to tell her about Victor. She held his gaze for a few seconds. He drew a deep breath. "There's more bad news, isn't there?"

He took Michael from Rose's arms. "I'm not sure how to say this."

"Just say it," Rose said.

"Kate was worried about Victor because he missed your birthday. She said that he'd been sick on his last few visits."

Rose nodded, "He said that he was better. He even looked better last time he was here."

"Well, because Kate was worried, I had Sebastian's firm look into it. He called me last night. I'm sorry, mom. Kate. Victor was killed six weeks ago in a security operation."

Kate gasped. In identical mother-daughter mannerisms, Kate and Rose lifted their hands to their mouths. After a moment, Kate asked questions, which Brandon answered based upon what Sebastian had told him. He omitted the sordid reality of the nature of Victor's business. Kate and Rose believed that Victor was a private security contractor of the legitimate sort, such as the type of agent who worked for Black Raven. Brandon saw no reason to tell them the reality of Victor's work. He waited for some kind of response, other than the unsettling calm that she portrayed.

"That's it?" Rose asked. "A couple of Black Raven agents believe that Victor died in an explosion?"

"That," Brandon nodded, "along with other intelligence gathered by Black Raven."

Rose shook her head. "Did someone see Victor's body? Are there photographs? Is there some kind of evidence?"

"No," Brandon said. His mother was strong. On the night of the fire, when they realized that Catherine had died, Rose was the sole stabilizing force for Brandon. His father had broken down, but Brandon didn't remember Rose even crying. In the following days and weeks, grief stole his father. Grief turned Victor into a fourteen-year-old who was bursting with anger, paranoia, and a dark side that was powered by a mean streak. Rose, though, had put on a brave front, and now, she shook her head. The initial shock had passed, and she looked as calm as ever.

"I don't believe it," Rose said.

"But he's never missed your birthday," Kate said. "No matter where he's been, he has always called. Or he comes here."

Brandon hadn't seen his brother in years, not since, according to Sebastian, Victor had become a mercenary with no morals. He didn't have personal knowledge of his brother's activities, he certainly didn't see him die, and if Rose put her tremendous force of will into denying Victor's death, there'd be no persuading her that Victor was gone. Not without Victor's body, which Brandon would never have. "Maybe one day I'll believe it, but not now. I'm his mother," Rose said, holding Brandon's gaze. "I'd feel it."

Brandon had expected tears and grief. He hadn't contemplated that Rose wouldn't believe him. He looked at Kate, who gave him a subtle shrug and a light shake of her head.

"Victor told me a few months ago," Rose said, "actually in one of our last conversations, that he might not be able to call for a while. He was starting a job that required the utmost secrecy. He said not to worry, no matter what I heard, even if he didn't call." Brandon could tell from the way Kate's glance was bouncing from Rose to Brandon, that Rose's doubt was contagious. "Victor said not to worry," Rose repeated, "and though I worry why he didn't reach me on his birthday, I certainly will not believe that he is dead." She glanced at them, then stood. She gave Michael a soft kiss on the forehead, and told Brandon, "I'll come to see Michael on Sunday morning. Is ten o'clock good for you?"

"Of course," Brandon said, not knowing what else to say.

"Mom, would you like me to stay with you tonight?" Kate

asked.

Rose gave her daughter a soft smile, then shook her head. "That's very nice of you, but no. I have work to do. If you stay, Brandon will have to drive on the Causeway alone with the baby," she shuddered, referring to the 24-mile bridge that spanned Lake Pontchartrain, "and I'd hate for him to have to pull over if Michael starts to cry. Now, if you two will excuse me, I have evening exercise and feedings with the dogs, and I have grooming and paperwork to do before tomorrow's show." She slipped through the back door. Brandon stood and watched Rose walk across the yard to the newly-built, red barn that housed the kennel and her office. Whether she believed him or not, his news about Victor had to be disturbing. The news about Lisa was also terrible.

He fought the urge to follow her. He got it. He understood her need to be alone, but busy, so that she could sort through her feelings. Or just forget about feelings.

Restlessness simmered within Brandon throughout the drive home. By the time they arrived, it was after five. Kate helped him with Michael, then, once they were inside, she said, "You look like you're wound so tight that you're going to have a stroke."

"I shouldn't have bothered with Victor," he said. "It was a waste of effort and time."

"Victor told her not to worry, and a son telling his mother not to worry isn't a bad thing," Kate said. "If she isn't going to be distraught, that isn't a bad thing either. Let her live in denial."

Some of Brandon's anger ebbed. Kate was correct. Denial was better than grief. It had to be. "And you?" he asked his sister. "Are you all right?"

Kate nodded. "I'm sad," she said, "but until mom lets go of her hope, I'll have some as well."

In light of Sebastian's expertise, the hope was foolish, but Brandon didn't steal it from her.

As Kate left, Brandon attempted to settle Michael in the pack-n-play, but Michael started crying the second that Brandon's hands left him. He couldn't be hungry. Brandon wondered whether he was tired. He hadn't napped since

Brandon had picked him up at three for the drive to Rose's house. He lifted Michael, as his sobs became louder and more jarring. Brandon was relieved when Laura, the day nanny, stepped into the breakfast room.

"I've unpacked the boxes from his mother's house that were brought over, and laid everything out in one of the rooms upstairs," Laura said.

"I don't know what's wrong with him," Brandon said.

She scooped Michael from his arms and checked his diaper. "He's wet. That's probably why he's crying." Brandon felt useless, because he hadn't thought to check the diaper. It seemed like he had changed it a second ago. Laura's dark eyes gave him a soft glance. "You'll get the hang of this. Esme and I made a list of a few more things that he needs," Laura said, "and she's shopping now."

"I need some exercise. Can you handle everything for a while?" When Laura nodded, Brandon continued. "A friend of mine is stopping by with decorators to pull together a room for him." He scribbled a note for Taylor. "This is for her. She'll be here around 6:30."

Brandon went upstairs and changed into a pair of running shorts and shoes. He didn't bother with a shirt. The temperature had topped a hundred degrees and the pavement had spent all day absorbing the heat. The run was going to be brutal, but it was what he needed. He mapped out his run in his head as he laced his shoes. He started slow. By the time the first mile was behind him, he was in autodrive.

Lose it, he told himself. *Lose the irritation. The feeling of ineffectiveness. The feeling that something was wrong. Victor wasn't worth it.*

Whether Rose or Kate wanted to believe it, Brandon knew that Victor was dead. Black Raven was good, and Sebastian was the best. If they said Victor was dead, he was gone. Good riddance. By mile five, after winding his way though City Park and circling the art museum, his anger ebbed. Until Kate or Rose brought him up again, he would not think of Victor.

At mile eight, he turned into Lakelawn Cemetery, then sprinted along tree-shaded pathways for the half mile to the tomb where Amy and their unborn child were buried. He reached it, out of breath, and stopped. After they died, he'd been ripped apart by a sadness that manifested itself in uncontrollable rage. Now, he was better, and especially now, with Michael in his life, he had to be better. He stood next to the tomb of Amy Adams Morrissey and Catherine Adams Morrissey, their baby who had never been born, and told them, in his thoughts, of the changes that had taken place in his life since his last visit to the cemetery, only three days earlier.

Single parenthood. Life with an infant. How Lisa had died. Waves of sadness and its ever-present friend, guilt, filled his thoughts. He deserved guilt, because on the night of the accident, he and Amy had decided to take two cars so that Brandon could work for another hour. He had one more pleading to read, a stack of cases to re-read, and one more walk-through on the appellate argument he was giving the next day. So he wasn't driving when, on Amy's way to her father's birthday party, an eighteen-wheeler, the driver hyped on amphetamines, had crashed into her. Tonight, his survivor's guilt had a new twist. He was getting to experience fatherhood, when Amy had never experienced motherhood, when Catherine hadn't experienced life.

He didn't handle sadness or guilt well, and those emotions turned to anger that coiled through his gut. Anger, his go-to emotion, was always there, festering. To repress it, he forced his mind to search for something to assuage the pain. He found a lifeline when he remembered the night before, when Taylor told him to focus on Michael's breathing. Her idea had worked. He stood, touched his index and his middle finger to his lips, and pressed a fingertip kiss onto the A in Amy's name and the C in Catherine's name. He glanced at his watch as he started to run. It was 6:45. He was two miles from home. He'd be there at seven or shortly after. Taylor should still be there, and he felt better with that thought.

Damn.

Other than the fact that she was a Bartholomew, born with more privileges than money could buy, born into a world where he'd never be welcome, she was irresistible.

***

Taylor left the D.A.'s office at four thirty and drove to the HBW Tower. She had to be at her father's house for a five-thirty meeting with the party planner and staff who would be handling the Saturday evening patron party. She had only a few minutes, but it should be enough time for her to look for original design drawings of the Hutchenson Landing Craft in the corporate library. She'd find the drawings, figure out whether the drawings that were in the private library matched the museum's design drawings, or whether Benjamin Morrissey's name was on the originals, and then she'd let Brandon know the answer. She didn't want to be the one to burst Brandon's bubble, but she would. To the extent that his theory rested upon concealment of the identity of the true drafter of the design drawings, his theory was flawed.

She was certain of it.

She took the box of crystal desk items out of the trunk of her car, rode the elevator to HBW's private floors, and was met with the broad smile of the HBW receptionist. "Good evening, Ms. Bartholomew. I'm delighted that I'll be seeing you on a more regular basis. Would you like assistance with that box?"

"No thank you, Sam," she said. "It's small and light," she smiled at the elderly man, "and I'm not that much of a prima donna."

"Well, I didn't mean to suggest that you were," he winked, "but you wouldn't be the first person with an office on the top floor who fit that description." He had manned the reception desk since Taylor was a child. She had always loved his quiet manner, his stately presence, and his sweet chit-chat as she signed the register for the corporate floor. "Is my father here?"

Sam nodded. "Your father, Mr. Westerfeld, Mr. Hutchenson, and Mr. Landrum are meeting in your father's private conference room. They requested that they not be disturbed."

Avoiding interaction with her father was a good thing, but Taylor tried not to look relieved as she took the private elevator that led to the top floor of the high rise. The top floor housed suites of offices for the three members of the HBW Board of Directors and, as Taylor and Claude used to joke, the precious few others who would ascend to the thrones. The Bartholomew office suite consisted of her father's corner office, his private conference room, and, next to that, the office that was now hers. The hallway door to her father's private conference room, where the meeting between George, Claude, Andrew, and Lloyd was taking place, was closed. Two cubicles sat outside the Bartholomew suite. One would be for Taylor's secretary, who Taylor hadn't yet hired. She'd been so hopeful that she was going to stay at the District Attorney's office, she had put off interviewing secretarial candidates. The other cubicle, which was directly outside George's office, belonged to Judith Kaine, her father's secretary, who was on the phone. Judith wore a conservative black pantsuit, her dark hair was in a neat bun, and she wore red reading glasses. She put the caller on hold when she saw Taylor.

"Good evening Taylor. May I help you?"

"No, thank you, Judith. I'm only here for a couple of minutes." Judith nodded and resumed her call.

Taylor walked into her office, deposited the box on her desk, then drew a deep breath as she scanned the space. The best thing about the office was the wall of windows that overlooked the Mississippi River. She'd have to redecorate the office, which was filled with dark rugs and oil paintings that reflected her father's taste, not hers. The antique mahogany desk made her shudder. She couldn't work the rest of her professional life at that desk. It was too dark and too heavy. Taylor's office had a door that led into her father's private conference room. On the other side of the door, a loud *whack* resonated, as though something was slammed against a hard surface. Taylor jumped at the unexpected noise.

Claude's voice was loud enough to escape through the thick walls and door. "What do you mean you have no clue who is doing this?"

George responded, his voice authoritative and even, but equally loud. "Calm down. We have a problem, Claude." Some of his words were lost, as though he had turned in the opposite direction as he spoke. The words picked up with, "We are directors. We deal with problems."

She heard a voice that was slightly lower than Claude's and her father's. She recognized it as Andrew Hutchenson, Andi's father.

"Is paying..." again some of the words disappeared, "...an option?"

George answered, but although she could identify her father's voice and sharp tone, she couldn't make out his words. She stepped closer to the door, trying to hear. She heard, "We need to be dismissive." She heard, "Hutchenson..." then more unintelligible words, then, "letter," and more words that she couldn't decipher.

Claude asked, "What the hell does that mean?"

"A hoax," George said. "It isn't complicated. Fraud. Lloyd?"

After a pause, then words that she couldn't decipher, Lloyd responded, "The timing. Don't you think..." more words disappeared, "...that this could..." his words were gone. Taylor thought she heard "police."

Her heart raced. She thought she heard all kinds of things, but the reality was she couldn't make out Lloyd's words. Whatever Lloyd said prompted George to say, "Absolutely not under any circumstances."

More conversation ensued, but the words were muffled. The conference room's hallway door opened. Whoever departed went in the opposite direction from her office. Taylor took the departure as a cue to leave. She made her way to the corporate library, saying goodbye to Judith and nodding to other staff that she passed along the way.

Taylor used her access card, opened the library door, and, as the lights automatically brightened, she walked past shelves of books, to the area that housed design drawings. From the company's inception in 1934, various original designs of the naval architects at HBW had been noteworthy. Drawings of those vessels were archived in the library, in an elaborate filing system that consisted of hanging, custom-made, glare-proof sleeves of clear plastic, with wooden bindings. Taylor began at 1934 and started flipping though the drawings. In the years 1937-1942, where drawings of the Hutchenson Landing Craft should have been, there were drawings for other vessels, but none for the landing craft.

"Looking for something?"

Taylor's heart raced as she spun around. Claude stood an arm's length behind her. He wasn't wearing his suit jacket. His tie was loose. His shirt was starched and neat, but the top button was open. "I saw that your office light was on. Judith saw you come in here."

Dark circles formed crescents under his blue eyes. Taylor said, "You look exhausted."

"It's been a long day, and it isn't over yet." He glanced around the library, then focused on the stacks where Taylor stood. He met her eyes with a puzzled glance. "Looking for naval design drawings from the 1930s?"

"As a matter of fact, yes."

"Why?"

"The Tulane student who was murdered was preparing her thesis on spies of World War II, in particular focusing on the treason case involving the Hutchenson Landing Craft. Her notes indicated that she interviewed you. You didn't tell me that last night when I asked you about her."

The fatigue in his eyes was replaced with an intense, bright burn of worry. "Taylor, drop it. As of today, you're no longer an assistant D.A., and the murder isn't your concern. Now you're corporate counsel for HBW, which means that you work for your father." His bitter tone was out of character. "Like we all do. He rules this place, and he wouldn't want you to be asking questions."

"Why not?"

He shook his head. "I've already told you too much."

"You haven't told me anything. I overheard some of the conversation from the conference room. What was that about?"

He glanced at the entrance to the library, then back at her. "Stop with the questions, please, for once. I can't discuss board information with you."

Claude had always been more than a friend. He was a few years older than Andi, Taylor and Collette and, at times, he'd been as much of a big brother to Andi and Taylor as he was to Collette. There weren't secrets between them. At least there hadn't been, until now.

"Are you serious?"

"Deadly serious." Claude said. "Information around here is on a need to know basis." He paused as a flush turned his cheeks red. "And your father is the person who decides who needs to know what and when. Just because you're going to be general counsel, that doesn't mean you're going to know everything the board discusses. I've got to get back in to the meeting," he said, looking over her shoulder at the stacks, to where the drawings of the Hutchenson Landing Craft should have been. "And you need to figure out something else to do with your time." He turned and headed for the door.

She followed him. "Wait."

"I warned you before and I'm warning you again." Claude turned to her one last time before stepping out of the library. "You won't like being in orbit of your father, Taylor. You won't. Trust me. Don't waste your life working here."

George stepped into the library as Claude stepped out. "Hello, Taylor. I didn't know that you were here." George's black-brown eyes gave her his typical hard once-over, he glanced at his watch, and frowned. "Weren't you going to be meeting with the party planners now?"

"I'm on my way," she said, pushing past the anxiety that his frown inspired. From here on out, she was going to be working *with* him, not *for* him, she reminded herself. She had to stop feeling like the daughter who couldn't get anything right.

"The conversation that you were having in the conference room. It sounded heated. What was it about?"

"Don't worry about it," he said, "at least not this weekend. Did Lloyd mention that you will be providing the remarks on behalf of the families at the gala on Sunday?"

Taylor recognized the brush-off, and Claude's comments had primed her for an argument. She lifted her chin, drew a calming breath, and said, "The fact that the board is having a private meeting now means that the issues won't be discussed in tomorrow morning's board meeting, doesn't it?"

"Yes, Taylor," George said. The harsh look in his eyes said *deal with it* in a way that made further words unnecessary. A pulse beat at his temple. Taylor knew that the pulse signified irritation. He had steered HBW for more than forty years and he was easily capable of harsh decisions, yet he had no idea how to relate to her. He didn't appreciate her academic achievements, and, at times like now, all she had to do was speak, and he'd be irritated.

Once, as a teenager, he had told her to stop acting as a silly girl. The disdain he used for both *silly* and *girl* had cut through her and, at that moment, Taylor understood why he always looked at her as though he was disappointed, no matter what she did. She had yelled that she was sorry that she hadn't been born a male. He had snapped that he was sorry, too. It had been a childish comment on her part, but she'd never forgiven him for his response, which had inspired her to play up her feminine side, in every way that she could. She'd never broken the habit, and that's why at the gala, she'd be giving welcoming remarks in a red silk halter dress with a plunging neckline that was anything but conservative. She'd chosen the dress before she had learned that she was giving a speech. He wouldn't approve, but attire was the least of her problems.

She held her father's gaze, undeterred by his annoyance. "When Lisa Smithfield, the Tulane student who was murdered, talked to you, what did she ask you, and what did you tell her?"

A flush formed on his cheeks, yet his voice was calm and controlled. "I don't recall anything very interesting or noteworthy." He paused. "Now you're going to be late for a meeting that I was counting on you to lead. As we discussed yesterday, I need you to responsibly handle your duties this weekend. Government personnel and elected officials who are in charge of the submarine-contracting decisions will be at Saturday's party and Sunday's gala. I'd appreciate it if you would stop worrying about things that are none of your business, such as closed-door meetings and the unfortunate murder of a Tulane student, and pay attention to things for which you are responsible. Right now, your priority needs to be that the patron party goes off without a hitch, then you can turn your attention to the gala."

George turned his back to her, stepped into the conference room, and shut the door.

Chapter Ten

Even after driving for ten minutes, Taylor was still furious with her father and angry with Claude. She made it to her father's house a few minutes late, composed herself as she put on lipstick in her car's make-up mirror, then smoothed her hair. She drew a deep breath, and let herself into the foyer, where Clara Mullins, the party planner that she and her father used, and John Mancke, her father's personal assistant and house manager, were waiting on her with the caterer, the photographer, the florist, and the head of her father's internal housekeeping staff. The meeting took a half hour, with a walk-through of the residence. They stopped in each room that would be open for the party, and ended in the rear yard, where a white tent was being erected, complete with chandeliers and a dance floor.

After, Taylor went home and found Carolyn waiting for her in her bedroom, with a seamstress for final alterations on the dresses that she was going to wear for the Saturday party and the gala. Taylor apologized for running late. She took a quick shower before trying on the dresses, staying under the warm water long enough for a soapy rinse, but was careful not to wet her hair. "I have to be in Old Metairie at 6:30, so I'm in a rush."

Carolyn glanced at her watch and frowned. "You might not make it."

"I know. Let's try on these dresses fast, all right?"

Carolyn's sharp eye and the seamstress's insistence that every tuck and seam be perfect tried Taylor's patience. The red dress for the gala gave the seamstress an easier time than the ivory chiffon and silk cocktail dress that she was wearing on Saturday. The problem was underwear lines, which Taylor changed three times. Carolyn laid out the accessories and jewelry that Taylor would use each night, glancing at Taylor for a nod or a shake of the head. As Taylor stood still while the seamstress pinned, then unpinned the waistline, mental images of Anna Maria's angelic brown eyes, the young girl's pink and chartreuse satin ribbon, and Marvin's machine gun flashed through her mind. She saw 2813 Melody Street, and Lisa's apartment, where Lisa had been packed and ready for a new life with Michael. Michael, crying inconsolably, while in Brandon's arms, was a fitting reaction to the tragic circumstances of his mother's absence. The world was tragic and sad, and, as she glanced at the ladies who were working hard to make sure that she looked her best at the weekend's parties, reality was oceans away from her pampered existence.

"Taylor," Carolyn said, interrupting her thoughts.

"Yes?"

Carolyn gave her a perplexed look. "We're through." The seamstress was packing her bag. "You need to slip out of the dress."

"Sorry," Taylor said. "I was daydreaming."

Carolyn said, "Your schedule for today didn't include a meeting at 6:30."

"I'm doing a favor for a friend, and I have people meeting me there," Taylor explained to Carolyn as she went into her closet for a pair of jeans. She stopped, suddenly aware of the excess that confronted her. She didn't have only a few pairs of jeans from which to choose. She had countless jeans, organized in a neat row by color, size, and whether they required heels or sandals. Brandon's words from earlier in the day flashed through her thoughts. *The fact that someone cannot see past the exterior is more of a reflection of them that it is a reflection of you.* As she paused, she wondered if he was correct. Had she become, on the inside, the prissy rich girl that her wardrobe suggested? *Dear God. She hoped not.* Without thinking too much about it, she chose a pair of jeans that, hopefully, minimized her butt, a white linen blouse, nude, peep-toe heels, and a matching thong and brassiere that were made of beautiful, intricate swirls of lace in crisp white.

She sat at her vanity. As Taylor smoothed her hair, Carolyn said, "Is everything okay?"

Taylor nodded. "I'm fine."

"I know the work transition is going to be hard on you,"

Carolyn said, "but you were late last night, distracted this morning, and this evening your thoughts are a million miles away." Carolyn narrowed her eyes. "What's going on?"

"I just have to hurry. This is really important."

"Are you doing this favor for a friend who is a man?"

"No," Taylor said, "his son."

"Oh," Carolyn said, "so there is a man involved. Is he the person you were talking to on the phone when you arrived home last night? The one who was worried whether your alarm was working?"

"Yes," Taylor said as Carolyn studied her. "There was a murder this week. He knew the victim. The baby was theirs."

"Good Lord."

"He's compelling. He's," she paused, "different. Intense. It's complicated." Taylor blushed as she thought about the night before, how his arms had been strong and hard, how his kiss had made her knees weak. *Oh. My. God. I want him. It could happen. This is what it feels like. Anticipation, with a capital A. This is why I'm shaking at the thought of going to his house.* She shook her head, but couldn't stop thinking about Andi's advice.

Just do it and move on.

"Well?" Carolyn asked. "What's complicated?"

"It's nothing."

Carolyn gave Taylor a soft smile, "Looks like something to me."

Taylor shook her head. "Tomorrow, early, I have a board meeting."

"I know that."

Taylor glanced again at herself in the three-way mirror. "Do I look fat?"

"Of course not," Carolyn said.

Taylor often joked with Andi and Collette that she had Beyonce's butt, without the voice. Glancing at herself made her think of that joke and that she hadn't heard from Collette. She dialed Collette's cell, but there was no answer. Taylor left a message. "Hey. I thought I'd swing by your house later. Call me. We can do a late dinner, or I'll hang out with you at your house." She dialed Collette's land line. There was no answer there, either. She left a message.

"Hey. Call me. Soon."

***

Normally he felt great after a kill. But this Friday, he was tired. After he was sure that Collette was with her mother, he was too tired to stage her death so that it looked like the accident that he planned for it to be. He found a sheet, one that he would take, laid it next to her, and, for a few minutes, he indulged himself by laying on the floor and sleeping. When Collette's cell buzzed with a text, he awakened. He read Taylor's text. He smiled. Taylor was coming. Later, but she was coming. Taylor would find Collette. He would be there, watching. His joy dissolved as he received a phone call from his person on the inside, who said, "There has been no decision as of yet."

"The board does not believe that Lisa's murder is connected to the extortion attempt?"

"The Board is not worried about Lisa's murder."

He looked at Collette. Her blue eyes stared vacantly at the ceiling. People who knew him knew what he was capable of, how he could extinguish life without raising alarms. It was his signature. These people, though, did not know him. Collette's death might break their hearts, or at least it would break the heart of Claude Westerfeld, one of the three board members. That would be gratifying, but it would not secure twenty-five million dollars. He would have to do a better job with his next kill. He thought through the best way that he could accomplish his goals. He had to sound alarms. George Bartholomew needed to be worried.

He had options, he reassured himself. Many options by which he could destroy the lives of Andrew Hutchenson and George Bartholomew by killing their daughters. Options by which he could rob their lives of joy and make them meet his demand.

***

Taylor arrived at Brandon's house at 6:45. Max, the painter

and carpenter, was there, as was Sarah, the decorator and designer. They stepped out of their cars, as Taylor parked to the side of Brandon's driveway. Max had curly brown hair, large brown eyes, and an easy smile. Sarah, the more serious of the two, had short black hair, dark eyes, and a peaches and cream complexion.

"Sorry I'm late," Taylor said.

"Honey, we'd wait a week for you," Max said as he gave her a head-to-toe glance. "Those are the new Louboutin's aren't they?" When Taylor nodded, he said, "Fabulous. And those jeans are divine."

Taylor chuckled, glad that she'd met his razor-sharp scrutiny. "Thanks, Max."

"So," Sarah said, "how are you involved in this?"

Taylor explained as best she could as she walked to the front door then added, "The last thing on Brandon's mind is how to decorate a nursery, and Lisa, the baby's mother, was trying hard to get that sort of stuff right. I want to pull it all together, fast." Taylor knocked on the door. "That's where you two come in."

The nanny answered. Taylor extended her hand and introduced herself to Laura, with whom Taylor had spoken on the phone the day before. "Mr. Morrissey left this for you."

Brandon's handwriting was neat and elegant on thick, heavy paper. *"Pick any two rooms upstairs that make sense for a baby/toddler's bedroom, along with a playroom. I don't care about the specific furniture or color, etc; Budget is whatever is reasonable. As for theme, I'd like it to feel happy. I'll be home around seven."*

Sarah, Max, and Taylor entered, as Laura disappeared down a hallway. Max paused in the entryway, gesturing with his chin to the wall of living room windows. "Stunning pool. The Lin Emory sculpture is a perfect piece for a focal point, and," he looked around the spacious living room, "this is certainly minimalist, but done well. If only there was more furniture, some art, and personal touches, it would be perfect." They climbed the stairs, where a hallway led to open French doors. Max paused, studying the doors. "They're steel." He looked at the upper corner of one of the doors. "Smile, because we're on camera," he glanced at the hinges, "and there's an automatic shut mechanism. Goodness. His upstairs is a giant safe room."

The doors led to a wide center hallway that was large enough to contain a seating area, but there was no furniture or decoration of any kind. "This area would make a great open-air study, with plenty of bookshelves and photographs," Sarah said.

"I'll tell him," Taylor said, her heart twisting, because she knew why Brandon's house was devoid of family photographs. All six upstairs rooms were open. The first five that they looked into had no furniture. One had neat stacks of baby things, on the floor, that Taylor recognized from Lisa's house. Their footsteps echoed on bare limestone floor as they moved around the rooms.

"Well," Sarah said, "I thought downstairs was sparse. Did he just move in?"

The articles that Taylor had found the day before about Brandon killing a man in self-defense had indicated that the incident had happened in his home on Northline Street, which is where they were. Taylor said, "He's been here at least two years."

"We've done a few houses in this area. Sarah doesn't pay attention to the chatter, but I do," Max said, "He's the lawyer who does the Morrissey Minute." He lowered his voice. "You know, the hunk in the suit. He and his wife bought the property after Hurricane Katrina. After that, his wife died in an awful automobile crash. He was going to sell, but when it was finished he moved in. A couple of years ago, he killed an intruder, in this house."

"So decorating hasn't been a high priority. Finally," Sarah said, at the door of the final room. "Signs of life."

Minimal furnishing decorated the master suite, but the furnishing that was there, an oversized king size bed, side-tables, a dresser, a gentleman's desk with a chocolate-velvet upholstered chair, had the rich look of hand-made items. Sarah and Max stepped into the room, while Taylor felt more comfortable viewing his private space from the doorway. Sarah's gaze fell on the bed, which was adorned in crisp white linens. She said, "Yves deLorne. Gorgeous." She looked around the room and gave a nod to the furnishings. "The man's got great taste."

He favored light, grainy woods. A cream-colored area rug softened the hardness of the limestone floor. A neat stack of hardback books and an iPad sat atop a side table. A laptop computer was open on his desk. Floor to ceiling draperies were made in lush, cream-colored raw silk, with a chocolate-brown border. The only decoration was a built-in waterfall, framed in copper, which filled most of the wall that was across from his bed. Water cascaded over smooth rocks and disappeared into the floor. The gentle, rain-like sound, the light colors, the white linens, and the uncluttered furnishings gave the room a spa-like feel, yet it felt undeniably masculine. The ambience of Brandon's bedroom, coupled with the memory of his arms around her and his taste as he kissed her, made Taylor's legs go weak, her stomach twist, and a flush creep up her chest.

Anticipation.

God. She was going crazy.

Just do it.

"Baby's suite," Taylor said, bringing everyone's focus back to the matter at hand.

When they agreed on which two rooms made the most sense, Max measured the rooms and the windows. "Plantation shutters would be perfect. Also, I think a build-out in each room for a desk. One room can have a desk for play, while the other can have a desk that's for homework. I'll do design plans for each." Max took more measurements, mumbling about an entertainment console, while Sarah pulled out paint chips and fabric samples.

Taylor checked her phone for messages from Collette. There were none. She put the phone and her purse down next to the baby's things, as Sara looked through the items that Lisa had selected for her baby. After a few minutes, Max asked, "What does Brandon want for a theme?"

"Happy," Taylor said, remembering his note.

Max shook his head. "Seriously? No theme? No direction on build outs? Nothing but happy?"

"Happy," Taylor said. "That's it."

"Boats would be nice," a deep voice said from the doorway,

"if you can work that in."

Sarah, Max, and Taylor turned in the direction of his voice. Sarah's soft intake of breath matched her own. Max's under-his-breath, but audible, "Oh my word," was less subtle.

Brandon held a half-empty plastic bottle of neon orange sports drink. His hair was wet. He wore only a pair of loose runner's shorts, which sat on his hipbones and stopped at mid-thigh, and running shoes. Yards of lean, muscular limbs and smooth, flushed-from-heat skin were exposed. Beads of moisture accentuated muscles that ripped across his not-too-hairy chest. His abdomen was flat and taut. The stained glass fleur-de-lis tattoo on Brandon's right bicep was one of several. A wing-like outline, in shades of gray, charcoal, silver, with touches of white, started at his heart, arched over his left shoulder, and covered his left forearm. Small Chinese letters, in dark purple with lighter borders, formed a lace-like paragraph that spanned from the bottom of his right ribcage to the waistband of his shorts. The tattoos were done with a light hand and were almost whisper-like across his body. The designs were, well, elegant was the only word that came to Taylor's mind. They softened his hard body and didn't bring any of the knee-jerk "ick" factor that she usually felt when she saw tattoos.

No, Taylor thought. *No ick.* More like positively, deliciously compelling. With his lean runner's body damp with perspiration, and wisp-like tattoos skimming over his ripped muscles, he looked wicked, in the best sort of Hugh Jackman or David Beckham-ish way. Taylor dragged her eyes to his as a heated flush formed on her cheeks. His green-eyed gaze was on her. She squared her shoulders and said, "We can do boats."

She introduced him to Sarah and Max.

He gave them a nod from the doorway. "Thanks for coming out so fast. Taylor says that you're good at expediting these things."

Max cleared his throat. "Depending on the build-outs for media, we can get this done in ten days. We'll give you a couple of alternate plans and budgets tomorrow afternoon, and we can get started after that."

"Great. My assistant, Pete, will be your contact." His gaze fell on Taylor. "I have to shower. You'll be here a while?"

She nodded. Brandon turned away from the doorway, revealing broad shoulders and a muscular back that was covered with a tribal maze that looked about halfway complete. It shimmered in hues of silver, gold, and black. He was gone only a few seconds before Max whispered. "Taylor, please tell me you're getting some of that."

Taylor shook her head. "Max. Don't say things like that. He's only a friend."

"I don't know if I'd get involved with him," Sarah said, a worried expression in her eyes as she held Taylor's gaze. "Think about his recent history. Heck. Look at him, because it's written all over him. Literally. The man has more issues than muscles, and," she gave Taylor a stern look, "there's plenty of those. Be careful."

***

Brandon showered, pulled on jeans and a polo shirt, then answered a call from Marvin. "Yo, Brandon, I got something, and it isn't 'bout Tilly, cause so far I haven't found the fucker and the cops haven't either."

"What is it?"

"Neighborhood chatter from a kid. Problem is, he won't talk to me. The little shit won't talk to you, either. He's six years old. Got issues with men. His auntie said that he might talk to a woman."

"Will he talk to the cops?"

"Not likely. His auntie is more likely to bother the kid for your green incentive than for NOPD brass."

"What do you think he knows that might be helpful?"

"Well, if rumors are right," Marvin paused, "I think he saw something that gives me more doubt about whether Tilly did it."

Brandon paused, thinking for a moment. "Would he talk to Taylor?"

"Your date last night?"

"She wasn't a date, but yes."

"Well, she ain't a dude. It's worth a shot."

"All right," Brandon said. "Where and when?"

"Central City. The high rise that borders Calliope Street. Now is best, cause I don't think you want to drag your lady friend through there too much after dark."

Brandon hesitated. The buildings that made up the Central City project, and what went on in them, had inspired rap artists to write chilling lyrics about violence and hopelessness. "I'll let her decide," Brandon said, pretty sure that Taylor wouldn't consider saying no. He detoured downstairs and scooped Michael from the pack-n-play. Michael, who had been having his last bottle of the night when Brandon came in from his run, was crying. As Brandon lifted him, he seemed momentarily happy at the change of scenery. He sat with Michael a few minutes. His diaper was dry, his skin was pink, and the fresh scent of baby powder wafted around him. Everything seemed all right, but Michael's lower lip started trembling, and his ensuing wail was desperately unhappy. Jett started to pace around the kitchen and gave Brandon a glance that said *do something, stupid.*

"Why is he crying?" he asked Anna, who had taken Laura's place at seven. The sisters both had auburn hair, with some gray, dark brown eyes, and freckles. They were of medium height and build. He guessed that Anna was the older of the two, but they both looked about sixty-ish. They had a quiet calmness that he found reassuring.

"I think he's getting sleepy," Anna said. "We're pushing it with an eight o'clock bed time."

"I think Lisa had him up as late as seven. Is an hour that big of a deal?"

"It can be," Anna said, "and right now, everything is different for him."

Brandon paced around the kitchen. Jett followed, and Michael became quiet. Brandon carried Michael upstairs to the rooms that were going to be his, with Jett at his heels. Taylor, Sarah, and Max were deep in conversation. Michael gurgled, interrupting them. Brandon said, "The little guy wanted to say thank you before he goes to bed."

Taylor, Sarah, and Max crossed the room. "He's big for a two-month old," Sarah said. Brandon smiled.

"Those full lips," Max said, "His eyes. Gosh. That black

hair. No mistaking that he's yours.'"

Taylor reached towards the baby and, with her left index finger, she smoothed a cowlick in his dark hair. "It looks like you're doing better with him than yesterday," she said. "Good job."

Her deep gaze told him that she understood more than the sadness of the circumstances. He'd bet that she understood that this odd twist in his life was a good thing, even a great thing.

"Would you like to hold him?" Brandon asked.

She answered with a confident reach, slowing, for a second, as he shifted Michael into her arms. He leaned towards her, hoping to detect her fragrance. It was light. She hadn't over-applied it. While his body responded to the essence of gardenia, her soft smile as she stepped away from him and pressed her lips to Michael's forehead stole his heart. Her gaze rested on Michael, then her eyes found Brandon's. She whispered, "He's falling asleep."

Max mumbled something about being done for the evening. Sarah agreed. They said goodnight, leaving them alone. Taylor said to Michael, "Your rooms will be wonderful and happy, with boats and a gorgeous black lab who will never leave your side."

"Thank you," Brandon said, meaning it more than he could express.

She held his gaze. "You're welcome."

His eyes lingered on hers for a moment, then he mentally shook himself. *Damn it.* No more long looks, he had told himself earlier in the day. No more. "Marvin called a few minutes ago. There's a kid with information in Central City. He's six years old and scared of men, so we thought maybe you'd talk to him."

"Of course," Taylor said, letting him take Michael. "Should I follow you?"

"No. One car would be better in that neighborhood."

They deposited a snoozing Michael with Anna on their way out. When they reached the interstate, she asked, "What happened to this child that makes him scared of men?"

"I don't know," he said. He watched her shiver. He reached

over and gripped her hand. "You don't have to do this."

"I know," she said. "But I'm going to."

He left his hand on hers a second more, then slowly pulled it away when his grip become more about touching her soft skin than reassuring her.

"I went to the corporate library," she said. "There's plans and drawings for hundreds of boats, but no plans and drawings for the landing craft. My father's private library may have them. I didn't have a chance to go in there tonight, and..." She shook her head, then didn't complete her thought.

Brandon glanced at her as he took the exit ramp onto Claiborne avenue. She was nibbling on her lower lip, a mannerism that seemed inconsistent with her usual poise. "And?"

"Tomorrow there's a party at my father's house. I'll be able to break away and see what is in his library then."

"You seem troubled," he said.

"Rough day, that's it." She drew a deep breath. "While I was looking for the nonexistent drawings, I topped off the day with an argument with a friend, who told me that working with the company will be the biggest mistake of my life, and I followed that discussion with an argument with my father."

"Is your friend in a position to know?"

"Yes," she said. "He's Claude Westerfeld, newest and youngest member of the HBW Board, who is struggling with his duties. After speaking with Claude, I asked my father about any conversation that he may have had with Lisa, and he told me not to worry about it. He said it was none of my business. So, while the board is conducting heated, behind-closed-doors meetings, my father reminded me that my duties this weekend are to make sure that the parties go smoothly. Now, I'm wondering why. Why have I signed my life away to work for my father? I feel like I've voluntarily agreed to a death sentence."

"There's no delicate way to say this," he said, "but the reality is that your father won't be there forever."

"He will never retire and he's not slowing down. He could conceivably be a force to reckon with for two more decades. I can't do it. I'm suffocating, already, and I haven't even started."

"I don't have the answer for you," he said as he turned the car into the run-down neighborhood. "But you don't strike me as the type of person who will let others, even your father, suck the life out of you."

He pulled up to the high-rise buildings of the Calliope projects as the sun set. Pete pulled into a spot on the opposite side of the street. Before Brandon locked the car, Marvin was at his side of the car, with two young men. Marvin and his two men wore bulkier clothing than the July night warranted. Brandon, who had a pistol tucked into a holster that he wore around his waist, under his loose shirt, didn't doubt that everyone except Taylor was armed. Brandon glanced at Taylor. "I'm coming around to your side of the car. Me. Pete. Marvin. Whatever happens, stay within touching distance of one of us. Got it?"

She gave him a wide-eyed nod, then he stepped out of the car to get her.

"One of my guys will stay with the cars," Marvin said as they walked together. "We gotta go through the quadrangle." His voice was lost when two police cruisers sped past them, sirens blaring. "It's the third high rise on the left. It's a second-floor apartment, one that looks out onto Calliope Street, where they found Lisa's stuff."

"Tilly Rochelle's mother lives in one of these buildings," Taylor said, remembering what she had learned while looking though Rochelle's records.

Marvin was on one side of Taylor, Brandon was on the other, and Pete was right behind her. "Yeah, but Tilly's mom hasn't seen him in years," Marvin said. "Tilly lives with his grandma, when she'll let him in, and that's about twelve blocks from here. So the fact that Lisa's things were found near Tilly's mom isn't something that connects Tilly to Lisa's murder." Marvin gestured with his chin to the courtyard. "Anyway, according to what this little boy's auntie told her hairdresser, this kid saw who dropped the stuff on the sidewalk. The auntie went outside in all of that rain and picked up Lisa's bookbag and purse. She called the police the next day, when the news broke of Lisa's murder. She told the police she found the things. She didn't tell the cops about the boy seeing who had dumped the stuff. Then when news hit the streets that Tilly was tagged for the murder, she talked at the beauty parlor. Auntie knows Tilly and so does the boy. Those Rochelles are notorious here, and not for good reasons. According to the auntie, the boy says Tilly didn't dump the stuff, but I know we need to hear it from him."

"He should be telling the police this," Taylor said.

"This kid's scared of men," Marvin said. "He probably thinks policemen are aliens."

"There are police *women*," Taylor said.

"Cops are cops," Marvin answered, as they reached the third building on the left. "Up the stairs, then last door on the left."

The hall was a concrete corridor with industrial lights. Most weren't working. There was no air conditioning. The stairwell was hot. It stunk of stale urine. Brandon reached the door, as Marvin knocked. A black woman with dark hair styled in neat curls answered. She wore a pair of jeans that had a sharp crease, a New Orleans Saints t-shirt, and white tennis shoes. She eyed them, then looked past Marvin, Brandon, and Pete, to Taylor. "I'm Callandra Washington, Anton's auntie. I'm hoping he'll talk to you, but if you want him to talk, the three of you men can't come in. Maybe one of you men, but even that's pushing it."

Chapter Eleven

Brandon left Marvin and Pete in the hallway and shut the door behind him and Taylor. As Brandon led Taylor into the apartment, he made a mental note to tell Marvin to pay Callandra even if Anton didn't talk. The apartment was neat and clean, a window unit cooled the space, and a kid's crayon drawings were pinned to one of the living room walls. The drawings were signed by Anton. A skinny little boy was on a couch, wearing Spiderman pajamas and gripping a teddy bear tight.

"Anton," Callandra said, "these people want to talk to you about what you saw two nights ago."

His hair was in a short afro, and his eyes were wide with fear, but also curiosity. As he eyed them, Taylor stepped forward, and gestured to Brandon with her hand behind her back, to stay put at the door. She went to the couch, then got down on one knee.

"Hello, Anton. I'm Taylor."

The child was more interested in his teddy bear than Taylor.

"What's your bear's name?"

The boy didn't say anything, but he glanced at Taylor, then shot Brandon a wide-eyed glance.

"I have a bear that's about that size," Taylor said. "Mine's a girl. She's fluffy and soft. She has a pink ribbon. Her name is Annie and she's scared of the dark."

He giggled. "Bears aren't scared of the dark."

"Annie is," Taylor said, "she lives in my bedroom, and I can never turn out the lights because she doesn't like the dark."

"Bears aren't scared of the dark because they live in caves."

Taylor shook her head. "Annie doesn't live in a cave."

"They sleep all winter."

"Annie doesn't," Taylor said.

"Well, maybe Annie really ain't no bear," Anton said, with a serious head shake and a big smile.

Brandon chuckled as Taylor laughed. Anton handed Taylor the bear for closer inspection. "His name's Teddy. I use him as a pillow," Anton explained, "and sometimes to hide my eyes if I get scared, because he's a bear and he's never scared."

"I have a friend I use like that," Taylor said. "He's standing in the doorway."

Anton shot Brandon a wide-eyed glance, then he moved closer to Taylor. "Is he a nice man?"

Taylor nodded. "Super nice. His name is Brandon. He's like a great big teddy bear."

Anton glanced at Brandon, then started giggling. "He don't look like no teddy bear." His auntie started laughing when she heard the child's laughter, and Taylor did as well. Taylor sat on the couch next to Anton, then, after another five minutes where conversation focused on Spider Man, other superheroes, and school, she steered the conversation to two nights earlier. "I was sleeping," Anton said, "but the thunder was loud. I looked out the window for lightning. Wanna see where?"

Taylor went with Anton into his small bedroom. Brandon followed and stood on the threshold. "A big black car pulled up. Big and black and shiny. A white guy got out, and dropped the stuff on the sidewalk. Right where the bad man killed my mommy."

Brandon's stomach rolled. Taylor shot Brandon a pained over-the-shoulder glance. He watched her draw a deep breath. She said, "I'm really sorry to hear about your mom." She reached for Anton's shoulder and rested her hand there. "The person two nights ago, can you tell me what he looked like?"

Anton shook his head. "But he wasn't Tilly. Tilly don't have no car, and that man's white."

"How do you know he was white?"

"I saw the skin on his face. He white." He nodded in the direction of the door, to Brandon. "Like him."

"Was he small or tall?"

Anton was silent for a second. "I dunno. He seemed tall. Like him."

Taylor asked, "Fat or skinny?"

He nodded again in the direction of the door, towards Brandon. "Like him. Maybe skinnier."

"What was he wearing?"

"Black clothes. Black gloves."

"Glasses?"

He shrugged. "Don't think so."

"Can you remember anything else?"

Anton shrugged. He shook his head.

"You'll get your auntie to call me if you remember anything else?"

He looked at her and gave her a full smile. "Yes, m'am."

They walked back to the car, with Taylor between Brandon and Marvin. Brandon told Marvin what Anton said. He waited for Taylor to chime in, but she didn't. Once in Brandon's car, Taylor rubbed her arms. "Wow."

"You were great with Anton," Brandon said. "Really, truly great."

"Thank you," she said. He watched her take a deep breath, square her shoulders, and straighten her posture.

"Hey," Brandon said, as he drove out of the neighborhood. "Are you all right?"

Taylor glanced at him and gave him a slight smile that didn't reach her eyes. After a second, she nodded. "Trying to shake off the sadness. So, the person who dumped Lisa's things was definitely not Tilly."

"If Anton is telling the truth," Brandon said.

"There's no way that child is lying. We have to let Joe know about this."

"Marvin will be doing that, but Joe will want your impression," Brandon said, "after he grouses about you talking to a witness."

"So you think Joe will be ticked off at me for talking to him?"

"Probably. You're no longer an assistant D.A., so you can't use that as an excuse for doing police work," Brandon said. At a red light, he watched her dig though her purse. "Do what I do when I deal with the police."

She looked up at him and asked, "What's that?"

"Tell them what they need to know, then ignore them."

She shook her head. "I'm not good at ignoring those in authority."

"Good lawyers know the rules, but make their own. If you want to win the hard cases, sometimes you have to ignore authority. That's where the fun comes in."

"I'll remember that when you're opposing counsel to HBW."

"When I'm opposing counsel to HBW," he said, "you won't need a reminder."

"Is that why you became a lawyer and didn't stay on the police force? Problems with authority?"

He chuckled. "One of many reasons, but yeah. I wanted to be the boss. The money didn't hurt, either. After my father died, my mother raised three kids on a nurse's salary. We weren't poor, but we struggled, and she worked hard, long shifts."

He got on the interstate, and, with a few sideways glances, he saw her take her wallet and a brush from her purse. She unzipped a compartment, then shook her head and shut her purse. "I left my phone in your house. Probably by the baby's things." She paused. "Anton said that the guy was in a big black car. That sounds like my description of the car at the crime scene that flashed the lights at me. It is too much of a coincidence. Isn't it?"

He nodded. It also sounded like the car that he saw when they were at the courthouse earlier in the afternoon. "It's time for you to tell Joe about your visit to the crime scene, if you haven't already."

"I haven't. I tried calling him earlier today, but he hasn't returned my call."

She was quiet as they drove to his house. When they were almost there, she said, "May I ask you a personal question?"

He laughed. "Since when have you asked for permission to ask a question?"

"Really personal."

Warning signals flashed, because there was one subject that he wouldn't talk about, and he didn't want to have to tell her that. He said, "I'll give you one."

"You said that you're an insomniac. What do you do at night after a bad day, when you know that you won't be sleeping much?"

He breathed easier, then glanced at her, worried. "Your day was that bad?"

She nodded. "Well?"

"Do you want glib, or do you want the truth?"

"The truth."

"I've never slept much. As a teenager and in my twenties, I'd watch TV, study, read, or work. About five years ago," he paused, "my insomnia became worse. I got into street fighting. It was a fad. For me, it was my only release. I got involved with an underground club. At first the fights weren't organized, but then they were, then there was money on the line."

"The scar on your cheek?"

"A knife fight." He paused. "I'm lucky he didn't cut my eye out. I had broken ribs, a broken nose, countless black eyes, and a few concussions. My life five years ago, four years ago, and even three years ago, was an all-consuming buzz to forget something terrible." God help him. He still couldn't say it, not even to this compassionate woman. *My wife died. Amy. Our baby. Catherine.* He couldn't say, *I went crazy after my wife died.* He was on Metairie Road, driving past the cemetery where they were entombed, and he couldn't say their names, couldn't admit out loud, in words, that they were gone. Taylor didn't pry by asking a question. Instead, she gripped his hand. *She knew,* he thought. He turned his hand in hers, holding hers, gripping it tightly as he swallowed back the heartache.

"I didn't intend to make you revisit something so terrible."

He shook his head. "I didn't sleep. I fought. Thank God I had filled my law firm with some serious talent, and they were able to take up the slack when I was at my worst. I met some bad characters," he glossed over the reality, not wanting Taylor to know the absolute depravity of that time. "And then I met some guys who were involved in a murder for hire scheme, one of whom was a cop with the NOPD. They were targeting a witness who was fingering a cop with criminal activity. I wasn't so sick that I didn't realize how fucked-up they were. I went to the police chief. Joe got involved, and that's what he referred to in yesterday's interview. I thought the cops had it under control, or at least were doing something about it, but then the whole thing exploded, when one of them tried to kill me. I killed him instead." He glanced at Taylor as he drove. She had the good grace not to look too appalled. He continued, "It was my reality check. That was about two years ago. I gave up fighting, but I still couldn't sleep. I started working again through the night. Sometimes I exercise. But if I do that, sleep doesn't come at all. There are times that my brain can't handle another legal thought," he frowned as he pulled into his driveway, "so I started getting tattoos."

"Oh," she said, giving him a look that he couldn't read. She'd gotten an eyeful of them earlier. He figured that she had found them appalling, so gross that she couldn't tear her eyes off of them.

"There's an artist I met in my fighting days. It is tedious and slow. I lay on the table for hours. It hurts a bit. Something about it makes me fall asleep, which really should be a reason to worry, I guess." He shrugged. "I don't care. It keeps me out of trouble, because the biggest problem with not sleeping is that there's all this restless energy that goes with it. Then there're women." He shrugged. "Nothing serious. And boating. I have the one that you saw yesterday, the Frayed Knot, and I have a smaller go-fast boat that I keep docked near her."

"Women and boating seem to be the healthier of your alternatives."

He chuckled. "You don't like the tattoos?"

"Actually, I didn't mind them at all when I got a view of them this evening. I've never seen anything like them. They shimmer."

"I bet you're not around too many men," he paused, "or women for that matter, with tattoos."

"That would be true, except for the random tiny act of rebellion, and always in a place where it won't show."

"You could get one, if you're fond of them."

She frowned and gave a quick head shake. "The boat that I saw yesterday is a beauty."

He chuckled with her change of subject. "Sometimes I take that one out, drop anchor, and stare at the moon and the stars. The smaller one, I run at night, in the lake and in the waterways that surround it."

"Sounds risky."

He shrugged. "Only if I go really, really fast."

"I bet that you do."

He laughed. "I love it on the water, in the dark." He pulled his car into the garage. He led Taylor inside, and nodded to Anna, who was sitting in a chair in the casual living room that adjoined the kitchen, reading. Michael was sound asleep in the pack-n-play. Jett was laying in her bed, which was next to the pack-n-play. The dog's big brown eyes followed Brandon and Taylor's progress across the room, but aside from a tail wag, she didn't seem particularly concerned that Brandon was home.

Anna said, "I hope it's okay that I pulled the dog bed over to Michael. Poor thing was laying on the floor. She doesn't leave the baby's side."

"Of course it's all right." Brandon glanced at his watch. It was almost nine thirty. He told Anna, "In about an hour I have some people who are coming over for work in the study. With the hallway door shut, it stays pretty quiet in here, so we shouldn't bother you. When Michael wakes up for his next feeding," he paused, "let me know, if you don't mind."

Brandon led Taylor up the stairs so that she could look for her phone. "One day I'll have to take you out on the boat."

She hesitated on the top step, then gave him a look that he couldn't read. Before entering what would soon be the nursery, she said, "Well, I have an idea of what really happens on those boats of yours."

She knew about Lisa. She had talked to Sandra. "Damn it. I'm not hitting on you, I swear." He'd love to, but he wasn't. He stopped inside the doorway and watched Taylor retrieve her phone from near the stack of baby clothes.

She put it in her purse, walked straight to him, then past him, and shut the door so that they were alone in a mostly empty room. "That's a shame," she said as she stepped into his personal space. "Because I really, really wish that you would."

Brandon stepped back a few inches. Not so far that he couldn't reach out and grab her, but far enough to get a true read. "Are you serious?"

She stepped closer. *Damn.* "Do you have time now?"

"I only have casual sex, Taylor, and until now, like this very minute," he said, deadly honest, because that sudden come-on look in her hazel eyes made him think he'd been about as wrong about her as he could have been. "You didn't strike me as the sort to look at sex as casual recreation."

"We've both made assumptions about each other that are best forgotten." She closed the distance between them and her cheeks had a slight pinkness, a blush that made him think that her internal fires were already stoked. Her eyes had a half-closed, sultry look. Her lips were only a couple of inches from his. Her sweet fragrance sifted into his consciousness, altering his reality to one where *sex now* made perfect sense. Brandon closed his arms around her, lifted her hair, and found the spot on her neck where his lips had been the night before. She raised up on her tiptoes and turned her face to him. The touch of her tongue on his was even more silk-like than he had remembered. The small part of his brain that knew his instincts couldn't have been so wrong about Taylor, screamed at him to *stop. Now.* This woman was not into casual sex. There was nothing casual about her.

Stop.

But while his instinct hollered *stop,* desire tamped down rational thought. At the last possible second when *stop* could win, he broke away from the kiss.

"Now?" he asked. "Are you serious?"

***

Taylor hadn't expected Brandon to be such a gentlemen. She was basically begging, and he was giving her time to think. She wasn't going to think.

Just do it.

Something needed to go right on this day where nothing had been right. "I want to focus on what feels good. And this," she whispered as she leaned forward and planted her lips on his, "feels good."

He bent to her, pushed her against the wall, and gave her the deepest kiss that she'd ever had in her life. Her insides clenched with want. She heard herself moan. He broke the kiss, opened the door of the baby's room, lifted her into his arms and carried her to his bedroom, where he set her on his soft bed, then knelt on the floor in front of her, between her knees.

Green eyes held hers while he unbuttoned her blouse, pulled it off, then removed her shoes. He unbuttoned her jeans, then inched them down, not needing her assistance. He left her lace bra and her thong panties on. Nothing about him was touching her, except his eyes, which studied every inch of her.

"You're gorgeous."

Oh God. This was a mistake. *Just do it* was an easy thought, but in reality, she wasn't sure of what to do.

"Stand," he said.

When she did, he said, "Take off the rest."

She hesitated.

He reached behind her, unhooked her brassiere, and lifted the straps off her shoulders. His eyes fell to her chest as the bra dropped to the floor. Her breasts were large. Unfashionably large, she often thought, but they matched her butt. From the way Brandon's gaze locked on her chest, she guessed that he didn't mind their size. She hooked her thumbs in her panties and slipped them down. The lights were on in the bedroom and his face was eye level with her hips. He looked up at her, his eyes smoldering. A sultry half-smile played at his lips.

"You're absolutely amazing."

He stood and softly pushed her onto the bed, then followed her there. His kiss was long and deep, while his fingers toyed with her breasts. He broke the kiss before she was ready, then closed his mouth on her left breast, his tongue rough on her nipple as his teeth nipped at her. He kneaded one breast with his hand while he sucked at the other. Electric shocks slashed through her body, with all energy pointing between her legs. He moved his mouth from her left breast to her right, taking his time. Her insides clenched.

"Please," she whispered, letting her legs spread.

He lifted her so that she straddled him as he sat on the edge of the bed. Her legs stretched behind his hips, then hooked around them. She could feel his erection through the rough denim of his jeans. His mouth was still at her breasts, teasing and suckling and gently biting, as his hands cupped and kneaded her buttocks. "God," he said. "I love your butt."

"Too big," she mumbled.

"No. Perfect." He moved his hands between them, and she felt his fingers on the soft skin of her inner thighs. "Yes," she whispered, as fingertips moved to the soft flesh between her legs. As one finger was dedicated to soft pushes, another found her entrance and dipped in. His fingertip swirled inside of her, but it was enough for her to feel that desire had made her wet.

"Oh God," she whispered, as her world focused on the feeling of his fingers, his hands and the rough denim of his jeans. An urgent need for an an orgasm slammed through her. "Oh. My. God," she almost screamed. He studied her as the orgasm tore through her. "Ohhhhhh. Brandon. Oh. Oh."

He didn't stop using his fingers to toy between her legs until she was limp and panting and somehow, she was lying on her back, and he was standing. He unzipped his jeans. When his erect penis sprang free, she stared. A hint of unease gripped her. Everyone said that the first time hurt, and he was so big it certainly looked like it would hurt, especially since his body was nothing but lean, hard muscle. He didn't give her time to dwell on it. He reached towards his nightstand, opened a drawer, and ripped open a condom packet. He slipped it on. With his palms on her knees, he spread her legs, lay between them, then bent to kiss her where his fingers had been.

"Amazing," she said as his tongue made the pressure build again. "Oh God." She felt more alive than she'd ever felt in her life and with each stroke, each nibble, each lick, it became better. With his lips and his tongue pressed against her, he toyed with her opening with a fingertip. "Ooohhh," she couldn't keep quiet as he gazed at her from his vantage point between her legs. He swirled his finger at her entrance in a slow, circular motion, his only contact with her body, then he moved it slightly in, then out, increasing the movement as her moans grew. His eyes bounced back up to hers. "You're so, so tight."

She thought about telling him why, but she could only moan as her hips shifted up and down. It was the slightest movement, but one that she couldn't control. He accepted her invitation and pressed his mouth again to her sex. As his fingertip toyed with her entrance, he licked and nibbled between her legs until she was almost to the point of orgasm, again.

"Oh God," she said, clenching fistfuls of his hair as her hips thrust forward, pushing her flesh into his mouth. "Oh," she whispered. "Yes. Yes. Yesssss. Please don't. Please don't stop."

As quickly as Brandon brought Taylor to the edge, he broke her free fall by stopping all contact. He hovered over her, his elbows on either side of her chest, with the rest of his body weight on his toes. Core strength wasn't a problem for this man, who centered himself over her so that the head of his penis was poised at her entrance. She could feel his flesh parting her, pushing and probing, but not sliding in, as he looked into her eyes and lowered his mouth to her breast. "Please," she said, not ashamed to beg, because if his mouth and his fingers could feel so good, having him inside of her would ultimately be nirvana. Right? The wet heat of his tongue on her nipple sent more shock waves through her. "Please."

He broke contact again, then looked at her, eyes intent, and asked, "Please what?"

She lifted her hips and hooked one leg behind his back. "*Just do it.*"

He gave her a half-smile as he pushed in. She expected a second or two of discomfort. More than anything she had ever wanted in her life, at that moment, she wanted the full length of him inside of her. Forget what she wanted, and forget discomfort. Reality hurt. Before he started to push into her, she'd been wet. Now, suddenly, she felt dry. Desire had disappeared and was replaced with an uncontrollable clenching urge. She started to close her legs and would have succeeded, but he was there. Her thighs gripped his hips, while her hands found his shoulders and pushed. He gave her a puzzled look. He shifted his hips, still moving in. It was too much. She pushed harder against his shoulders as her pelvic muscles clamped shut.

"Stop," Taylor said. "Please stop."

Brandon knew what stop meant. Thank God. He was barely inside of her, but any more forward progress and she would have screamed with pain. He asked, "Are you all right?"

She shook her head. "Hurts," she whispered. "Bad. Stop. Now. I need you to stop." He started to pull out, his eyes concerned. Even that hurt. Jesus. "Slow," she said, gritting her teeth. "Please. This hurts. Go slow."

"I'm so sorry. I thought that you were ready. Hell. You said that you were ready. Has it been a while?"

"Forever," Taylor mumbled, relieved when he was finally out of her. She wanted to run and hide, but he was doing that hovering thing again, the one where he was balanced only on his toes, his legs were between hers, and his elbows were on either side of her shoulders. He wasn't touching her, but she was effectively pinned.

He looked down at her, his green eyes wide. "Forever? Like a year, or two, or please don't say you mean that literally."

She winced. "Literally."

He rolled away from her with a groan, but not before she got yet another glimpse of his penis. It was straining against the thin condom. It was so long that the tip of it hit above, far above, his belly button, for goodness sake, and it too thick to fit where it was supposed to go.

Holy Mother of Jesus. No wonder why it hurt. He was huge. How was that ever supposed to feel good?

She drew a deep breath, pulled her knees to her chest and sat up, covering as much of her nakedness as she could, at an absolute loss for what to do.

"Forever, as in you were, or," he frowned, "are, a virgin?"

She nodded.

His eyes widened. "Are you fucking kidding me?"

"No," she whispered, so humiliated that she wanted to die.

"You should have told me. Somewhere between oh and now and please," he said, throwing back the few words she had managed to say in the past fifteen minutes, "and don't forget *just do it*." He gave her a narrow-eyed glare. "You could have thrown in the fact that you're a virgin."

"Then you wouldn't have believed that I was ready for casual sex."

"Well, obviously, you weren't." He drew a deep breath. "A little honesty would have helped here. I'm damn glad I was able to stop." He swung his legs over the side of the bed. "You might not be so lucky with your next victim."

She winced.

His glare softened. "Aw hell. Put your clothes on before I say something else that I regret."

He walked away from the bed, across the room, and into his adjoining bathroom. He slammed the door, leaving Taylor feeling humiliated, vulnerable, and immature. The sound of water from the shower prompted Taylor to get moving. She grabbed her clothes and dressed as fast as she could, thanking God that the shower kept running. She opened the door to his bedroom, then shut it softly behind her. As she went down the stairs, she made sure she wasn't forgetting her cell phone. She opened the front door as Pete was stepping out of his car. She mumbled "Hello," and "Have a nice evening," without pausing.

Taylor got in her car. She thought about calling Andi. Darnit. Andi was on a date. She still hadn't heard from Collette, but that didn't stop her from driving straight to Collette's house. God, she hoped that Collette was there. She needed to check on Collette anyway, and Taylor really, really, really felt like being with a girlfriend. Not that she was going to tell a soul about what had happened.

God. How awful. How absolutely embarrassing. She was an idiot. Stupid, stupid, stupid. Her phone rang fifteen minutes later, when she was pulling onto Collette's street.

It was Brandon.

A hot flush crept across her cheeks. She thought about

ignoring his call, but then figured she needed to take the medicine. Grow up and deal with it, she told herself.

"I can't believe that you left."

She didn't blame him for sounding annoyed. "It seemed like the right thing to do after you ordered me to get dressed, then slammed the door."

"You asked me to stop, Taylor. When a woman says that, it only means one thing. It was damned hard to do, but I stopped."

"I only wanted it not to hurt."

"Well then," he paused, "we certainly had a lapse in communication. Are you ok?" His voice had softened from the irritated bear tone that he had used earlier. His concern was unexpected and touching, in a way that reminded Taylor that Brandon was nothing like she expected him to be.

"I'm mortified and embarrassed. I behaved in a manner that was unacceptably childish," she said. "I'm sorry. You're correct. I should have told you." She hesitated. "I really, really feel uncomfortable talking about this. I wasn't expecting it to feel like that, but I should have known."

"If you had told me," he said, "I could have figured something out. I don't usually get complaints, Taylor."

"If I had told you," she said, "we wouldn't have even kissed."

"I at least would have tried to persuade you not to waste your virginity on me."

"Better to waste it on you," she said, "than to marry some poor guy because I'm horny and promised myself that I'd wait until marriage when I was a chubby seventeen-year-old bookworm with more than a little acne."

She heard Brandon chuckle as she pulled into Collette's driveway and parked next to Collette's Jaguar. She took his chuckle as a good sign. Maybe he wasn't furious with her, but the memory of his erect penis was too vivid in her mind to believe that he wasn't suffering residual effects. As her cheeks flushed with heat, she asked, "Are you all right?"

"I'll live," he said, "but that won't happen again."

"No," she agreed, but wondered precisely what he meant by *that*. "Definitely not."

"Goodnight, Taylor," he said.

"Goodnight, Brandon."

All the lights on the street side of Collette's house were off. Maybe she wasn't home, even though both of her cars were there. Taylor went to the door and rang the bell.

There was no answer.

Taylor called Andi, who picked up on the second ring. "Is your date that good?"

"Actually, we're walking out of the movie, and I just ducked into the restroom. Your timing is perfect. Taylor, he's precious. Nice. Not from here." *Not from here* meant a lot to Andi. She was a serial dater and hated locals, men who never seemed to get past the Hutchenson name and the wealth that it stood for. "We're going out for a few drinks and some appetizers. Why don't you and Collette join us?"

Andi's question assumed that Taylor had made contact with Collette. "I haven't been able to reach her. I'm at her house now. Her car is here, but the lights are off, and she's not answering the door. I was wondering if you and she talked?"

"Last I spoke with her was this morning, and I know that she didn't have plans." Andi said. "This doesn't sound right."

"I'll call Claude. Maybe she had dinner with him."

There was a pause. Taylor could imagine Andi's eye roll. "Right. Claude's been so freaking self-centered since he ascended to the Westerfeld seat on the board that he hasn't realized his sister is dying from grief." She paused again. "Okay. That was all true, but really mean."

"Hey," Taylor said, thinking of Claude's abrupt comments earlier in the evening. "I'm not arguing with you."

"Well," Andi said, "call me after you talk to him, or when you find her."

Taylor walked along the side of Collette's house, to see whether lights were on in the park side of the house. As she walked, she dialed Claude. When he answered, she heard conversations and glasses clinking. "Hey, Taylor. What's up?"

"I'm looking for Collette."

"She's not with me."

"Do you have any idea where she is?" The flagstone path was narrow and not well lit. Beyond the path and Collette's front garden there was the park, which was beautiful in the daytime. At night, it was too much dark, empty space. Taylor swallowed back sudden fear.

"No." Claude didn't seem concerned.

Taylor said, "Thanks, Claude." She broke the connection.

From outside, there were no visible lights in the living room or bedroom, both of which overlooked the park. Taylor rang the door bell. As she waited, she dialed Collette's home phone. She could hear it from outside. There was no answer. The hair on the back of her neck stood as she sensed that someone was watching her. She turned, quickly. A shadow moved, twenty yards into the park, in the direction of a tree. Everything else was still. She turned back to the house and heard water. It was either a faucet, or a drip, coming from somewhere. She stepped back, wondering whether she was hearing a nearby garden fountain.

No. It was coming from inside Collette's house. Maybe. She couldn't tell. She bent to the pane of etched glass that was in Collette's door, but there were no lights on and she couldn't see in. Taylor tried the knob. It wasn't locked. Fear raced through her, yet she pushed the door open. Collette's alarm should have made noise, but there was nothing. Taylor's eyes adjusted to the interior darkness. Water was falling through the living room, from the part of the ceiling that was directly below where she knew Collette's bathroom was located.

Taylor took the stairs two at a time. She ran across the landing, through Collette's bedroom, and pushed open the door of the bathroom. Collette was sleeping in the tub, not paying attention to the water that was overflowing.

No. Not sleeping.

"Oh God."

Collette was unconscious, her long red hair floating around her. Taylor lurched toward the tub, slipping on water that covered the tile floor, while pulling her friend out of the cold,

cold water. Good God. Collette was cold. Too cold.

"Collette," she screamed. "Wake up."

She couldn't drag Collette to the carpeted bedroom. She was heavy and stiff, and, without clothes, too slippery. *God.* Collette's lips were blue. *Help.* She needed help. Taylor found her cell phone on the floor. It was wet, but it worked. She dialed 911, tried to stay calm as she gave the address, then said, when they asked for a name, "Collette Westerfeld. She's unconscious. Hurry. Please."

"Come on, baby. Wake up," she begged. "Please wake up." She tried to open Collette's eyes. She slapped her cheeks, at first gently, then harder. She tried C.P.R., or what she remembered of resuscitation efforts from a long ago class. Collette didn't respond. She was so, so cold. Taylor hugged her, trying to warm her. *Please. No. Good God.* "Wake up, Collette. Wake up. Please. Please."

Taylor heard sirens. Doors slammed and footsteps ran up the stairs. A hand fell on her shoulder. Warm brown eyes looked into hers. "We'll take it from here."

"She's cold," Taylor said, as one of two young paramedics pried her arms off of Collette. The other paramedic turned off the faucets. They laid Collette on the floor and checked for vital signs. Taylor sat on the floor, her eyes locked on Collette, as she answered their questions. "She was unconscious when I got here. I tried to revive her."

"Do you know what she took?"

"She's been on antidepressants," Taylor choked on a sob, "and she uses sleeping pills. She lost her mother and brother recently."

The paramedic with the brown eyes glanced at Taylor. He said, "Westerfeld. The plane crash?"

"Yes," Taylor said. It had happened as they were landing in Houston, but it had been covered on the local news.

One of the paramedics glanced towards the tub. Taylor glanced there with him, to where prescription bottles stood among bubble bath and bath salts. Taylor counted four open bottles. One of the paramedics examined the bottles as the other attended to Collette. "Sleeping pills, antidepressants, and anti-anxiety meds." He found another bottle. "Migraine medicine. Most of these are empty."

The two young men exchanged a long look. The one who was working on Collette kept trying to revive her. After a while, he shook his head. Both of them focused their attention on Taylor. By the way they no longer seemed to care that Collette wasn't breathing, by the way the rush to save a life had gone still, she knew that Collette was dead.

"No," Taylor screamed. "No. Good God. No."

The brown-eyed paramedic came to her. He rested a comforting hand on her shoulder, as he used a towel to dry some of the water that surrounded Taylor. The warmth of his hand helped her control her screams. She stood, aware that her jeans were dripping with water, but not caring. She leaned against the counter, trying to breathe.

"Are you all right?"

She nodded, even though the answer was no. He handed Taylor her cell phone, which he had dried, and had checked to see that it was working. He asked, "Was the man who directed us here a neighbor, or is he related to her?"

"What man?"

The paramedic glanced at his partner. "He met us at the street and led us up the stairs. He was here, in the doorway, until a minute ago."

Taylor shook her head. "I don't know. I didn't see him."

"Well, is there someone you can call?"

Taylor's first thought was to call Andi. Or Claude. But she knew that she had to call her father, before the others. George was the clearing house for all serious emergencies that affected the HBW families, especially emergencies in which Taylor was involved. When he answered, emotion choked her, and she could only sob.

"Taylor?"

She fought for words, but when she spoke, she stuttered. "D-d-dead. Coll-Collette."

"Taylor," George said. "Compose yourself."

Taylor somehow got out a couple of meaningful sentences

around the words *Collette* and *drugs* and *overdose*.

"Do not call anyone. This does not need to be made public. I'm on my way. I'll call my doctor."

"I did," Taylor said, breathing deep. "I called 911."

"Do you have any goddamn sense?"

Taylor saw herself in the bathroom mirror, wild-eyed and pale. *Sense?* Evidently, she didn't have the kind that her father valued.

She doubted that she ever would.

Chapter Twelve

At eleven thirty Brandon was finishing a discovery strategy session with Mitch and Pete. Much of what Mitch needed to find out in the case would involve Pete's investigative skills rather than Mitch's legal skills. As they left, Brandon walked to the kitchen area, where Anna was rocking Michael, who let out a loud cry as Brandon's cell phone rang. He answered Sebastian's call, saying, "I have to call you back."

"What the hell is that noise?"

"A long story," Brandon said, taking the baby from Anna as she stood to prepare a bottle.

"I have time," Sebastian said.

"I don't. I have a house full of lawyers," Brandon said, "and a crying baby."

Michael cried again. Sebastian asked, "Who thought it was a good idea to bring a baby to your house?"

"Let me call you in a few hours."

"Don't forget, because now you've got me curious."

Brandon took the bottle from Anna, made sure Michael was going to start taking it, then returned to the study with Michael and Jett. He introduced his son to Steve, one of his more experienced junior partners, and Noel, a third year associate. Brandon sat and fed Michael and listened.

The Alford case had bad injuries and decent facts for liability. The trial was to begin on Thursday and would last at least three trial days. They talked jury strategy and, when the bottle was empty, Brandon stood, placed Michael against his shoulder, and patted his back.

"Pretend I'm a distracted judge," he said, "and give me your opening." When Steve completed the argument, Michael's burp filled the silence. "Success," Brandon said, "all around."

Brandon had promised Steve and Noel his undivided attention and, after depositing Michael with Anna, for three hours he gave it to them. At three in the morning, Steve and Noel packed their litigation bags and left.

He wondered whether he should try for sleep. After checking on Michael, who was snoozing, he climbed the stairs, then paused at the threshold of his bedroom, which had been completed after Amy's death. Until tonight, it hadn't been a place for sex, not with anyone. He kept condoms there, but they were for taking elsewhere. More often than a place for sleeping, his bedroom was a solitary space where his thoughts drifted to what his life would have been had he stopped working on April 5th, five years earlier, and driven Amy, his witty, sharp, compassionate wife to the birthday party. He either would have avoided the accident that had stolen his soul, or he would have died with her. Either scenario was better than what he was left with, a life without his precious wife and their unborn child, and guilt over their deaths.

Tonight, his bedroom's hue wasn't of distant, fading memories, and it wasn't about missing what could have been. The normally neat bed linens were in a disarray. He bet that he'd be able to smell Taylor's perfume on the sheets.

A virgin.

He wasn't going near the bed until Esme changed the linens in the morning. Taylor had said that she was ready to lose her virginity. *Great. Just great.* She could do that with someone else. He didn't want the drama. Sex would be important to her. It wouldn't be to him.

Right?

Doubt about whether his limitations were real or imagined was such an original, unexpected thought, that he almost didn't detect it. The only solace in the fact of her virginity was that his instinct about Taylor had been dead on.

Yet even now, while his mind said stay-the-hell away, he started getting hard at the memory of his mouth on her breasts, his fingers toying with her, her soft moans, and her throaty cries. *Aww fuck.* Getting partly inside of her had been incredible. She might be composed in public, but in bed, she was anything but cool, calm, and controlled. *Damn it.* He made a call as he went downstairs. Velvet answered by saying, "Hello, gorgeous."

"Do you have time for me?"

"I'm finishing my last client now," she said, "Give me a few minutes and I'll be ready."

Brandon broke the connection with Velvet, than sent Sebastian a text. "*You up?*"

His phone rang within a few seconds. Sebastian asked, with a groan and a yawn, "Do you ever, ever sleep?"

"Not often enough," Brandon said. "Sorry I couldn't talk earlier."

"It was eleven-thirty on a Friday night and you were in a room with a crying baby. What the hell is that about?"

"He's mine."

Silence. Then, "No shit?"

"None at all."

"Babies don't appear out of nowhere. How old is he and when were you going to tell me? Who is the mother? Hell," Sebastian paused for a breath. "I didn't know that you were serious with anyone. Did you marry someone and not tell me about it? Son of a bitch. Last I heard, and it wasn't that long ago when we had that discussion, you were never doing serious again."

"He's two months old, he's the product of a one-night stand, and DNA has confirmed that he's mine. One of the condoms that I used that night was obviously defective, if you can believe that."

"Don't tell me that shit."

"It's true. His mother was murdered Wednesday night, I'm not a suspect, thank God, but I'm now the sole parent, and I'm trying like hell to make sense of her murder."

"When were you going to tell me about this?"

"I found out about him two weeks ago. I didn't even know that she was pregnant. You were out of the country. It's been a whirlwind," Brandon said, "and I wanted to tell you in person."

"Some things shouldn't wait, dumb ass. She was murdered?

What the hell?"

Brandon told Sebastian what he knew about Lisa's murder. When he was through, Sebastian asked, "Do you need help?"

"With the baby?" Brandon chuckled. Sebastian had never been married and as far as Brandon knew, had never held or cared for a baby.

"Don't laugh. I could help with something. Not with changing diapers, but with something. At least I can help with whatever you're doing to figure out who murdered her. I know you well enough to know that you're trying," Sebastian paused, "and I know a thing or two about investigations."

"Black Raven doesn't need to get involved. This is a local matter."

"The world's small. Everything is local," Sebastian said, "Besides, you have access to any and all Black Raven assistance."

"I can handle this."

"Well, at least agree to keep me informed."

"Agreed."

"On another note," Sebastian paused, "I was calling to tell you a few more things that I figured out about Victor. Odd things that are out of character for your brother and," there was a long pause, "you know I don't like odd things."

Brandon returned to the keeping room as he listened to Sebastian talk about Victor's financial status before his death, and where they'd been able to trace some of Victor's money. Michael was still sleeping, Jett was snoozing, and Anna was reading. Brandon whispered to Anna, "I'm going out. Call me if there's any problem."

Brandon started his car as he listened to Sebastian run through more of the facts that he had uncovered about Victor's bank accounts and expenditures over the last year. "So, to sum it all up," Sebastian said, "your brother had been paid well, but he spent big, mostly using a few aliases that I have solidly traced to him. I think that he acquired a few properties in the States last year. We're working on locations. Some of his accounts are impossible to trace, and he used so many aliases it's a nightmare to trace all his assets. What struck me most was repeated payments over the last four years to the Zurich Health Institute. Ever heard of it?"

"No." Brandon exited the interstate, took the Vieux Carre exit, turned onto Esplanade, then pulled in front of Velvet's two-story house, parked his car, and stepped out.

"They serve medical needs of the super wealthy. On a cosmetic level, they specialize in identity-changing plastics. They also do private donor organ transplants and they're a pioneer in alternative cancer therapies."

"Kate and mom knew he was sick. They weren't sure what he had. Mom says that he'd been getting better."

"Anyway, over the the last four years, Victor spent almost four million there, in regular installments, until three months ago. Don't know what for yet."

"But intel tells us Victor is dead," Brandon said. "So why do I care about his financial data or what medical procedures he was getting?"

"Well, coincidentally, three months ago, a full month before we think that he died, all of his account activity stopped. And I mean everything, not only payments to Zurich. He drained his accounts and sold assets. We're looking for credit card activity, flights, phone calls, border crossings, but so far we're finding nothing with any of his aliases. He went totally off the grid, even the grid that his kind of paranoid mercenary lives on." Brandon knocked on Velvet's door as Sebastian continued, "It's as though he was planning on disappearing, and that's bothering me. I'm also concerned that there's something that I'm not seeing, like aliases that we haven't figured out. Given his prior activity, the sudden lack of activity is out of character. I'm starting to think that his death may not be what it appears to be. I mean, why would all activity stop a full month before his death? Unless, of course, he was trying to disappear."

Velvet wore a white leather halter top that did little to conceal high, tight breasts. Jean shorts exposed most of a flat midriff and long, lean, muscular legs. Her dark hair was long and in a neat, high ponytail. When she saw that Brandon was on the phone, she stood on barefooted tiptoes and gave him a silent kiss on both cheeks. She led him to a spa-like room. He continued his conversation with Sebastian as he sat on Velvet's table.

"So you're starting to doubt that Victor really is dead?"

"I hate to admit that I could be wrong and I'm not willing to admit it yet. Really. I'm sorry, Brandon. I don't know. I'm looking into it more," Sebastian said, "and Ragno's team is also trying to figure this out."

"He told my mother that he had to disappear, for whatever that's worth."

"You told Rose that I think that he's dead?"

"Yes," Brandon said, wishing that he had waited. "She doesn't believe it."

"I hate to say this, but given the financial shenanigans, I'm wondering if he staged his death. I'm sorry. I shouldn't have called you last night without analyzing the financial data."

Brandon thought about giving Sebastian a hard time, but the reality was he'd known the guy almost all of his life, and Sebastian didn't usually make mistakes. "Hey. Don't beat yourself up."

"I'm not yet saying that he's alive. I'm saying this is weird and I didn't want to keep it from you."

Velvet pressed a glass with a healthy pour of dark rum into Brandon's hand as he ended the phone call. He drained it, and she poured him another as he unbuttoned his shirt. The smooth tone of her voice matched her name, as she said, "That didn't sound good."

"It wasn't," Brandon said. He slipped off his shirt and took off his jeans.

Velvet turned on her overhead light and bent to examine the tattoo on his waist. The letter to Amy and Catherine was something that he'd written in his darkest days. He had it translated into Mandarin, and Velvet had inked the delicate lettering onto him. It had been her most recent work of art to be completed. "You've healed well. So what do you want to work on? The maze, or something new?"

"The maze." Brandon finished the rum. He lay face down. With the machine's hum, his mind drifted. Fatigue came with the needle's first sting, and dreams came with sleep. Randomness coalesced to thoughts of the house fire that had suffocated his sister, destroyed their home, and the documents that Marcus had gathered in his lifelong quest to prove Benjamin's innocence. The fire was ruled an accident. Victor, fourteen at the time, had insisted that there were no accidents. Anger, a dominant Morrissey male trait, made anything good in Victor disappear.

No accidents.

Victor had blamed the fire on a man. A man, who was watching their house. A man. *A really smart man,* Victor had yelled, *can make anything look like an accident. It takes a smarter man to see through it,* he had yelled. *The fire marshall was an idiot.*

His father had killed himself six months after the fire. Victor's reaction was equally destructive, but not self-directed. After that, other fires mysteriously started in their neighborhood. Brandon suspected Victor, but no one else did. More disturbing than the fires, which didn't result in loss of life, was the fate of animals in River's Bend. From the time that Victor was fourteen, until Victor left home at the age of eighteen, animals in their neighborhood were found dead. The deaths were written off as accidents. Odd accidents, though, because a Labrador retriever who could swim drowned. A roof of a rusty shed fell on a cat and smashed its head, when the cat should have been able to dart away. A toy poodle who never left its yard was found half-eaten, streets away, in a yard where a pit bull lived. No one knew how the poodle got there. When squirrels died, people found their furry corpses in unusual places, in unusual positions.

From Brandon's perspective, no one had suspected that the killings were anything but accidents, except Brandon, who watched his brooding brother interact with animals. On the evening before Beauford, the sweet old beagle who who rarely wandered far from home, was found dead on the side of railroad tracks that were more than a mile away, ten-year-old Brandon had watched Victor place a hunk of meatloaf in a bag. When their mother left to work a night shift, leaving Victor in charge, Victor waited until eleven in the evening to leave the house. Brandon, who was only ten years old at the time, tried to follow Victor undetected. In an overgrown field, seventeen-year-old Victor had turned and backtracked.

Brandon didn't realize that his brother was on to him until Brandon lay, face down, on the dirt path. The element of surprise gave Victor superiority that made the strength of his more mature body impossible to overcome. Victor flipped Brandon onto his back, clasped his hands around Brandon's neck, and choked him. With moonlight overhead, Victor's dark eyes staring into his, Victor's hands choking him, and Victor's knees digging into his ribcage, Brandon understood that his brother was capable of killing him.

Victor gave Brandon his first ever kick in the balls, then left. The bruises were bad. Brandon tried to hide them from his mother and he was able to do so, until after school the next day. When Rose saw the marks on his neck, he told her he had an after school fight. He refused to tell her with whom. When pieces of Beauford's body were found, the neighbors had concluded that he'd gotten on the tracks and couldn't get out of the way of an approaching train. Brandon, though, wondered whether a smart dog who never wandered so far from home had simply wandered, or whether he had been guided. He didn't dare ask Victor anything about it. To his knowledge, no one ever did.

With Velvet's hand on his shoulder, Brandon awakened and became aware that the needle was silent. There was a dull ache in the center of his back. Velvet said, "You keep moving."

"Sorry," Brandon said, shaking off the feelings brought on by the dream, awkwardly real feelings of being a ten year old who was scared of his big brother. "Have I messed you up?"

"No," Velvet stood and stretched. He did the same. Brandon glanced at his watch. It was five twenty. "I need your back for another hour. I started another part of the grid," Velvet said, pointing to an easel that held a paper drawing of the maze that she was etching on to his back, "and I can't stop. The colors are gorgeous, by the way. More rum?"

He shook his head. He lay back on the table and this time, as he drifted, he saw Taylor, placing her lips on Michael's cheeks. Yes, he thought, as he drifted closer to sleep. Now that was a dream worth having. He saw Taylor, taking charge of decorating the nursery. God. Those almond-shaped, greenish-brown eyes. Her questions. Her sharp, inquisitive mind. He couldn't reconcile the composed, slender, yet shapely and sensual woman he knew as Taylor with the thought of an awkward and chubby seventeen year old who had promised herself that she'd be a virgin until marriage.

Taylor, talking to Anton, making the scared little boy smile while coaxing words out of him. He saw the beautiful rise and fall of Michael's chest as he slept. He didn't know if he'd have focused on the subtle movement, were it not for Taylor. She was not only irresistible. She was intuitive, and more important than knowing how to ask questions, how to push a person's buttons, she knew when not to say anything at all. Last evening she had held his hand when he couldn't say the words, *when my wife died*. Her soft grip had let him know that he didn't need to say the words.

She got it.

***

Taylor watched Carolyn tie back the silk drapes while leaving the filmy gauze panels in front of the windows. With each quiet move, more light seeped into the bedroom, bringing with it the harsh reality of Collette's death. Fresh tears stung Taylor's eyes. Andi, who had returned with Taylor to Taylor's home in the early morning hours, rather than going to her own home, was still sleeping in Taylor's king-size bed. Andi stirred with the light, her long brown hair in disarray over her face and across the pillow, but she kept her eyes shut.

Carolyn said, "Your father, Claude, and Mr. Andrew will be here in an hour. I'm getting things together downstairs."

As Carolyn slipped out of the bedroom, Taylor checked the time. It was seven thirty. Last night, after George had arrived at Collette's house, Andi, Andrew, and Claude had arrived. George had his assistant take notes and make phone calls, and he postponed the Saturday board meeting until Wednesday morning, assuming that the services for Collette would be on Tuesday. Andi had pleaded with George to cancel the patron party and the gala. He wouldn't. The events had to go on, he reasoned, because the events were important to HBW and to the museum, and they couldn't be sidetracked or delayed because Collette had chosen this weekend to overdose.

If Andi couldn't pull herself together to attend the patron party and the gala, George had said, she didn't need to be there.

He had given Taylor a harsh look that didn't need accompanying words.

Taylor didn't have the option of not attending.

While they were at Collette's house, George had contacted the owner of the funeral home and the city coroner. Both men would be at Taylor's house at eight thirty in the morning. They would have had the meeting at George's house, but he did not want to have such a private meeting at his home, where party preparations would be in full swing.

Taylor's phone vibrated with a text. It was on her bedside table. A text from Brandon read, *"Wheels up at 11:33; departing from Eagles Terminal A; on ground in Dallas for about three hours; land in NOLA on return at 5:10."*

Oh God. She had forgotten about the trip with Brandon to see Rorsch's documents. She responded with a text. *"I can't make the trip."*

Andi was looking at her. "What was that?"

Taylor was going to explain, but tears started to stream down Andi's cheeks, and Taylor felt her own eyes fill. Andi said, "I can't believe that she's gone."

"I know," Taylor said. Her phone vibrated with a return text. *"Why? Still embarrassed about last night?"*

Her stomach twisted at the memory of what had happened between her and Brandon. Collette's death, though, minimized the importance of the humiliating event. She felt an urge to tell him about the rest of the night, but she couldn't reduce Collette's death to a simple text. Tears slipped from her eyes. She wiped them away and typed, *"The night got worse after I left your house."*

"Everything OK now?"

"I can't talk now. Will call later."

Taylor put down the phone, spent a few minutes consoling Andi, then, when her own tears stopped, she stepped into the shower. Memories of Collette and all of that awful, cold water made her shiver.

More tears flowed as she turned up the hot water. It soothed her as it flowed over her body. She washed her hair and combed conditioner through it. When she got out of the shower, Andi was still in bed, but she was sitting up and holding Taylor's cell phone.

"What happened last night with this person named Brandon Morrissey? These texts are interesting."

Taylor shook her head. "Nothing and you really shouldn't read my texts."

"He's asking if you're still embarrassed about last night." Her dark green eyes studied Taylor. "It sure sounds like something happened."

"Please drop it, Andi."

"I would," Andi said, "except my friend who is always composed is beet red, and that same friend who rarely even seems interested in men is getting texts that I cannot decipher. So no," she said, "I'm not dropping it."

"Dad's getting here in a half hour, with others. I need to get dressed. I don't have time to tell you about it." She started the blow dryer and glanced at Andi. "Aren't you getting out of bed?"

"Not until you tell me what happened to prompt these texts."

What had happened between her and Brandon was awful and humiliating, but compared to Collette's death, it was easy to think about. She sighed. She eventually would have told Andi, anyway. She started with her idea that she no longer planned to wait until marriage to have sex. Andi responded with eyes-wide-open surprise. She sat up in bed, alert, a pillow on her lap.

"For the last year, I knew I couldn't follow through with it," Taylor explained, glancing at Andi, "so I thought I'd take your *just-do-it* advice."

Andi waved Taylor's cell phone in the air. "Wow. So tell me about him."

"I've never met anyone like him. He's complicated. He's not judgmental. He doesn't care about who I am, how much money I have, and he certainly wouldn't run around the country club talking about how he's the guy who got to take my virginity." She chuckled. "He isn't the country club type and he doesn't strike me as the type to talk. He's the toughest guy I've ever met, but he's also one of the nicest." Taylor felt her cheeks burn.

"But it hurt. So I asked him to stop."

Andi gave a slight head shake. "Wait. What did you just say?"

"It hurt. I asked him to stop. He did," Taylor said, "and I'm mortified about the whole thing."

Andi buried her face in a pillow. Her shoulders shook with a silent laugh, then she looked up, and asked, "How far was he in before you asked him to stop?"

"Please stop talking about it."

"It's his fault," Andi said, rallying to Taylor's defense. "He must have gone too fast. Jerk. What did he do? Give you a ten-second kiss then go at it?"

"No," Taylor said, remembering the feel of his mouth on her breasts, his fingers inside of her, and the pressure of his tongue between her legs. "God, no. But he didn't know it was my first time."

Andi went slack-jawed.

Taylor added, "He didn't know until after I asked him to stop."

Andi rolled her eyes, "No wonder he's asking if you're," she breathed in deeply, then howled with laughter, "embarrassed about last night. I know you have a subscription to Cosmo, because I've sent the magazine to you for the last five years for your birthday. Don't you read the articles? It was only going to hurt for a second or two. Really. Don't you know that?" Andi started laughing again, so hard she could barely speak.

It took Taylor a minute to see any humor at all, but then it was so pathetic that it was funny. Sort of. Taylor started laughing. Once she started, she couldn't stop, and somewhere along the way, her laughter turned to tears, which became sobs.

"Collette would have teased me forever about this," Taylor said.

Andi started crying as well, then she shook her head. "The Collette we used to know would have loved it, but she hasn't been herself for years, even before Alicia died." Andi paused, then glanced again at Taylor's phone, reading Brandon's texts. "What were you two doing in Dallas today?"

Carolyn returned to the bedroom with a tray of coffee and juice, then slipped into Taylor's closet, leaving the door partially open. Taylor gave Andi a few details about Brandon's involvement with Lisa and Lisa's incomplete research. "From what we can tell, Lisa's research echoed the long-held suspicion of Brandon's father that his grandfather, Benjamin Morrissey, was framed."

"Wait, wait, wait," Andi said. "He's *that* Morrissey? The Morrissey treason case?" She narrowed her eyes. "He's the lawyer that's in those commercials, right?" Taylor nodded. "He's gorgeous, but good God. Taylor. Your father will have a freaking fit over your involvement with him."

"I'm old enough to have a personal life without regard to my father's approval or disapproval."

"Well," Andi said, "that should be true, but is it?"

Taylor sighed. "I really shouldn't care whether my father approves or disapproves, but obviously," she drew a deep breath, "I do. Otherwise I wouldn't be working at HBW. My father wouldn't even want to be in the same room with Brandon, much less want to know that I was involved with him. Besides, I'm not *involved* with Brandon."

Andi shook her head. "You can tell yourself that, but I was watching you talk about him, and it looks like you're more involved that you think."

"You have sex with men that you're not involved with," Taylor said, "don't you?"

Andi frowned. "Not as often as you're making it sound."

"Well, men you aren't in a serious relationship with."

"Okay," Andi said, "yes."

"Why can't I?"

"Wait," Carolyn said, as she stepped out of Taylor's closet with an arm load of laundry, "have I missed something really important in this conversation?"

Taylor drew a deep breath, glanced at Carolyn, and shook her head. Carolyn was more than a friend. She was a mother figure to Taylor, and, although she ultimately told Carolyn all details of her life, Taylor wasn't ready to give Carolyn details of what had happened the night before. "Nothing important."

Carolyn nodded, but her eyes were serious. "All right. If you say so."

"You're not me, Taylor. It's taken years of practice to think of sex as only sex, and I know that you're not there." Andi shook her head, dismissing Taylor's not-in-front-of-Carolyn-glare. "Carolyn's going to figure out all of this anyway, and you know it. My advice was always just do it and *move on*," Andi emphasized the last two words. "I don't think that you paid too much attention to the move on part," she paused, then started laughing, "or the *do it* part."

"Stop laughing," Taylor said, but she had a sinking feeling that Andi was correct, because at this point, Taylor couldn't imagine not being with Brandon again. She wanted to see him, to talk to him, to see if she could bring out that gorgeous smile. But instead of acknowledging that Andi was right, Taylor repeated, "Brandon and I are not involved."

"Honey, if you could see yourself from my point of view right now," Carolyn said, "you might not be so quick to say that."

"He doesn't do relationships."

Carolyn shrugged. "How do you know that?"

"He told me."

Andi said, "I think that you should still go with him today."

Taylor shook her head. "What are you talking about? You tell me my father will have a fit, then you tell me to go with Brandon."

"When you talked about him, you seemed," Andi paused, "different. I don't want your father to influence who you fall for. So go. This afternoon. Why not? We're planning everything for Collette's services this morning, right? Actually," she frowned, "you know darn well that your father is going to take the lead on all of the plans. And there are more people working on the patron party and gala than it would take to build a pyramid. All you and I are going to do this afternoon is sit around and cry," Andi said, "and as much as I'd like to have you with me to do that, I think you really should take a break for the afternoon. I'm actually going to skip the party and the gala," Andi narrowed her eyes, "as your father invited me to do last night. *My* father will understand."

Taylor's heart sank. "I wish that I had that option."

"You do, Taylor. For once in your life, tell your father no. If you don't start now, when? You know damn well he's going to live until he's a hundred and he's going to be a force that you need to deal with, sooner or later, or else he'll keep making your life miserable. It just isn't right to get all dressed up, make small talk, and pose for pictures at a party tonight with Collette gone. I'm going to go to the beach house, stare at the waves, and not return until Monday."

"Please don't leave me," Taylor said.

"I can't go to those parties, Taylor." Andi started crying. "I can't do it. I'm sorry. I can't act composed when my heart is broken. I can't be like you. Please don't ask me to stay here."

Chapter Thirteen

The day and the night belonged to Andi Hutchenson. Andrew Hutchenson would lose his youngest child, his only daughter. He had twenty-four hours to make it happen, but he'd been planning this for weeks. It was not going to be difficult. At ten-thirty in the morning, he entered The Chocolate Croissant and ordered a double-shot cappuccino and an everything bagel with cream cheese. As he waited for his order, he glanced at the offerings on the news and magazine racks.

In addition to the usual local and national newspapers, the coffee shop had glossy social publications, the kind that catered to Southern society women. On the cover of one of the July publications was Collette, his redhead, Andi, his brunette, and Taylor, his honey-blonde piece of perfection. He selected the magazine with his women on the cover, another magazine, and two newspapers.

He sat and opened his iPad, where the GPS application reduced Andi to a blue dot. The tracking device was triggered by a sensor that he had placed in her car's bumper. Actually, he had placed it in the bumper of both of her cars. She had two, after all. One sporty, the other more functional. Today, Andi was driving her SUV.

He chuckled.

Technology was wonderful. The blue dot departed from Taylor's house then turned onto the interstate, and then west. The dot took the airport exit. He frowned. Surely she wouldn't leave town. Her friend had died, and there were important events to get through for the weekend.

Unease knotted his stomach. Important events didn't mean that Andi would stay in town. Andi wasn't Taylor, and Andi's father wasn't George Bartholomew. Andi, unlike

Taylor, didn't have high expectations to live up to. The knowledge he had gathered about Andi indicated that she could do what she wanted, when she wanted to do it, and she did. She had finished college, but barely. It took her six years to complete a degree in art history. She called herself an artist, but he couldn't find exhibited works. He guessed that artist was code for a rich girl who didn't need to work and had no interest in it.

Of the two who remained, Andi was the one who was unpredictable. Predictably unpredictable, but unpredictable nonetheless. If Andi got on a plane with plans to disappear, killing her in the next twenty or so hours would become more complicated. He thought through the scenarios, which all began with him figuring out where she was headed. He could make it happen. He had the capability of tracking her through the use of cell phones and credit cards, two things that she could not live without. He drew a deep breath. He was tired, but that was the disease. There was nothing wrong with his mind, and when he needed it, he would have the energy. The hunt that led to a kill always gave him energy.

***

Brandon arrived at the airport at eleven, parked his car, and talked to Joe as he carried his briefcase to the jet. Joe had talked to Taylor prior to calling Brandon, and Joe was going to talk to Anton later.

"I'm not sure you'll get anything out of him," Brandon said, "but I was watching last night. The kid was certain that it wasn't Tilly that dumped Lisa's stuff on the sidewalk."

"Taylor told me about her trip to the murder scene and her feeling that someone was watching the two of you when you were at Lisa's house on Thursday night. Do you think someone was there?"

"I didn't see him if he was there, and when I was outside I didn't see evidence of him." Brandon boarded the ladder and nodded hello to the two pilots. The jet could seat twelve, with two passenger areas. The rear compartment was designed for rest, with a long couch and two reclining chairs. The forward compartment had a table in a booth-like configuration and two separate, stand-alone chairs. Brandon settled into the jet's forward compartment, at the table, and placed his briefcase on the bench next to him.

"Taylor was on edge," he explained. "I had taken her to Marvin's house, and she'd already been to the murder scene. Still, she doesn't strike me as the type to hallucinate. I saw the same kind of car yesterday, and I'd swear whoever was in it was watching us, because he sure as hell sped away when I spotted him."

"Tell me more about Lisa's research," Joe said. "Taylor's got me curious."

Brandon gave Joe some background. "Lisa's theory seems to be that my grandfather was framed." He drew a deep breath. "And I can't figure out why that was her theory, because her laptop was stolen and it looks to me like chunks of her research are missing. There's boxes that are taped and sealed that are labeled research, and all that's in there are empty binders. I think someone went through her work," Brandon said, "though the place doesn't look like anyone was in there. I think we need to at least explore whether her research could be related to her death."

"Maybe so, but right now," Joe said, "Tony and I are focused on finding Tilly Rochelle, though with Anton's statements to Taylor, I'm seriously doubting whether that's going to be productive."

"As of nine this morning, Marvin had a lead on Rochelle's location in Jackson, Mississippi. If he's there, Marvin will bring him to you. I'm flying to Texas in a few minutes. Lisa talked to the granddaughter of Rorsch, the man who caught my grandfather. She went to Texas to read his memoirs. You're more than welcome to come with me. Wheels are up pretty soon though."

"You need to stop doing police work."

"You can't stop me from talking to someone about history that involves my grandfather. Besides," Brandon said, "the NOPD owes me leeway."

"We made a mistake back then. We don't owe you anything." Joe paused. "I should be pissed, but hell. Reality is that I barely have time to do anything on the Smithfield case. Tony and I are in it up to our chins on last week's triple shooting, and we're both set to give another interview to the feds today on internal matters. If I get to talk to Anton and if we get Tilly in for questioning, that would be a home run of a day. I certainly don't have time to go to Texas. I might never have that kind of time. But promise me one thing."

"Depends on what it is."

"If things start deteriorating, let me know before you jump on a fast train to hell, all right?"

"Sure. Will do." Brandon broke the connection, then stood and walked to the cockpit, where the pilots were performing final checks. He'd flown with both of them before. Brandon talked to them for a few minutes, then he settled at the table, opened his briefcase, and pulled out pleadings for an argument that he was giving on Wednesday.

"Mr. Morrissey?"

Brandon looked up at the pilot.

"Are you expecting anyone?"

Brandon glanced out of the window. A silver Mercedes SUV had pulled up next to his car. As Taylor stepped out of the passenger side, Brandon's heart beat faster and he let out a deep breath. *Damn it.* He wished that he wasn't so glad to see her.

"I guess so."

The driver, a young woman with dark brown, waist length hair in a sleek ponytail, stepped out of the car, hooked elbows with Taylor, and the two walked to the jet as Brandon stepped down the boarding ladder. The two women, wearing large sunglasses, lightweight dresses, and sandals, exchanged a hug at the foot of the boarding ladder. "I decided that I could make it." Taylor spoke loud so that she could be heard over the whirr of the engines. "Is that all right?"

Brandon nodded. "Of course."

"Andi," Taylor said, "Brandon."

Andi extended her right hand and gave Brandon a firm handshake. "Nice to meet you," she said, then leaned forward, with her mouth only inches from Brandon's ear. "Please take care of her for the next six hours, then see that she gets home safely, no later than six, so that she can get ready for that damn party that she's insisting on going to. Promise?"

As Brandon nodded, he shot a glance at Taylor. If Taylor heard her friend's odd instructions, she gave no indication. Andi stepped back, the two women shared a long hug, then, after they exchanged a few sentences Brandon could not hear, Andi returned to her car, and Taylor climbed the jet's boarding ladder.

She placed her purse and a soft leather satchel on the table, next to his work, then sat at the table where Brandon's work was spread out. She didn't remove her sunglasses. She sat still. Her hands were clasped, but gently. She wasn't frowning and she wasn't smiling. Brandon sat next to her, puzzled. He'd seen her give off an aura of coolness, but he sensed that now she was fighting for poise.

The pilot gave them a two-minute warning, requested that they fasten their seat belts, then shut the door to the cockpit. After fastening his seatbelt, he reached over and lifted her sunglasses from her eyes. Her hazel eyes, more green than brown today, those beautiful, sharp, inquisitive eyes, looked into his and welled with tears as the jet started its ascent. His heart twisted.

"Please tell me that those tears aren't about what happened between us."

She shook her head. She mouthed a silent, "No."

She wore no make-up that he could discern, but she was still beautiful. "Taylor?"

She wiped at her tears with her index finger. "Last night, after I left your house, I went to my friend's house. Collette. I found her. She was," she shuddered, "dead. It looks like an overdose of prescription medicine." The jet taxied, then lifted. "I told Andi that I shouldn't make this trip. I'm fine." She reached into her purse and found tissue as uncontrolled tears fell. "Then this happens. And I have to get my act together, because we have the party tonight and the gala tomorrow night, and I have to be at both. I can't imagine getting through the next hour. Or two. Without these tears. How am I going to give a speech tomorrow night?"

He had told himself that he'd keep his distance, but distance no longer seemed important. This wasn't about sex, although one part of his body didn't seem to get that message.

This was about trying to ease her pain. He unsnapped his seatbelt, reached for her, then put his arms around her. She leaned into the space between his arm and his chest and pressed her forehead to his shoulder. Her body shook with sobs.

"I'm so sorry."

"I should have known." Her words came as her sobs eased. Taylor lifted her head. Her heartbreak was visible in her eyes. He softened his hug, giving her space. She sat up, reached for her satchel, and dipped her hand into the bag. She didn't find what she was looking for. She pulled out *Gracious Homes and Glorious Gardens,* a magazine that Brandon recognized as being a gossipy, society publication about wealthy citizens of the deep South. He wouldn't dream of paying for it, much less reading it.

She placed the magazine on the table then returned to her satchel, where she finally found more tissue. She swabbed at her eyes. "Andi and I both knew that Collette was having a rough time." Her gaze fell on the magazine. Brandon glanced at the cover, where Taylor was photographed in a chair, with Andi standing at her left shoulder. A petite red head stood at Taylor's right shoulder. They were dressed in classic feminine suits and looked fresh, rich, poised, and confident. The tag line read *Andi Hutchenson, Collette Westerfeld, and Taylor Bartholomew, three best friends, are planning the Fall's most important social event.*

They looked to be about the same age. Where there were three, now there were two. Only three days earlier, a woman looking into the Morrissey treason case, a part of HBW history, was murdered. Now, a Westerfeld was dead. Although his heart pounded, he kept his voice calm as he asked, "There's no suspicion of foul play?"

"No. If my father has his way, the official report will be that it was an accidental overdose of prescription medication." She frowned. "It is the option that was most palatable to my father at our meeting with the coroner this morning. He wouldn't dream of letting the coroner use the word suicide."

Out of nowhere, in the same way that he got hunches about legal theories, cases, and juries, something told him that the timing of Collette's death was too close to Lisa's death to be coincidental.

Hell.

He made a mental note to talk to Joe about it. Murder could easily be masked to look like suicide. Collette, a young socialite, who probably had never encountered a sociopath, would have been powerless in the crosshairs of one.

Taylor continued, "We knew that Collette was too dependent on meds. Antidepressants. Anti-anxiety pills. Sleeping pills. I was supposed to check on her yesterday, but I didn't go there until I left your house. If I had gotten there at seven-thirty, or eight, I could have saved her." She paused as fresh tears fell and her voice dropped to a whisper as she said, "Or maybe it wouldn't have happened at all."

Brandon focused his attention on the grief stricken woman next to him. He caught a tear with his index finger, then smoothed back her hair. His hand fell on her shoulder and rested there. He wished that he could impart to her some of his hard-earned strength. Instead, he only had words that portrayed his own journey with grief and guilt, a journey of which he had never spoken. Hazel eyes were seeking comfort. Waiting.

Aw. Damn. There was something about Taylor that he couldn't resist, on every level, even this deeply personal one.

He drew a deep breath as he searched for words that he could actually say about the worst time in his life, thinking that she might benefit from his mistake. "In my experience, grief can hurt so badly that it can derail your life. It can make you sick, physically and mentally." Brandon hesitated as he fought through the gut-twist of memories and pain. "Grief, no matter how it comes at you, is a hard enough burden. Layer it with guilt, self-imposed or for good reason, it doesn't matter, and grief becomes toxic."

More tears fell. "I should feel guilty. I should have been there for her."

He shook his head. "Focus on being sad that Collette is gone, but don't destroy yourself with guilt. You can't undo her death. No matter what you think that you should have done in the time that led up to it." He traced the line of her high cheekbone with an index finger, then lifted her chin, so that she had no choice but to look into his eyes. "Don't start down the road of unending guilt. It's addictive. Stop thinking about what you should or could have done. Just stop."

Seconds passed, then minutes, as they stared into each other's eyes. She reached to his cheekbone and touched the thin scar that was a souvenir from a time when he had wanted, more than anything, to die. She asked, "Are you through with guilt?"

His heart picked up its pace as he drowned in her gaze. "I'm trying to be. Some days are better than others."

"Thank you," she said. He reached for her, hating that she looked so damn miserable. Fresh sobs wracked her shoulders as he closed his arms around her. She buried her face into his shoulder and cried. After long minutes, when her sobs eased, Taylor wriggled deeper into the space between his shoulder and his chest, kicked off her sandals, then tucked her feet under her. Nestled close, she reached her left hand across his body and clasped his right hand, and then she was still.

Hell. Since Amy's death, Brandon had been with women. The women he liked enough to contemplate as sexual partners were typically nice, intelligent, and, in some way, attractive. Sex, though, was only sex. Sometimes it was great, and, as his body was reminding him, a bit of it right now wouldn't be a bad thing. His steadfast insistence on casual relationships robbed all interactions of intimacy, that deep feeling that came with two connected souls, the special feeling that he had shared with Amy. Casual was casual. There was nothing intimate about it.

This, though, this holding hands and consoling Taylor, telling her of his own experience with guilt so that she might learn from his mistakes, was not casual. It was a sharing, on a deep emotional level, of his most private pain, and, although the words had flowed, he wasn't ready for this. He shouldn't be sharing such thoughts with her, or with anyone. Having her tucked against him, giving her comfort, willing her to draw upon his strength, had nothing to do with sex and nothing to do with casualness. It was contact on a deep, emotional level, the closest contact that he'd had with a woman since his life with Amy. His heart pounded.

He wasn't ready for this. He had to *stop.* He should put distance between Taylor and him. At least a few inches.

His arms, though, didn't listen to his brain, and no matter how he wished it, he couldn't stop willing that Taylor not suffer. If holding her made her feel better, he wouldn't stop.

Yet he *wasn't-fucking-ready-for-this*. Being this close to any woman meant that he was ready to move past his grief, and that meant he was ready to forgive himself for Amy and Catherine's death. It meant he was ready to have a life without them. He swallowed. He wasn't ready.

Not now.

Not ever.

Right?

***

When the blue dot left the airport, he breathed easier. As Andi got back on the interstate, his tension unknotted. She bypassed New Orleans, and continued on I-10, towards Mississippi. He allowed himself to smile, because this made sense. His research was paying off. She was heading in the direction of Florida. There, five hours from New Orleans, the Hutchenson family had a beach house in the wooded and sand-duned, private neighborhood of Water's Edge. Gated, exclusive neighborhoods, the kind where rich people built multi-million dollar homes and stationed underpaid guards in gatehouses, were easy hunting grounds for him.

Andi Hutchenson, who didn't have to attend parties when she didn't feel like it, could easily jump on the interstate and head to her family's beach house, sit on the porch, and watch the waves as she cried over her dead friend. Because of the parties, which everyone else would likely be attending, except for the spoiled, youngest offspring of Andrew Hutchenson, she might even be going alone. He chuckled. If that was the case, making her disappear would be easy. He left the bakery, got in the car, and followed Andi through Mississippi.

***

The First Trust Bank of Dallas was closed, but the lobby, which served both the First Trust Storage Vault and the bank, was open. There were two guards, but only one customer. Her ash-blonde hair was pulled into a neat twist. She was slender and wore a crisp white linen shirt, tailored khaki pants, and black, closed toe loafers. Brandon guessed that she was in her late fifties. "Madeline Rorsch?" She nodded as Brandon introduced himself and Taylor.

Madeline's sharp blue eyes inspected Taylor, then she glanced at Brandon. "I was not told that anyone would be accompanying you."

"I apologize for that," Brandon said.

"I'm sorry," Taylor said, "if my presence presents a problem."

Madeline shifted her head a bit to the left and studied Taylor. "Bartholomew. As in George Bartholomew?"

Taylor nodded. "The first was my grandfather. The second is my father." Taylor had been quiet during the drive to the vault. She had sat next to Brandon in the rear seat of the chauffeured car, her leg pressed against his, her hand in his. More than once she had wiped fresh tears from her eyes. Now, as she responded to Madeline, she was subdued, but composed.

Madeline nodded to a guard, who led the way. "Precious few have requested access to my father's collection, and that may be because of the subject matter. He focused not on weapons, but on less interesting things such as first edition books, maps of battles, letters, and transcripts. Most of it relates to his work as an FBI agent, then later with the Office of Secret Services." They entered an elevator, which opened into a long hallway on the third floor. "Once documents from the cases that he handled became public record, he added them to his collection. His material related to his work in the Gulf Coast states, including the Morrissey case, is extensive."

As Madeline and the guard stopped at a door and entered codes in a keypad, Brandon asked, "How is your father?"

Madeline turned to Brandon, a serious expression on her face. "You will soon see. My ninety-six year old father is in the vault, waiting to meet you."

The Rorsch vault was large, with wood paneling, dark brown carpet, and soft light. One side was lined with tall mahogany file cabinets. Another side had floor to ceiling bookshelves. Maps covered a wall, with more maps placed in sleeves that hung from wooden arms. Medals, documents, and plaques hung from another wall. A reading table that sat six was centered in the room. Phillip Rorsch was at one end. It only took one glance to know why Lisa had made more than one trip to Texas to pursue the Rorsch angle. He had a magnetic allure. Although he was in a wheelchair, he sat erect. He had his daughter's ice-blue eyes. They were filmy with age, but he had a sharp, mesmerizing gaze. He was bald and thin and more than a little wrinkled, yet he was dressed in pressed slacks and a starched shirt and nodded as Madeline introduced them and explained Taylor's connection to HBW.

After they introduced themselves, Phillip asked, "How did it come about that a Bartholomew and a Morrissey are here together?" His voice was weak, with a breathy rasp.

"Lisa's death brought us together," Brandon said, "and her research is of interest to both of us, as it involves our families. We saw that she came here a few weeks ago to look at your documents."

Phillip shook his head. "When Lisa last came here, she did not come to see my documents. She did that months and months ago." He glanced at Madeline. "Was it January or February?"

"January," Madeline said.

Rorsch nodded to a box that was in the middle of the table. "These old papers are sensitive. Please wear gloves to handle the documents."

Brandon opened the box and pulled out gloves for Taylor and himself. "We're wondering whether you can shed light on what Lisa knew, because her research, from what we've been able to find, is incomplete. I believe, though, that she was echoing what my father said years ago."

"I spoke with your father of his beliefs," Rorsch said, "over the telephone and in person."

The hair on the back of Brandon's neck stood on end as he learned of this connection. "You knew my father?"

Rorsch nodded. "He came here a couple of years before he died. I told him what I told Lisa. If you open the second drawer in the third stack," Brandon pulled on the gloves, then followed Rorsch's instructions. "Those are transcripts of your grandfather's trial. I was the primary witness in the Government's case in chief. I testified about how I'd been contacted by Benjamin Morrissey, who was attempting to reach

Nazi spies that had infiltrated the Gulf Coast region. I was a new agent and under deep cover."

Brandon pulled a chair out for Taylor and sat next to her. As Rorsch spoke, Brandon leafed through the first of two transcript volumes, positioning it between himself and Taylor. Hazel-green eyes held his gaze for a second, reflecting his excitement. Not only were they looking at a 1940's trial transcript, they had the key witness from the trial giving them his thoughts. "The only time Benjamin and I spoke to each other was at a restaurant named Antoine's. I followed his instructions as to time and place, all of which was delivered by courier. When I arrived, he was there, waiting. I entered a bathroom stall. He was waiting in the adjoining one. His shoes were polished black leather wingtips. He wore black pants with cuffs that were crisp and clean. I saw the bottom of a black wool coat, and nothing else. I did not see his face. I would not have recognized him, in any event. He identified himself as a partner in HBW and provided information that only a partner would have known. There was a leak in a bathroom faucet." He shook his head. "My remote memory is so strong. I listened to how he spoke each word, trying to pinpoint his background. When he told me what he was attempting to sell, I almost lost it. I was barely twenty-two, I'd been an agent for maybe two months, and he was trying to sell me important information. We arranged the exchange of the plans for the landing craft and the price, then and there. He was also going to supply the number of units that were being ordered, which was a key Government secret."

The breathiness of Rorsch's voice became more pronounced, and his pauses more frequent. "When Benjamin arrived at the Bienville Street wharf, the river fog had not cleared. As we had arranged, he arrived precisely at 7:30 a.m., he was driving a black Ford, he parked it on the far side of the lot, away from the river, where I was waiting with two other agents. The other agents carried a trunk that looked large enough to hold two million dollars. He had a satchel and a case of drawings. He stopped at the designated spot, I took the satchel and the case, and the other two agents dropped the trunk and apprehended him. It took maybe a minute. The other agents processed him." Rorsch's blue eyes leveled on Brandon, and he drew a deep breath. "They handled the post-arrest interviews. I stayed in the field, far from the offices, to protect my cover."

After a few breaths, Rorsch continued, "My point is that after that meeting at Antoine's, I did not speak to your grandfather. Not for five more years, and that was more than a year after his conviction. That is a very important point."

Taylor said, "Why is that important?"

"Benjamin consistently denied that he was involved in selling the plans. No one believed him. He gave his version of the events at the trial, but I wasn't there to hear him testify."

"The rule of sequestration was in force," Brandon said, guessing that the rule where witnesses were excluded from hearing other witnesses testify was used at the trial.

Rorsch nodded. "Correct. I was only at the trial for my testimony. I was not present when Benjamin testified, or when the verdict was read, or when he personally pleaded for leniency at sentencing. When he was convicted, I knew nothing of Benjamin Morrissey, except I knew that his name was spoken in the bathroom stall, and he was the person who arrived, as we had agreed, at the wharf. When he was tried, numerous other cases that I had worked in the field went to trial. I was constantly traveling, preparing for one case as soon as I left the courthouse from testifying at another. As my cases went, Morrissey's was open and shut."

"Morrissey showed up with documentation of military secrets and handed them to someone he thought was a Nazi sympathizer with the intent to exchange the documents for cash," Taylor said. "The essential elements for treason are there."

"But there's more, isn't there?" Brandon asked.

Rorsch nodded. He took a few breaths, then said, "Benjamin testified that two days prior to his arrest, and after he and I met at Antoine's, the Government had finally shown real interest in the landing craft." Brandon listened as he found his grandfather's words in the trial transcript. "What was only a dream of HBW&M when I met with Morrissey in Antoine's, over the ensuing week, became a reality. Because the company ended up with government contracts for the boats, the information that Morrissey was trying to sell to the enemy had suddenly become priceless war strategy. What had been worth only what Morrissey could con the Nazis into paying for it, had become a multi-million dollar contract for HBW&M, and it secured a future for the company."

"So desperate men who had poured their money into research and development of a worthless, odd-shaped boat were no longer desperate," Brandon said.

Rorsch held Brandon's eyes as he nodded. "And the company had to produce the boats quickly. They were scrambling to activate employees, acquire real estate, build warehouses, and get the assembly line production in place. The night before the exchange was to take place, an informant whose name was never obtained contacted local FBI headquarters and let them know that Brandon Morrissey would be arriving at the Bienville Street wharf in the morning, meeting a Nazi spy, and was planning on selling military secrets."

Taylor said, "I'm still not sure I understand why it was important that you didn't hear Benjamin testify at trial."

Rorsch took a deep breath. "I'm getting to that. Benjamin testified that on the morning that he was arrested, he met with George Bartholomew and Andrew Hutchenson. They told him that they had acquired a lease for the Bienville Street wharf. They handed him what Benjamin thought were designs for the production buildout and asked that he deliver it to contractors who were at the wharf. In reality, the case that his partners gave him had design drawings for the landing craft. He went where they told him to go, handed the documents to the man who was waiting there, then was arrested."

Brandon heard Taylor draw a deep breath. She asked, "Are you saying that my grandfather and the first Andrew Hutchinson set him up?"

Rorsch nodded to Taylor. "That is Benjamin Morrissey's testimony." He gave Brandon time to find his grandfather's words in the trial transcript. "The jury didn't believe it. After all, my testimony indicated that he was the person I met in Antoine's and he showed up with the documents. After his conviction, Benjamin wrote to me. Simple, handwritten letters. He asked for a meeting. He told me that I'd understand once I met him." Rorsch paused. "His letters were so insistent that I could not forget them, but I did not immediately act on them."

Rorsch directed Brandon to a file cabinet and a folder that was labeled "Morrissey. Letters." Brandon sat and opened the folder. His heart twisted as he saw the careful, print handwriting. *"Please meet with me. I have been wrongfully convicted. Please help me."*

"By the time your grandfather was writing to me," Rorsch said, "I was in charge of the Southeast Division of the Office of Secret Services. A year or so after Benjamin was convicted, I happened to be where he was incarcerated. I asked to speak to him." Rorsch paused, drew a deep breath, then clasped together hands that were knobby with arthritis, and shook his head, "Here's the answer to your question, Ms. Bartholomew. When he spoke to me, I knew that I had never heard his voice before. He was not the man who made contact with me. I knew that he had testified correctly."

Brandon's heart skipped a beat. He asked, "Why were you so certain?"

"He had a thick, heavy accent, one that I recognized from my work in the Gulf Coast region. It was a Cajun-French accent. It wasn't the educated, smooth voice that I heard in the bathroom stall at Antoine's. I would have sworn to that. Actually, I did swear to that. I gave him an affidavit to that effect." Rorsch's voice was fading with each sentence that he spoke, and his pauses for breath were more frequent. "It is in these files, in a folder regarding his appeals."

Taylor stood, went to the file cabinet, and found the affidavit. Brandon glanced at the document, which was dated almost three years after Benjamin's trial. "His direct appeals were over by the time that you prepared this," Brandon said.

Rorsch nodded. "His only hope was to present my affidavit as new evidence, in an application for post-conviction relief, via the writ of habeas corpus."

Brandon frowned. "The odds of winning that type of case are slim."

"In the 1940's, an era of wartime hysteria, for a man convicted of treason, the odds were impossible. After he lost his post-conviction appeals, I drafted a letter to President Truman requesting a pardon. In the same folder with the affidavit, you'll see my pardon letter." Brandon stood, found the letter that was dated December 1946, then sat down, hard. "My request for a pardon would have had a negative impact on my career," he said, "and I hesitated. Your grandfather died of a heart attack in 1946."

"My father never believed that his father died of a heart attack," Brandon said. "Benjamin was still a relatively young man. No autopsy was performed. The family learned of Benjamin's death days after it occurred."

Rorsch nodded. "I know. Your father told me that. But the death certificate lists heart attack as a cause, and that is what I was told then. I had no reasons to suspect otherwise. Because Benjamin died before I sent the letter, that was the end of it as far as I could tell. I never sent the letter."

"If Benjamin Morrissey was not the man at Antoine's," Taylor said, "who was?"

"It is plausible to believe it was one of his partners. It also explains why the informant called the FBI office."

"How so?" Taylor asked. Brandon glanced at her. Her arms were folded. Her cheeks were flushed. He could understand why she wasn't liking Rorsch's theory, which implicated her grandfather.

"Once the military was interested, really interested, the last thing Bartholomew, Hutchenson, or Westerfeld wanted was to let the plans get in the hands of the Nazis. They wanted the FBI to intercept the plans," he said, "and, instead of following the option of simply not showing up, setting Morrissey up as the spy ultimately meant they didn't have to share profits with him."

"My grandfather had already designed the boat," Brandon said. "He was expendable."

Rorsch nodded, then continued, "They made him a partner because he was a genius in boat design. The speech pattern of the man in the bathroom was that of a well-educated man. Morrissey didn't even get through grammar school. He was self-taught. He would not have arranged a meeting at Antoine's, which was then one of the city's most expensive restaurants." Rorsch fell silent for a minute. "I believe my testimony led to the conviction of an innocent man."

"Did you ever publicize this?" Brandon asked.

"No," Rorsch said. "But I have not hid it, either. In the late 1970's, I was contacted by Lloyd Landrum, a professor of history at Tulane University." Taylor glanced at Brandon, whose heart was pounding. "Landrum was writing a book on the history of World War II, from the domestic perspective. He also told me of his dream of creating a World War II museum. I allowed him full access to my documents. I allowed him to make copies. I explained my thoughts about Benjamin Morrissey. I showed him my affidavit." He shook his head. "There was no mention of my concerns in any of Landrum's books. He told me the museum, which was in the planning stages at the time, would have more documentation. When the museum opened, I went to it. None of my doubts regarding the Morrissey case are evident from the museum's collections."

"Mentioning your concerns would require highlighting the fact that Hutchenson and Bartholomew told my grandfather to go to the meeting," Brandon said, his gaze locked on Rorsch's blue eyes. "This, coupled with your belief that my grandfather was not the man in the bathroom stall, indicates that they set him up. In a museum that was funded, in part, with money from the HBW families, such facts would not be trumpeted."

Chapter Fourteen

Taylor stood. At first, the vault had seemed large. Now, the room, devoid of natural light, was stuffy. "There's got to be an explanation. You're not simply talking about events that took place in the 1930s and 40s." She met Rorsch's gaze. "You're suggesting a cover-up in more recent times, aren't you?"

"You're correct, Ms. Bartholomew," Rorsch said.

The walls seemed to move closer. Her heart beat faster, inspired by a sick feeling of dread. Taylor glanced at the memorabilia that adorned the windowless room. She glanced at Rorsch, who was so, so old. She decided that age had distorted Rorsch's memories. "A more recent cover-up implies guilty knowledge among men who are living. Men I know. My father is included in that group."

As a slight flush crawled up Rorsch's neck, Taylor turned to Brandon. His jaw was set. Crystal-clear green eyes were studying her. Taylor turned back to Rorsch, and continued, "Couldn't the most plausible explanation be that while this fact now seems so important, in the total history of World War II, when you think of all the facts that are there to be told, your doubts about Benjamin Morrissey's conviction just aren't, and I apologize Mr. Rorsch, aren't so significant that they need to be mentioned?"

"I could agree, Ms. Bartholomew," Rorsch said, "but Landrum billed himself as an expert on the amphibious invasion of Normandy. The museum was originally named the D-Day Museum, and the first exhibit is the Hutchenson Landing Craft. In telling the story of the Allied invasion of Normandy, the facts are not complete without discussing the Morrissey treason case. Once anyone talks to me," Rorsch's voice was getting louder, while his breathing was becoming labored, "the facts must include my belief that Benjamin Morrissey was wrongly convicted."

"I didn't mean to upset you," she said. "I'm only looking for an explanation, one that doesn't suggest sinister motive on the part of men who were not convicted of a crime."

"There's more that you should know before you are so dismissive."

Taylor sat. More dread built. Rorsch conveyed a passion for his beliefs, and as much as she didn't want to admit it, he was believable. "More?"

"The first Andrew Hutchenson wrote a confession letter that explains that Benjamin Morrissey told the truth at his trial. He wrote the letter shortly before he died, in 1979."

Taylor's heart stopped. She remembered the words that she had overheard from her father's conference room the day before. *Hutchenson. Letter. Hoax.* The words had not been in a sentence, but had been spoken in the same conversation. Yesterday, the words had made no sense. Rorsch was weaving sense into two of the words, but there was no way that he was correct. Absolutely no way. Rorsch could be making all of this up. He could be senile.

"There's no way," Taylor said, "that my grandfather would have done such a thing."

Brandon put a hand on Taylor's hand, as Madeline said, "Ms. Bartholomew, if you insist on arguing with my father, I'll have to ask you to leave."

Taylor drew a couple of deep breaths. *Listen*, she told herself. *Listen. Don't react.*

Rorsch's eyes bounced from Taylor's to Brandon's. "I take it that neither of you have ever seen the Hutchenson letter?"

Brandon shook his head, as Taylor said, "No."

"The first Andrew Hutchenson instructed his lawyers to deliver the letter to three recipients upon his death," Rorsch said. Brandon and Taylor were both leaning forward to catch each of Rorsch's words. When Rorsch had started speaking, she'd been worried about Brandon as he listened to the story of how his grandfather had committed treason. Now, the tables were turned. Brandon's hand, gripping hers, was comforting.

"One recipient was Lloyd Landrum," Rorsch said. "Another was the Board of HBW." In 1979, Taylor's father was in his second year as a member of the HBW Board.

Taylor shook her head, dismissing Rorsch's commentary. "If my father had known of this fact, he would have made it public knowledge."

Both Rorsch and Brandon gave her long, questioning glances. She shook off growing doubt, but stayed silent.

Rorsch continued, looking at Brandon. "Another recipient was your father, Brandon. He called and told me about it, first, when he received the letter, and later, when Landrum's book came out." Rorsch frowned. "Landrum's book came out in 1981, with no mention of anything that I had told him, and no mention of the Hutchenson letter. The only reference in the book to the treason case arising out of the Hutchenson Landing Craft was that Benjamin Morrissey was convicted."

"And after that my father killed himself."

Rorsch took a breath. "When Lisa first came to see me, she indicated that Landrum was one of her faculty advisers. I mentioned my concerns to Lisa regarding Landrum. I told her not to trust him," he said, "yet she seemed to. I did not tell Lisa of the letter. You see, I didn't have it and had never seen it," Rorsch said. "I only had your father's word that it existed."

"And you doubted him," Brandon said.

Rorsch frowned. He gave Brandon a slight nod. Taylor didn't like his pauses, because they were followed by more words, more sentences that shook her belief in bedrock facts. "When Lisa was last here, she came to show me the letter. She had an original. She wouldn't tell me who gave it to her. She had already told Landrum about it. I advised her to make it public, before showing it to other individuals."

"You didn't copy it?" Taylor asked.

"No," Rorsch said, "I did not copy it. It was Lisa's discovery. I didn't want to add it to my collection before she had an opportunity to publicize her research. Evidently, the person who gave it to her told her not to tell anyone of the source. She did not want to reveal her source, and I did not press her on it. However, going back to the three original recipients of the letter, I assume that no one on the current board would have given the letter to her, and Landrum wouldn't have given it to her." Rorsch shrugged, his gaze locked on Brandon. "So that would only leave someone with access to your father's documents."

Brandon shook his head. "My father's documents were destroyed in a house fire, in 1980, before he killed himself."

"Not all of your father's documents were destroyed in the fire."

Brandon asked, "Excuse me?"

Rorsch leveled blue eyes on Brandon. "Not all of your father's documents were destroyed."

Brandon pushed his chair away from the table and folded his arms. "How do you know that?"

"He told me that some of his documents were saved. He blamed himself for your sister's death, because he managed to save the documents, but not her."

Taylor glanced at Brandon. His jaw was clenched. A pulse throbbed at his temple. He looked at Taylor with a pained expression in his eyes, and explained, "My sister, Catherine, was ten years old. She died of smoke inhalation."

Taylor's heart pounded as she digested this part of Brandon's history. She watched him turn to Rorsch and Madeline.

"Mr. Rorsch, I'm sorry if it sounds like I'm doubting you," Brandon said, "but yesterday I asked my mother about my father's documents. She confirmed that everything burned in the fire."

Rorsch shook his head. "I'm only telling you what your father told me."

"My father was angry, he was obsessive, he drank too much, and he was delusional." Brandon paused. "So if I had to take the word of either my mother, or my father, I'd take the word of my mother."

Brandon glanced at his watch, then at Taylor. "If we don't leave soon, we'll be late for our departure."

Thank God, Taylor thought. She wanted to be out of this closed-in room of old memories and away from Rorsch's words of supposition and innuendo. She needed to think, and she couldn't do it there. She and Brandon both thanked Madeline and Rorsch as they peeled off the gloves.

Before they could leave, Rorsch said, "Wait." Taylor paused, with her hand on the door. "Please don't falter. If there is anything that I can do to help you two expose the truth, please let me know."

Taylor's stomach twisted as she stared at Phillip Rorsch. *The truth?* His theory couldn't be the truth. She opened her mouth to tell him that, but Brandon gripped her elbow and led her from the vault. Outside, in bright sunlight, she breathed in deep, pulling fresh air past the knot that had formed in her throat.

Brandon asked, "Are you all right?"

She nodded as Brandon opened the door of the waiting car, then slid in next to her. She wasn't all right, though. She had lost a good friend, and, if Rorsch's words had any basis in reality, the world no longer made sense.

At least *her* world no longer made sense. The only thing that was tangible and real was Brandon. She lifted her face to his. Only inches separated them. Somewhere between last night's aborted attempt at sex and her crying on his shoulder on the flight from New Orleans to Dallas, the typical amount of inches that separated non-intimate partners had become a thing of the past.

"There's got to be an explanation," she said, "like maybe the poor man's thoughts are just, well, not really grounded in reality?"

"I can think of several explanations," Brandon said, one arm draped around her shoulder, his other hand clasping one of hers. "And that might be one. The other explanations I'm thinking of aren't anything that you'd like. Hell. I don't like some of what he said, because he suggested that my mother lied to me."

"What are you going to do about that?"

He shrugged. "Call and ask her."

He took his phone out of his pocket and dialed. "Mom. Hey." He paused, then said, "Michael's fine. Look. I had a meeting this afternoon with someone who indicated that not all of dad's documents burned in the fire." Taylor could hear a female voice, but, because Brandon didn't have the phone on the speaker setting, she couldn't make out the words. "If you really do have dad's documents, I need to see them. What they reveal could tell us what Lisa's research indicated."

Taylor heard more female words.

"I'm not mad." Brandon softened his tone. "I don't care if you hid the documents from me, but now I need the truth. Do you have dad's documents? Mom?" He paused. "Yes. I'll be home in two hours. Would you like me to come to you?" His words were gentle as he gazed at Taylor, but listened to his mother. "I'll see you at my house around seven."

He broke the connection. "She wants to talk face to face." He frowned. "Maybe Rorsch isn't crazy."

Other than his words, Rorsch didn't seem senile, but he had to be, Taylor thought. Otherwise, her grandfather was a criminal and her father had actively concealed her grandfather's crimes.

"Does your mother have your father's documents?"

"She wouldn't say."

She drew a deep breath and looked into Brandon's eyes. "I can't call my father and ask about the things that Rorsch said. Not like you just did with your mother. That kind of direct, out-of-the-blue approach would not work with him."

Brandon's gaze was serious. "From what I've seen, you're pretty good at asking questions. Damn good, as a matter of fact. Figure out what you want the answer to, and ask it. Handle him however you can, directly or indirectly."

"Handle? I don't handle my father. No one does."

"Then let's focus on how we get information by going around your father. In 1979, when the Hutchenson letter would have been circulated," Brandon asked, "who was on the HBW board?"

"After the first Andrew Hutchenson died in 1979, Andi's father was on the board, and he still is. Alicia Westerfeld was on the board throughout that time, as was my father." Taylor paused. "My grandfather died in 1977. Since then, my father has always been the most dominant personality on the board, even though Alicia was tough as nails. Andrew, Andi's father, is gentle. He follows my father's lead. So does Claude, Alicia's son who took her place when she died."

"I know that you're ultimately going to talk to your father about what Rorsch said," Brandon held her gaze, "but if you really want to figure out the facts, talk to Andrew as well. As a matter of fact, I'd start with Andrew, because if the Hutchenson letter exists, and if it was concealed in 1979, then the dying wish of Andrew's father, that the truth be made known, wasn't honored. I don't think that could sit well with a man who has any integrity. Andrew's guilt might make him more inclined to be truthful."

Her heart skipped. "Are you suggesting that my father will lie to me?"

"I've never met your father in person. I do know how he directs his lawyers to fight on behalf of the company," he paused, "and they fight dirty."

"You said that you don't follow rules," she said, trying to defend her father.

"I don't withhold evidence or tell my clients to lie. Your father's lawyers do. When you start looking through the cases that your company has been involved in, look to see how many times I've won sanctions against your lawyers."

"As of today," she said, "I'm general counsel. I'll fight hard, but not dirty."

He chuckled. "Good to know, because this morning I did a search of my files. My firm has twenty pending cases against HBW. A few will result in sizable judgments."

"Don't count your cash before the verdicts come in, counselor." In response to his laughter, and as the driver turned into the airport, she added, "And it sure sounds like we shouldn't be sitting so close, because if we're on opposing sides in that many cases, we have current day conflicts, regardless of what may have transpired between your grandfather and mine, and your father and mine."

"You have outside firms that can handle the cases, and I can let other lawyers handle them on my end. We can build Chinese walls, if we need to." He shrugged. "And as far as what transpired between our grandfathers, well, the past is the past. We can't change what happened. We can only figure out what happened, figure out whether any of it is relevant to today, and do something about it if it is."

That Brandon had an answer for everything wasn't bad. Especially not when he was logical, when he articulated such reasonable thoughts, and when she was sitting so close to him that she could feel his warmth. He smelled of woodsy soap, vanilla, and clove, and the aroma inspired her body to crave the pleasure that he'd given her the night before, regardless of the multitude of conflicting interests they had.

The driver parked the car next to the jet, then stepped out. Brandon bent closer to her. Her heart stuttered as his green eyes found hers. He grazed his lips on her cheek. She turned her lips to his, but he didn't kiss her. "Our hour and a half plane ride is about to be an hour and a half too long," he said, "I don't have enough willpower when you look at me like that."

"I don't want you to have willpower," she said. "I want to forget about how much I miss Collette. I want to forget everything that Rorsch said." She dropped her voice to a whisper, "I want something worth remembering, like what we did last night, and I won't ask you to stop."

He gave her a serious look, studying her until his cheeks were flushed. He guided her into the jet, and, when the pilots disappeared into the cockpit and shut the door, he pulled her to him and gave her a hungry, mouth-wide-open kiss. She lifted her arms to his shoulders and rubbed against him. Their clothes separated them, but didn't conceal his desire for her. He reached behind her and gripped her butt, then lifted her against the wall of the jet. While he held her, his fingers started inching her dress upwards, exposing her legs, then her thighs, then somehow, her legs were hooked behind his hips and the only thing that covered her sex was a sliver of lacy thong. He pushed it aside, groaning as his fingertips slid through her moist folds. She shivered, then moaned louder as he dabbled in her wetness, swirling a fingertip into her. He gently lowered her to a standing position, reached for his wallet, looked into it, then kicked the table's pedestal as he dropped the wallet on the table. "I can't believe this."

"What?" she asked.

"No condoms."

The pilot announced over the intercom, "We will be taxiing in a minute."

Brandon sat down with a thud at the table that they'd been sitting at on the ride from New Orleans to Dallas. She sat and leaned into him. He gently pushed her away. "No condoms, no sex. Fasten your damn seatbelt."

"Pregnancy's not a problem. I've been on the pill since I was nineteen."

He frowned. "Why?"

"Acne. My mother wanted me to look perfect for my debut year."

"So she orchestrated the metamorphosis of a chubby, acne-ridden bookworm into you?"

She laughed. "So, you listened when I explained the circumstances of how I came to be a twenty-seven-year-old virgin?"

"I listen to everything that you say." His eyes were so serious they stole her breath.

"I had curves, but too many in all the wrong places. I could afford the best clothes, but I was too self conscious to wear them. Carolyn and I protested the extreme efforts," Taylor said, "but my mother, like my father, was a strong force, and I succumbed. After all, I wanted to be pretty for my debut year. My mother took charge with diet doctors, exercise trainers, and, because I was prone to acne, the pill, and it helped me with cramps, so I've stayed on it. So," she said, leaning towards him, as the plane started taxiing, "I give you permission to have sex with me without a condom."

He scowled at her. "Condoms don't simply prevent pregnancy."

"I know that, but you normally wear them, don't you?"

"Always. Even with Lisa."

"Given the circumstances of my virginity, and your," she felt her cheeks flush with heat, "size, won't it will feel better if you're not wearing one?"

He unfastened his seat belt, then hers, and guided her into the jet's rear compartment, shutting the door. As the jet began its ascent Brandon untied the halter top of her sundress and slid it down to her waist. She shivered with anticipation as he took off her strapless bra then spent long minutes nibbling and sucking at her breasts. He pushed the sundress down her hips, removing her panties with the dress, then slipped off her sandals before he planted a trail of kisses from her breasts to her belly, and lower. When she moaned, he stood and stripped, exposing his lean, muscular, painted body. He was erect and straining for her. He sat on the sofa and guided her into a kneeling position, with her knees on either side of him. He slid his fingers through the folds of her sex, then applied steady pressure between her legs with his thumb.

"Oh," she said as her body pulsed with need. "That feels so good."

He inserted two fingers into her. The pressure of his knuckles, inside of her, sent shock waves through her body.

"Yes," she whispered, as her nerve endings sizzled.

He rubbed the hot, smooth head of his penis against her most sensitive flesh while his fingers thrust deep inside of her. "Oh," she said, "Oh Brandon." She gripped his shoulders, as his mouth latched onto her breast. Her body jolted with pleasure as she started to climax. "Oh. My," she said, "God." He removed his fingers, shifted his hips, reached for her hand and wrapped it on his thick shaft. As he pushed into her, he let her control how much and how fast. It felt great, until he was a few inches inside of her, then it felt like he was ripping her apart. Blinding pain suddenly outweighed her pleasure.

Not again, she thought, as she froze.

"Taylor?"

"Just do it," she whispered, "fast."

He put both hands on her hips, gripped her tight, then paused. Green eyes locked on hers, questioning. When she nodded, he pushed her hips down. She gasped. Where pleasure had hit her with lightning bolts, pain sizzled. He held her tight and moved both of them, so that he was laying on top of her on the sofa, never slipping out of her as he kissed away tears that she had realized were falling. "Are you okay?" She nodded, but the real answer was no. He moved slowly, barely an inch in, an inch out. "Does this hurt?"

It burned, but she could bear it. She hoped that it didn't take him too long to have an orgasm, because his thrusts were hot-friction torture. One. Two. She drew a deep breath. Three. She stopped counting as she tried to think of a way to forget about the pain. She opened her eyes, wondering how long they'd been closed. Worried green eyes looked into hers. A pulse throbbed at his temple. His teeth were clenched. His hips were still. "I'll stop."

"No. Just go slower."

"If I go any slower I'll die."

"This is fine then," she said. "Really."

He shook his head. "I'm not going for fine." He was hard, throbbing, and deep inside of her, but he stopped thrusting. He moved his mouth to her breast and licked and nibbled at her nipples. He balanced on one forearm and his toes, and reached between her legs with his free hand, rubbing her clitoris with a soft, whisper-like touch that finally coaxed faint ripples of pleasure through her body. As the ripples grew, she forgot about the pain. When she moaned, he started thrusting again, slowly. He glanced into her eyes, gauging her reaction. She loved the concern that she saw there, the worry for her that gave him the willpower to barely move his hips, even though beads of perspiration had formed on his forehead and on his shoulders. Tension rippled through the muscles in his arms and his chest as he made only tiny thrusting movements and kept his weight off of her. The pain diminished, and as more waves of pleasure broke, she was able to relax. Once she relaxed, the hurt disappeared. Tiny waves of electricity rippled from her core, and, finally, her hips moved with him, allowing her to absorb his full, warm erection.

"That's it," he said, as her muscle-clenching resistance disappeared. He pushed in a little bit deeper. Once. Twice. "Hurt?"

"No," she said, "really. No."

He almost pulled out of her, then he went in a little faster and a little harder. "Feel okay?"

Against his hard, smooth flesh, her walls felt tight and hot, and a fresh wave of arousal made her wet. Her walls flexed with pleasure, drawing him in.

"Talk to me," he said.

She whispered, "I didn't know," she moaned as he slid deeper into her, "that it could feel this good." He moved faster and harder. She spread her legs wider. She met his thrusts with her hips, sighing louder each time he slid into her.

"You feel like heaven," he said.

She lifted herself onto her elbows and watched him pull out of her, then push in. She let her head fall back as he planted his mouth on her breast. Electricity sizzled across her body as he thrust deep into her and he nibbled at one nipple, then the other. "Oh. Oh. Ooooohhhhh," she said, unable to say anything else, until passion and arousal came together and, with his penis deep inside of her, the tension broke. She screamed, "Brandon. Oh. Oh. Brandon."

He lifted his face and stared into her eyes, as he thrust, fast and deep. He ground his hips into hers, never breaking eye contact, until he shuddered and moaned. When he stopped thrusting, and when her own spasms stopped, she buried her face in his shoulder, her cheeks flushed and hot. She caught her breath. "Oh God," she said, "I screamed."

He lifted her chin so that he could look into her eyes. "I love the way you moan, the way you talk when you're coming, and how you sound when you scream. It drives me crazy. No one heard you. No one but me." He gave her a deep, lingering kiss. He rolled with her, then lifted her so that she lay on top of him. He positioned her legs so that they were draped on either side of him, her hips were pressed into his, and he was cupping her butt with his hands, kneading her flesh with strong fingers. His eyes were intense. She thought he had climaxed, but he was still hard and deep inside of her.

She asked, "Did you have an orgasm?"

He chuckled. "Questions, questions, questions. That's my favorite one so far. Yes. I did." He kissed her, deep. "But I've been aroused since last night." He broke the kiss and looked into her eyes. "Can you handle more?"

When she nodded, he pressed her hips into his, pushing deeper, then easing the pressure, then doing it slowly, again, and again. Her body responded with none of the prior pain and only warm, wet pleasure. An involuntary moan escaped from her. God. She bit her lip and pressed her palm against her mouth, trying to keep quiet. He took her palm away and held both of her hands behind her back in one of his hands. The flight had been smooth. Now, the jet bumped a bit, enough to make her slide down him, hard, with no resistance.

"Oh. Oh," she said, "oh yes, Brandon," when she didn't mean to say anything at all. He gave her a deep kiss, gliding his tongue over hers. He let go of her hands, lifted his hands to knead her breasts, and rubbed the tips of his fingers on her erect nipples. She was on her knees and balanced on his chest with the palms of her hands. He raised his hips, with his feet pressed into the couch, and lifted her with him so that he was inside of her as deep as he could go.

Waves of pleasure, more intense than before, built from inside as she rode him. "Brandon," she said. "Oh." She bit her lip, trying not to scream, then gave up. "Oh. Yessss. Brandon."

He groaned, gripping her and guiding her hips, slowly, so that she slid up and down his shaft, then plunging deep inside of her as he pushed her hips forward and back. She knew by the way his eyes were half closed, by the way his breath quickened, what felt good to him, and what felt great. Their bodies melded perfectly, and the grinding movement that felt great to him made her quiver. "Oh," she said, "You. Feel. So. Good. "Oh," she whimpered, as she climaxed, "Yes. Yes. Brandon. Yessss."

He arched his back and held her hips tight against his. He was so engorged that she felt each spasm. This time, his orgasm was intense and lasted longer. After, he drew a deep breath, and held her close on top of him, his arms tight around her. Breathing, together, was all they could do. Before they could say anything, one of the pilots announced that they would be beginning their descent in a few minutes. Brandon gave her a long kiss, and said, "You're amazing." He started to disentangle his limbs from hers, and said, "Stay here. I'll help you."

At first, she didn't understand why he wanted her to wait. She got to her feet and felt a way-late rush of modesty as she realized that their activities had produced more than a little moisture. She darted for the bathroom at the rear of the cabin.

With the bathroom door shut behind her, and with water running, she paused when she saw her flushed face and chest in the mirror. Her hair was wild. Her pupils were dilated. More red came to her cheeks. She'd been completely uninhibited. She had even screamed. More than once.

The jet's descent reminded her that the real world was fast approaching and she inexplicably felt a sudden need to cry. She needed Collette, and she didn't need to be in her father's presence. She didn't need to look at her father and wonder if Rorsch was correct, that somehow her father knew of the Hutchenson letter and hadn't done anything about it. She needed not to have to rush home, get dressed, go to a party and make small talk to hundreds of people. She needed to enjoy the afterglow of making love for the first time, of the incredible feeling that came with having Brandon deep inside of her.

No, she thought. *They hadn't made love. It was casual sex.* It shouldn't feel so earth-shattering. Maybe it wouldn't have, if the day itself had been better, if she hadn't already felt like her life was upside down.

Brandon knocked.

Casual sex, she reminded herself. *Be casual about it.*

He asked, through the door, "Are you all right?"

She stepped out. He was almost dressed, but his shirt was unbuttoned. She tried to give him a smile as he handed her clothes to her, but her smile didn't quite make it to her lips. "I wish we could stay on this jet."

Serious green eyes held her gaze. "Me too."

As she slipped into the sundress, he reached for her, lifted her hair, tied the halter tie, then planted a soft kiss on the back of her neck. A hard bump of turbulence separated them. The pilot announced that if they didn't already have their seat belts on, now would be a good time. They finished dressing, then returned to the table in the forward compartment and fastened their seat belts.

He kissed her. A sweet kiss, on the lips. Then once again, deeper.

Yes, she thought, as he wrapped his strong arms around her. *This is what I need. This. I need this.* He made her feel centered. Casual, she reminded herself. Act casual.

As the jet rolled to a stop, she had a moment of uncertainty. "How do I act as though nothing happened?"

He frowned. "Wait. Casual doesn't mean that you have to act like nothing happened.

"Not with you," she said, gesturing with her chin to the cockpit, "with the pilots. I know they heard me."

He chuckled. "I'm not sure they could have, but do you really care what they think?"

She stared at him, wondering if he was joking. "I was raised to care about what everyone thinks."

He chuckled. "Do your composure thing. Stand up, shoulders back, your lips straight, and your eyes direct. Like when you were sitting across the interview table from me, when Joe was interrogating me. Act aloof, as though you're above it all."

She laughed. "I didn't, and don't, act like that."

"You did and you do." His serious expression was transformed by a delicious, wicked smile. "But now that I've been inside of you, and listened to you scream my name as you come, I know better."

She tried not to blush as the cockpit door opened. They unfastened their seat belts and stood. The pilot who had greeted her earlier stepped out and nodded to them. Taylor squared her shoulders, put her chin up, and prayed that he hadn't heard her scream.

Chapter Fifteen

Before they stepped out of the jet, Brandon pulled Taylor to the side. In a nod to her sense of decorum, he made sure that both pilots were out of sight, and then bent his forehead to hers. Hazel-green eyes gazed into his as he kissed her, deeply.

At some point he'd realized that it wasn't simply that he wanted to have sex with her. He wanted all of her. Her mind, body, and everything about her, especially that low purr that was a verbal invitation to slide inside of her. Without breaking eye contact, he reached for the hem of her sundress and moved his hand to the inside of her leg. She sighed into his mouth as he lifted the dress and traced a line up her thigh.

"Well, well, well. You really are busy these days."

Son of a bitch.

Brandon broke the kiss and took his hands off of Taylor, as he turned towards Sebastian. At six feet five, Sebastian was an inch taller than him, and he had managed to climb the jet's boarding ladder without Brandon hearing him. Every female who worked for Brandon told Brandon that Sebastian was a gorgeous hunk of a man. He had dark brown wavy hair, a sculpted body, and dimples in both cheeks that made him perpetually boyish. Even Amy, who only had eyes for Brandon, would become mush when Sebastian worked his charms. Now, Sebastian had a shit-eating grin, and his blue eyes had a head start on laughter that Brandon didn't want to hear.

"Sebastian Connelly," Brandon said, stepping away from Taylor, "this is Taylor Bartholomew."

Taylor's cheeks were flushed with red, yet she drew a deep breath, smoothed her dress with her right hand, her hair with her left, and squared her shoulders. After only a second's hesitation, she extended a hand to Sebastian. "Hello."

"It is a pleasure to meet you, Taylor. Pete gave me your

schedule." Sebastian explained to Brandon, and when Brandon got a close look at his friend, he realized that the laughter had faded from his eyes and, in its place, there was worry. "I coordinated my arrival time with yours so that you could give me a ride. Didn't you see my jet when you landed?"

"I was busy," Brandon said.

"You should look happier to see me," Sebastian said. "After all, I dropped everything to fly here and meet my godson."

"Who said anything about you being his godfather?" Brandon gestured for Sebastian to lead the way, then led Taylor down the stairs.

Once in the car, Sebastian sat in the back seat and stared at Brandon in the rearview mirror. Blue eyes, filled with unasked questions, held Brandon's gaze. His friend didn't attempt chit-chat, and Sebastian's quiet manner as Brandon drove across town, to the Garden District, made him uncomfortable. Sebastian was usually only quiet when when he was seriously worried. He was miked, as always, to Black Raven's home office. A tiny telephone, almost invisible, was hooked to his ear. It was controlled by buttons on his watch band. As they drove, he received at least three phone calls that Brandon counted. He answered questions with short, almost cryptic, one-word answers, and at one point he simply said, "Ragno. Talk to me."

Taylor was quiet. She wore her sunglasses. Every now and then she glanced at Brandon, but with her calm, outward composure, and those damn shades, he had no idea what she was thinking. She pulled her phone out of her purse, and, out of the corner of his eye, he watched her type a text. On Saint Charles Avenue, she turned to look at her father's mansion. It was five minutes to six. Men in black pants and white shirts were unloading catering trucks in the side driveway. A white canopy covered a red-carpeted path that led from the sidewalk to the front door. The wrought iron archway that welcomed guests was decorated with greens and white flowers. A New Orleans Police Department horse trailer was in front of the house, indicating that mounted police officers would be providing security.

Taylor made a phone call. "Clara, the valet stand is too close to the Saint Charles corner. There will be a traffic jam." As Taylor gave instructions, she turned to get a better view of the house.

Brandon glanced in the rearview mirror, and saw that Sebastian watched as Taylor assessed the mansion. Sebastian locked eyes on Brandon. Sebastian mouthed a silent, *what the fuck?*

Taylor, still on the phone, asked, "Are there any problems?" She listened. After a pause, she added, "No." Taylor glanced at her phone and pressed a button. "Oh. Yes. He did. Twice." She sighed. "I'll call him. I'll be there in under an hour. Call me if you need anything."

Brandon walked Taylor to her door, then lifted her sunglasses so that he could see her eyes. Her gaze was weary, as though she was processing too much. "One minute, two minutes, three."

She stared at him. "Excuse me?"

"The night will be over before you know it," he kissed her forehead. "If you need a friendly voice, call me."

***

Taylor's body ached from her afternoon with Brandon, and she craved a steaming, hot bath. Before she stripped and stepped into the tub, she dialed her father, who answered with, "I've tried to call you."

"I know," she said, "sorry. I'm having phone issues."

"Claude won't be here tonight." Her father's disapproval was evident in his tone. She shut her eyes. Of course Claude wasn't going to be there. It hadn't been twenty-four hours since Collette's death. It was only natural for him to need time away from HBW duties. George continued, "So you need to help with business contacts. I need you here early so that I can give you names."

Taylor glanced at the clock. It was ten after six. "I'll be there by seven." She could make it there then, but she needed plenty of help. Carolyn knocked, then stepped into the bathroom. Taylor stripped and pulled her hair on top of her head in a tight ponytail, then looped the end of it so that it formed a bun. She didn't have time for her hair to get wet. She turned, caught a glimpse of her body in the mirror, and met Carolyn's wide-open eyes.

"Well, my goodness," Carolyn said as she and Taylor both got an eye full of small bruises, left by Brandon's thumbs, as he had gripped her hips. She turned, slightly. His fingertips had left bruises on her butt. Her left breast, inside of the nipple, had teeth marks and tiny suction bruises that seemed to darken as she stood there. More light teeth marks were on her right breast.

"Oh, no," Taylor said, warm with sudden embarrassment.

"We can cover all of that with clothes," Carolyn said. She stepped closer to examine the side of Taylor's neck. "But that bruise is going to require a lot of concealer, and your hair cannot go up tonight. I only hope the make-up doesn't rub off on the neck of that dress. It's low in the front, but high in the back." Carolyn studied Taylor's face. "Good Lord. You even have stubble burn on your chin. It's faint, now, but as the night wears on, it's going to smart. You're going to have to reapply concealer at the party. Now hurry. Get in the shower. There's not time for a bath. Make the shower cold. Warm water will make those bruises turn darker."

"I didn't realize he was leaving marks," Taylor mumbled, stepping into the cold shower, lathering, then stepping out. Bundled in a terry cloth robe, she sat at the make-up counter.

Carolyn studied Taylor's eyes, and gave a slow, knowing nod. "You're okay, right?"

Taylor nodded, "It was wonderful." She tried to stifle the need to cry, but when she drew a deep breath, fat tears started to fall.

Carolyn held Taylor's gaze in the mirror. "If it was wonderful, why are you crying?"

"I think I'm in love." The words came out even before Taylor had formed the thought. Carolyn's brow furrowed with concern. "I swear it's not only because we had sex, but, my God, it was unlike anything I've ever felt before."

"Well, of course not. Honey, you'd never had sex before. Great sex is well," Carolyn blushed, "it's great. There's nothing else like it."

Taylor shook her head. "This isn't just about the sex. He's amazing. Strong-willed. Smart. Stoic. He's witty and tough, but he's caring and considerate. He makes me feel as though I'm important to him. He studies me, as though he can't get enough of me. He sees *me*. Not a Bartholomew. No one," she frowned, "aside from you, and Andi, and Collette," fresh tears started as she said Collette's name, "no man has ever made me feel like they would think the world of me, even if I wasn't named Taylor Marlowe Bartholomew."

"If he makes you feel so wonderful," Carolyn asked, "why are you crying?"

Taylor explained the circumstances of Brandon's wife's death, how he almost killed himself with grief, and how he couldn't talk about his wife, or her death, even five years later. "He'll never love me. He won't let himself."

Carolyn shook her head. "I would think that a man who once loved a woman that much wants to love again."

"I know. That's what scares me. Because even if I could convince him to love me," Taylor drew a deep breath, "I shouldn't, because I'd be leading him on. We would never have a future. My father would never, ever accept him, for many, many reasons." Taylor's shoulders shook, and tears started flowing again. "I shouldn't have made love to him. I can't be casual about it and I can't move on, as Andi would say. It was," she paused, "so much more than a one-time thing. It felt like the beginning of something. Only there will never be anything there, because of my last name."

"Well, you are more than your last name. From what you've said, this man seems to know that," Carolyn said, "and one day, you're going to have to stand up to your father, otherwise he'll push you and push you until you're a shell of yourself. I don't know if this man is the reason to do it, but for now, Taylor, honey, please compose yourself. When your father couldn't get you on your cell, he called the house phone twice. He is in quite a mood. You need to get ready and go. Now."

***

When Brandon returned to the car, he found that Sebastian had moved to the front seat.

"You've lost your fucking mind."

Brandon had a good idea what Sebastian was talking about, and he didn't want to hear it. His thoughts were too muddled, his senses too raw.

"Drop it."

"You said Bartholomew when you introduced me to her, but it didn't occur to me that she was *that* Bartholomew." Sebastian knew Brandon's family history and, because Sebastian had been raised in the outskirts of New Orleans and still spent time in the city, he knew of the continued prominence of the Bartholomew family. "She's a blue-blooded heiress, for God's sake. Besides that," he narrowed his eyes as he studied Brandon, "she looks young."

"You don't get to weigh in on my choice of women," Brandon said. "Have you had any kind of meaningful relationship with a woman in the last, um, decade?"

"Don't make this about me. You're the one whose personal life is in a state of upheaval right now."

"At least I have a personal life."

"Fuck you too," Sebastian said, his tone serious. "So answer my question. What the hell are you doing falling in love with an heiress with the last name of Bartholomew?"

"I'm not in love," Brandon said as he drove. "Lust, maybe. Love? No."

"You were gazing into her eyes..."

Brandon's stomach twisted. "You almost caught us in the act, asshole."

"You didn't hear me walking up the freaking stairs, and I wasn't trying to be quiet."

"So I was looking into her eyes," he shrugged, "big deal."

"After being with her from Dallas to New Orleans, you didn't have enough? Nobody *gazes* like that unless they're in love. In the car, you kept glancing at her. I haven't seen you look at anyone like that since Amy."

"Leave Amy out of this. It isn't love. I just met Taylor. On Thursday, to be exact. Two days ago," Brandon said.

"So?" Sebastian retorted.

Aww hell. Brandon didn't want to hear what he knew was coming. He floored the accelerator, jumped past traffic, then veered into the exit lane, as he glanced at Sebastian in time to see his friend shrug and shake his head.

"You told me you were going to marry Amy after your first date, which occurred within twelve hours of meeting her," Sebastian said. "You and Amy never spent a night apart after your second date, which was the night after your first date. Amy reciprocated, at least."

Brandon tried to tell himself that he wasn't pissed, but Sebastian had finally gotten to him. He pulled into his neighborhood, forced himself to do the speed limit, then drew a deep breath and asked, "What the hell is that supposed to mean?"

"You don't fall often, Brandon, but when you do, you fall hard," Sebastian said, "and I can't freaking tell how this woman feels about you. Once her goddamn blush faded, she was cooler than ice."

Brandon shrugged. "So she's a challenge."

"Hah. I knew it. You are in love."

"Change the goddamn subject, Sebastian," Brandon said.

"How do you know her, anyway?"

Sebastian wasn't going to stop. Brandon couldn't start talking about how he knew Taylor, though, without giving details about Lisa. They sat in the garage, with the door open, and the air conditioning running, for another fifteen minutes. Brandon concluded with their trip to Dallas and told him what Rorsch had said.

"Has it occurred to you that you and Taylor have divergent interests?"

Brandon wanted to punch him. "Yes, asshole. But what we're really trying to figure out is whether this could be related to Lisa's murder and, when it comes to that, I don't think either of us cares very much about what happened in the past."

Sebastian frowned, as though he didn't believe Brandon. "I'll indulge you, for a while," Sebastian drew a deep breath, "so in 1944, your grandfather was convicted. According to Rorsch, your father obtained this letter, written by the first Andrew Hutchenson, in 1979, and the letter proves your grandfather's innocence. Your father tried to make the letter public, but nothing ever happened. Right after your father obtained the letter, your home burned in a fire, and, until now, you believed that all of your father's documents, including the letter, burned in the house. According to Rorsch, Taylor's father is somehow implicated in the cover up that took place in the late '70's, early '80's?"

Brandon nodded. "Yes, and Lisa had the Hutchenson letter. We know that, because Rorsch saw it. I've been through Lisa's house. The letter isn't there. Nothing she may have written about the letter is there."

"And the letter hasn't been made public before?"

Brandon nodded. "That's right. Lisa talked to the members of the HBW Board, George Bartholomew included. Her notes tell me that. I know that Rorsch advised her not to confront the HBW board members with the letter. I don't know whether she took his advice."

"Would anyone with HBW kill Lisa to keep the letter quiet?"

"Concealing a crime is one thing," Brandon shook his head, "murder is something else entirely. I just don't know."

"Victor always said that there was a man watching your house when it burned," Sebastian said, "didn't he?"

In the days after the fire, Victor's paranoia and anger took flight. Sebastian and Brandon had been inseparable friends then, and Sebastian had witnessed Victor's rages. "The fire was caused by a gas leak at the hot water heater," Brandon said, "no matter what Victor claimed."

Sebastian nodded. "That's what the officials told us then, but we're no longer kids. Think, would you? Men start gas leaks, Brandon. It happens every day. What if your father confronted the HBW board members with the letter? The first Andrew Hutchenson was dead and it's safe to assume that the board members weren't so happy about revealing the truth. Burning your father's letter would be a good way to make it go away."

"You're sounding like Victor."

"That's what I'm trying to do."

Brandon's heart started pounding.

Sebastian continued. "What do you think Victor would have done with this information? Today. Now. If he had known that

Lisa had the letter?"

No, Brandon thought, yet he couldn't deny it. *Fuck no.* The niggling workings of his instinct had manifested itself in a nightmare about Victor while he lay on Velvet's table. When Taylor told him of Collette's death, his instinct had also prompted certainty that the timing of her death wasn't a coincidence, and the thought that a sociopath could have killed her and masked it to look like suicide. He pounded his fist on the steering wheel as certainty hit him.

"Victor's not dead," Brandon said. There was no relief as he voiced the words. "Is he?"

Sebastian's cheeks were flushed and his blue eyes were deadly serious. "That's why I came here. I don't fucking know whether he is alive. It's driving me nuts and it's driving Ragno nuts. She never gets things wrong. Never. We're finding more and more discrepancies in his financial data. My hunch is that Victor planned his disappearance, and now, with everything weird-as-shit that you're talking about," Sebastian drew a deep breath, "what really keeps bugging me is that the few clues that I have as to where Victor might be are pointing here, or near here."

"Damn it to hell," Brandon said. "What clues?"

"Right before the explosion at the Ali Bin Laden compound, Victor, or someone using an alias that he used before, wired a sizable amount of cash to a New Orleans's law firm that specializes in real estate transactions. I've tried to get information from the firm, but that's a non-starter. Attorney client privilege," he said, "and they're invoking it, big time."

"Who is it?"

"Stone, Lipske, and Lewis."

"Well, that sucks. In addition to real estate transactions, they do insurance defense. I've won big against them, and I've had to play hard ball to do it. They won't be doing any favors for me. Besides that, they have notoriously high ethical standards and they won't bend on the attorney-client privilege."

"Property transfer records aren't online here," Sebastian added, "and the records office is closed for the Fourth of July holiday."

"NOPD might be able to get us to the records office, but still," Brandon shook his head, "it could require a court order to get the city to open the office outside of regular hours. On the weekend before the Fourth, I don't see a court order happening for a records search. It won't be officially open until Tuesday."

"I can get in unofficially," Sebastian said. "It will require a bit of planning. Problem is, this records search could take a while."

"Let me check if Marvin knows anyone who worked in the Orleans Parish Office of Mortgages and Conveyances."

"Marvin?"

"One of my local guys. With his local knowledge, in this arena, he's worth at least five Black Raven agents."

Sebastian ignored the comment, and continued, "Also, in the week after the explosion at the compound, an alias that Victor used for international travel in the past gave us a hit for travel from Frankfurt to Atlanta," Sebastian paused, "and the same name rented a car in Atlanta."

Brandon swallowed. "What kind of car?"

"A black Mercedes S550. Four doors."

"Son of a bitch." Brandon explained that a Mercedes look-alike had scared Taylor on Melody Street. Taylor had said that the man in the car had broad shoulders. Anton had seen a big black car. He had said the man was white. "Hell, I saw that car, watching us."

Sebastian continued, "Victor could be here. I wanted to tell you in person, even before I knew what you told me about Collette Westerfeld, and I wanted to tell you I'm sorry. I never should have told you that Victor was dead. Obviously, I didn't have enough information to make such a call."

"An apology isn't necessary," Brandon said, "but I appreciate the visit."

"I also need to see my godson."

"Careful. Not that you'd recognize the emotion, but you might actually fall in love."

Sebastian smiled. "I'll let you know if that happens." His eyes turned serious. "I really think Victor is here."

Brandon's mind spun with thoughts about what Victor would do if he had the information that Rorsch had told Brandon and Taylor. "If Victor thought that anyone with HBW had knowingly concealed the truth, he'd make them pay," Brandon said. "He'd hurt them. If he needed money, he'd do it financially. No matter what, if somehow he was here and focused on HBW, he'd find a way to make them suffer. Like my father suffered. But why now? After all these years?"

"Finding the Hutchenson letter could have been the catalyst," Sebastian said. "Plus, he's sick."

Brandon said, "He's always been sick."

"I'm not talking mentally," Sebastian said. "That's a given. He has some kind of cancer. We're still working on cracking the diagnosis codes for the Zurich Health Institute, but he's been in and out of there for the last four years. I now believe that he visited there after the date of the fire at the Bin Laden compound. The alias that he used then has an appointment in two weeks for what might be a bone marrow transplant. It looks like a year ago, he had a liver transplant, if we have that code right. He's spent millions on health care. Victor needs money and he needs to disappear," Sebastian paused, "because the slime-ball company that he previously worked for has a bounty on his head."

"Are you here to claim it?"

Sebastian shook his head. "Raven's don't go hunting to collect bounties, Brandon, and neither do our agents. We protect. There's a big difference, and you know that."

Brandon thought about the last meeting of Ravens, the men with ownership interest in Black Raven. Brandon had been there, serving as legal counsel. "The lines are getting blurred, though."

"True."

"There's no telling what Victor would do, once he unleashed his energy here." Brandon's stomach twisted as he remembered the glossy photograph on the cover of the magazine of the three best friends. He explained to Sebastian what Taylor had told him about Collette's death. "The coroner is calling it an accidental overdose."

Sebastian shook his head. "Timing is off."

"I know." Brandon glanced in his rearview mirror. "Mom's here," he said, watching Rose step out of her car with a box that was the size of a packet of printer paper, "and you've got a godson to meet." Sebastian and Brandon agreed not to tell Rose their doubts about Victor's death, or their suspicions that Victor might be in New Orleans. Being quiet in front of Rose about Victor's activities, whether or not they were certain of the activities, was something to which Brandon and Sebastian had long been accustomed.

Rose handed Brandon the box, then hugged Sebastian. "Sebastian," Rose said, "Brandon has told me about your findings. You know that I trust your judgment. But I believe that you're mistaken. I'd feel it if my son was dead," she shook her head, "and I don't feel it."

"I hope that you're right," Sebastian said, hugging her, while giving Brandon a hard glance. Brandon guided them into the kitchen area, where Laura was sitting in a barrel chair, holding Michael. Jett thumped her tail against Brandon's leg while he patted her on the head, then she did a jogging lap around Rose.

"My son," Brandon said, as Sebastian reached for the cooing, kicking bundle.

"My God."

"I know," Brandon said, "amazing, huh?"

Brandon nodded to Laura to let Sebastian feed Michael. As Anna arrived, Laura gave them all a quick run down on the day. Rose watched Sebastian hold Michael, and the worried look in her green eyes eased a bit. Laura left, and Anna, seeing that Michael had enough hands to tend him, took Jett for a walk.

"Mom," Brandon said, eyeing the box that his mother had brought with her, "I won't be angry with you, no matter what you tell me."

Sebastian stood, with Michael in his arms, as though he was going to give them space by leaving the kitchen area, but Brandon shook his head. "No. Stay," Brandon said. He watched as the nipple slipped out of Michael's mouth and formula dribbled on his chin. "Concentrate on what you're doing before you give him a bath in the stuff."

To Rose, he said, "Lisa's death is an open question, and I've got to try to resolve what happened," he paused, "for Michael. Phillip Rorsch today suggested that dad's documents weren't destroyed in the fire. He also suggested that Lisa may have gotten information from you. I need to know if that's true."

"I can't bear thinking about Lisa," Rose drew a deep breath, "that something I may have told her could have been a factor in her death."

Brandon thought that his heart was going to explode in his chest.

Hell. Holy fucking hell.

"Mom. What did you tell Lisa?"

***

At six thirty he stopped at a Brooks Brothers outlet and purchased the type of lightweight beach clothes that a normal, well-to-do male would wear on the Fourth of July weekend at the beach. He wore the clothes out of the store. He sat in the parking lot and, using his iPad, scoured the website for the Water's Edge community and their on-site map. Secure communities shouldn't post maps online, he thought, especially not maps with street addresses, with layouts of parcels of land, with legends that showed every detail of the community, even dotted lines that showed that the beaches there were public, as were all beaches in Florida. The house that was on the most secluded point of the Water's Edge property, on what he bet had been the most expensive parcel, was the Hutchenson house. He could avoid driving into the community entirely, and avoid the minor hassle of the guard gate, by parking his car in the adjacent state park and walking on the beach. He parked in an area with plenty of cars. The state park had a beach front, a wooded area with hiking trails, a campground where tents were allowed, fishing lakes, and a large pad where RV's were stationed.

At seven he walked along the beach, his sandals in his hand. He enjoyed the feel of the powder-fine, pure-white sand as he approached Water's Edge. Large sand dunes, some as high as two-story buildings, were covered with wispy sea oats that fluttered in the Gulf breeze. Aside from the broad expanse of pristine beach, the sand dunes were the hallmark of the development. The public park crowd was behind him and there were fewer people on the beach that fronted the gated development. Tall dunes separated the beach from the houses, and separated the houses from each other. The Water's Edge developers had built raised walkways throughout the community. The raised paths linked the houses and meandered around small interior lakes and dunes. The secluded walkways provided many, many opportunities for mayhem.

He didn't have to go to the house to find her. Andi was sitting on a beach towel, wearing gym shorts and a bikini top. She had her arms around her shins, with her legs drawn to her body. Her long brown hair was loose and blew with the wind. With her chin on her knees, she stared at the crashing waves, seemingly oblivious to anyone. While she gazed at the water, he went to the Hutchenson beach house. He entered through a side door with a lock that was easy to pick. He figured out which room was hers. He disengaged alarm contacts that would allow him to reenter the house when he came back to do his business with Andi Hutchenson, then he'd return to New Orleans, where Taylor waited.

Chapter Sixteen

"Mom? Did you say that you're worried that something that you told Lisa could have been a factor in her death?"

Rose nodded. Tears slipped from the corner of her eyes.

Son of a bitch.

"But yesterday you said that you didn't talk to her."

She frowned. "Well, now that you've talked to Phillip Rorsch, I can't keep denying the truth. I met with Lisa twice. Not only once, as I told you yesterday. The first time, I told her some things. The second time," she drew a deep breath and held Brandon's gaze, "I allowed her access to your father's documents."

His heart pounded. "She didn't tell me. Not that I wanted to talk about it, but she didn't even try to tell me."

"I allowed her access on the condition that she never talk to my children about the documents or the subject matter until after her dissertation was final, after the material became public."

Brandon drew in a deep breath. Well, hell. Rorsch wasn't crazy after all.

Rose continued, "I lied after the fire, I lied your entire life, anytime you asked me about it, and I even lied yesterday. That fire took my daughter. It broke your father, and it turned Victor into something," she paused, "something that scared me. Maybe he was like that before the fire, but, after the fire, I couldn't deny it. I wasn't going to let you delve into your father's obsessions. I wasn't going to lose you. The only good thing that the fire gave me was the ability to tell you children that your father's documents were destroyed. So that is what I did, to protect you from your father's obsession. I was scared that it would make you crazy as well."

With the reality shift that came with his mother's words, Brandon felt like he had been punched in the gut. "Where have the documents been all of these years?"

"Various places. In the beginning of this year, once my new office in the kennel was finished, I moved them out of a storage unit that I had kept for years." She shrugged, "I was tired of paying rent. Victor came to visit in January, right after I moved the documents there. I kept them in locked cabinets. I didn't think anyone, not you, Kate, or Victor, had ever looked at them, but now," she drew a deep breath, "I think Victor looked at them in January. The second time that I met with Lisa, after Victor was here in January, I let Lisa take some of the documents. Victor was here again shortly after that." She paused as tears dripped from her eyes. "He asked where the documents were. He always had a way of getting around a lock, you know. I didn't tell him that I'd given them to Lisa."

"Are you certain of that?" Brandon asked.

"I never mentioned Lisa to Victor." Fresh tears fell from her eyes. "Three months ago, when I met her for the second time, when I gave her the documents, Lisa was eight months pregnant. I didn't know anything about her circumstances. I didn't know that she was carrying your child. She didn't share her personal life with me. I wanted to be rid of the burden that your father's work placed upon me. She provided an opportunity for the true story to be told. Maybe the truth was simply going to sit in a scholarly article." She shrugged. "I didn't care what the end result was. I just felt like there was a chance the facts could be aired by someone who was objective." She drew a deep breath. "A few days after I gave the material to Lisa, Victor was there, and somehow, he knew that some originals were gone," she shuddered, "and he was furious. I was worried. Worried that he'd try, some way or another, to get them from her, so I didn't tell him who had the original. He left that night."

"Victor's last visit. When was that?" Brandon asked.

"Right after I met with Lisa. Almost three months ago. Something about him," she shuddered. "He had aged. He was thin. It's as though life has gotten the best of him, and he's always had a dark side, even as a child. I wasn't blind." She drew a deep breath. "And he always behaved when I was around, but I knew that I couldn't influence him. I knew that he tormented you, but that you never told me about it."

Brandon hated that his mother looked so worried, but he had no words to make her feel better about Victor. His pulse beat fast as he asked, "Was there a letter, drafted by the first Andrew Hutchenson, that you let Lisa take?"

"Yes. Your father had an original. I gave it to Lisa. It had a raised seal. I have copies." His heart pounded, as Rose gestured to the box that he had carried into the kitchen for her.

Brandon lifted the lid of the box, his eyes drawn to the handwritten, scripted words. The top document was a copy. It wasn't notarized and it didn't have signatures of witnesses. Maybe the original document's raised seal would be an indicator of authenticity, but without a damn good handwriting expert, or an admission by someone who saw Andrew Hutchenson write the document, the copy would not be admissible in court as evidence.

"I gave the original to Lisa, but I kept the many copies that your father had made," Rose said. "Victor was furious that I gave the original away."

To the current members of the HBW Board, Marcus Morrissey, and Lloyd Landrum,

It is 1979. My death is near. I write of a heinous wrong that I and others perpetuated. In 1940, George Bartholomew Sr., Charles Westerfeld, and I panicked when the military wasn't interested in purchasing the landing craft. At the time, HBW&M had no other designs under military contract and we could not keep our company afloat. Benjamin Morrissey wasn't bothered by his lack of money. He was a simple man who was used to living in a lean manner. Bartholomew, Westerfeld, and I were facing financial ruin. We conceived a plan to sell the design of our worthless landing craft. We decided to use Morrissey's name, the name of our least powerful partner, as it was plausible that he would have the information, and we did not want to sully our own names. At the time, we did not believe that Morrissey would be in jeopardy of being caught. However, because Morrissey had already designed the landing craft, his value was limited. He was expendable.

Bartholomew established communication with German spies who had infiltrated the Gulf Coast. When Bartholomew agreed to the terms of an exchange, we did not dream that the landing craft would become a military secret of the United States. We were simply making the Nazis believe that we were selling something that was priceless, when in reality, we were selling worthless plans for a boat that would never be built. Immediately after Bartholomew set up the exchange, the disinformation that we had attempted to sell became real contracts. We panicked. We contacted authorities with an anonymous tip that Morrissey would be meeting the Nazi spies. We did not know then that Bartholomew's contact was really an undercover agent of the U.S. We only learned that fact after Morrissey was apprehended.

Once Morrissey was arrested, I was sickened over the fact that my actions would lead an innocent man to be convicted. I wanted to contact my sources in the Government and attempt to have the charges dropped, even if it meant confessing my involvement. Bartholomew and Westerfeld persuaded me otherwise by appealing to my greed and my pride. With Morrissey out of the way, we did not have to share profits with him. More importantly, the boat would be known as the Hutchenson Landing Craft. I would receive credit as the original designer. I wanted MY name on the boat that would ultimately be used to defeat the Nazis.

I allowed Morrissey to be blamed for our crime.

Although George Bartholomew Sr. and Charles Westerfeld have predeceased me, and did not breathe a word of this to anyone, I cannot go to my grave without telling the truth. I apologize to all who have suffered, and who will suffer, because of my lie.

May God have mercy on my soul.

"I hope the son of a bitch is burning in hell," Brandon said. For the first time in his life, Brandon understood the depth of his father's frustration. He handed the letter to Sebastian. In exchange he received Michael, who had finished the bottle. Brandon grabbed a soft yellow cloth from a basket that sat next to the pack-n-play, placed it on his shoulder, and held Michael in one hand, balancing him against his shoulder. With his free hand, Brandon looked through other documents. There were multiple copies of the Hutchenson letter and below those, there was correspondence between his father and Lloyd Landrum, dated in 1980 and 1981.

To Rose, Brandon asked, "Victor saw these letters to Lloyd Landrum?"

Rose nodded.

"Then it didn't matter that you didn't tell Victor that you gave the original Hutchenson letter to Lisa. These letters could have prompted Victor to go to Landrum, who could have told Victor about the Tulane student who was about to expose the Hutchenson letter to the world."

She shook her head. "What are you saying?"

Brandon drew a deep breath, then decided to be as direct as always. "Victor would have figured out a way to profit from the Hutchenson letter, mom. I think that once he saw this letter, he planned to destroy those who kept the letter secret. He would have made sure that Lisa was incapable of making it public. He would have claimed the original for himself."

Rose drew in a deep breath, but she didn't try to tell Brandon that he was wrong. "I'm sorry, Brandon. At some point before now, I should have let you know about all of this."

Yes, she should have, but she hadn't. He reached across the table and gripped her hand with his free hand. "I'm glad that you told me today. I'll figure this out, mom. Don't worry." He paused. "What about all of those drawings of the landing craft that dad had?"

She shook her head. "Those did not survive the fire."

He swallowed back his disappointment, because the

original drawings would be further proof that his grandfather had been the original designer.

"I need air," Brandon said, as Anna returned with Jett. He handed Michael to Anna, then stepped into the backyard. Sebastian followed him. He turned to Sebastian. "If you wanted to destroy someone as powerful as George Bartholomew, what would you do?"

"Take his money."

"What else? I mean really destroy him."

"Go after someone he loves."

Brandon held Sebastian's gaze as he dialed Taylor. He glanced at his watch. It was a couple of minutes past seven.

Answer, he thought. *Please answer.*

It took three rings, but she did.

"My mother has a copy of the Hutchenson letter. She gave the original to Lisa."

Taylor gasped. "Did Rorsch accurately describe the contents?"

"Yes," Brandon said. "Exactly."

There was silence as she digested the ramifications. "I'm shocked."

"I know," he said.

"I have to walk into the party," Taylor said, "and I need to do it now. I'm sitting in my car, outside of my father's house, and I'm late."

"There's more," he said.

"It has to wait."

"It can't," he said. "I'm worried that you could be in danger."

"Brandon," she said, as he heard a car door shut, "I don't have time to talk about this. Besides, this party has security, and lots of it. The idea that I could be in danger here is preposterous."

"Taylor," he said, as his tension built, tightening the muscles in his upper back and neck. "This is more important than the damn party. Stop. Listen to me for a few minutes."

"Right now nothing is more important than this party," she said, "and I'm late. I'll call you as soon as I can. Okay?"

Son of a bitch. She wasn't exactly blowing him off, but, well, she was.

As Brandon ended his call with Taylor, Sebastian leaned against the back door and shook his head, his blue eyes full of skepticism. "Do you really think that she didn't know about the Hutchenson letter?" Sebastian asked. "She's a Bartholomew, for God's sake."

"Taylor said today that she didn't know of it and she sure as hell sounded surprised just now." Brandon sat in one of the chairs that was at the pool. He breathed, deep.

Once.

Twice.

He had to calm the hell down, because frustration led to anger. He didn't need to go down that road. He needed to think. Rationally. "Victor has to be using the original of the Hutchenson letter to profit. It was worthless if Lisa exposed it to the world, so Victor stopped her. Victor could be using it to extort the HBW Board."

"Given what I know of your brother," Sebastian said, "and given the personal stake that he'd feel with this information, I'm not sure that he'd stop with financial extortion."

Brandon nodded. "That's what I'm worried about. What if Collette's death wasn't an accident? What if he's trying to send a bigger message to them? Like pay, or else others will die. Or maybe he wants to make them miserable, like they made my grandfather's life miserable and my father's life miserable. If I wanted to make George Bartholomew's life a living hell, I'd go after Taylor. She's his only child. Hell," Brandon tried to shake off the foreboding feeling that he couldn't contain. He was sweating, damn it, as he rose and paced along the side of the pool. His phone rang. When Brandon answered, Marvin said, "Yo. Tilly will be at NOPD headquarters in Joe Thompson's custody in ten mins."

"Thanks, Marvin."

Brandon brought Marvin up to speed on the Hutchenson letter and his concerns about Victor. Marvin was silent for a few seconds, long enough for Brandon to wonder if he'd told Marvin enough about the historical angle for Marvin to grasp the potential importance of the facts to Lisa's death. Marvin said, "That's some crazy shit. So you think your brother went after Lisa so he could use the letter against the HBW Board, and that Taylor, she's a Bartholomew, right?"

Brandon chuckled with relief. Marvin got it. "Yeah." He explained a few more things about Victor.

Marvin said, "Sounds like we gotta be prepared for almost anything."

"That's exactly right," Brandon said. "Hey, do you know anyone who works in the Orleans Parish Office of Mortgages and Conveyances? I need to get in there this weekend."

"Let me do some thinking on that one."

After their conversation, Brandon showered and changed into a suit. When he went down the stairs, he found Sebastian in the study, on his phone, with three computer monitors working. Brandon's computers were password-protected, but that wouldn't stop Sebastian, who broke the phone connection as he eyed Brandon's attire.

"Are we going out?"

"We? No. I'm going to the Second District station." Brandon told Sebastian about Tilly, who Joe was going to be interviewing there. "Then after that, I'm going to a party. Anything new on Victor?"

"No, but I'm working on it. Two of my best analysts are pulling a Saturday night shift back in Denver. Two of my field agents are on the way here. Just in case." Sebastian frowned. "From what I could tell of your side of the conversation, it didn't sound to me like Taylor invited you to the mansion for the party."

"She didn't. It's a fundraiser, though. I don't think they'll turn away people who write checks at the door."

Sebastian stood. "I'll go to the station with you. After, can you drop me off at the condo?" Brandon nodded. Sebastian kept a condo and a SUV in the warehouse district. "And if you're going to that party to confront George Bartholomew, I have to go with you."

"Confront him?" Brandon shook his head. "I'm not planning on it."

Sebastian shook his head. "I'm not sure I believe you."

"Look. I'm not my brother. I'm rational. George Bartholomew and the rest of the HBW Board obviously didn't publicly air the Hutchenson letter. However, I don't have hard evidence that tells me exactly what they did, so I'm not going to barge into his house and accuse him of anything. Plus, investigators looked into the fire at our house and they didn't find evidence of foul play, so I'm certainly not going to blame George Bartholomew for it, thirty years after it happened. Right now, I care about figuring out what happened to Lisa," Brandon paused, "and I care about Taylor. I'm going there to warn George Bartholomew about Victor."

On the way to the station, Brandon called Pete. It took most of the fifteen minute ride to give Pete what Brandon felt he needed to know about Victor. "Until I figure this out, I need you at my house. There might be nothing to this, but keep the alarm on, your favorite weapons nearby, and be on the look out. I don't know what Victor will do. If he murdered Lisa, I'm bringing him down," Brandon paused. His brother wouldn't voluntarily surrender to authorities. There'd be a fight. His stomach twisted. He had to prepare himself for all possibilities. "Once he realizes that, then I'm a target. If I don't have my own eyes on Michael, I want your eyes on him. I'm not scared of much..."

"Hell," Pete said, "I know that."

"My brother scares the living shit out of me."

"Say no more. I'm headed to your house now," Pete said. "Michael will be safe."

"Corey, Marvin's son, will be back-up and he's bringing Boy, a big, beautiful Rottweiler."

"Cool," Pete said.

Brandon broke the connection as he pulled into the station's parking lot. Sebastian, who had listened to the conversation, said, "Good call."

With those words, the night got darker.

"Great," Brandon said. "Fucking great."

"What?"

"I was hoping that you'd tell me I was being paranoid."

"Not in my book," Sebastian answered. "I called in some Black Raven agents. We need to find your brother, and we need to do it fast."

Tilly and Joe were in the interview room. Brandon and Sebastian joined Marvin and Joe's partner, Tony, in the adjoining room, where they could see and hear the interview. Tony said, "I told Joe that you were on your way. He'll take a break when he feels it's right. So far, Tilly's admitted that he told Marquis Rochard and a couple of others that he killed Lisa, but Tilly now says that he was lying. He wanted to get into the Kings, as we thought." Tony shook his head. "This kid's got no sense, because killing a harmless college student isn't the way to get into the Kings. Now, Joe is trying to figure out what else Tilly might know, if anything, and Tilly has clammed up."

"Oh. I'm sorry," they heard Joe saying. "I forgot to wish you a happy eighteenth birthday. It was three months ago, right?"

Tilly wore an oversized New Orleans Saints football jersey, three long, thick gold chains, and a black rosary with an silver crucifix. A gold baseball cap, which sat on the table, had left an imprint in his short afro. His skin was dark black. Brandon couldn't see his eyes or his facial expression because the wiry teenager was looking down, at the table.

Joe continued. "Did you know that the fact that you're eighteen makes you eligible for the death penalty?" Tilly shrugged, but didn't look up. Joe continued, "I love the death penalty. It's a shame those appeals take so long. Because once you're convicted, you're going to be sitting on Angola's death row for a long time. You won't be in candy land with other juvies. The Angola inmates are going to have plenty of time to get a piece of your sweet, eighteen-year-old ass."

The kid finally looked up. His lips were in a sneer, but there was fear in his wide, dark eyes. "You don't scare me. I didn't do nothing. So what if I lied?"

"Well that goes to show how stupid you are, because you've all but admitted that you killed her. I'd be shitting on myself if I were you."

"I didn't do it, and you ain't got evidence that says I did."

"You told Marquis Rochard that you did it, and others, and you admitted that you told them. Why? Why the hell would you be bragging to these people if you didn't do it, and how the hell did you even know that it happened if you didn't do it?" Tilly chewed on his lower lip then spent several long minutes examining the table as he ignored Joe.

"Oh," Joe said, "another thing. You told Marquis that you shot her in the head. No one knows that. No one but me, my partner, the coroner, and the killer. So, you're not me, you certainly aren't my partner, and you aren't the fucking coroner. That only leaves one other possibility. So happy eighteenth birthday, cause that gives you two things to look forward to now."

Tilly glanced at Joe, then back down at the table.

"Two things. Prison rape and death by lethal injection."

Brandon watched Tilly look into Joe's eyes. The punk's sneer was gone. There was a pleading glance in his eyes.

"I need protection."

"From what?"

"The killer."

"Why?"

Tilly gave Joe another long, pleading stare. "He was freaky. He wasn't a homeboy. Hell. I know most of the people in that neighborhood. It was a hit. An honest to God, professional hit," his black eyes were wide with fear. "I swear. I don't want that dude coming after me."

Brandon drew a deep breath. "Well, I'll be damned. He saw the murder."

Joe leaned forward. "You saw it?"

Tilly nodded. "The whole thing. I knew she was shot in the head because I saw it happen."

Joe said. "Tell me about it."

"There's an abandoned house that I sleep in sometimes on Melody Street. I was on the lookout that night for some punks, so I was paying attention to street noise. Not too many people know my secret spot, but some do. Anyways, this guy pulled up and got out of his car. Dude drove a fancy black Mercedes sedan with tinted windows. I was like, where the fuck this dude be going on that dumpy street? He got out of his car and stood near some bushes. I was like, what the fuck? What's he hiding for? It was creepy as shit."

"What did he look like?"

"Tall. Sort of had muscles, like he worked out, but sort of thin. Pale white face. He had on a cap, but fuck, it was hotter than hell, and muggy too. He took off the cap once and wiped his forehead with it. He didn't have no hair. She walked up, and then I saw the gun that he'd been holding. He moved fast, man. Didn't see the gun before then, cause it blended in with all that black shit he had on. Dude even wore gloves. He lifted that gun, pulled her by the hair, and pressed it against her head. I was too far away to tell what it was. It was black. Maybe a Glock. He had an awesome silencer, because I didn't even hear a pop. I didn't know silencers could be so good, ya know? It was like a whisper. The homemade jobs don't do that. You always hear something. A pop. Or a whoof. This one, well, I barely heard anything. I saw her fall."

In the outside room, Brandon glanced at Tony. "Did ballistics come in consistent with the use of a silencer?"

Tony nodded. "And a silencer that would be that quiet would be a damn good one."

Joe asked, "Then what?"

"He grabbed her shit and left her there. He walked to his car and that's when he hit a part of the sidewalk where the streetlights shone. He looked my way, but by then I was so far in the shadows, there was no way he was seeing me, and that's when I saw his eyes." Tilly paused. "I'll never forget that dude's eyes."

"Why?"

"They were this weird shade of green-gold. Fucking freaky, in that white face, with the streetlight shining on them. About the only thing I ever saw with eyes that color was a cat."

"What else?"

"That's all I got. I didn't see anything else."

Joe stood. He entered the surveillance room. He looked at Brandon, then Sebastian. Instead of greeting them, Joe said,

"Fuck." Joe had known Sebastian when Sebastian was on the force with Brandon. The two had become reacquainted two years earlier when Brandon had killed the intruder. After a second, Joe added, "If the two of you are here together, looking that serious, it tells me the fast train to hell has left the station. Start talking."

Brandon told Joe everything that he could about Rorsch, the Hutchenson letter, how it was connected to Lisa, and Collette, and then he polished it all up with his concerns about Victor. He concluded with, "I think Tilly just described Victor. Let Tilly see me. I look like Victor," Brandon shrugged. "Sort of. We're about the same height. His face was always thinner. Our eyes are the exact same color, except his might have a tinge of light brown. In the dark of night, with streetlights, I would imagine that the light brown tint could look gold."

Joe frowned. "That would be quicker than getting an artist to draw what Tilly saw, and if he says yeah, that's the dude, well then, case closed. I get to arrest you, because you're identified as a murderer, and then I can go home for the night and get a great night of sleep."

Sebastian shook his head. "Brandon, I don't think so. Weren't you a suspect as recently as two days ago?"

Sebastian had gone to law school with Brandon, but had never practiced law. Still, Sebastian knew enough about the law, from both a legal perspective and a cop perspective, to make Brandon pause. Then he shook his head. "If he identifies me as the killer, there's several ways to get this identification thrown out. Overly suggestive. Not a proper line-up. Whatever. Let him look at me."

"If you're not going to take my advice, call Randall," Sebastian said, his eyes serious. "He would advise you not to do this."

"I'm not expecting Tilly to finger me. I'm expecting him to say, sort of, but that's not him," Brandon said. "I'd bet my life on it."

Sebastian said, "You might be."

"Hell, I'm game," Joe said.

With Brandon on one side of a one-way window, Joe let Tilly get a good look at Brandon. After, Joe said, "It went exactly as you said it would. Tilly said you were sort of like the guy that he saw, but the guy that he saw seemed leaner than you, and bald. There's more angles in his face than in your face. Your eyes, though, Brandon, were just like the perps. Except, according to Tilly, your eyes didn't glow as much. No shit. He really said the word, *glow*."

"Find my brother, and you've found Lisa's killer." Brandon thought through a few scenarios of how to approach George Bartholomew and tell him that his daughter was a potential target of someone who wouldn't think twice about killing her.

"Joe," Brandon said. "Want to go to a party with me?"

Chapter Seventeen

Clara pointed Taylor in the direction of the study, where George was reviewing the guest list with Andrew and Andrew's two oldest sons, Phillip and Mark. Her father and Andrew wore neat seersucker suits and white dress shirts. Phillip and Mark wore cream-colored linen suits. Tom Hood, HBW director of security, was there, his earpiece evident, and Lloyd Landrum stood next to George, who stopped in mid-sentence at Taylor's entrance. He gave her a dark-eyed appraising glance, accompanied with a frown due to her late arrival, then returned his attention to papers that he held in his hand. Judith, her father's secretary, crossed the room and handed Taylor a paper that contained names of important guests, with details about each name.

"Taylor, I'd like you to remember these names in particular," George said, as he rattled off names. John, her father's personal assistant, was at the computer. Photographs of each person appeared on a large computer monitor that hung from the wall. "All three have authority regarding the submarine contracts." George said some other names and remarked upon their military standing. John showed more photographs that Taylor tried to commit to memory. "The senators from Louisiana are here and also, because we're doing the full court press for the contracts, our competitors are here."

The private meeting ended, and, after a champagne toast, led by George, "To submarines," they all took their positions at various places in the house and on the grounds. Taylor and George, the official hosts, stood in the foyer, a few feet from the reception desk. Taylor followed Brandon's advice and focused on one minute, then two, then three. She tried not to think about the Hutchenson letter, but a hard knot of dread was in the back of her throat.

She believed Brandon.

She believed that his mother had something, but whatever document she had, it couldn't be true. It just couldn't be. Her grandfather and her father couldn't be the bad guys. The bad guy had been Brandon's grandfather. A jury had convicted him. In his phone call, Brandon had spoken with urgency. Something was wrong, because, from what she could tell, Brandon didn't overreact. She had ended the conversation quickly so that she could get to the pre-party meeting and appease her father, but now she needed to know what was wrong.

Taylor made small talk about the July heat with a woman whose name she should have known, but couldn't remember. As soon as that guest stepped away, a male guest gripped Taylor's forearm and introduced himself. He was one of the people on her list, someone who had authority over the submarine contract. He introduced her to his wife, who had a pretty, easy smile.

One minute. Two minutes. Three minutes.

For an hour, Taylor greeted guests while at her father's side in the front entrance. At nine, she took a break, retrieved her purse from the study, and climbed the stairs to her old bedroom on the third floor. She took her cell phone from her purse to call Brandon. Before dialing, she saw that at eight p.m. Andi had sent her a picture of the beach, with soft evening sunlight casting a pinkish hue on crashing waves, and a text, *"Collette would have liked this gorgeous sunset. Hope you're doing ok. Sorry I'm not there with you. Can you talk? Dying to hear about your day."*

Taylor responded, *"Party ends at 11:30. I'll be in bed by midnight. I'll call you then."*

"Great. Leaving beach now. Can't wait to talk to u. Status of your v. pledge?"

Taylor chuckled because Andi couldn't resist. She responded, *"Gone."*

"Moved on?"

Taylor hesitated. She glanced at herself in the dresser mirror and automatically reached into her purse for concealer to cover the bruised area on her neck. She wanted more. More time with him, more kisses, more touches. More times when she could make him laugh. More. To say that she wasn't ready to move on was an understatement. *"Not quite. Still reeling from it all."*

"Maybe u shouldn't move on."

Taylor was about to dial Brandon when George knocked, then opened the bedroom door. "I'm sorry, Taylor. I know that Collette was a good friend. Thank you for rising to the occasion and attending the party." Taylor hadn't expected empathy or appreciation, and those two emotions, coming from her father, added a new jolt to the roller coaster ride that she'd been on ever since learning of Lisa's death, from her first glimpse of Brandon, to Collette's death, to the flight home from Dallas. He continued with, "You're doing a fine job."

Her father's approval, something that she had always wanted, was something that she had rarely received. A quiet, "Thank you," was all she could say.

"Shall we return to the multitudes?" He gestured for her to walk ahead of her.

She hesitated. He was there. She had his attention. She wanted to know what he would say about Rorsch's comments, and, taking a page from Brandon's playbook, she chose the most direct route possible.

"What does the Hutchenson letter actually say?"

"Excuse me?"

Good God, Taylor thought, as she watched her father's eyes widen and his face lose all color. His reaction told her that Rorsch wasn't a crazy, hallucinating old man. The Hutchenson letter actually existed, and if it could make her father go pale, it must say exactly what Rorsch had suggested. She reminded herself to breathe, but the ball of anxiety in her throat wouldn't allow the air to hit her lungs.

"Did you just ask me about the Hutchenson letter?"

She nodded.

He narrowed his eyes. A small bit of color returned to his cheeks. "How do you know of it?"

"Lisa Smithfield," she said, "the Tulane student who was murdered. Her research led me to it."

He studied her. "Did she have the letter? Do you have the letter?"

"No," Taylor said, forcing herself to think and not give in to anxiety. With rational thoughts, she was able to breathe, and then able to speak. "There's a trail that suggests that she had it. The letter explains that Benjamin Morrissey was innocent, doesn't it? That the three men who originally founded HBW let Morrissey be falsely convicted of treason."

George's dark eyes, deadly serious, held her gaze. He gave her a slow nod. "That is exactly what the letter says," he paused. A steel-trap door of anxiety threatened to close off her throat, making breathing impossible. "The letter is a fraud."

She gasped. She shook her head. "A fraud?"

"Yes," he said. "A total fabrication."

Momentarily blindsided by his instant dismissal, she shook her head. "What do you mean?"

When George saw her reaction, he said, "Goodness. Please don't tell me that you've fallen for that outlandish conspiracy theory. The letter was prepared by Benjamin Morrissey's crazy son, who was obsessed with his claim that his father was innocent, and the content of it is nothing but a lingering conspiracy theory regarding the Benjamin Morrissey treason case. The conspiracy theory resurfaces every other decade or so. I'm afraid that Lisa Smithfield had fallen for it."

Palpable relief coursed through Taylor and de-iced her veins. Thank God. He had an explanation. She was able to breathe, really breathe. *Hutchenson. Letter. Hoax.* Those were the three words that Taylor had overheard the day before, and the words now made sense. Even Brandon said that his father had been obsessed. Had Marcus Morrissey been that crazy? Thank God. There was an explanation, and it made sense, more sense than thinking that her grandfather had committed a crime and framed someone else. The explanation made much more sense than thinking that her own father was complicit in concealing a confession by the first Andrew Hutchenson.

"Do you have any further questions?"

Her mind flashed to Brandon, the day before, at the museum. Telling her how his father would show him the drawings, night after night, and that the drawings were signed by his grandfather. "Who actually designed the landing craft? Who put pen to paper, did the drawings, did the engineering? Hutchenson or Morrissey?"

He frowned. "Why do you ask?"

She drew a deep breath. "Lisa Smithfield believed Morrissey did the design, but didn't receive the credit."

"That's part of the conspiracy theory. The reality, as far as I know, is that Andrew Hutchenson designed it," George said. "Benjamin Morrissey was a minor player. He had some innate knowledge, but not enough to put his ideas on paper in a meaningful way, much less go from paper to the beaches of Normandy." He frowned. "Any other questions?"

A million, she thought, but she couldn't articulate any. She was too busy wrapping her mind around relief.

"Then we have a house full of guests who need our attention."

She replaced her phone and make up in her purse, then carried it with her so that it would be in the first floor study and close to her, in case the bruise on her neck started to show through the make-up. She followed George and, as she started down the curving staircase that led from the third floor to the foyer, she glanced to the first floor, where one guest in particular captured her attention and made her heartbeat soar. Brandon was in the entry way, bending slightly to listen to a woman who was working the reception desk. He turned towards the stairway. She watched him look around the grand foyer, his eyes taking in the sparkling chandelier, the oil paintings that adorned the walls, and then his eyes fell on her, his expression, for a moment, unreadable. In a navy-blue suit, light blue dress shirt, and a tie with green, yellow, and blue, he looked elegant and gorgeous. Joe was at Brandon's side. Joe was wearing clothes that fit in with the party, or at least with the men who had decided that dress pants and a sports coat were formal enough for a hot Saturday night in July. Nothing about Joe's appearance suggested that he was a policeman, but as Joe scanned the entryway, the grim look in his eyes indicated that he wasn't there for fun.

Taylor knew the moment her father saw the star of the Morrissey Minute, the man whose law firm had more than twenty lawsuits pending against HBW Shipbuilding Enterprises, the man whose not-quite-sane father had drafted the Hutchenson letter. George and Taylor were midway down the curving stairway when her father stiffened and muttered, under his breath, "Well, what the hell." Brandon and Joe were both looking at them. "Do you know them?" George asked.

"Yes," she said, while Brandon's eyes held hers. She glanced at her father, and said, "Yes, I do."

There were questions in her father's eyes, but she glanced away. When they reached the final stair, Brandon and Joe stepped towards them. "Brandon Morrissey," Taylor said, "New Orleans Police Officer Joe Thompson. My father. George Bartholomew."

***

Taylor's introduction came as Brandon told himself, *It was just a house. A damn big house, but just a house.* Brandon had almost succeeded in not being bothered by his surroundings, until he entered the foyer and saw a spotlighted oil painting. In it, Taylor was flanked by her parents. The canvas was at least eight feet tall, yet it wasn't too large for the formal entryway. A slightly younger version of Taylor was standing in a formal, white, sheath-like sleeveless dress and long white gloves. A glistening diamond tiara was perched in her long, golden brown hair. Brandon knew that women who were Mardi Gras royalty in the exclusive krewes and women who were debutantes wore tiaras at various social events. But Taylor didn't look like a mere carnival queen or a silly debutante. In the painting, she looked like real royalty, not pretend royalty. She looked like she belonged there, with a crown of diamonds in her hair, in the mansion, at the pinnacle of society in New Orleans.

Fuck. The very thought rattled the hell out of him.

Tonight, she was gorgeous, in a form fitting ivory-colored dress, with her hair flowing to the middle of her back. Composure had robbed her face of expression. She had the look of a polite, gracious host of an important social event, present, but her mind on a million other things. Brandon couldn't equate this version of Taylor with the images of her that were implanted on his mind, images of a grief-stricken woman, an inquisitive woman who had not wanted to believe Rorsch's theory, and a sensual woman looking up at him with passion as he made love to her.

As Taylor introduced Brandon and Joe to her father, Brandon forced himself to turn from her to George. George was almost Brandon's height. He stood erect. He wasn't smiling. His dark-eyed attention was focused on Brandon, then Joe, then back to Brandon. He gave them an abrupt nod, but didn't offer his hand.

Joe said, "Mr. Bartholomew, I'm the detective who is working the Lisa Smithfield murder case. I need to talk to you and Andrew Hutchenson."

"We're busy," George said with a slight head shake.

"So am I," Joe said.

A slight pink flush crawled up Taylor's cheeks. She glanced at Brandon with a pained expression, but it was there for only a second, then she put on her unreadable party face.

"My house is full of important guests," George said. "You are welcome to enjoy the party, but if this visit is about police work, you may contact my office and set up an appointment for after the Fourth. This isn't the place or time."

Brandon had tried to be open-minded, but his openness ended with George's words and the superior tone that he used. He decided that George was a pompous bastard.

Joe responded, "Then I'll start talking here. In front of your important guests."

A man with an earpiece approached with a questioning look. George gave a slight head shake to the man, and said, "Find Andrew and Tom."

George gestured to Brandon and Joe to follow him though a thick-paneled doorway, off the foyer, and into a study. Taylor, for a fleeting moment, was at Brandon's side, then, as Brandon slowed his pace to allow her to step ahead of him, he detected a faint wisp of her gardenia-scented perfume. He wanted to take Taylor away from there, to take her anywhere where decorum didn't strip the life out of her eyes. George's superior attitude had inspired a banal reaction, and he felt like telling George that Taylor belonged with him.

She's mine now. Mine. And with me, she can be whatever the hell she wants to be.

The thought sent panic through his gut, because, once in the study, where Taylor deposited her small evening bag on a desk, then stood closer to her father than to him, the message in her body language made him realize that merely claiming her wouldn't make it so.

Brandon watched George look at his daughter. "Taylor, I need you to tend to the guests."

She shook her head. "I'm general counsel. I need to be here."

"If this were anything serious," George said, with a slight shake of his head, "that would be true."

"It may not be serious to you, Mr. Bartholomew, but," Joe said, "I can assure you that this murder investigation is very serious."

Joe's words inspired the full wrath of George's glare. Brandon and Joe had discussed how they would proceed, with Joe taking the lead, but Brandon didn't have patience. He pulled a copy of the Hutchenson letter out of his pocket and pressed it into George's hands. George looked at the piece of paper. He put it down on his desk, dismissing it as though it was yesterday's newspaper. Taylor reached for it. Color left her face as she read the first few sentences, then her eyes held Brandon's, as George started to chuckle.

Son of a bitch. Brandon said, "You think this is funny?"

"You do know, Mr. Morrissey," George said, "that the letter is a fraud. A hoax."

"No," Brandon said, his eyes bouncing from George to Taylor. Her eyes conveyed pain, but not surprise. "I don't know that."

"It is quite simple," George said. "Andrew Hutchenson did not write this letter."

Brandon's heart did a stutter beat. "Then who the hell did?"

"Your father."

"No," Brandon said, feeling the world tilt off-kilter as Taylor glanced at him, then looked away. "My father would not have done this."

"Your father was a sick, pathetic man who was unable to

make anything of himself, except what his obsession with his own father's purported innocence would allow."

The study door opened. Three men entered the room. "Andrew Hutchenson," George said, to a man who was dressed in a seersucker suit, "meet Brandon Morrissey and NOPD Officer Joe Thompson." Andrew Hutchenson was a little bit shorter than George. He had a full head of gray hair and blue eyes. He looked to be about George's age and seemed like a kinder, more genteel version of George. At least he didn't automatically look down his nose at Brandon. Unlike George, Andrew had the good sense to look curious, as though actually wondering why Brandon and Joe were there. The other older man, who wore white linen, was Lloyd Landrum. He had thinning salt and pepper hair and brown, expressive eyes. He wore frameless eyeglasses. Like Andrew and George, he was fit and seemed younger than his age. Tom Hood, the director of HBW security, a man who Brandon guessed was about his age, had auburn hair and dark brown eyes.

George explained, "Mr. Morrissey has brought us a copy of a letter that he believes was written by the first Andrew Hutchenson. I've explained that the letter is nothing new to us, that it is a hoax that was created and perpetuated by his own father."

Focus, Brandon thought, as he watched Andrew Hutchenson grow pale, swallow, reach for the copy of the letter, then sit down hard in a chair and read it. It was a curious reaction for a man who was staring at something that he knew to be a fraud, but, at that moment, Brandon didn't care about Andrew or what he thought. Lloyd stood behind the chair where Andrew had plopped, and, at Andrew's shoulder, read the letter. Brandon didn't care about Lloyd, either. Brandon cared about Taylor, who still didn't seem surprised by what her father was saying. When Taylor looked away from Andrew, to Brandon, Brandon asked her, "You knew about this?"

Taylor gave him a slow nod. "I just learned about it."

His stomach twisted, as his heart sank. He should have listened to the warning signals that Sebastian had been blasting his way. "A heads-up would have been nice."

"Minutes before you walked through the front door, I asked my father about the Hutchenson letter."

He shook his head. "You believe that it's a hoax? Without question? After what Rorsch told us today? The letter confirms his suspicions, which he had decades before the letter was written. Rorsch documented those suspicions, in his affidavit and in the pardon request. Aren't you at least questioning whether the content of the letter is the truth?"

Taylor didn't answer him. She didn't have to. He saw in her eyes that this inquisitive woman, who asked question, after question, after question of him, believed her father, without one. Disappointment, in himself, and in her, pierced his heart. He had fallen for the woman who he thought that she was. Evidently, he'd given her too much credit. At least when she was around her father, she wasn't the woman who he had believed her to be. She might never be that woman.

"How is it that you have the right to question my daughter about any of this?" George asked, glancing at Taylor, then back at Brandon. "As a matter of fact, how exactly do you two know each other?"

Brandon hoped that his glare told the man to back-the-fuck-off, but he wasn't sure, because George didn't look intimidated. His dark eyes were sharp, his cheeks were flushed, and he just looked pissed. "I'll let Taylor answer those questions."

Tom, who had been standing in the corner of the room, approached George. He spoke into his mic, received feedback through his earpiece, then said, "Senator Landusky has arrived. She will be here for thirty minutes, exactly. You wanted to deliver your speech while she is here, correct?"

George nodded. He asked Joe, "Are we done?"

"No," Joe said. "We're not here to debate whether the letter is true," encompassing George and Brandon in his gaze. "We believe that whoever killed Lisa believes that the Hutchenson letter is the truth, and if we're correct, we think that you could be in danger."

"This is crazy," George said.

"My brother, Victor, may have recently acquired an original of the letter," Brandon said. Taylor's deep breath interrupted him.

"As of yesterday you believed that Victor was dead. Right?"

Taylor asked.

Brandon bit back a flash of irritation as he understood the rules by which Taylor played. Those rules gave her license to doubt him and question him, again and again, but not her father.

"New intelligence indicates otherwise," he said to her. "If Victor believes the letter to be the truth, if he believes that the HBW Board acted to conceal it," Brandon glanced at George, Andrew, and Taylor, "you aren't safe. If he believes that you caused my father pain, he will hurt you. Financially, emotionally, whatever it takes. My brother is a killer. He gets paid to do it. He makes deaths look like accidents," Brandon said, stating as facts concerns that he had never stated to anyone other than Sebastian. "That's his calling card."

Brandon expected skepticism. He expected, damn it, he expected questions. Yet he was greeted with stoic silence, from George, Andrew, Taylor, and Lloyd. Brandon looked at Joe, who met Brandon's eyes with a wide-eyed, *what-the-fuck* expression.

"Based upon the information that Brandon has provided," Joe said, "and recent developments in the Smithfield murder investigation, we're considering whether Victor Morrissey was involved in Lisa's murder." Taylor gave a surprised gasp. Finally, Brandon thought, there was an appropriate response from her. "We have forensics doing a sweep of Collette Westerfeld's home."

"And who the hell gave you permission to do that?" George asked.

"Last I checked," Joe said, "I don't need permission to investigate a possible homicide. Ms. Westerfeld's brother and my partner are at the house with the crime lab technicians."

"It wasn't a homicide. It was an accidental overdose," George said. "Obviously, you haven't done your homework by speaking to the coroner."

"The coroner didn't know what we now know."

"You are invading the privacy of a troubled young lady. I will see to it that the chief of police is aware of how you acted."

"Go right ahead," Joe said, "because there's nothing wrong

with anything I've done. Besides, last time my superiors didn't listen to Brandon Morrissey, we had an ugly situation on our hands." Joe focused his attention on George, then Andrew. "Lisa Smithfield was researching the Morrissey treason case. If anything unusual has happened in that regard in the last few weeks, days, I need to know now."

There was silence. Andrew stood. He placed the letter on George's desk. George, in turn, placed it in the top desk drawer. Andrew walked to the window, which overlooked the rear yard, and seemed to be interested in the party. Lloyd sat in one of the chairs, glanced from George to Andrew, then his eyes settled on Brandon, who wondered what, if any, exchange had occurred between his father and this man who gave the appearance of being sophisticated and scholarly.

Joe repeated, "Has anything happened?"

George asked, "In what regard?"

"Don't play with me," Joe said. "If Victor Morrissey stole the original of the Hutchenson letter from Lisa, it stands to reason that he'd have contacted you. So, let me be perfectly clear. If anything has happened in the last few days that is related to this letter, and you're not telling me about it now, I will consider your silence to be interference with a police investigation and I will see that you are prosecuted. I can, and I will."

Andrew turned from the window, his attention focused on George. Lloyd also was focused on George, who was silent for long enough that Brandon knew, no matter what George's answer was going to be, that the real answer was yes. Something had happened. A threat. A demand. Something. Yet George shook his head. "You're threatening me for no reason. This letter is a hoax. It is nothing more than a bad joke that is more than thirty years old. Even if I were somehow threatened with this letter, I would not make the threat a matter for the New Orleans Police Department to investigate. I will not allow it to become such. Once I talk to your superiors, you will understand that this letter is a private matter."

George's words, though full of bluster, didn't fool Brandon. He glanced at Taylor, who was staring at her father with worry in her eyes. He wondered whether George was fooling his daughter. Brandon said, "You haven't answered Joe's question."

George glared at Brandon. "This conversation is ridiculous. I have given you enough time. I have a speech to give."

As George walked towards the door, Brandon said, "I think that Victor believes that, after my father received the Hutchenson letter, someone from HBW, set fire to our house in 1981 to destroy all of my father's documents, including the Hutchenson letter."

George turned to Brandon. "That's preposterous."

Brandon shrugged. "I'm not saying that it's true. I'm saying that my father painted HBW as the bad guys. Victor was and is imbalanced. Right or wrong, he believed what my father said. My sister died in that fire. My father never recovered from his grief." Brandon locked eyes with Taylor, then turned back to George. "Victor knows what the death of a daughter does to a man."

Andrew's gasp stole Brandon's attention. Brandon detected a shake in Andrew's hand as he watched the man wipe his brow.

George asked, "Are you suggesting that Victor would go after our daughters to get to us?"

"That's exactly what I'm suggesting."

Brandon wanted George to be so scared that he'd ask Brandon for help. He waited. No request came. Instead, George narrowed his eyes and shook his head. "Taylor indicated that as of yesterday, you believed that your brother was dead. Is that correct, Mr. Morrissey?"

Brandon nodded, ready to explain more, but George continued, "Sanity, or the lack thereof, runs in families. There's a gene, you know, the absence of which can make people delusional. Simple tests determine the presence or the absence of the gene. Given your father's delusions, you, Mr. Morrissey, should avail yourself of those tests, or, at a minimum, undergo a psychiatric evaluation." Brandon would have crossed the room to strangle the man, except Joe grasped Brandon's forearm and kept him anchored. George continued, "Leave my house," he drew a deep breath, "and leave my daughter alone."

George, Andrew, Lloyd, and Tom left the study. A security guard stepped in, holding the door open for Taylor, so that she could follow her father, and, Brandon assumed, for Brandon and Joe to exit the premises. Brandon turned to Taylor. Her cheeks were flushed red.

"I'm sorry that he insulted you."

Molten anger coursed through Brandon's veins. He tried not to direct it at Taylor, but hell, he was almost as angry with her as with her father. She was looking at Brandon with doubt in those hazel-green eyes, as though she believed her father, as though Brandon was destined for an asylum. "You don't question anything that he says?"

"I do question him," she hesitated, "but I've learned *how* to do it. He's my father."

"He may be that, but he's also rude, arrogant, and pompous," he forced himself not to yell, "and I'm not crazy."

Joe interrupted, "Taylor. We've got Tilly, who saw the murder, and gave us a description of the murderer that fits Victor. With Tilly's description, I can't ignore Brandon's theory." Taylor went pale. Joe added, "If your father had given us the time, instead of throwing insults, we'd have given him that fact."

Taylor glanced at the security guard. "I need a minute."

The guard hesitated, still at the open door. "Your father would like you at his side when he gives the speech, which will be any minute now. "

Taylor stood her ground. "Please. Step out."

The guard acquiesced. Brandon and Taylor stood maybe five feet apart, staring at each other. Her hand shook as she lifted it to her forehead and smoothed back her hair. Her glance fell on Joe, then Brandon, and her gaze stayed there, with him. As seconds ticked by, some of his anger dissipated. A minute fell away and he felt a little less like exploding. She looked so damn miserable that he tried to find the right words, something, that would make him feel better about leaving her there. Something that would make him feel like she would be safe, that precautions would be taken. He couldn't find the words, though.

Joe cleared his throat. "Brandon, I'll wait for you outside."

They were alone and still he didn't know what to tell her, because his every thought was balled up with the miserable *oh-shit-why-have-I-messed-with-her* feeling that had flooded through him the second he stepped into the mansion and saw that damn oil painting. George alone had cemented the *oh-shit* feeling, and the interaction between George and Taylor made him physically ill. He should have never touched her.

Taylor said, "So it doesn't really matter whether there is any truth to the Hutchenson letter or whether there really was a conspiracy to hide it. What you're saying is your brother is capable of killing, and you believe he has Andi and me in his sights?"

"Yes," he said, "and I don't for a second doubt that he'd go after you. Especially now that I've gotten a glimpse of your father, because I can't think of an easier way to extract revenge on him than to go after you. Does your father care for anything or anyone else?"

She frowned. "Money. Power. Status."

He nodded. "It would be easier to kill you than to rob him of those things." She flinched. He continued, "Also, because of the timing of Collette's death, and that damn magazine cover that I can't get out of my head, with you, Andi, and Collette, I think he'll go after Andi, because she's Andrew Hutchenson's daughter."

Brandon placed a hand on Taylor's shoulder. She stepped closer, as though seeking comfort, but instead of giving it to her, rational thought returned. Touching Bartholomew royalty was a thing of the past for him. He let his hand fall away and stepped away from her.

Her eyes widened. From the pained expression she shot at him, she understood the meaning. Now that he understood her reality, he couldn't go down that delusional road of wanting her and needing her. There would be no more touching, but there was one more thing that he needed to do while in the mansion. He wanted to see the Bartholomew library's version of the architectural drawings of the landing craft. He said, "The library. Where is it?"

Tom opened the study door and said, "Your father will be giving the speech in two minutes. He directed me to find you."

As Taylor moved past Brandon, towards the door, she bent towards him and whispered. "Third floor. Locked and alarmed. Give me twenty minutes. Service stairway is third door on the left in the main hall. I'll meet you in the far bedroom on the left on the third floor."

It took her twenty-five minutes. He spent the time on the phone with Pete, making sure that things were all right at home. He called Kate and Rose individually, not telling them that anything was going on, but checking to see whether they'd say if Victor had contacted them. They didn't mention Victor. Finally, he called Sebastian, who told him that there was nothing new to report on Victor's whereabouts. When Taylor stepped into the bedroom, he broke the connection with Sebastian. Her cheeks were flushed. Her eyes were bright. His arms ached to hold her, but he repressed the urge. No more of that, he reminded himself. He couldn't do that to himself.

Chapter Eighteen

Brandon's green eyes were serious as she entered the bedroom. She'd run up the narrow, steep stairway. She tried to catch her breath.

"Before the library, I need to check on Andi."

He nodded. She called Andi, who answered on the third ring. "Hey. Are you all right?"

"Yes. Dad called," Andi said. "He hired an extra security detail and the alarm's on. I'm fine, but what the hell is going on over there?"

"Too much to tell now. I'll talk to you when I get home. Around midnight. Stay safe."

To Brandon, she said, "Follow me."

On the far end of the third floor, down a long hallway, was the entrance to her father's library. It would be locked, she knew, but the same code that allowed her to enter the house would allow her to access any interior rooms. She reached the door, used her access code, and slipped into the dimly lit room with Brandon, shutting the door behind them. It took her a while to get her bearings. She couldn't remember the last time she had been in her father's private library. She walked past neat bookshelves. Table-height display cases caught her attention.

The cases held original drawings of various HBW vessels, organized by year. In a case with drawings from the years 1938 through 1940 she saw drawings of the Hutchenson Landing Craft, the same drawings that were in the World War II museum. Multiple, movable shelves were in the case. A button on the outside of the case shifted the shelves. She pressed the button, looking at drawing after drawing. A ball of anxious dread in her throat made breathing difficult. The drawings in the case were the same as the drawings in the museum that she had looked at with Brandon the previous day, except there was one glaring difference. Each and every sheet was signed by Benjamin Morrissey. The same drawings that were in the museum had been signed by Andrew Hutchenson. Good God. She'd seen these drawings before, but there were so many drawings of naval architecture. She had never focused on her father's private collection of HBW designs, had never focused on the drawings of the landing craft, and had never noticed the discrepancy that was now obvious. Brandon was correct. Brandon's father had been correct. Benjamin Morrissey was the designer of the landing craft and, she drew a deep breath, not two hours earlier, her father had lied to her.

Brandon said, "Holy shit."

At the same time, she said, "There's got to be an explanation."

He turned to her. His jade-green eyes were wide. His cheeks were flushed. "Are you fucking serious?"

Dread flooded her veins. She lifted her chin and stood her ground, but she felt like running and hiding. "Yes."

His upper lip lifted in a sneer. "I'm sure your father has one."

She shut her eyes. "Please don't do that."

"Do what? State the obvious?" Brandon whacked his palm on the display case. It rattled in protest. He was so close to her that she could smell his musky cologne and a faint hint of soap. If she stepped one inch closer they'd be touching. Yet they weren't touching. She knew that he was doing that on purpose, as he had backed away from her in the study. He hadn't been able to keep his hands off of her all day. That he was keeping his distance from her signaled to her that what had previously been about history and about others was now between the two of them.

"This is one more indication that the Hutchenson letter is the truth, that it isn't some crap that was made up by my father, and that Rorsch's theory is correct. Yet if your father gives you an explanation, no matter how implausible or unfounded, you're going to believe him. Aren't you?"

"I need time," she said. "To digest this."

"Fine," he shrugged. "Take it. I don't have time to wait for you to face facts."

He stepped closer to the display case and lifted the lid.

"What are you doing?"

He reached into the case and gently stacked five of the drawings together, then rolled them. "That should be obvious."

"You can't take them."

"Don't tell me what I can do with *my grandfather's* drawings."

He rolled the documents into the shape of a neat cylinder. As he stepped away from the case with the drawings, her heart twisted. "Wait. Please wait."

"You can tell your father these will be in the museum, as soon as I figure out how the hell to get them displayed there."

"Wait," she said. "Please, and I'm not going to argue about you taking the drawings. I just need to talk to you."

He paused before turning to her, long enough that her heart stuttered, because she didn't think that he would stop. When he did finally turn to her, the look in his eyes was hard and cold. He shook his head. "Whatever it is that you want from me, I don't have it to give. I see the obvious. You don't." He ran a hand through his hair. "I can get past a lot, Taylor. I can get past your names, and what they mean in terms of social hierarchy. I can pretend that we come from the same worlds, though we don't. Hell, I'd probably even suffer through dinners at the country club if that's what would make you happy. But this," he lifted his chin and held up the hand that held the drawings, "I can't do this. I can't watch you live in denial. You're smarter than that. I'll never be able to be in the same room with your father and be civil. He's lying. Not only that, he's so goddamn fucking arrogant that he's kept these drawings, with *my* grandfather's signature on them. He's kept evidence of his lies for years and years and years, as what? Proof to himself that he can get away with manipulating the truth?" He shook his head. "I can't stick around and watch you interact with him. Your questions," he hesitated, "God. I love that about you. You question everything, Taylor. Your questions are astute and relevant and they reveal a witty, sharp mind and a beautiful desire for knowledge. Yet you don't question him."

Taylor walked to him. Her heart had skipped as he said *love*, because she knew that was a word that he didn't use lightly. As she got closer, she saw pain in his beautiful green eyes and a furrow at his brow. She understood then that a pendulum had swung. This afternoon, as he had kissed her, held her, and made love to her, he had been on one end of the emotional spectrum. Now he was on the other. "You said casual," she whispered.

"Well," he shrugged as he looked away from her, then back, "I was fooling myself, and now we both know the truth."

She reached for his hand, but he stepped back.

"Don't touch me."

She bit the inside of her lip and held back a sob. No tears, she told herself. Do not let him see you cry. She could tell by the hard set of his jaw that he was determined to take the only way out, and her tears were only going to make his departure uglier.

"I fell for you," he said, with a beautiful half-smile and sadness in his eyes, "so fast that I didn't realize it was happening. This has only happened one other time in my life. I can't," he paused, "I can't handle more heartache. I'm all tapped out on misery and disappointment. Tonight, seeing you with your father, watching you believe him without question," he shook his head, "tells me that the barriers between us are insurmountable. One day, you'd have to choose, and I can't be the one left out. At best, you're drowning in uncertainty. I don't have the mettle to stick around until you figure it out, because if these designs, signed by my grandfather, don't seem significant to you," he shrugged, "nothing I can ever say or do will persuade you otherwise. I've warned you and your father about Victor. I'm done here."

She couldn't breathe. Taylor squared her shoulders and stared into his hard green eyes. He was right. She might never figure it out, at least not in a manner that was acceptable to Brandon, and it wasn't fair of her to ask him to stick it out until she did.

Brandon didn't say anything else. He left her there, alone, in the library, where she let miserable tears fall. *Think*, she told herself. *Think*. Her only rational thought was that the drawings proved that her father had lied to her when he'd said that

Benjamin Morrissey did not design the landing craft. With that thought, Taylor dried her tears, reapplied her make-up, and went downstairs. She slipped into her father's study, where she opened the top desk drawer and retrieved the copy of the Hutchenson letter that Brandon had delivered. She read the entire letter, then slipped it into her purse. After, she mingled throughout the party. When it was time for the guests to leave, she stood at her father's side as they told the guests goodbye, even though a hard ball of dread had formed in her throat. Her dread grew as the guests left. If their guests only knew what she now suspected.

If only they knew.

When the last guest left, her father said, "You should stay here tonight."

She turned to him, arms folded, and said, "Your library has original design drawings of the landing craft. They were signed by Benjamin Morrissey."

He gave her a hard glance. "Not now, Taylor."

"If not now, when?"

"This is an important weekend. It has to go smoothly. The issues regarding the landing craft are complex. One day you'll be better schooled in the nuances of our business. There's so much for you to learn."

"Like how to lie?"

His face flushed red. Anxiety made her heart race and stole her breath, but she fought past it.

"If I kept looking in your library, would I find an original of the Hutchenson letter there as well? One that you would admit that Andrew Hutchenson wrote?"

A pulse formed in his right temple. "I should have let you go to the beach with Andi."

"You lied to Brandon, didn't you?"

He didn't respond. She thought about telling her father that Brandon had taken the drawings. She knew she should. George didn't give her time to say anything more. He dismissed her by turning and walking away from her. As he stepped away, she said, louder, "And me. You lied to me."

She needed air. She could no longer breathe in her father's home.

***

He approached the Hutchenson beach house at ten thirty. A Water's Edge security car was parked in the driveway. Hell. He called his contact. "Has something happened?"

His contact explained what had transpired with Brandon Morrissey and Joe Thompson's visit to George Bartholomew. As he listened, he tried to stay calm, but he knew that he was losing control. When his contact relayed George Bartholomew's explanation of the Hutchenson letter, he forgot about being calm.

His blood boiled.

"A hoax? A conspiracy theory? The product of a deranged mind?"

"Yes."

He broke the connection. Spiraling bands of anger coiled from his gut, burned through his heart, and pulsed through his body. Out of control. This was fucking out of control. He thought through a new plan, one that had nothing to do with finesse or discretion. The plan didn't require any special talent. It only required a bit of strength and, lucky for him, with fury he was always strong, even now. The HBW board members needed to understand that he would hunt them, one by one, until they paid his demand. He drove to a twenty four hour Wal Mart, where he purchased sturdy line, electrical tape, cigarettes, and black permanent markers.

Andi Hutchenson was soon to be his burnt-flesh billboard.

He went through the back of the house. The security guard was in the front, unaware of what was happening. Andi was awake when he opened the door to her bedroom. She lunged for her cell phone, as he lunged for her. He was faster, grabbing her by the neck and pressing his gun to her head. He wanted her to remember most of what was happening, so that she could tell the others. He wanted her to feel fear, so he subdued her with an injection of only a small dose of GHB. The drug made her easy to carry. It was going to be messy, so he took her from there, though the back, using a path that he had planned earlier, on a wooden walkway and around a sand dune, then another. The security guard who sat in the front of the house, in the driveway, saved his life by not seeing them and not messing with their quick exit.

Andi struggled when he placed her in his trunk. He closed it and returned to Louisiana, to his camp, anticipating what would happen when burning cigarettes singed Andi's pampered, soft skin.

Her cell phone sat on the passenger seat next to him. At a quarter past midnight, Taylor sent a text. "Hey. Call me. I'm home."

He typed. "Exhausted. Sleeping. Let's talk in the morning."

Taylor's next text came a few seconds later. "Seriously?"

He replied. "Really. Can't keep my eyes open."

Taylor didn't respond.

He smiled.

***

At midnight, Brandon stepped into Sebastian's condo. Three Black Raven agents were in the living room, wearing running shoes, black cargo pants, and white shirts that were emblazoned on the front pocket with an embroidered Black Raven logo. They were sitting on the couch, their legs were stretched out on the coffee table, and their eyes were focused alternatively on a large screen television and laptop computers. Two pizza boxes were on the coffee table. They stood when Brandon entered and introduced themselves. Sebastian was sitting on a stool at a concrete island, the centerpiece for his modern kitchen, working on two computer monitors, while eating his way through a bag of Oreos. Brandon went to the bar, poured several fingers of rum into a tumbler, added some ice, then sat down with Sebastian.

Sebastian's blue eyes scanned Brandon as he sipped the rum. "How did it go at the mansion?"

"Her father didn't welcome me. She made it clear that when it comes to believing stories, she'll go with her father's version." Brandon gave Sebastian a few details and told him about the drawings. "I slipped the roll of them under my suit jacket and walked out of the mansion. No one tried to stop me. I warned them," he shrugged, "now I'm through."

"With?"

"Her."

"This afternoon you said that you were ready for a challenge," Sebastian said.

Brandon's heartbeat faltered as he remembered the near-euphoria that he'd felt after making love to Taylor, and before seeing her with her father. Then, he'd been confident that she was worth whatever obstacles might be in their path. "Well, I was wrong. I'm not fighting that battle."

Sebastian narrowed his eyes. "It's been almost two hours since you texted me that you left the party. Where'd you go?"

"Checked on Michael," Brandon said.

"Where else?"

Brandon paused. Sebastian would ultimately get an answer. His friend never rested until he did. "Then the cemetery, and then I drove past Taylor's house to make sure there was security there."

Brandon hated the worry that he saw in his friend's eyes.

"How much time do you still spend at the cemetery?"

"Not that much. I go there to think." Brandon knocked back the rest of the rum. He thought about pouring more, but he didn't. He could drink the whole bottle and it wouldn't make him feel any better. "I'm fine. Really. I never should have barged into that party, even with Joe."

Brandon's phone rang and Marvin's voice started the moment he picked up. "Yo. What city office you said that need to get in?"

"Orleans Parish Office of Mortgages and Conveyances."

Marvin was silent for a second. "What building is that in?"

"City Hall. Main Annex. It's the third floor."

"Dude. Why didn't you just say you needed to get into City Hall?"

Brandon shook his head. "This office is under different lock and key."

"So? Wouldn't someone who works in janitorial services at City Hall have a key?"

Brandon's pulse picked up. "Probably. You know someone like that?"

"I'm working on it. Everybody's in different places with this damn July 4th holiday. I can't find my regulars. I'll get back with ya later."

Brandon glanced at Sebastian. "Joe's working on an entry into the office through official channels, but, given that it's a holiday weekend, my money's on Marvin."

"To do a real estate transactional search," Sebastian said, "you're going to have to use multiple names."

"I'd probably limit the search to aliases that are associated with bank accounts."

"So far," Sebastian said, "Ragno's found six."

Brandon made a mental note to call some of his lawyers and paralegals in the morning. Without an address, and with multiple names, the title search in the notoriously disorganized Orleans Parish records office was going to take more than one person a boatload of time. Brandon asked, "What have you discovered in the last two hours?"

"Nothing," Sebastian said.

"Well, that's great."

"I'm sorry, but Victor's off the grid. Totally. He's using cash, or he's using aliases that we don't have. That car that he rented," Sebastian shrugged, "is gone. Hasn't shown up anywhere that we can see. So, if you're thinking that you're going to find your brother, I'd keep an eye on what you think he's going to go after."

Brandon nodded. "There's HBW Security in her driveway. At least Taylor or her father had the sense to do that. Joe's going to have cars drive by. After what I told them, I thought that she'd stay at her father's house." He shrugged. "I wasted my breath."

"Does she at least have a really good alarm system?"

"I wouldn't know. I've never been in her house," Brandon paused. "Aw *hell*."

"What?"

Brandon stood, in a lightning flash forgetting his *through with her* attitude. "We've got to get there. Her alarm was giving her problems."

The drive to Taylor's house took fewer than ten minutes. He and Sebastian took two cars. The agents went with them. Brandon parked down the street, with a side view of Taylor's house. Sebastian parked behind him and walked towards Brandon's car. Several lights were on, both downstairs and upstairs. Sebastian knocked on the driver's side window of Brandon's car. Brandon lowered it. Sebastian asked, "What are you waiting for?"

Brandon said, "I'm not going into her house."

"You're just going to sit here?"

"We had a fight. I walked out on her."

"Well, call her. Otherwise, I'm walking up to the front door, knocking on it, and I'm going to have to explain why I need to check her alarm system, while you're sitting in the car."

Brandon dialed her number. She picked up on the second ring. "I'm outside of your house. I want Sebastian to check your alarm system. He's an expert."

"The alarm company was here yesterday."

"Damn it, Taylor. Humor me."

A minute later, Taylor opened the door, with her cell phone in her hand. She waved the HBW security guard away as he stepped out of his SUV. At least he stepped out to watch them approach her porch, even though he hadn't thought to check on why five men had pulled up to Taylor's house. *Hell.* These people had no fucking clue.

She wore a cream-colored robe that looked like softly spun silk. Her initials were monogramed on the lapel in dove grey. The robe was tied at the waist, but the deep v-neck revealed a small amount of pink lace and more cleavage than he cared to see. Her hair was loose. She was barefoot. Her make-up was gone, revealing natural, soft beauty and a tired, nervous, and vulnerable expression in her eyes. His chest tightened as she introduced Brandon and Sebastian to Carolyn. Sebastian had Carolyn lead him to the alarm's control panel, in another room. Taylor held Brandon's gaze with one that was serious. She had no trace of a smile.

Brandon said, "I thought that you'd stay at your father's tonight. It would be safer, at least until the police rule out foul play with Collette."

"No," she said, although her face became pale at the mention of Collette. "I'm more comfortable in my own home."

They were in a staring match. He could break it by reaching for her. He ached to hold her, to comfort her. Hell, holding her would make him feel better. He couldn't do it, though, because he didn't want to risk the inevitable hurt that would come with caring for her. Call it cowardice. Whatever. He didn't give a damn. He couldn't handle falling for, and losing, another woman.

She broke the silence first. "You walked out on me."

He swallowed. "I had to."

"I'm angry."

"So am I."

Sebastian reentered the room and said, "There are echoes throughout the system."

Taylor turned to Sebastian. "What does that mean?"

"Some of the contacts have been electronically disabled and they're jumbled," he shrugged, "so there's no way right now to know which ones are working."

"The system is supposed to beep if contacts are loose," Taylor said, "and someone from the alarm company was here yesterday. He checked it."

"This isn't the same as loose contacts, like from wind hitting a window, or a door. Your alarm system is a computer, it has a virus, and evidently, the alarm company didn't get past the false positives." Sebastian explained. "Nothing would happen if someone entered at more than half of the entry points."

"Can this happen randomly," Taylor asked, "or did someone tamper with my system?'

Sebastian shot her a look of exasperation. "Lightning could cause this, but there'd be other evidence of lightning. Given our concerns about Victor, Lisa's murder, and Collette's death, I'd say a really good tampering job is a hundred percent more likely than lightning." Sebastian paused. "Whoever did this is good. He could walk into your house, and you wouldn't know it."

The color drained from her face. "Can it be fixed?"

"Electronics need to be reconfigured before this thing is secure, and some rewiring is probably needed. In a house this size, it could take days, and then, the system isn't that great to begin with. I'd recommend a new one." He focused his attention on Taylor. "You shouldn't stay here."

"I'm not leaving," she said.

"Look. I'm an expert in risk assessment and protection. I advise you to leave. Go somewhere more secure. A high-rise hotel, with one door into the room, and a few good guards, would be a hell of a lot safer than this place."

"What's the name of your firm?"

"Black Raven."

Taylor looked at Brandon. "Is Sebastian as good at what he does as you are a lawyer?"

Brandon didn't hesitate. "Better."

Taylor turned to Sebastian. "You're hired. Make me safe and my home secure. Do whatever it takes. Get the necessary personnel. Redo the alarm system. I presume that you have enough manpower to start now?"

"Tech personnel for the system can be here tomorrow, midday. I have three field agents here. I'll need a retainer to get started." Sebastian threw out a number that would have made most people cringe. "And that's the friend-of-Brandon discounted figure."

Taylor nodded. "That's fine."

"Once you hire Black Raven, Taylor, you have to do as they say for your safety," Brandon said.

Taylor frowned as she glanced at Brandon. "This is between me and Sebastian."

"No. I provide legal advice to the company. If you don't agree to that term, I'll advise Sebastian not to do business with you."

She turned from Brandon and nodded to Sebastian. "Fine."

She dialed a number and told the security detail that was in her driveway that Black Raven would be providing additional security personnel.

"My men will stay the night. One inside, roaming the house. Two outside. They'll assume their positions as soon as we make sure that no one is already in your house. The agents will work the perimeter, the attic, and any crawl spaces. Brandon, I'll take downstairs." Sebastian gave him a hard glance, one that told Brandon he was setting him up to deal with Taylor. "You take upstairs."

Chapter Nineteen

Brandon checked every upstairs room, window, closet and space. He ended at the room that he saw Taylor walk into, where the door was half open. He knocked as he pushed it open the rest of the way.

Bedside lamps and floor lamps gave the room soft light. She was sitting on the bed, hugging her knees to her chest, with her feet pulled in close, under the hem of her robe. White bedding with satin trim was turned down. She was covered from shoulders to toes in her robe, but she still looked sexy as hell. Sexy, and worried and way too vulnerable. Her eyes followed his progress as he pushed drapes to the side and checked the room's floor-to-ceiling windows, then shut the drapes. French doors, with a simple lock system that wouldn't take much expertise to crack, led to a balcony. It was empty. He relocked the doors.

Her closet was huge. A red, halter-tied ball gown was on a mannequin that was shaped like Taylor. Matching red silk shoes with high, skinny heels were on a small shelf next to the dress. A black-velvet jewelry case on a table sparkled with diamond bracelets, rings, necklaces, and earrings. He walked out of the closet. "You need a better security system just for your damn jewels."

"So that I understand what you were saying in my father's library," she said, "you may have feelings for me, but you're worried that my father will come between us. You believe that I will choose my father over you, and you're not even going to start down the road of having feelings for me, because you don't want to fight a losing battle."

Brandon shrugged. "That's about it."

Taylor lifted her chin. Her cheeks were flushed. Her eyes were filled with tears, but she didn't give in to crying. Instead, she drew a deep breath, and her voice didn't waver as she said, "Most people in my life have been attracted to me because I am a Bartholomew. You, though, are using that as a way to not even get close."

"I wouldn't say that the problem is that you're a Bartholomew. I'd say that the problem is," he paused, "well, you're acting like one."

He needed to leave her bedroom. He had said enough. But he couldn't make himself walk towards the open doorway that led out of her bedroom. He couldn't even turn from her. Invisible tethers kept him from moving, even when his mind told him he had no business being there.

From the doorway, Sebastian said, "Taylor, my agents are in position. I'm headed back to the condo."

"I'm headed out with you," Brandon said.

Sebastian gave him a head shake. "Look, if I manage to figure anything out about Victor's whereabouts, you'll be the first to know. But really," his friend's blue eyes locked on him, "I don't need the company."

Sebastian turned and left, shutting the bedroom door behind him. *Damn it.* Once again, he was alone with Taylor.

"I'm not sure of myself, but," she hesitated, and a slight twinge of pain in her voice yanked at his heart. She continued, "Is it too much to ask that for the moment you believe that I'll ultimately do the right thing?"

"That isn't how it works," he said, turning from her, as she eased herself off of the bed and started walking to him. "People who don't have faith in themselves rarely live up to the high expectations of others. That's why low expectations suck. People usually meet them. They never realize their true potential. I don't want to stick around and watch you do that."

"Can we just focus on right now? Stay," she said, "Please. I don't want to be alone."

He wanted to say no, but she untied her robe and let it fall to the floor. A pink lace camisole was stretched over her breasts. It draped down her waist and stopped about three inches above her hips, where matching lace barely covered her. "Please stay for a while. This is casual," she said. "It doesn't have to mean anything."

His mind said *leave*, but every other molecule in his body said *stay*, because he could think of nothing else but how it had felt to be inside of her.

"Please," she repeated.

He needed to go. *Hell.*

"Stay," she said, "only a few minutes."

He yanked her to him and opened his mouth onto the thin lace camisole, nibbling and tonguing her nipples through the fabric. He ripped off her camisole and panties. Lamplight revealed marks that their earlier lovemaking had left on her. The bruises and bite marks became primal, arousing evidence that he'd been there before. He knelt on the floor, opened his mouth to her sex, parting her folds with his tongue, tasting her, while breathing in her sweet, earthy essence. He slipped two fingers inside of her. She gripped his shoulders and moaned, softly, then held her hand to her mouth to keep her cries quiet. He tongued her until she whispered his name, then kept going, until she slid down him, to her knees, panting for breath. He gave her a soft push so that she fell onto her back, pushed her legs apart, then knelt between her legs.

He dragged his eyes from her damp, inviting sex and met her gaze as he undid his holster, placed it on her bedside table, took his switchblade out of his pocket, and placed it next to the pistol. He kicked off his shoes and unzipped his pants. She helped him push them down. He kicked them off then pulled her legs around him and up, until her knees were hooked in the crook of his elbows. He slid his full erection into her warm, tight channel with one strong stroke. She gasped and tensed, but didn't ask him to stop. He couldn't, even if he wanted to. Desperation for her drove his body, fueled by the certainty that there was never going to be another time that they'd be together, that he was having one last taste of something he could never again have. He plunged into her so hard that together, with each thrust, they slid across the soft carpet. Moist walls gripped him and natural, tight pulses deep inside of her made him lengthen and become harder, even after they'd been at it for so long that time seemed suspended and he had lost his breath. It took willpower, but he paused, and, in case he was misreading her moans and gasps, he asked, "Are you all right?"

Her chest was flushed. Her eyes held his in a sultry, pupils-dilated gaze. "Yes. Good God. Yes. Please," she paused. "Don't stop."

"Tell me," he said, plunging deep, "that you'll never forget how I feel."

"Never," she sighed, as she lifted her hips to meet his. "Oh. Brandon. Never."

His thrusts had pushed them to the wall. They used it to brace themselves. Her hands were stretched over her head, exposing her full, round, breasts and erect nipples. Her breasts bounced with each move, calling him. He shifted so that her knees were hooked over his shoulders. She was as open to him as she could be and it was such a goddamn turn-on that he still felt a hot, pulsing build-up of need, when he should have been spent. He closed his mouth on one nipple, then the other.

She whispered, "Never. Yes," she said, "Don't stop." Her juices made his slide in and out of her a wet, hot, squeeze, unlike anything he'd ever felt before. Her moans, sighs, and soft whispers kept him going, fast, hard, and deep. Finally, when she called his name, once, twice, three times, and her body shuddered with an intense orgasm, he exploded into her.

After, he lay on top of her, with most of his weight on his arms. His spine tingled and every muscle in his body was spent. She didn't say anything. He couldn't say anything. He shifted his weight and lay on his side. She curled towards him, asleep.

After several long minutes, when she didn't awaken, and he had regained some of his energy, he stood and pulled back the duvet and the top layer of covers and sheets on her bed. He lifted her and placed her there, then pulled the sheet to her shoulders. Taylor barely stirred.

His heart twisted with that sick feeling that came with wanting what he couldn't have. Damn it. He needed to stay away from her.

He got dressed. He slipped on his shoes, then looked at her again before tying the laces. *Aww hell.* He had to tell her goodbye, but she was sleeping. In his world, sleep was sacred, and, after the last few days, Taylor deserved whatever relief came with a few minutes of good, hard sleep. He couldn't wake her, but he also couldn't simply have sex with her, then leave, without telling her goodbye, because this goodbye would be their last. He kicked off his shoes and got into bed with her. He sank into the bed and soft pillows, almost groaning with sudden exhaustion. She moved towards him, then pressed herself against him, and, with his arms around her, and her head on his shoulders, she breathed in and out in deep sleep. He felt himself drifting, gliding away from consciousness as he breathed with her. His last thought before crossing into slumber was that Taylor was pure, unexplainable magic.

***

Taylor's phone beeped with a text. The sound pulled her out of her dreams. She flashed back to the raw need and power with which Brandon had made love to her. Then, as she became more fully awake, she thought of her father. She felt the dread that had formed at her belief that her father was lying, and at her now certain knowledge that Brandon would soon disappear from her life. Brandon wasn't going to wait for her to find the courage to stand up to her father, and she didn't blame him. Right now, though, his arms were around her, so at least he hadn't taken the easy way out and disappeared while she was sleeping. Sometime during the night, he had dressed. When she looked up at him, in the soft lamplight that filled her room, jade-green eyes were focused on her.

She asked, "Did you sleep?"

"Yes," he said, with a slight smile. He let go of her and stretched, then he reached for his phone and hers. "Amazing. I slept for almost three hours." He frowned. "Do you often get texts at four thirty in the morning?"

She shook her head. Each text sent two signals, separated by a minute. The second buzz sounded as he handed her phone to her. Andi's text read, "*I'm on the levee. One hundred yards downriver from the intersection of River Road and Cold Storage Road. Please come. Alone. Hurry.*"

When she gasped, Brandon took the phone from her and read the text.

"Call her."

Taylor did. There was no answer.

"Call the land line at the house in Florida where she's

staying."

Taylor winced. "I don't know the house number."

"Call her father. Tell him what's happening. This is a ploy to get you out of your house here," he hesitated, "or maybe to get you to that part of town. She might still be in Water's Edge."

Taylor called Andrew, explained what was happening, and broke the connection so that Andrew could make phone calls. Brandon called Sebastian and agreed to meet Sebastian at Cold Storage Road. Taylor dressed, pulling on jeans, a bra, a tank top, and a long-sleeve t-shirt.

"The text says for me to go alone."

"Like hell," Brandon said. "You shouldn't be going at all."

"I have to go," she said.

Out of habit, Taylor called her father. He answered on the second ring. She read Andi's text to him, then told him that she had hired Black Raven. He wasn't pleased, until she told him that her alarm system was not operating properly and that they were alarm experts. When she broke the connection with her father, Brandon said, "I'll drive."

"My father will have a fit when he sees us together."

Brandon gave her a hard glance that told her that he didn't give a damn what her father thought. "I'm not letting you walk into danger because of that."

Taylor explained what was happening to the HBW security agent. Two Black Raven agents rode with them, in Brandon's car, while one Black Raven agent and the HBW security agent stayed to monitor Taylor's house.

"We need to call Joe," Brandon said, once they were in his car.

"My father said if needed, he'll alert the authorities," she said. "He'll arrive with Tom, the director of HBW Security."

"*If* needed?" Brandon drew a deep breath, shook his head, and glared at her in a way that made her insides tremble. "I'm calling Joe. I really don't give a damn what your father has to say about it."

When Joe's phone went to voice mail, Brandon left a message as he raced through dark downtown streets. "Call me.

It's urgent."

He drove through the French Quarter and then the Marigny, and found the intersection of Cold Storage and River Roads on his car's GPS system. Funky residential neighborhoods that were downriver from the French Quarter gave way to a commercial district of warehouses and wharves. The streets were dark and, given that it was a holiday weekend and a Sunday morning, empty.

"Cold Storage Road is about a mile from here," Brandon said, his eyes on the rearview mirror as he flashed a *get ready* glance at the agents in the rear seat.

Taylor's phone rang.

Andrew said, his voice shaky, "Security informs me that she's not at Water's Edge. Her car is still there, though, and the house is locked. There's no sign of a struggle. It's as though," he gasped for air, "good God. It's as though she simply disappeared."

Taylor felt rising panic as she broke the connection with Andrew and reported what he said to Brandon.

"We'll find her." Brandon's words were reassuring, but the expression on his face was grim as he called Sebastian and gave him the news. When he turned on River Road, the car's lights shone on the red eyes of a river rat that looked to be about a foot long. It scurried across the road, then disappeared into shadows.

Taylor shivered. "Hurry."

Joe called. His voice, over the car's intercom system, was gravelly with sleep. "What's urgent?"

Brandon explained the text. He added, "Taylor's with me. We're almost to Cold Storage and River Road. George Bartholomew is on his way, as is Sebastian. Two Black Raven agents are with me as well."

"I'm on my way."

As they approached Cold Storage Road, they hit a stretch where there were no streetlights. Brandon's headlights barely made a dent in the inky night. He turned on the high beams as he slowed the car. "After I get a flashlight out of my trunk, I'm coming around to your side. Whatever happens, stay with me, and I mean touching me. Do not step away from me. No matter what."

"I don't see her," Taylor said, her eyes scanning the tall levee that bordered the Mississippi River, where all she could see was darkness.

Brandon parked. He left the headlights on. She stepped out of the car when he opened her door. With Brandon on one side and a Black Raven agent on the other side of her, they climbed the levee, as Sebastian pulled up. His headlights gave the dark night more light. The other Black Raven agent walked ahead of them, using a flashlight to scan the area. Damp grass hit Taylor midway up her calf. On the levee's crest, light slid across pale flesh of a body in a fetal position.

"Oh, my God," Taylor said.

Without slowing his stride, Brandon dialed 9-1-1 and requested medical assistance. Taylor would have broken into a wild run, but Brandon's grip on her forearm kept her close. Together they hurried to where Andi lay, nude, her long hair tangled in the grass. Andi's eyes were rimmed with black bruises and swollen shut. Her nose was swollen and crusty with blood. Her wrists and ankles were bound together with multiple ties of rope and electrical tape.

"Andi," Taylor said. Her insides clenched in panic. "Is she alive?"

Brandon was behind Andi. Taylor saw his eyes widen. He hesitated, then reached over Andi, and pressed at her neck. "Her pulse is faint. Talk to her. Tell her she's fine."

"Andi. I'm with you," Taylor said. "You're safe now. We're taking you home."

Andi moaned. Her eyes opened into bare slits, and Taylor leaned over her, smoothing her hair back from her forehead. She held Taylor's gaze for a second, then shut her eyes. Brandon used his switchblade to cut away at the layers of twine and tape that bound her ankles and wrists. As Taylor moved around Andi to let Brandon cut the bindings, she saw Andi's back, where smears of black ink formed letters that were randomly accentuated by festering, oozing circles of burned flesh. "Her back. Brandon. Dear God. What the hell happened to her?"

"Taylor," Brandon said, "Get that tape off of her mouth. She's having a hard time breathing through her nose."

Taylor stared at the lines and holes that spanned from Andi's buttocks to her shoulders. As her eyes adjusted to the dim light, she read the three lines of text.

"Pay my demand by July 4th or more children will suffer for the sins of their fathers."

"Taylor," Brandon voice was calm. "Don't worry about her back. It's nothing. She's going to be fine. The tape. Get it off of her."

Taylor met Brandon's hard, worried gaze. He had seen Andi's back, because that's where he had been when they first approached Andi. His serious gaze told Taylor that he knew that the injuries to Andi's back were most definitely not nothing, but Taylor understood that Brandon was trying to keep Taylor, and especially Andi, from panicking. In her work at the district attorney's office, she had handled an assault that had involved cigarette burns. The photographic exhibits of the burns and the scars they'd left on the victim had been unforgettable. Cigarettes were the only weapon that Taylor knew of that could make such a precise circle, and more than a hundred burns dotted Andi's skin, accenting each of the black-inked, crude letters.

Brandon continued, his voice soothing. "I'm almost done with her wrists and her ankles." As Taylor eased the tape off of her mouth, Andi gasped a rugged, rough breath of air, then gagged.

"Taylor. Talk to her," Brandon said, as Andi tried to breathe, and, when Brandon had finished cutting the ties that bound Andi's wrists and ankles, Andi reached her arms for Taylor, choking with pain as she did so.

"If she's been bound for a while, movement hurts."

"It's going to be all right," Taylor said, holding Andi at her shoulders and trying to avoid scraping the burns on her back. "You're fine now. Fine. We're with you. I won't leave you."

From where they were on the levee's crest, Taylor could see the distant city skyline. A ship glided by on the water. "You're all right," Taylor said, careful not to let her arms touch too firmly on Andi's back. "Breathe easy."

George arrived, then Tony. George ran to Taylor and Andi. He studied Andi's back. He went pale. He stayed close to Taylor, who stared into her father's eyes. Taylor whispered, "What is this about?"

George shook his head. He reached for Taylor, pressing one palm against her back, the other hand on her shoulder. If she hadn't been holding Andi, Taylor would have slapped her father's hands off of her. She couldn't bear his touch. She tolerated it, though, focusing on calmness, for Andi, because if she started screaming at that moment she wouldn't stop. She glanced over her father's shoulders, to where Brandon was watching the two of them. When her eyes found Brandon's, he turned away.

Andrew arrived. He took one glance at his daughter, then looked at George. He said, "This is your goddamn fault."

George stood. He stepped away from Taylor and Andi and turned to Andrew. "Do not forget that you have been with me every step of the way."

Joe arrived at the same time that an ambulance sped to the edge of the levee. Taylor absorbed their words. It was all she could do to resist demanding an explanation from George and Andrew. Keeping Andi calm was more important. She'd fight for an explanation later. She focused on Andi, laying in the levee grass with her, holding her, and repeating, "You're fine. You're going to be all right. Help is on the way." With Andrew kneeling at her side, Taylor stayed as close as she could to Andi as the paramedics assessed the injuries. She heard, "Third degree burns," "Possible broken ribs," and "Broken nose." The first morning light was a pink strip on the horizon as the paramedics moved her, chest down, face to the side, on the stretcher. Andi was conscious then, with her hand gripping Taylor's hand. Taylor saw Joe turn towards George.

Joe yelled, "Extortion? The Hutchenson letter? I asked you that. Last night. I asked you, not eight hours ago. You said *no*. You goddamn arrogant son of a bitch."

Once again, it took all Taylor had to keep from joining Joe in his argument with her father. There'd be time for that later. Andi was more important, she reminded herself. She held Andi's hand and watched her friend slip into unconsciousness as they lifted her into the ambulance. One of the paramedics turned to Taylor and Andrew. "There's room for one."

Andrew was pale. His hands shook. "I'll go."

Brandon handed his car keys to one of the Black Raven agents, who drove Taylor to the hospital.

Minutes turned into hours in the hospital. Due to the level of pain and shock that Andi exhibited when conscious, and the fact that Andi had seemed unable to tell them information about what had happened, the doctors decided to keep her sedated. Taylor breathed slightly easier when she learned that there were no signs of rape. At eleven, in a private room, with two HBW security guards and one Black Raven agent outside the door, Andi lay face down, asleep, with her back exposed.

The emergency room doctors had done preliminary cleaning of her back, but a physician who specialized in burns, with two nurses, began a painstaking cleansing process, using magnifying glasses, a syringe of fluid, a sharp, needle-like instrument, gauze swabs, and gel. The doctor finished at two-thirty, layering salve on Andi's back and applying a thin, cellophane-like dressing. The ink was gone. Where there had been letters and words, now there were only round burns.

The doctor gave Taylor and Andrew a tired glance. "Most of the burns are third degree. She must have suffered excruciating pain. As long as we can fight infection, she will heal."

Taylor sat on one side of Andi's bed, with Andrew on the other. Without medical personnel surrounding her, Andi slept easier. Andrew was ashen and he seemed much, much older than his age. At times, he reached for Andi, to touch her, as though to make sure she was still alive. Taylor remembered, just yesterday, what Brandon had told her. *Start with Andrew. Ask Andrew questions.*

Taylor whispered, "The words on her back. *Pay my demand by July 4th or more children will suffer for the sins of their fathers.* What does it mean?" Heavy blue eyes looked into hers. He stayed silent.

"Andrew," she said, "Please don't treat me as my father would."

He sighed as he glanced at Andi. "I will never forgive myself. I should have stopped the madness years ago."

Dread built in her chest. Taylor drew a deep breath. He continued, "We received a demand letter last week. Someone threatened us with public exposure of the Hutchenson letter unless we pay his demand."

Taylor cringed. "Joe asked my father about that last night. My father didn't admit it."

"I know."

Taylor asked, "How much was the demand?"

"Twenty-five million."

Taylor's heart raced. With that kind of demand, the extortionist must think that the Hutchenson letter was worth something, that the letter was more than a hoax, that it represented more than the conspiracy theory that her father claimed it to be. She drew a deep breath.

"Your father really did write that letter, didn't he?"

Andrew nodded. "Yes. I was there when he did so. He was in his sound mind and he wrote of events that actually happened."

Her world shifted, but instead of feeling the dread that had come the day before with Rorsch's words, she felt fury. Fury with her father for lying to her. Fury with herself for believing the lies.

"You and my father chose to conceal it."

Andrew nodded. "Alicia was on the board then as well. She was also determined to keep it under wraps."

"Does Claude know about it?"

"Claude knows about the Hutchenson letter now, but he did not know until last week, when we received the extortion demand." Tears streamed from Andrew's eyes as he looked at Andi. "I will never forgive myself for letting this happen to her."

She hesitated. "Will you admit it, now? Publicly? That your father's letter is the truth?"

He held Taylor's gaze. "Yes. It is the only way to stop this madness."

For long minutes, Taylor couldn't see anything but her father's sneer, the night before, as he lied and said that Brandon's father had prepared the letter. She paced around

Andi's hospital room, thinking.

Truth was the antidote to a lie. In this instance, truth would be more powerful than an antidote to a lie, because it occurred to Taylor that the Hutchenson letter only had value if it was concealed. If it was no longer concealed, the value would disappear. Once the value disappeared, the threat would as well, and the extortionist would have no power. An idea, one that she kept to herself, formed.

"Don't tell my father that I know the truth. Not now."

Her phone rang with a call from Joe. She stepped out of the room and nodded to the Black Raven agent, who walked down the hallway with her. After Taylor gave Joe an update on Andi, he gave Taylor information about Collette. "I put a rush on toxicology reports that the coroner already ordered and, on a whim, ordered a test for some additional street drugs." He cleared his throat. "She tested positive for a whole slew of prescription drugs, but she also tested positive for GHB."

Taylor knew of the date rape drug from her time with the D.A.'s office. She drew in a deep breath. "Collette wouldn't have taken that."

"People usually don't take that voluntarily," he said. "There's nothing else that we've found at her house, but I thought that I'd let you know. The perp could have started her off with that, then she wouldn't have resisted as he forced her to swallow the rest of the drugs."

As Taylor remembered something that she had forgotten, her hands shook. "Joe. Call the paramedics who arrived at Collette's house. One of them said someone was there when they got there. I didn't pay attention, then. In fact, I forgot about it. Until now. Maybe he was just a neighbor, but, wouldn't a neighbor have stayed? This guy was there when I got there, he led the paramedics up the stairs, and he," she paused, "watched. Then he disappeared. I didn't see him. The paramedic's description might help."

"Whoever he is, he's attacked your two best friends," Joe said. "He's extorting your father. He watched you at Collette's house, and he contacted you last night about Andi. Listen to Brandon and the Black Raven agents. Be careful, Taylor."

Taylor broke the connection with Joe, shut her eyes, and

focused on breathing. She needed to be calm, but anxiety made each breath difficult.

One minute. Two minutes. Three.

She had a plan, she would try like hell to stick with it, and the night would come and go. She had a plan, she reminded herself, as she called her father. He sounded concerned for her and also for Andi. "I'm fine and Andi is resting," she said. She shut her eyes. "I wanted to let you know that I will attend the gala and give the speech."

"You don't have to do either. As a matter of fact, it might be best if you stayed home tonight."

"No," she said. "I will not do that. Would you ask Lloyd to prepare comments for me and drop them by my house at five? I'll go with whatever he writes."

"Are you sure?"

"Yes." She broke the connection, not waiting for a reply.

She nodded to the Black Raven security agent, who had walked a few steps away to give her some space as she talked on the phone. Serious brown eyes glanced at her. He looked to be about her age. He was slim and fit, he stood ramrod straight, and he wore a firearm, in plain view, on a holster at his hip. He'd been nice to her as he had driven her to the hospital that morning, speaking calmly and reassuring her that Andi would be fine.

"Robert, right?"

He nodded.

"Would you mind giving me a ride home?"

Robert still had Brandon's car. There was a faint trace of Brandon's cologne in the warm car. Taylor hadn't heard from him. When they arrived at Taylor's house, Sebastian was downstairs, directing two agents at the control panel of her alarm system. Sebastian turned to her.

"Brandon told me that Joe called with news that there was GHB in Collette's system," he said.

She nodded. "I guess it would have been too much for Brandon to call and ask me whether I'm all right after hearing the godawful news that my friend didn't commit suicide, that she was murdered, and maybe his brother did it?"

Sebastian frowned. "We need to talk."

"About Brandon?"

He nodded.

She folded her arms. "Talk."

Sebastian walked towards the kitchen, away from the other agents. Taylor followed. Carolyn was fixing a tray of sandwiches. Fresh fruit was in colanders. "It sure seems like all these men who are working here should be fed." Carolyn's dark brown eyes glanced at Taylor. "How is she?"

"Sedated. Thank God."

"Are you all right?"

Taylor nodded. "Yes. Thank you, Carolyn."

Sebastian helped himself to a bunch of grapes, ate a few, then said, "Has Brandon ever talked to you about Amy?"

She shook her head. "No. I know a little about the accident though."

"He loved her like nothing I've ever seen. Not sappy love. Just good, deep, make-love-everyday kind of love."

She wondered how a friend could know so much about the inner workings of a relationship. "Did he tell you that?"

Sebastian shook his head. "No. It only seemed that perfect to me. It was soulmate kind of love," he shrugged. "Hell. I'm not doing it justice. For everyone who knew them, it was what we all wanted."

"Why is this relevant to what's happening now?"

"You asked me why Brandon hadn't called you to deliver bad news."

"I didn't ask why. I observed that he didn't."

"This is why."

"I'm not sure what you're trying to tell me," she said, "because all I'm getting is that Brandon and Amy had a relationship that's impossible to follow."

Sebastian held her gaze with a serious look. "Not impossible, but I'd say damn hard. That's why it took him so long. You see, Brandon knew Amy was the right one for him, from the minute he met her. I think he thought that about you, but he hadn't admitted it to himself. He fell for you, until he caught a load of your father's crap, and watched you with your father." Taylor flinched with the reality of Sebastian's words. He continued, "Then he realized that you'd always have divided loyalties. He's not going to set himself up for disappointment. He's my best friend, Taylor, and I understand that. I watched him shatter when Amy died. The only reason he didn't kill himself in the years right after her death," he paused, "is because he watched his father commit suicide and he believes that it's the coward's way out."

Taylor's heart ached for Brandon. "Why are you telling me this?"

He ate a few more grapes as he studied her. "Because I can't imagine that you're not in love with him. In case you haven't figured it out, he's that great. He's a one-in-a-million kind of guy. You'll never find anyone with a stronger moral compass, more integrity, or more capacity for love. So, if you have feelings for him, give him a chance. If you do that, he'll fight for you. Choose him over your father, or," he paused, "let him go. I love the guy. I can't stand to see him hurting. He's done that for too long."

She thought of her plan. Public exposure of the Hutchenson letter wasn't only a tool to diffuse years of lies. It wouldn't just steal the power from the man who was using it to extort HBW. Her heart raced, because, if she had the courage to do what she intended, Brandon Morrissey was going to figure out that she was worth the fight. She studied Sebastian. "I've got to attend the gala tonight at the World War II museum."

He nodded. "Robert told me about it. I advise against it."

"The real threat begins tomorrow. Right? His message on Andi's back," Taylor shuddered, "was that if his demand was not met by July 4th, then more people would be harmed, correct?"

Sebastian nodded. "That's what he said. But I don't trust that he'll wait until tomorrow."

She folded her arms. "Not attending is not an option."

"The risks are too great. I don't control the site, I have no idea what kind of security is in place," he glanced at his watch, "and it's already after three. I can't guarantee that you'll be safe, and that's what you're paying me for."

She heard him, loud and clear. "I'll assume the risk."

Serious eyes held hers. "I was worried that you'd say that. I have a rent-a-tux guy coming," he glanced at his watch, "soon. I'm going to accompany you with three of my agents, but you have to be careful, stay close, and keep your eyes on me and my guys."

"I'm slated to give a short speech at 7:15."

He nodded. "Understood."

Taylor gave a silent prayer for courage. She would need it. She looked into the eyes of Brandon's best friend. A direct gaze and unsmiling expression revealed serious undercurrents to his blue-eyed good looks. He seemed genuinely concerned about the situation that had evolved between her and Brandon.

"You might want to make sure that Brandon is there for my speech."

She turned, walked out of the kitchen, and went upstairs. Taylor stripped, climbed into a hot bath, and, facing sudden exhaustion, fell asleep in the tub. She stirred when she felt Carolyn's hand on her shoulder. "Taylor," she said, "It's time to get dressed."

Chapter Twenty

At five thirty, Brandon was elbow deep in property records of the Orleans Parish Office of Mortgages and Conveyances, with four lawyers and two paralegals from the Morrissey Firm, when Sebastian walked in, wearing a tux. Brandon and his people were manually searching property transfer files for the last six months, using Victor's aliases that Sebastian had provided, hoping that they'd find a property transfer to one of the names. If they found property that Victor had acquired, it would at least give them a place where they might find Victor. They had been at it for two hours, as soon as Marvin's wife's second-cousin, director of janitorial services for City Hall, had opened the door.

Brandon said, "No luck yet."

Sebastian sat next to him. "It's a shot in the dark, anyway."

"Well, that's fucking inspiring," Brandon said.

"He could be using a hotel room. The property transfer clues may lead nowhere."

Brandon shook his head. "No. He's got to have a place. He tortured Andi. No one could do that in a hotel room, or anywhere that someone might hear him. He wouldn't risk renting," Brandon said. "There's too many questions. Too many eyes. I've had my lawyers double-check the work of your agents. The neighboring parishes all have conveyance records that are on line. He didn't buy property in any of those parishes," Brandon opened another conveyance book, "so it has to be here, in this colossal disorganization."

"Taylor is insisting on going to that fundraiser tonight."

Brandon opened another conveyance book. His pulse picked up with the thought of Taylor, but he shook his head.

"She hired you, so officially it isn't my problem."

Sebastian leaned closer to Brandon. "I would like you to go, even if just for a little while. I could use a hand tonight, because I can't guarantee her safety there. I've told her that, and she's insisting on going. The museum isn't my site. I don't control it and I haven't had time, or personnel, to do the necessary work."

Brandon glanced around the room. From his assessment, it had taken them two hours to go through one-fourth of the records that they needed to search, transaction by transaction, title by title, page by page. The work was beyond tedious, but his gut told him that this was the only way they were going to find his brother.

"I'm busy."

"Yeah," Sebastian said, "busy avoiding your feelings for her."

Brandon didn't know what to say, because the truth was he had no words for how amazing Taylor made him feel, when they were having sex and when they weren't. God. He'd even managed to sleep with her in his arms. She was a soothing tonic that he'd never have enough of, and that was exactly the way he'd felt about Amy, from the moment he met Amy until the moment she died. At least, that was how he felt about Taylor, until he watched her with her father. Then he wanted no more.

Sebastian continued, "One of her best friends is dead, likely killed by your fucking brother."

Brandon couldn't deny it. Joe had also told him that due to the interstate nature of the kidnapping offense against Andi, the FBI was getting involved. Joe expected a team to be assembled by the evening, and he wanted Brandon and Sebastian to be at the station when they did a task force briefing.

Sebastian added, "And thanks to your brother, another of her friends is tortured. Taylor is figuring out that everything that she's ever been told about her family history is a lie, that her family is the bad guys, not the good guys. I'd think that if you cared for her, you'd at least be there for her tonight."

"That's what her father is there for," Brandon said, remembering the morning, on the levee, when George had stayed at Taylor's side, virtually squeezing Brandon out of the equation. "It's difficult to get around him, when she listens to everything that he says."

"You're hardheaded," Sebastian said. "She's up to something. I have no idea what. She's giving a speech tonight. At seven-fifteen. She told me you should be there for it."

His heart pounded. "Why?"

"Hell if I know," Sebastian stood. "But even aside from whatever Taylor has up her sleeve, hasn't it occurred to you that your brother might be mingling in the crowd tonight, planning what he's going to do to the woman with whom you've fallen in love? You might recognize him, even if he's in disguise."

Brandon instructed his lawyers to keep looking. At six ten, he was in his car, headed home. By six-forty-five, he was showered and dressed in a tuxedo. He kissed Michael goodbye, then arrived at the museum at five minutes past seven.

***

As Taylor put the finishing touches on her make-up, Carolyn handed her the comments that had been delivered to the house on Lloyd Landrum's behalf. Taylor scanned the comments, then put the piece of paper to the side. Carolyn helped her step into the red dress and zipped it for her. She slipped on the high heels, retrieved her handbag from the previous night, read, then reread the Hutchenson letter, and tucked it in the handbag that went with her dress.

One minute, two minutes, three minutes, four.

The museum sparkled, people were beautiful, voices filled the atrium, and cocktails flowed. Taylor mingled with guests, with Black Raven agents and HBW security at her side. The security personnel were discrete, yet still a presence. At six forty-five, Taylor sat at her father's table. He gave her a nod as he talked to the guests at the table.

Taylor observed him, wondering how much strength it took for him to behave as though nothing was wrong, because he was doing it really well. It took every bit of her willpower to act naturally, and still she was unable to focus on anything that anyone said. Conversation was impossible. All she could think of was her speech, and how her father was going to react. She glanced around the atrium, hoping that she'd see Brandon. She didn't. At a couple minutes after seven, she stood, walked into the backstage area, and, with shaking hands and a nervous ball of fear rising in her throat, she watched Lloyd Landrum approach the podium and waited for him to introduce her.

***

His pulse raced as he followed Taylor backstage. Sexual desire was rare for him, but she made him rock hard. Neither Collette nor Andi had been his type. Collette was too petite and Andi too boy-like thin. Taylor, though, was perfect, with thick golden hair that spilled past her shoulders, a small waist, a slender neck, and curves that he'd love to abuse. Some people called his sexual proclivities deviant.

He called it fun.

The blood-red halter dress accented her small waist and her much-more-than-a-handful breasts. He'd like nothing more than to fuck the lights out of George Bartholomew's daughter, with George watching.

A simple tuxedo and an earpiece, one that he'd taken from the stash that was being used by the HBW Security Team, was all that he needed to look like event security. It gave him the added benefit of hearing the agents talk to each other. As security, no one questioned the tell-tale bulge of a pistol under his tuxedo jacket.

Lucky for him, there was disorder with the two groups providing security. With dark brown eye contacts, thick-framed glasses, and a good hairpiece, he didn't worry that Sebastian would recognize him.

With each move that Taylor made, his mind raced through the variables, the likelihood of seizing her. Taking Taylor from the gala was his desired option. If he felt like he could get a kill shot, and get away, that was option two. He'd love to fire off a good shot while she was giving her speech, so that she crumpled in front of George Bartholomew's eyes.

There were stairs on either side of the stage. Taylor was poised to enter on the right side of the stage. Two Black Raven Security agents that had accompanied Taylor were on either side of the stage, looking at the audience. Sebastian was next to Taylor. He was so close to them that he could hear their conversation.

"My father will not like my speech," Taylor said to

Sebastian.

He wondered what she meant by that. His pulse quickened. He didn't like uncertainty.

She added, "Please do not let him interrupt me."

Sebastian nodded. He turned from Taylor then, and spoke into his lapel mic to an agent who, presumably, was in the audience. "Let me know if George Bartholomew leaves his seat. Or moves."

Sebastian reached for his cell phone, read a text, then said into his lapel mic, "Meet Brandon at the right entry door."

With Sebastian focused on communicating with the other agents, he was able to position himself next to the stairs, next to her. Taylor hesitated, with one foot on the bottom stair. He reached for her forearm, and helped her stabilize. With his fingers on the soft, bare skin of her forearm, an electrical flash of sexual energy coursed through him.

Taylor's high-heels were not made for stair climbing. With a gentle hold on her elbow, he guided her up the stairs. Her hair flowed long and loose, and ends of her hair tickled his hand. He let go of her arm as she reached the top. He caught a whiff of dick-hardening perfume as she turned to him. He held his breath, wondering if she could sense anything about him, if on some level she knew his connection to Lisa, Collette, and Andi.

Taylor looked into his eyes, and said, "Thank you."

He nodded. "You're welcome."

He watched her cross the stage, turning to the crowd of more than a thousand people as she walked. The sea of elegantly dressed people became quiet as she approached the podium. An enormous flag provided a backdrop. Silk swatches in red, white, and blue adorned the walls of the museum. Tables had tall vases of white flowers. His eyes were drawn to the khaki green Hutchenson Landing Craft. The boat, and other museum displays, had been untouched by the party planners. The starkness of the displays reminded him of the serious nature of his business. His eyes fell on George Bartholomew, who was watching his daughter.

After greeting the audience, Taylor said, "I speak to

correct an injustice, to reveal a truth that has been concealed for decades. This letter was prepared by the first Andrew Hutchenson. Today I have learned that it is the truth."

As Taylor started to read the Hutchenson letter, shocked calm seized him. George Bartholomew stood. His face was mottled. He headed towards the door that led to backstage. His eyes scanned the crowd. As Taylor continued to read, mouths fell open. Eyes widened. People were still. Lloyd Landrum was pale. Motionless. Brandon stood near one of the entrances, on the right, his face turned towards Taylor, the green of his eyes visible even in the distance. Brandon's eyes widened. Brandon seemed to be the only person in the atrium who realized that Taylor's very public reading of the letter had more to do with what was going to happen in the current world, than what had happened in the past. Sebastian had his arms full with George Bartholomew, who was attempting to climb the stairs to the stage, as though by stopping Taylor he could undo the damage that she was causing.

Taylor had told Sebastian to keep her father from interrupting her speech, and the Black Raven agents followed her instructions, physically blocking George from climbing the stairs to the stage.

Calm. Stay calm, he told himself, as he kept his eyes on the red-dressed prize. He could simply shoot her as she read the letter. He counted six security agents, other than himself, who were backstage. She would die, but he would not get away.

Think, he told himself. *Think.* He needed money. It wasn't a want. It was a goddamn need. He wanted to destroy George Bartholomew. Now, with the Hutchenson letter exposed, there was only one thing that was worth any amount of money to George Bartholomew and only one way to destroy him. That thing was wearing a red silk dress, high heels, and was standing not more than twenty feet from him. He breathed in, deeply. He was calm. He looked for options.

As Taylor neared the end of the letter, he was jostled by one of the Black Raven agents who was helping Sebastian restrain George. HBW security, loyal to George, were trying to keep Black Raven agents away from George.

He didn't join the push and pull.

There were two ways off the stage. One would lead Taylor to her father and the pandemonium that now surrounded George. He walked to the other side of the stage, which was guarded by only one Black Raven agent. He knew which stage exit he would take if he were Taylor, and that was the exit that led away from her father.

She finished the letter, glanced at the stairway that she had used to enter the stage, saw her father, and the scuffle that surrounded him. She turned to the other stage exit, to him. He met her at the top of the stairs. She was pale. He guided her down the stairs by the elbow. She was trembling, and almost stumbled.

"I need to step outside," she said. She gave him and the Black Raven agent an uncertain glance. "Would you mind stepping outside with me? I can't breathe in here."

He and the Black Raven agent, a twenty-something young man who seemed to have no idea of the earth-shattering importance of Taylor's speech, guided Taylor to the nearest exit. Once outside, in a parking lot that was full of cars but no humans, he pulled out his pistol, and shot the agent in the head, before the agent could say anything into his mic. He reached out fast, grabbed a fistful of Taylor's hair, wound it around his hand, and pressed his pistol into her mouth.

"Don't even think about fucking giving me any trouble."

***

Brandon's gut twisted with the certainty of impending doom as Taylor read the Hutchenson letter. She was stealing thunder from a demon. Victor was going to be pissed as hell, and Taylor was going to be the target of his wrath. For a while, he stood there, stunned, but as Taylor neared the end of the letter, an urgent need to get to her propelled him forward, through the cavernous atrium to the stage. He dodged shocked party goers. He opened the door that led backstage as Taylor finished the letter. There, he saw one man in a tuxedo punch another tuxedo-clad man. One of Sebastian's agents had George Bartholomew pinned against the wall.

Sebastian was yelling, in George's direction, "Calm the hell down," but Sebastian's eyes were searching the stage. Brandon saw Taylor glance towards her father, then exit the stage on the opposite side of where he was.

"Let George go," Sebastian yelled, "and secure Taylor. Now."

Once he was free, George climbed onto the stage, and started speaking, putting a spin on Taylor's revelation of the Hutchenson letter. His tone was calm. Brandon didn't listen to him. Brandon was one step behind Sebastian as they ran behind the stage, to the other side. One of the first doors was a restroom. No one was in there, and the other interior doors, likewise, didn't reveal Taylor.

Sebastian yelled into his lapel mic, "Where the hell is she?"

A Black Raven agent stepped up to them. "Robert guided her off the other side of the stage. There was HBW security with them. She needed to step outside for air."

Brandon ran out the nearest exit door, which opened onto an alley, a side street, and a parking lot that was in the back of the museum. There was no movement. The street was empty, and the parking lot was full of cars and well lit, but there were no people in it. He ran through the alley, tripped, and almost fell over a lifeless man in a tuxedo with a bullet wound to his head. Once he regained his balance, he ran through the parking lot. He died a bit with each step that he took, each yard that he crossed without a glimpse of her.

"She's gone," he yelled to Sebastian. "He's got her."

Brandon called Joe, who arrived within minutes, with Tony and other NOPD officers. Two FBI agents who had been meeting with Joe at the station also arrived. The FBI Agents called for reinforcements. The NOPD officers and the FBI Agents, milling around the backstage area and the parking lot, together with HBW Security and Black Raven agents, looked to Brandon like a goddamn cluster-fuck of manpower.

Footage from a security camera stationed outside the museum's exit showed Taylor stepping out the museum with two tuxedo clad men and showed a man's effortless kill of Sebastian's agent. The tape showed the man yanking Taylor's hair and subduing her with a Glock pressed into her mouth. Brandon stared at the grainy image as it was replayed. The man was almost recognizable as Victor. The darker eyes could be a result of contacts, he wore glasses, and it could easily be fake hair. The man had managed to disappear into thin air with Taylor, after stepping out of the range of the camera.

Tony pressed replay on the video footage. Brandon's gut roiled as he stared again at the image of the man, the handgun, and Taylor. It took a certain kind of man to put the business end of a pistol in the mouth of an innocent person, and this man did it with the unflinching ease of someone who had no soul. The smooth, easy movement told Brandon he was looking at his brother. George Bartholomew walked into the security room in time to see that frame. George stood at Brandon's side, drew a harsh pull of breath, and mumbled, "Good God."

Brandon turned to him. His hands were balled into fists, which he longed to put into George's face. The look of abject horror on the man's face, though, kept him from physically wounding the man who suddenly looked old beyond his years.

Brandon simply said, "Your arrogance did this."

Sebastian stepped between Brandon and George. Brandon looked at his friend, drew a deep breath, and almost said, *Son of a bitch, You were supposed to be protecting her*, but his cell phone rang and blocked his ill-advised words of blame. The caller was one of his lawyers who was at the Mortgage and Conveyance Office. "I've got two properties that are linked to one of the aliases. I'm texting you and Sebastian the addresses now, with GPS data. One is a boathouse. The other's a camp. I think. From what I can tell, it is in New Orleans East, almost on the edge of the parish."

As Brandon relayed the information to Joe and Sebastian, Joe motioned for the lead FBI agent to join them. "Victor won't be at the boathouse," Brandon said. "It's too congested there, in the marina area. The boathouse has to be Victor's jumping off spot to get to the camp, which is in a more isolated area."

Joe said, "We can check the boathouse pretty quickly, but the camp address isn't a street address. It's on the marsh side of New Orleans East, in the outflow canal area. On water. I don't think that you can access it by roads."

"You can't," Brandon said. "I know the area, because I take my boat out there. Hurricane Katrina took out the road that was there, and it was never rebuilt. The camp is only accessible by water. I know how to get there. I'm going. Now."

"You can't just go," the FBI agent said. "We need to plan logistics. We need boats. If he's there, we'll need negotiators. Marksmen."

"Bring whatever you need," Brandon said, "but I'm going now. You don't have time to plan every detail. You'll only screw up if you delay."

Brandon's eyes fell on George, who said, "He wants my money. Or he wants me. He can have anything." George choked back a sob, then regained composure. "I need to be with whomever gets there first. I need to tell him he can have anything."

"Not a good idea," the FBI agent said.

George's wrath fell on the agent. "You are not going to tell me what I need to do to save my daughter." He turned to Brandon. "Please. Take me with you. To save Taylor, I will give him whatever he wants, even if it means my life."

Brandon held George's gaze. He nodded. Brandon turned from the group. Within seconds, the FBI agent was at his side, with George and Sebastian.

The FBI agent said, "You need to wait."

Brandon kept walking, but glanced at the agent. "I didn't get your name," Brandon said.

"Agent Todd Reeves. Who are you?"

Agent Reeves had big brown eyes and a short hair cut. He looked ridiculously young and inexperienced and he actually stepped in front of Brandon, as though to stop his forward progress. *Jesus.* Victor could kill this guy with his eyes closed.

"I'm Brandon Morrissey. The man who took her is my brother. I'm responsible for her. She's mine," Brandon said, his pulse racing. "Mine," he added, and shot a glare at George Bartholomew. "She doesn't know it yet, because I only realized it when she gave that damn speech, and now I have to rescue her before my brother hurts her, or worse." Once Taylor was safe, he needed to figure out how to persuade her that he wasn't the dumbest fuck-up that she'd ever met. "Get the hell out of my way."

Agent Reeves didn't move. Brandon wondered whether he could punch the agent, knock him out, and get away with it, but then Reeves was joined by another FBI agent who also stood in front of Brandon.

Reeves asked, "You have a boat?"

"Yes," Brandon said, "a fast one."

"You know the waterways?"

"Yes."

"I can't condone vigilante action, and," Reeves said, "as a matter of fact, I can take steps to keep it from occurring. However, we need local knowledge. I'm not familiar with that area and none of the other agents who are working with me are boaters. My concerns regarding your actions would fall to the side if you accept an offer of myself and another agent to accompany you and let me take the lead when we're there."

Brandon nodded, while thinking, *like hell.*

"Back up will meet us once they're able to secure the necessary equipment."

"Orleans Marina, A Dock, slip 16," Brandon said. "I'm headed there now. If you're not there when the engines are fired, I'm leaving you."

Joe was ahead of Brandon and let him know that Victor was not at the boathouse, but there was a black Mercedes sedan parked there. Brandon pulled away from the marina in his go-fast boat, with Sebastian, two Black Raven agents, Reeves, another FBI Agent, and George. He used every bit of the boat's seven hundred and fifty horsepower.

Within twenty minutes they were about a hundred yards from the camp, with the engines barely a notch above idle speed, and as near to silent as the engines could be. The camp stood on high pilings. Lights were on. Sebastian's two agents had stripped down to their underwear and had slipped into the water. Brandon's depth gauge indicated that they were in thirty feet of water. A flat boat with two engines that powered the boat with five hundred horsepower was on the far side of the camp. Brandon didn't see a ladder or any other way up to the camp.

When they were fifty yards out, someone hit a switch on a spotlight. Brandon's blood turned to ice. Taylor was tied to a column that cornered the second-story porch. She was on the outside of the porch, without her feet touching any part of the structure. She was suspended in the air, her back to the wooden column, stabilized, it seemed, by only a rope that snaked around her legs, her torso, and her arms. The rope was cutting into her skin. Blood was dripping from gashes in her wrists and falling into the dark, murky water that surrounded the camp. Lead weights were tied to her arms and feet. Where the red dress wasn't anchored to her by the rope, it hung, limp and lifeless. She lifted her head. Wide-eyed with fear, she met Brandon's gaze.

He locked his gaze on hers, communicating with her with only a look. *I'm here. You'll be fine.* As soon as I figure out what the fuck to do, *you'll be fine.* The tear streaks that ran down her face made him insane with fury.

Victor stepped from behind the column, his body partially blocked by Taylor, with a handgun in his hand that was trained on the occupants of Brandon's boat. Brandon didn't feel one ounce of brotherly anything for this lunatic. All he wanted to do was kill the fucking bastard.

On their approach to the camp, Sebastian and the two FBI agents had lifted their weapons. In a calm, loud voice that the quiet night air easily carried over the water, Victor said, "Weapons in the water, gentleman."

"FBI," Reeves yelled. "Drop your weapon."

"You don't have a good shot. You're more likely to kill her than me, and you know it. So drop your goddamn weapon, or you're dead," Victor said, his tone quiet.

"My guys are going to have to shimmy up a piling," Sebastian whispered, as he threw one of his pistols into the water. Brandon reached for a hand-held radio, one that he knew would sink, instead of his Glock. He threw the radio into the water.

"He'll see them," Brandon whispered.

Agent Reeves hesitated before lowering his weapon. Victor shot him, in the forehead. Where there had been smooth skin, there was a red hole and the bullet went through, making it rain guts and bone on its exit. Reeves wasn't three feet from Brandon and the boat rocked as the agent's body coiled back. Sebastian grabbed Reeves before he fell overboard, then laid the body on the floor.

George Bartholomew yelled, "Good God."

Jesus. Brandon thought. From the vantage point that Victor had above their heads, he could pick them off, one by one, and there was nothing they could do about it.

Victor said, "The good professor alerted me that you were coming."

George said, "You son of a bitch. Let my daughter go."

A slash of silver shone in Victor's non-pistol hand. A six-inch gash appeared in Taylor's forearm. She screamed, then sobbed. Victor said, "Now say something else that's equally stupid." There was silence. "Hello, Brandon."

Brandon said, "What do you want in exchange for her?"

"Now that is exactly the right question you should be asking. I'll trade Taylor for George Bartholomew, on my deck, with twenty-five million dollars wired into my account, then a free exit," he said. "And by the way, she's losing blood."

The remaining FBI Agent whispered. "This is against protocol. We need reinforcements."

George said. "He'll kill her. Let me go up there." Dark, intense eyes leveled on Brandon. "I'll give him anything that he wants. Save her. Please."

Victor said, "There's a ladder that I'll drop on the third piling to your left. Guide the boat there and let George climb the ladder."

Brandon guided the boat to the piling. The ladder was remote controlled. As George climbed the ladder, Victor hit the switch that pulled it back up. "Move that damn boat where I can see all of you. Now. Or they're both dead."

Brandon guided the boat about twenty feet from the camp, to a spot where he felt they'd have a better shot at Victor. Victor smiled at Brandon, shook his head, and held his blade against Taylor's neck. "If I hit the carotid, she's gone, baby brother, so don't get smart. Move the fucking boat to the left about ten feet. If anyone lifts a hand, George is dead, Taylor is dead, and so are you."

Brandon's heart raced as Victor trained the handgun on Taylor, which Victor kept there until Brandon had the boat positioned where Victor wanted it. *Damn it.* He had to do something, or she would die. He was powerless. His mind flashed to when he held Amy's broken body in the hospital. He couldn't let this end the same way.

He could see everything that was happening on the porch, but neither he nor Sebastian could get a good shot at Victor, and neither one of them wanted to show that they had a weapon unless they were certain they had a kill shot. He felt a glimmer of hope when he saw Sebastian's two agents surface on the far side of the camp. With hand signals and barely perceptible nods from Sebastian, they stayed in the water. Brandon agreed with Sebastian's call. Shimmying up the piling would make noise, and Victor was too tense.

Victor stayed with Taylor. He told George, "Sit at the table."

George complied. "Please let her go."

"The money. There's a phone on the table. The wire instructions are with the phone. I'm not releasing Taylor until my banker calls me and tells me that he has the money."

George shook his head. "I don't have bankers on call at this time of night."

"Well, if you want Taylor to live, I suggest you find one. Twenty-five million. Now."

"It's going to take time."

There was another flash of silver and another gash on Taylor's arm. This time, she didn't scream with the pain, and the silence for Brandon was worse than her cries. She was unconscious, either from pain or from loss of blood.

"You're running out of time," Victor said.

George made a call. He spoke for a minute, then was silent, then yelled. "You are not understanding. This is a life or death situation. Transfer me to someone with authority." Finally, George nodded, read Victor's wire instructions into the phone, and held onto the phone, silent again. He nodded, then glanced at Victor. "The transfer is happening now."

Victor said, "Tell your banker to call mine and have my banker call me when the transfer is complete."

Minutes later, Victor received a phone call. He mumbled a few words, then glanced at George and said, "Come closer to me."

Victor looked at the boat, at Brandon, and pointed his pistol at Brandon. "Don't move."

Brandon tensed. Not because of the pistol, but because he could see that Victor was using the blade to slash the rope that held Taylor to the column. He was going to drop her into the water, and let George see her sink. The weights at her hands and ankles guaranteed that she was going to drop straight to the bottom. It was deep, dark, murky water.

Hell.

He'd never find her if he didn't get a head start. Brandon didn't think about the consequences. As he dove off the boat, to where he thought she would fall, he threw his pistol to Sebastian. He heard gunfire, knowing that he was his brother's target. Searing pain ripped through his shoulder and his leg. He heard a splash as Taylor hit the water. He ignored the pain as he swam in the direction of the splash, and got there in time to grab her arm.

The weights that were tied to her drug both of them straight to the bottom. Through the water he heard muffled sounds of gunfire. He couldn't see anything. He was a strong swimmer, but he couldn't pull her up.

Hell.

He had to cut some of the weights off of Taylor before he could pull her up. He pulled out his switchblade. Tightness in his chest told him he needed air. *Damn it.* Letting her go wasn't an option. He'd drown with her. He managed to cut one ankle weight off, but he couldn't kick hard enough to pull her up, and he was choking. He found her arm, cut another weight off of her, then tried, again, to kick. He couldn't do it, not with the arching pain in his shoulder that almost immobilized his left arm and with the gunshot that seemed to rob his left thigh of strength. He felt others around him, pulling him, and Taylor, up. The water muffled the pops of gunfire. He heard an engine roar to life, then he and Taylor both broke the surface, aided by the Black Raven agents. She choked, then gasped for air. Her eyes found his and she whispered, "Brandon."

"I've got you," he said, then, as he cut the remaining weights off of her, he realized that her eyes had closed.

He held her head above the water. Victor was in his boat,

using George as a human shield. A boat with flashing blue lights had rounded the bend and was speeding towards the camp. Brandon thought he heard a chopper. The fact that reinforcements were arriving gave Brandon energy. He lifted Taylor by the waist and, with the help of the Black Raven agents, swam with Taylor to his boat. Out of the corner of his eye, he saw Victor fire a shot at George, then turn to face Brandon's boat. Brandon reached his boat in time to see Victor cock his arm back, ready to throw something.

Brandon knew what Victor was doing, even before one of Sebastian's men yelled, "Grenade."

Sebastian yelled, "Go underwater. Now."

Brandon inhaled as hard as he could, then pulled Taylor to him. She had slipped into unconsciousness. Before he pulled her down with him in the water, he looked over his shoulder, to where Sebastian was aiming his pistol at Victor. He heard a shot, and Victor, for a second, slumped. Brandon didn't have time to wait and see if Sebastian's shot was lethal. Taylor was going to die if he didn't get her underwater. He breathed in deep. He exhaled into her mouth, and said, hoping to God that she could hear him, "Hold your breath, baby."

Brandon pulled Taylor underwater with him as the grenade exploded.

***

Taylor drifted in and out of consciousness, never awake enough to remember details of what had happened, but knowing that she was getting help because, after a while, the pain wasn't as bad. By mid-morning, she dreamed, and, in a flash that was faster than lightning, she remembered details. She remembered her hands shaking as she read the Hutchenson letter, she remembered when her eyes fell on Brandon, and she remembered the cold metal of the pistol as Victor pressed it against her flesh. When her mind seized on the moment that Victor had cut the ropes off of her and she'd fallen into the water, her ability to breathe left her. She was drowning, bleeding, and too weak to swim to the surface. She sat up in bed, pulling IV lines with her, gasping for air.

Strong arms wrapped around her. "Hey. You're all right. It's over." Jade-green eyes held hers, but all she could do was shake her head as panic gripped her. "You're safe. Just breathe. It's over. All over. Breathe. One breath in. Come on."

She tried, but she couldn't get her breath past the hard knot in her throat.

"Breathe, Taylor," Brandon said. He was calm. He was close. Panic's iron grip started to loosen as she focused on the feel of his arms. "Just breathe. You can do it."

The first breath was the hardest, but it brought delicious, Brandon-scented, fresh air.

"That's it," Brandon said, holding her. As he rested his forehead on hers, she found strength in his gaze.

The second breath came easier. After a few more breaths, she nodded. He eased her back, so that she was reclined against pillows. She watched him sit down, hard, in the chair next to the bed. "You're getting a blood transfusion and your IV drip contains a painkiller, which is helping you sleep," he said. "The doctor ordered anti-anxiety meds. Would you like me to ring the nurse?"

She shook her head as she studied him. Now that he was sitting and she wasn't having an anxiety attack, it occurred to her that something was off about him. Aside from a worried expression, his face was pale. "Are you hurt?"

"A scratch or two," he gave her a one-shouldered shrug. "Not a big deal."

"Why are you in a hospital gown?"

He gave her a half smile as his eyes held hers. "My clothes were wet."

"You kept me from drowning."

He shrugged. "I couldn't lose you."

"Thank you," she said.

He smiled. A bit of color returned to his cheeks, and his eyes flashed with an intense light. "I'm going to want more than a thank you."

She laughed, which brought waves of pain. Dear God, it felt as though her arms and legs were being ripped from her body. With the pain, the light moment ended as fast as it began. "My father?"

"He's here, in critical condition, but alive," Brandon said.

Taylor shut her eyes. She didn't try to stop the anger that made her blood boil. "He had the option all those years ago to expose the truth. Instead, he concealed it." She drew a deep breath, as tears of frustration spilled from her eyes. "He's a fraud. I'll never forgive him. Never."

When she opened her eyes, Brandon was leaning towards her. He wiped her tears with tissue and gave her a slight head shake. "Don't focus on that now."

She said, "I should have talked to you or Sebastian before reading that letter. I thought it could end things, but it just provided a catalyst for Victor instead."

He shook his head. "Victor's catalyst came long before you read that letter."

"Did they catch him?" She prayed that they did.

Brandon nodded. "While you and I were in the water," she shuddered at the memory of dropping uncontrollably through the inky black water, "Sebastian got a couple of shots in him. It took Victor a while to die. He managed to get a few miles from the camp. They found his body an hour ago."

"Someone called him," Taylor said, "Someone told him you were on your way. We weren't there for five minutes when he got that phone call."

Brandon nodded. "Lloyd Landrum."

She gasped. She remembered more details, but the pain medicine made thinking difficult, and she fought against the sudden urge to sleep. "Victor said the professor had called."

"Lloyd is in custody now and giving them one hell of a story. Andrew is also talking to the authorities. They're still piecing the details together, but evidently, in 1979, when the letter was originally delivered to Lloyd, the HBW Board, and my father, the HBW Board paid Lloyd a sizable fortune to conceal the letter. He did."

Her thought processes were fuzzy, and waves of fatigue were making it hard for her to keep her eyes open, but she understood what Brandon was saying. She drew a deep breath, and he was quiet. She shut her eyes for a second, then opened them. "I want to know more," she said, "tell me what you know."

He swallowed. "Are you sure?"

She nodded.

"When Lisa showed the letter to Lloyd, he panicked. You see, exposure of the letter today would indicate that Lloyd had concealed facts earlier. At the same time, Victor, who saw my mother's correspondence between Lloyd and my father, went to Lloyd. Lloyd told Victor that Lisa had the original letter. We also think that Lloyd told Victor that the Board had paid him a small fortune to conceal the letter. Lloyd set the wheels in motion for Victor's murder of Lisa, to keep her quiet and so that Victor could reclaim the original. The rest was Victor's way of making money off of this and of making the Board of HBW, and especially your father, pay on an emotional level. I suspect that, once the extortion demand was in play, Victor was using Lloyd to learn what your father was thinking. Otherwise, Victor would have killed him."

"Do you know any more about the fire, the one that destroyed your home?" She drew a deep breath, and hoped that the answer to her next question was no. "Was it set by someone connected to HBW?"

He shook his head. "Both Lloyd and Andrew deny knowing that the fire was planned by anyone with HBW. All we really know about the fire is that it accomplished the goal of keeping my father quiet about the letter, and that may have been due to his grief over Catherine. The fire and my sister's death could have been a coincidence that played in HBW's favor."

Taylor looked at Brandon. "Was anyone else hurt?"

Brandon swallowed. "Victor killed one FBI agent. When Victor was attempting to get away, he threw a grenade, and instead of Sebastian diving for cover, Sebastian used that time to fire at Victor. The grenade exploded not far from where Sebastian was standing. The explosion knocked him off his feet, and he hit his head on something. They're evaluating him now."

"Oh Brandon," she said, scared by how Brandon had gone pale as he talked about Sebastian. "Is he going to be all right?"

"He's not conscious yet, but Sebastian is the toughest guy I know," Brandon said. "He's going to be all right."

His words didn't fool her. "You're worried sick, aren't you?"

He frowned, then didn't answer. A nurse came into the room. She checked Taylor's vitals, rearranged the IV lines, and asked Taylor if she was all right. Taylor said, "Yes. Really, really tired though, and numb."

"That's the morphine. Given the extent of your injuries, though, at least until tomorrow you need it in a drip, then we can start weaning you off of it." The nurse turned to Brandon. "I'm alerting the surgeon. Now that she's awake and alert, you don't have an excuse."

"Brandon?" Taylor asked, fighting through waves of drowsiness. "An excuse for what?"

He looked at the nurse. "I'm going to wait a while longer."

"Physically, Mr. Morrissey, she's in better shape than you are." The nurse pulled a cell phone out of her pocket, dialed a number, and said, "Mr. Morrissey is ready now." The nurse turned to Taylor. "Ms. Bartholomew, Mr. Morrissey was shot. Twice. Once in the shoulder and once in the the leg."

She didn't understand. "When? When did that happen?" She looked at him, then drew a deep breath. "When you kept me from drowning, you were already shot?"

He held her gaze. "I had no choice but to save you. Or die trying."

"And that's why he needs to get in surgery, now," the nurse said. "Most people wouldn't have managed to help you given the extent of the injuries he's suffered. He put his life at risk for you and it is still at risk. Now, he's bandaged and we've managed to stop the blood flow, but the bullets are in him. He's running the risk of irreparable damage and infection the longer he waits. Tell him to go, now."

The urge to sleep left her as concern for him made her heart race. She looked at Brandon. "Go."

The doctor opened the door without knocking. He glanced at Taylor, then Brandon. "Great. She's awake. Ms. Bartholomew is going to be fine until you get out of surgery."

"Five more minutes," Brandon said.

The doctor shook his head. "You have until the gurney arrives, which better be less than that."

The doctor and nurse stepped out of the room. Green eyes found hers. "I'm sorry," he said, "for all of this."

"You didn't cause any of this."

"Still. I underestimated you. I'm sorry," he said, "and I couldn't go into surgery without telling you that."

"I didn't have faith in myself," she shook her head. "I couldn't expect you to have it in me."

"The fact that you read that letter, in public, before all of those people, was an astonishing display of courage." Brandon leaned in closer. His eyes burned with a deep intensity. "There's something about you, Taylor, that's magical. You're captivating, witty, smart, and," he paused, "I want to hear your next question. I will never get tired of your questions. Never. In the last few days, you've made me experience feelings that I haven't felt since," he gripped her hand with both of his.

Her heart pounded as she watched him frown.

He shook his head. "Since..."

"You don't have to say it," she said.

Brandon bent to her, pressed his lips against hers, and looked into her eyes. "I want to. You've made me feel more alive than I've felt since Amy died." He paused. "I've never been able to say those words. Not until now. I died when Amy died. But now I can live again, and that's only because of you. You make me feel as though the part of me that died with Amy, the part of me that found joy in living, is still alive. You've given me hope that I might be able to have what I once had with Amy. My relationship with Amy had a rare beauty. It wasn't perfect. Amy and I had our differences," he shrugged, "and our disagreements, but that was just part of us. You've given me hope that I can have something special again in my life."

"Something special," she whispered, "with me?"

He chuckled. "Now you knew the answer to that question without asking it, didn't you?"

"Maybe." Her heart beat faster as she listened to him, and the pace had nothing to do with anxiety. He was hers. Really hers.

"Of course with you. Amy would have loved you. She would want me to be with you, because you make me feel as though

I'm at the very beginning of some of the best days of my life."
Brandon gave her a smile that made his seriousness fall away.
With his smile, warmth flooded through her. He continued, "As
soon as I get out of surgery, I'm going to figure out what I need
to do to persuade you that you can't live without me."

She breathed in deep, then let out her breath, her thoughts
suddenly crystal clear. "You've already made me feel that way."

"Was it something I said," his eyes light with a slight tease,
"or something I did?"

She chuckled, but didn't answer, because right when she
was about to speak, an orderly wheeled a gurney into the room.
The doctor followed, this time with a syringe in hand. "It's time,
Mr. Morrissey."

Brandon winced as he stood, and a shiver rushed through
her. *Please God,* she prayed, *let him be all right.*

He gave her a deep kiss, then broke it with a smile. One
hand caressed the side of her face with a soft stroke, while the
other hand held hers, tight. "I'll be fine," he said, as though
reading her thoughts. "By the time you wake up again, I'll be
through with surgery and back in here. I promise. But first," he
gave her an eyebrow arch, "I want an answer to my question.
When, exactly, did you start to feel that you couldn't live
without me?"

She gave him a soft smile and let go of his hand.

"I'll tell you after your surgery."

Epilogue

Three months after July 4th everything was different than it had been in June, before Lisa's murder. For Taylor, each day brought new challenges, and the first Saturday in October was no different. The morning didn't start with a challenge, though, because she awakened in Brandon's arms, with his eyes on hers, a half smile on his face as he toyed with her hair. They hadn't been apart for one night since July 4th, and he always awakened before her.

"Is he still asleep?" she asked.

Brandon looked over her shoulder, to the nightstand on her side of the bed, where the video monitor was placed, and nodded.

The question came naturally, because she now thought of herself as a mother to Michael. She would have loved him simply because he was Brandon's child, but there was even more than that behind her feelings for Michael. Bearing responsibility for Lisa's child was one way of undoing the ramifications of the fraud that had been perpetuated by her grandfather and her father.

Brandon said, "It's early. He won't be up for a while."

"Hmmmm," she said, welcoming his soft kisses on her forehead, her cheek, and on her neck. "Then we have time to kill."

"I'm glad you see it that way," he said, as he moved closer to her and methodically awakened every nerve ending in her body with slow lovemaking.

Afterwards, they showered, and then Michael was awake. He laughed and cooed through his morning bottle and bath, and laughed more when Laura arrived to take charge of him for the day.

Brandon and Taylor drove together to the monthly

Saturday board meeting of Hutchenson, Bartholomew, Westerfeld & Morrissey Shipbuilding Enterprises. As soon as Taylor had been able to gather her strength to confront her father, she went to his hospital room and demanded his resignation from the board. If he didn't resign, she told him, he'd never see her again. Her words had conveyed the coldness and the anger that she felt towards him, when she said, "And you may still never see me again. But if you do not resign immediately, you are guaranteeing that when I walk out of this room, all of my contact with you will be severed."

Andrew had immediately tendered his resignation, without any urging. Andrew's oldest son, Phillip Hutchenson, had taken Andrew's place on the Board. Both Claude and Phillip joined forces with Taylor to demand that George step down. By mid-July, George had resigned. He was facing criminal charges and, for now, was a lonely old recluse in his big mansion. Taylor didn't know if she was going to have any type of relationship with him going forward. What she did know was that if she had any contact with him, it would be on her terms.

The first business of the new board had been to send a formal apology to the descendants of Benjamin Morrissey and extend an invitation to Brandon Morrissey to become a board member to represent the Morrissey interest in the company. Aside from the necessity of such action from the public relations perspective, independent attorneys had advised Claude, Phillip, and Taylor that the Morrissey family had a viable fraud claim, aside from other civil claims against the company. Their claims, however, were tainted by Victor's actions. Whether the Morrissey family was going to act on their legal claim to the company was something Taylor doubted, given their mortification over Victor's actions. Besides, the fact that she and Brandon were in love made it unlikely that he would sue the company. However, to nullify the possibility that the company could be enmeshed in legal actions for years, and because they all agreed it was the right thing to do, Claude, Phillip, and Taylor invited the Morrissey family into the company. The legalities of how the business would be divided to include the Morrissey family would be resolved over time.

The Morrissey family, consisting of Rose, Kate, and Brandon, had resisted the invitation at first. After long conversations with Taylor, Claude, and Phillip, Brandon accepted on behalf of his grandfather. With Brandon as a board member, the board was working hard to salvage the company's reputation amidst the residual effects of the scandal. Taylor had let go of her dream of working in the district attorney's office; instead, she wanted to be there to guide HBW&M through this critical juncture. Without her father's presence, she believed that she could make a difference in the company, and that quickly became her new dream. Each of the four board members were involved in negotiations for the submarine contracts. Brandon's persuasive skills helped the board members focus on pros and cons of each tactical decision, then formulate presentations that focused on the strengths of the company. Despite the scandal, HBW&M was the most skilled shipbuilder in the maritime industry, and Brandon's presence on the board helped them present a unified front.

When the meeting ended at three, Taylor and Brandon went home. His house had become hers as well, and there, she fed Michael a bottle of formula, as lawyers arrived from the Morrissey Firm for an afternoon session of legal work. Brandon was juggling HBW&M responsibilities, law firm responsibilities, and a family life. From what Taylor could tell, he was thriving with the heavy workload. Before he disappeared with the lawyers into his study, Taylor said, "Be ready to go at six fifteen."

Brandon shook his head, "I didn't know we had somewhere to be."

She smiled. "We do. Michael too. Don't ask where. Just come along for the ride."

He gave her a wary glance. "You do know that I really don't like surprises. Don't you?"

"Yes. But relax. It's no big deal," she said, feigning nonchalance. There was nothing nonchalant about what they were going to do, and she didn't know how he'd react.

At six fifteen, when she and Brandon headed to the car, he deposited Michael into the car seat, then moved to get into the driver's seat. Taylor put a hand on his arm to stop him. "I'm driving." She pulled a scarf out of her purse. "And you're wearing a blindfold."

He gave her a hard look, then shook his head. "I love you, but no."

She was expecting that. She stood on tiptoes and planted a kiss on his lips. He responded by deepening the kiss and pulling her close. She broke the connection, pushing herself away from him with her hands on his chest. "If you want more of that anytime soon, you need to do this. Please."

"Damn it," he said, pulling her to him and kissing her hard, before saying, "That's not fair."

"I wouldn't typically use sex as a bargaining chip," she laughed, "but I can't let you see where we're going. Let me cover those eyes, or you're not getting any tonight. Or tomorrow, for that matter."

He took the blindfold from her then slipped into the back seat. "You're going to pay for this when we get home."

She shivered in anticipation of a long stretch of whatever he wanted to do to her body. "I can't wait."

She drove to the National World War II Museum, pulled into the parking lot, scooped Michael from the car seat, slipped the diaper bag onto Brandon's shoulder, then guided him into the museum. It was closed to the public for the evening. Aside from a few docents who had stayed for Taylor's show-and-tell, they were alone in the cavernous atrium. She pulled the blindfold off of Brandon and said, "There have been some changes since you were last here."

The displays had all been modified to tell the accurate story of Benjamin Morrissey's contribution to the landing craft. In the version that was now on the placards, Benjamin Morrissey was credited as the chief designer. Benjamin Morrissey's original design drawings, with his signature, were on display next to the landing craft. For purposes of the museum displays, the landing craft was now called the Allied Landing Craft. Taylor watched Brandon walk to each exhibit. He paused when he got to the final exhibit, the original Hutchenson letter that Taylor had read the night of the gala. The placard explained the crime and the decades-long cover-up. No details were left out. He turned to her. "You didn't have to do this."

"I didn't. The museum insisted upon accurately telling the history of the landing craft," Taylor explained. "All I did was assure them that they would not lose funding from me or the company. Claude and Phillip also agreed with that decision. There's still some fine-tuning that's needed in other areas of the museum."

He reached for her arm, then pulled her to him. "It's perfect." His eyes glinted with moisture as his gaze fell on her, then returned to the exhibits.

"This part of the museum has been closed to the public ever since July 4th. It reopens tomorrow. I wanted you to have a few private moments to absorb it before the modifications made the newspaper." He pulled her in closer, his hug encompassing both Taylor and Michael, who was in her arms. "Now Michael can walk in here one day," she said, "and be proud of all the Morrissey men who have come before him."

He looked at her, his eyes as serious as they'd ever been. "Thank you for knowing what this means to me."

"There's no need for thanks, and there's more for you to see tonight. A new exhibit has been in the works for some time. It's a live exhibit, where restorers will work on artifacts and explain the restoration process to the public. It includes a hands-on area where children will learn about the restoration process and about boat building." Before July 4th, the new exhibit area was going to be named after Lloyd Landrum, but Taylor didn't go into that. Landrum was facing criminal prosecution on numerous charges, including being an accomplice to murder. "The museum board unanimously voted to name it Benjamin Morrissey Hall. The exhibits are almost finished and the engraving of your grandfather's name was completed today. I consulted with Rose and Kate on this. They assured me that you would approve. Would you like to to see it?"

He lifted Michael from her arms, kissing her forehead as he did, then holding his son close. "We'd love to."

As she guided him there, she said, "I hope that you don't mind, but I have a few people meeting us there."

He laughed. She was never going to get tired of hearing his deep laugh. Like his smiles, his laughter was genuine and heartfelt and, usually, unexpected. "A few, or a hundred?"

"Just a few of the walking wounded." She used the term that she and Brandon privately used to describe those who had been affected by the fraud and secrets surrounding the landing craft and Victor's crimes.

At the Benjamin Morrissey exhibit hall, under the wide entranceway that bore Benjamin's name, Rose Morrissey gave Taylor a welcoming hug, then took Michael from Brandon. Kate greeted Taylor and Brandon with a hug and a thank you to Taylor.

Taylor shook her head. "I had very little to do with this."

"Except to guide the museum every step of the way," Kate said.

Rose, Kate, and Taylor had become friends. There had been uncertainty, at first, fueled by the responsibility each thought they should bear for the actions of their relatives. Rose and Kate sought Taylor's forgiveness for Victor's crimes, just as Taylor sought Rose and Kate's forgiveness for the actions of her grandfather and George. They were able to move forward after they agreed not to hold each other responsible for the terrible things that others had done.

Phillip and Andi Hutchenson walked through the small crowd, towards Taylor and Brandon. This was one of Andi's first public outings since the kidnaping and assault. Andi looked fine, on the outside, but Taylor had seen her friend frequently and knew that Andi was still haunted by what Victor had done to her. Brandon had apologized to Andi repeatedly for what his brother had done to her. She had finally asked him to stop apologizing, explaining that what Victor did to her wasn't Brandon's fault. Now, Andi approached Brandon and gave him a hug. "Recognition of your grandfather's accomplishments is long overdue."

Brandon returned her hug. "Thank you."

Sebastian arrived and crossed the room to give Brandon a bear hug, then he kissed Taylor on the cheek. "Great job, gorgeous."

"Thank you for coming, Sebastian. How are you feeling?"

"Never better," he said, giving Taylor his usual response. After the grenade blast, Sebastian had been in a coma for days. Surgery had been necessary. His scalp had been shaved, but his hair had grown back. He was still thinner than he had been on the day that Taylor met him, but he was looking healthier. After a medically-forced hiatus from work, he had just completed a two-week stint at Black Raven's home office in Denver, Colorado. He had returned to New Orleans to be at the museum on this night.

Sebastian had been a perpetual visitor at their home while he recuperated in New Orleans, to be near the medical team that handled his post-trauma care and surgery. As his strength returned, Sebastian had bonded so much with Michael that he now called for a nightly video chat at Michael's bedtime.

"We miss you," Taylor said.

Sebastian's blue eyes held hers with a doubtful glance. "You just can't help but be gracious, can you? Admit it. I was a restless moocher. Here you two are, practically honeymooning, and you didn't have one minute when I wasn't underfoot."

"I was glad to see you go," Brandon said, but his eyes were light, and Taylor knew that Brandon was joking. The truth was that Brandon was still worried about his friend's health. Sebastian didn't admit that he still felt sick, but Brandon talked to Ragno frequently. She reported to Brandon that Sebastian still had crippling headaches as a residual effect of the blast and fall. Besides the physical effects from the head injury, to Brandon, Sebastian seemed troubled. He explained to Taylor that Sebastian wasn't back to his old self yet. Taylor watched Brandon study Sebastian. Brandon added, "You look like you feel like hell."

Sebastian held his friend's gaze for a second with a serious look, then shook it off. "I'm fine. Hey. Speaking of honeymooning," Sebastian said, "when and where should I be showing up for the wedding?"

Taylor glanced at Brandon, whose expression was unreadable.

"Oh, come on," Sebastian said, lowering his voice. "You two haven't set a date?"

"I think the proposal comes first," Taylor said.

Sebastian's eyes bounced from hers, to Brandon's eyes, then back to hers. "What? He hasn't even asked you?"

"I was giving her time," Brandon said.

Taylor shrugged, "And I'm not pushing him."

"You two are hopeless," he said, as he shook his head. He spotted Rose and Michael, then turned and walked in their direction.

Brandon draped his arm over her shoulder. He pulled her close. "Let me know when you've had enough time to process everything that's happened."

She turned to face him. "I have," then held his gaze as she held her breath. "I never really needed time, you know."

His gaze was as serious as it had ever been. "Should I find a more romantic setting?"

Her heart pounded. She shook her head.

He glanced around the room. Her eyes followed the direction his took. People were milling around the exhibits. It didn't seem that anyone was paying attention to them. "Would you prefer privacy?"

"No," she said.

He rubbed the side of her cheek with the back of his hand. It was a soft gesture that he often did when he was gazing into her eyes, a signal that he was craving more than eye contact. She was never going to get tired of the way he touched her. "Are you sure you're ready to make a decision about the rest of your life?"

"Yes," she whispered, as her heart pounded.

His green eyes held her attention as he dropped to one knee, lifted her right hand, and said, "Taylor Marlowe Bartholomew, will you marry me?"

"Yes."

He stood, lifted her off of her feet, then cradled her in his arms. "When?"

"Before the year ends," she said, going with her instinct to throw one more event in the year of so much change. "A small celebration. Let's make something great happen this year. It feels right, doesn't it?"

"Great question. The answer is yes," he said, as he bent his head to hers, and their closest friends witnessed the long, first kiss of the newly engaged couple.

Watch for the next release from

STELLA BARCELONA

Shadows

A Black Raven Novel

Dear Reader,

Thank you for purchasing and reading *Deceived*. Please help me spread the word about *Deceived* by writing a review at Goodreads, Amazon, or wherever you purchased this book. Also, I love to hear from readers. Please visit me on Facebook, Instagram or at my website, stellabarcelona.com.

Various events in *Deceived* were inspired by the history of World War II. I'd like to thank all of the staff and volunteers who make The National World War II Museum, http://nationalww2museum.org, in New Orleans, Louisiana, the unparalleled resource that it is for information related to World War II.

Many people have provided invaluable support throughout my writer's journey. To name only a few, with heartfelt gratitude: my husband, Bob...He not only understands that every morning that I write makes each day better, he also tolerates the daily ring of an early-morning alarm at a time when he's not ready to awaken, and understands that there are times when I cannot do anything else but write; My sisters, Amy and Kathy...For keeping the colorful, fun, and crazy carousel of life revolving, welcoming me every time I want a ride, and understanding when I need to step off; My cousin, Joanna...For sharing so many summer days when we did nothing but read, and for being my first true friend and confidante; My almost-lifelong friend, Dee...for refreshing, no-nonsense wisdom, always delivered with a healthy dose of wit, that keeps me grounded when I freak out about...whatever; To fellow authors who have become treasured friends: my cousin, Tina DeSalvo...For graciously pushing and pulling me around conferences and introducing me to a world of writers that I never would have discovered on my own. Tina's unconditional friendship, wise critiques, and boosts of encouragement have sustained me for years; and Cherry Adair...For sharing her immense knowledge of the craft of writing, the business of publishing, and making room in her busy life for yet another friend who is a writer.

I also need to thank several people who have provided invaluable assistance in polishing *Deceived* and helping me on the path to publication. A big thank you to: Deborah Richardson and her talented team at Deborah Richardson Editorial & Marketing Services; Timothy Samaha, Marie

Goodwin; and Josh Friedmann of the Calliope Consulting Group. Also, thank you to Emily and Michael Naquin at the Beehive Hair Salon, who have, for many months, listened to me ramble about the endless projects that needed to be accomplished before *Deceived* went live; finally, thank you to Drew Bevolo, of Bevolo Gas & Electric Lights, for the use of the Bevolo Gas Lights Museum for my photography shoot and for being a friend who has gone out of his way to encourage my writing dream.

With Love,
Stella Barcelona

About the Author

Stella Barcelona has always had an active imagination, a tendency to daydream, and a passion for reading romance, mysteries, and thrillers. From her early days of reading, when she first escaped reality through the pages of a well-written novel, she knew that her daydreams needed an outlet, and she knew that her outlet would be writing.

In her day-to-day life, Stella is a lawyer and works for a court in New Orleans, Louisiana. Currently, Stella lives minutes from the French Quarter, with her husband of sixteen years and two adorable papillons who believe that they are princesses.

While she doesn't have a lot of free time, with her legal and writing careers battling for her every minute, she does enjoy any chance she and her husband get to go out on their boat. In addition she attends conferences, workshops, and retreats for writers. She is a member of Romance Writers of America and the Southern Louisiana Chapter of the Romance Writers of America.

* Photo by Zack Smith Photography at the Bevolo Gas Lights Museum